THE REPLACEMENT

A CULLING OF BLOOD AND MAGIC

The Replacement by K.M. Rives

Copyright© March 2021

Cover Art: Kiff Shaik @ Solidarity Squad

Editing: Whitney's Book Works

This book is a work of fiction. Names, characters, places and incidents are either a product of the authors imagination or are used fictitiously. Any resemblance to actual persons, living or dead, or to actual events or locales is completely coincidental.

This book in its entirety and in portions is the sole property of K.M. Rives.

The Replacement Copyright© 2021 by K.M. Rives. All rights reserved. No part of this publication may be reproduced, distributed, or transmitted in any form or by any means, including photocopying, recording, or other electronic or mechanical methods, without the prior written permission of the publisher, except in the case of brief quotations embodied in critical reviews and certain other noncommercial uses permitted by copyright law. For permission requests, write to the author.

Warning: This book contains sexually explicit scenes, adult language and may be considered offensive to some readers. This book is for sale to adults only, as defined by the laws of the country in which you made your purchase.

*For my kitties.
Despite your sharp claws,
you inspire me every day.
Meowrl.*

Chapter One

EMERY

What the fuck was she even doing there?

She knocked back her whiskey ginger like her life depended on it and signaled the bartender for another. Sitting on a barstool alone and tossing back alcohol like it was water wasn't the way she typically handled her issues. She was better than that.

Usually.

Emery surveyed the club and sighed. She'd grown up in a bar just like this one. In fact, that one would be hers if she stayed alive long enough. Unfortunately, her luck had finally caught up with her, and she was trapped in a dance with fate. One that could end her life, and regrettably, she didn't know the steps. As it stood, the Montgomery women didn't have a good track record for staying alive.

It should be a simple task. Wake up each day, put one

foot in front of the other, and keep breathing. But there she was…the last one alive.

For thousands of years, families like hers had been giving up their firstborn daughters for a chance to rule beside a vampire king.

Lucky for her, she was born second.

Too bad that didn't stop the universe from placing Emery, throat exposed, right before the very teeth she'd spent her life avoiding.

Replacement. Twin.

Two words that brought her to her current predicament. She was losing the only life she'd ever known, a life that promised the freedom to choose her own path. All because her sister, the chosen one, had to go and get herself killed.

It wasn't that she didn't love her sister, she did, but she never really knew Sloane. She was removed from Emery's life at the age of five, which didn't leave a lot of time for sisterly bonding. Still, she'd always felt the urge to know her twin. Always hoped maybe one day they'd be reunited. It was too late for that now, though.

And a part of her envied Sloane and the life she had at the castle.

There were other women her age. People to talk to. People with shared experiences. Everything Emery lacked.

The bartender brought her drink, his eyes everywhere but hers. "This one's on me, beautiful. Looks like you're having a rough night."

"You're not wrong." Emery smiled and lifted her glass, her eyes roaming over the handsome man. "Thank you."

Emery loved the bones of the place. A healthy mix of modern and vintage. Elegant, but with an underlying layer of blues and grunge where the metal tables met the worn wood floors. It felt like home.

The stage was small, the talent big. They were a mix of everyday Joes playing on a Tuesday night because it was what they loved to do. Those were Emery's people. People with a story. People with passion. People you could talk to for hours and never get bored.

The singer took his place at the microphone, and Emery closed her eyes. It was something her Uncle Miles taught her during all those years growing up in his bar back in Los Angeles.

He'd say, "Don't judge a band by their looks. Instead, feel the music. That's how you know you've got a winning act."

A deep, sensual voice filled the room. It was magic, lulling her mind into a false sense of contentment. Emery found herself swaying to the lyrics as the man belted out the first verse to "When a Man Loves a Woman." While not the typical song choice for a blues bar, the irony of the song in that particular moment wasn't lost on her.

That kind of love wasn't in the cards for her. At least not any time soon.

Despite the slight pang of sadness, Emery smiled. If it were her bar, she'd hire the man on stage in an instant. Hell, she'd marry him based on his voice alone. The low grittiness, the emotion it conveyed, she believed wholeheartedly he loved the woman he was singing about.

He could sing to her every night for the rest of her life, and she'd be okay with it.

Emery opened her eyes and took her time memorizing every last detail as she drank him in. He was gorgeous, dripping masculinity. Dirty blond hair, short on the sides but longer and tousled on top. A curl formed on his forehead that glistened in the stage lights. With a five o'clock shadow, collared shirt, and low-slung jeans, he nailed the struggling artist look. And yet, he held a presence she'd never seen in a man before. He commanded the room with his voice. Sitting on a bar stool center stage, he demanded every patron take notice with each subtle move of his body.

A slight reconsideration of taking her sister's place in the morning sifted through the dark recesses of her mind, not that it was a choice she could make. If it was, she'd be taking him back to her hotel room after his set.

She cocked her head to the side, her eyes raking over the singer. The royal family would never know if she took him for the night. They didn't say anything about her needing to be a virgin when she showed up to the castle. For the first time, she wanted to be with a man.

That man.

A shift in tempo pulled her from her thoughts. There was comfort in his voice. A comfort where she forgot, for a moment, her whole life would change in the morning.

That wasn't entirely true.

It changed the moment the fucking mark appeared on her wrist two days ago. All her dreams flew out the window in one gut-wrenching moment.

Her gaze dropped to where her thick-banded watch covered the silver vines circling her wrist, entangling themselves with her destiny. The mark sealed her fate, naming her as a woman of the Culling and ensuring if she ran, she'd be marked for death. The vines tingled as if it knew she stared at it, daring her to defy it by walking out the club door. To leave Chicago and her responsibilities behind.

With a huff, Emery tossed back the remainder of her

drink and slid from her bar stool. The room whirled as the effects of three whiskey gingers flooded her bloodstream. She stared longingly at the door, knowing one step toward it and the vines would sense her motives.

It was useless. Her fate solidified.

She made her way to the dance floor, turning her back on the door and any hope for escape. Couples danced in the center, but one stood out over the rest. They were slightly past middle-aged, but you'd never guess with the way they looked at one another. They might as well have been teenagers, young and in love. Tears pricked Emery's eyes. That's what love was supposed to look like.

While Emery wished someone looked at her like that, she didn't mind being a party of one. It's what she'd always known, and no one was rushing to change that. Not even herself. At that point, she'd be happy if she made it out of the Culling alive.

The voice of the sex-on-a-stick singer slowed, and a new song began. A popular sultry blues number she recognized immediately. She shifted her hips in time with the music, swaying as if she could drift away from the club and the family responsibility she owned.

Family.

It was a laughable term. Her biological family was dead. The woman who raised her, dead. Uncle Miles was all she had left, and he was every bit the fun uncle, not the adult she could count on.

There was Wren. Her best friend. Her only friend, if she was honest. But Emery had left her in Madrid in the middle of the night when the mark showed up. She didn't even bother to call and assure Wren of her safety after she'd spoken to the Culling liaison and confirmed she was to head to Chicago. The jury was out on if she'd still have a friend if or when she made it out of her adventure alive.

The music around her swelled, and tears burned the corner of her eyes. She may never see Miles or Wren again. A Montgomery alive at twenty-five? The odds were not in her favor.

Fear and anxiety flooded her veins, and the need to bolt for the door was all consuming. She didn't want to do this. She looked down at her wrist and, for a fraction of a second, considered chopping it off. She could live without her hand. Prosthetics had come a long way, and she'd survive the amputation. At least her life would still be her own. It wasn't glamorous, but she was just becoming who she wanted to be, and it was being stripped away. It was almost too much to bear.

The mark itched, as the heat from within burned up her entire arm. Emery's eyes flew open, her intent to run strong, but before she could move, she was paralyzed by the gaze of two piercing, steel blue eyes.

The singer's cold, intense gaze held her as he tripped over his lyrics, and his once golden face paled like he'd seen a ghost. His hands fisted and relaxed while he circled his wrists like he was preparing to throw a punch, and he never looked away from her as he regained his composure.

Emery met his stare until someone pulled on her hand, breaking the trance. "Excuse me, ma'am. Would you like to dance?"

"Ma'am?" Emery blinked and found a man standing beside her, the epitome of a Midwestern gentleman. Quite the opposite of the man on stage.

She scanned him from head to toe, trying to pinpoint who he reminded her of. Holy fuck. Emery bit back an alcohol induced laugh. The man was an honest to God Dudley Do-Right lookalike.

"So, would you?" he asked again.

"Uh, sure." She didn't have anything better to do but drool over the singer who could never be hers.

She was about to place her hand in Dudley's when the deep voice of a man rasped behind her.

"She's spoken for."

If the singer's voice was melodic sex, this voice was dominance incarnate. The tone raised the hairs on the back of her neck, freezing her in place. Maybe if she ignored him, he'd go away.

"How 'bout we let the l-lady speak f-for h-herself?" Even chivalrous Dudley was affected by the stranger.

Dressed in all black, the tall, dark haired stranger stepped between them, and Emery instinctively stepped back. He was a rock solid wall between her and Dudley.

"Leave." The man spoke in a layered tone that sent a chill down her spine.

Emery peeked around him in time to see Dudley's face go slack, losing all expression, his eyes dilated.

Every hair on her body stood on end. She swallowed hard, thanking the gods that for once Ada had the mind to teach her something about vampires. She knew what compulsion looked like. Sounded like. And the man before her was not a man, considering he'd just compelled Dudley.

Fuck.

Her guardians prepared her for that moment. Unfortunately, their suggested action was to run like hell and not get caught. Any witch, even a defective one like her, would be dead at the hands of a vampire. It was a miracle Sloane had lasted as long as she had at the castle. If Emery could run, she would, but the mark on her wrist ensured even if she did, she'd be dead.

Dudley spun on his heels and promptly left with Emery following right behind him. She made a beeline for the door despite the fact the vines sizzled upon her wrist. She made it two steps when a large hand claimed her forearm and spun her back to slam against his hard body.

Before she knew it, she was in the arms of the very being she'd been raised to hate. She struggled momentarily before she squeezed her eyes shut, wondering if she was about to be his next snack.

When she didn't feel the sharp cut of teeth at her neck, didn't feel her throat being ripped open, curiosity got the best of her. Emery craned her neck to peek at his dark features. He stared back, studying her in wonder. His short hair was disheveled and falling in his face, though it didn't hide his handsome chiseled cheekbones or strong jaw.

His obsidian eyes narrowed on her face. He leaned in, whispering in her ear, "Dance with me, Sloane."

Chapter Two

EMERY

Sloane.

He knew her sister.

Emery froze, confusion morphing into panic. Blood rushed in her ears, but struggling was no use against the strength of a vampire.

Finally finding her nerve, she tried to push away, but he wrapped an arm around her. "I'm not Sloane, you have the wrong sister."

The vampire reached up and fingered the strand of pink hair that had fallen into her face. "No, you're not. Still, dance with me." His hand dropped to her wrist, toying with the watch band as if aware of the mark beneath it.

Emery hesitated. He was a fucking vampire. Everything in her body said run, hyper aware of each and every way he could kill her, with no doubts he would. But he knew about Sloane, and that was enough to make her go against her better judgement.

"Tell me who you are, and I'll dance with you."

The stranger smirked, pulling her so close she could feel the chuckle rumble through his chest. "It's cute you think you have a choice in the matter." He pushed her out into a spin, bringing her right back to the spot against his chest, and dipped his head. His breath fanned her ear. "I know you know what I am. Don't worry, Emery, I've already eaten. And lucky for you, my family has interest in you untouched. You're the key to keeping us off the radar."

His words did nothing to calm her worry. Quite the opposite.

"Wait, what? How exactly am I going to do that? And what makes you think I'll agree?" Emery stopped dancing, meeting the vampire's stare with a false confidence she hoped he didn't see through. "I'll ask again. Who. Are. You?"

He looked over her head toward the stage and nodded. "Come with me."

Before Emery could turn around, he yanked her hand and went to lead her off the dance floor.

She jerked from his grasp. "Listen, asshole, I'm not going anywhere with you until you tell me what's going on. Promising me I'm not your next meal doesn't mean much considering what you are."

In a blurred movement, the vampire was on her, deadly still and breathing down her neck. "I would not feed from you if you were the last human on earth," he growled. Pulling back, his eyes warred with hers. She watched as they dilated followed by his layered voice. "You are going to follow me to our table so we can have a conversation."

Thankfully, the small amount of witch blood running through her veins made her immune to vampire compulsion. She played along, not willing to risk him knowing about her ancestry.

Even if she was defective.

She widened her eyes and did her best zombie impression. "I am going to follow you to your table so we can talk."

Creases formed at the corner of the vampire's eyes, as if he were trying to hold in a laugh. "I will admit, you're a good little actress. Your sister was too. Too much zombie, though, not enough passion. Keep it simple. Stick to the truth as much as possible if you must lie."

"What?" Emery gaped at the vampire. Why was he helping her?

"Sloane defied our compulsion as well."

"She did?" Emery had never known if Sloane had the same abilities as she did. Her sister never answered any of the letters she sent.

"Yes. I know what you are, but let's keep it our little secret. No one else at the castle knows."

Emery crossed her arms and raised her brow. "How did you know? What exactly *were* you to my sister?"

Without acknowledging her, he turned and walked away, seeming to know she'd follow.

The way she saw it, she had two choices: follow him and potentially find out more about her sister... or, she could run. Well, at least try to. She wouldn't get far.

So, one choice really.

Submitting to his silent request, she followed as he led her to a dark circular booth in the back, perfectly concealed from prying eyes, yet still offering a great vantage point of the entire club.

After sliding into the booth, Emery sat as far back from

the vampire as humanly possible. He flagged down a waitress. "Do you want anything?"

Refusing to acknowledge him, Emery spoke for herself, "Whiskey ginger please. Make it a double."

The waitress nodded and leaned over the table toward the handsome vampire, showing off her ample cleavage. "And for you?"

Emery rolled her eyes at the woman's display. Did she have no sense of self-preservation? He was good-looking, but also deadly.

"I'll have the same. Thank you, Cindy." The waitress tipped her head and sashayed her way to the bar.

Emery sat quietly, glaring daggers. She needed to determine his motives and how she could eventually get away from him once she found out his connection to her sister.

She had one card she could play, but doubted it would help. He stared back at her, silently watching her every move while giving nothing away.

Finally, the silence was too much. "Are you going to tell me who you are and why I'm here? More importantly, how did you know my sister?"

"I'm waiting for my brother, lest I say something he wouldn't approve of."

"So, you're his lackey? Can't handle the situation yourself?" She pushed him, knowing it was a bad idea, but not able to hold her tongue.

"I could handle you nine different ways right now. Eight of which you would love." He purred his words, giving her body the shock it needed to come alive. The vampire looked her up and down. "You know what? I changed my mind. You'd like all nine." He gave her a wink and a devilish smile before licking his tongue over a single fang.

Emery shuddered at the timbre of his promise and involuntarily covered her neck. What was his angle? One minute he was cold and distant, the next an asshole, and the next he said things that would make any ordinary girl's panties drop.

"I wouldn't do that if I were you." She unbuckled the watch on her wrist and showed him the mark. "I belong to your prince as a member of his culling, and I'm sure you don't want him finding out about your not so innocent innuendos."

"Do you now?" He leaned over the table, his breath fanning over her wrist as he spoke low and slow. "What if I told you my little brother doesn't mind sharing his women?"

"You expect me to believe you're the prince's brother? That doesn't even make sense. If he's your younger brother that would make you the crown prince."

Cindy arrived back at the table and placed the drinks down. Emery instantly grabbed hers and tossed it back like she'd done all night.

The vampire bore holes in her skull from across the table and slowly tipped his glass back, finishing it in a single swig.

"You know what? I'm already having a shit last night of freedom. I don't have time for this bullshit."

Emery slid out of the booth and did something she should never do in front of a predator. She gave him her back and attempted to run out of the bar. But before she could take three steps, she ran headfirst into the same brick wall of a chest. The air was knocked from her lungs, and his hands firmly gripped her arms. "Sit down, Emery. Now."

"No."

"I won't tell you again. You will sit, and you will wait for my brother. I will not be responsible for fucking this up."

"Too late," she mumbled under her breath before she registered what he'd said. "Wait, he's here?"

"Yes, sweetheart, he's here."

"Why would he be here, in a low-down club, when he's the crown prince of vampires?"

"Why wouldn't he be here? He owns this low-down club."

Of course, he did.

Fate was a motherfucker.

Emery slid into the booth and stared at her clasped hands on the table, her heart pounding in her chest. All she wanted was a night out before her life as she knew it ended but even that was too much to ask.

A shadow caught her eye coming to a halt at the edge of their table. It was much too large to be Cindy returning to flirt and show off her breasts. Emery inhaled a shaky breath, attempting to find her confidence, and looked up to see who'd joined them.

Her jaw hit the floor the same moment her stomach dropped.

The gorgeous man, who poured his soul out on stage, stood before her, but he no longer radiated carefree artistry. Instead, his jaw was tight, and he looked ready to murder someone.

"What's she doing here, Malcolm?"

So, douche canoe had a name.

"Relax, August, she stumbled here of her own volition."

August? As in Prince August? No. There was no way the gorgeous man was the prince. The vampire whose heart she was supposed to try to win. Fate was not this cruel.

"Really? Of all the bars in Chicago, she just happened to pick mine?" Annoyance flashed across August's handsome features.

Malcolm sipped his drink. "You have a little something on your lip, brother. Are you sated or should I find you something else to eat before you join us?"

August's tongue darted out to taste the trickle of blood on his full bottom lip, before reaching up to wipe it away. The action would have been downright sexy if he was any other man, and it wasn't the evidence of his latest victim. Emery's heart raced, as she was smacked once again by the reality of what these men were.

Her eyes searched the club for his victim, but she found nothing out of the ordinary.

The bar patrons carried on, unaware of the monster that drew them in. Hell, even she was torn between her predisposition to hate him for what he was and the urge to jump his bones. An ordinary human didn't stand a chance against the prince.

She shook her head, attempting to rid the memory of his smooth voice. It didn't matter the prince was sex personified, or that he called to her soul like a deadly siren, or that she very much wanted to get to know him on an intimate level. She couldn't forget what he was or that her sister was killed in his family's care. He was the reason she'd been pulled from her life to fulfill some archaic version of *The Bachelor*.

"I'm fine," August ground out. "What have you told her?"

"Nothing. I only took her captive until you were finished so we could discuss our plans for her."

Plans? If they thought she was going to play a part in

some nefarious plan, they were greatly mistaken. She had her own agenda, consisting of getting in and out of the castle with her life and gaining some clarity on Sloane's death.

The prince turned, looking her over with a glacial gaze. "I'm Prince August, but away from the castle, just call me August." He extended his hand out to her adorned by a beautiful ring that could have paid her mortgage for a year.

She cocked a brow. "Am I supposed to kiss it?"

August chuckled, sounding almost animalistic. "If you'd like. Although, I think a handshake is customary in the twenty-first century."

Emery rolled her eyes and hesitantly placed her hand in his, immediately regretting it. A buzzing sounded in her ears. Where the prince's hand met hers, a jolt of electricity erupted, catapulting its way straight to her heart. Her eyes widened, as her skin began to hum, vibrating from the inside out. She jerked her hand from his and yelped. "What the fuck did you just do to me?"

The prince masked any shock he may have experienced with a furrowed brow. "You have a mouth on you. That will need to be sorted before you go anywhere near the other women of my culling." August slid into the booth next to her, and Emery flinched. "As for what just happened," he shrugged, "static electricity."

She'd never felt static electricity like that. Like her body had been jump started from within. She slid farther away, ensuring they didn't touch again, even though her body protested the action.

Ignoring her clear objection to their proximity, August turned so his leg nearly touched hers. "So, you're the twin?"

She took a sip from her glass and allowed sarcasm to flow. "You're an observant one."

"Did Malcolm inform you of what we need of you?"

"No, your asshole brother thought to taunt me with his ability to talk in circles while we waited for you. He also informed me you like to share your women. I should let you know up front, I've never shared what's mine."

August growled, at the same time Malcolm spit out his drink with a cough. Served them right. If they wanted to be jackasses, she could be too.

"It's a good thing I'm not yours then, because I *do* believe in sharing. You, though, *are* mine. That mark on your wrist matches mine. It binds you to me until I decide otherwise. That means if I want to share you, I can do so at will."

Emery tensed at his words. Like hell she belonged to him. She belonged to no one.

"Would you like that, little one?"

She turned and faced him, not scared to lock eyes and challenge him. He wasn't her prince. "I'm. Not. Yours."

"We'll see." The bastard smiled and turned away. "I'd like to speak privately with Emery. Would you mind getting me a drink from the bar?"

"Oooh, bring me one too, *Malcolm*."

Malcolm hesitated, eyes locked on her, but she didn't have the faintest idea of what he was trying to silently say. He'd been all over the map for their entire conversation. Slowly, he got up and made his way to the bar, leaving Emery with August as a pit settled in her stomach.

When Malcolm was out of eyesight August spun on her, pressing her against the back of the booth. With his face hovering above hers, and his voice deadly smooth, his eyes dilated as he attempted to compel her. "What are you?"

Could he know what she was based on a single touch? Maybe it was a royal vampire trait. But Malcolm hadn't reacted, so that didn't make sense. She stared into the depths of August's oceanic eyes, but he gave away nothing.

Just like his brother.

Emery crafted her reply carefully, while simultaneously trying to keep her heartbeat steady. Malcolm's advice from earlier played in her mind, and despite the fact he was a jerk, she didn't want August to know about her witch blood. At least not until she knew his motives.

"I'm just a woman, forced to be in your culling like my sister before me."

"Why are you here tonight at my club?" He ignored her jab like it was his job.

She formulated her answer as close to the truth as she could. "I love jazz, and it's my last night of freedom."

August's gaze left hers momentarily, noting Malcolm's return. Seemingly happy with her answers, he ordered her to forget their conversation moments before his brother slid back into the booth.

Malcolm looked between them, slowly setting their drinks down. "Is she going to do it?"

"She doesn't have a choice," August stated, taking a long sip of his drink.

Emery shook her head, subtly pretending to come out of her compelled state. "Wait, I don't have a choice about what?"

"The culling. Your sister's death was untimely and has put my family between a rock and a hard place. Lucky for us, someone else in your family's line could take her place. That said, you'll be attending the culling not as yourself."

Who the hell would I be then?

She cocked her head at the prince in confusion. She knew she didn't have a choice. The damn mark on her wrist that matched his wouldn't even allow her to consider going AWOL.

"You will become Sloane."

Nothing could have prepared her for the words that came from his mouth.

Emery signaled Cindy to bring her another round. Maybe she should have asked for two. All she knew was she needed way more alcohol for the rest of their conversation.

Chapter Three

EMERY

Boom. Boom. Boom.

Emery rolled over in bed, reaching for a spare pillow and holding it over her face. She didn't know where the sound was coming from, just that she wanted it to stop. Her mouth was as dry as the Sahara, and she had an overwhelming need to pee.

Boom. Boom. Boom.

Shoving the pillow off her face, Emery finally opened her eyes, taking in the delicate cream wallpaper of a hotel suite and the sunlight peeking through a slit in a heavy curtain from a giant corner window. She was thrilled they hadn't been left wide open the night before because she doubted her hangover would appreciate the bright light. She didn't remember getting back to the hotel, but she was there. And alive. Which was all that mattered after a night with vampires.

Without a word of welcome, the door clicked and swung open. She sat up and covered her bare legs as Prince August entered the room without warning.

"Good morning, Emery." He smirked as he looked over her disheveled appearance. "You look like hell."

Still in shock by the fact he'd barged into her room without her allowing him in, Emery answered him with a raspy voice. "I feel like hell. Also, how did you get in my room?"

"I'm a vampire, Emery." As if that was answer enough. "As to *why* I'm here, I assume you don't remember us making plans after we got back to the room last night."

"Bold of you to assume I remember anything about last night." The sensation of the soft, white sheets on her bare skin sent a mortifying shock to her senses. If she couldn't remember the night before, and they'd been in her hotel suite, then… "Wait, did we? I mean, you know?"

"God no, Emery. You were far too drunk, and I like coherent women in my bed, not sloppy ones."

Ouch. It more than likely wasn't much of a stretch, but his comment made her feel like the gross mess she was. It was a good thing they hadn't done the deed the night before. She'd like to remember her first time, and as it stood, she couldn't remember a damn thing after her talk with the brothers in the booth.

"No. I tucked you and Copper into bed and left." The prince tossed her the water bottle he walked in with and stepped over to the window. "Who names their stuffed pet dragon Copper? Also, what grown adult has a stuffed animal?"

Emery ignored his condescending words and grabbed the ratty stuffed dragon, hugging it close. Copper was the one thing she had left from her mother. She'd gotten one each for Sloane and her on their second birthday. He'd been the constant in her life when she needed someone to hug after Sloane left. Ada hadn't believed in cuddling, but Copper never protested.

August pulled the darkened shades open, and to her horror, let in the overbearing sunlight. She felt as though *she* was the vampire afraid of light as her hangover strangled her senses.

"Wait, you can stand the sunlight?"

"I'm a created vampire, only turned vampires have a sensitivity to the sun. Now, I ordered you breakfast. Get cleaned up so we can talk."

She had no idea the difference between created and turned vampires, but at the moment, it didn't matter. All that mattered was lessening the pounding in her head.

She snagged the bottle and took a long chug, ignoring his implication she needed to hurry. Once the bottle was empty, she wiped her mouth and smiled at the uptight man who now had his arms crossed, as if to scold her for taking her sweet time. She was taking her time for a reason. She was nearly naked under the sheets, wearing only a camisole and lacy boy-cut panties. The last thing she wanted was the crown prince of vampires to see her in her underwear before a much needed shower. But he was about to because he wasn't looking away.

"Well?" He gestured to the bathroom and raised his brows at her. "Get a move on."

In a manic attempt at bravery, Emery dropped Copper and threw off the covers. Exposing her bare legs, she hopped over to her duffle bag. If she was going to be half naked in front of him, she would at least be confident about it. As she bent over, the prince's eyes roamed over her body. He didn't even pretend not to look at her ass. She couldn't fault him, though. She had a great ass. And she gave it a wiggle to see if he'd squirm.

Turned out, vampires were like any other man, in love with the female form.

"Like what you see, Your Majesty?"

Color flooded his cheeks, and he cleared his throat. "It's Your Highness, and yes. I find I quite like your ass." There was a hint of an accent in his voice, but it was faint and hard to pinpoint its origin. The British Isles, if she had to guess.

Emery gasped, covering her mouth. "Oh my, the prince has a mouth on him. Maybe we'll get along after all. Especially if you aren't as stiff and uptight as your clothes make you seem. A three-piece suit on a Wednesday morning? You've got to be kidding me."

August grinned and cocked an eyebrow. "You'd be surprised what I can do in a suit."

The prince was behind her before she could blink. In one swift motion, he pulled her ass against him and righted her against his rock solid chest. Her breathing labored and fear took hold. Fear...and something else entirely. Her body hummed as she leaned into him.

She ground her ass against his groin, feeling the evidence of just how much she affected him growing in his expensive suit pants. She was glad she had no intention of becoming this man's bride because she would likely be torn in two.

August shuddered against her, gripping her hips to halt her movement. His punishing hands held her in place.

"That smart mouth of yours is going to get you in trouble." He moved his hands from her hips and raked his fingers down her arm, eliciting a shiver over hypersensitive flesh. "And I can think of plenty of ways to silence these lips should it become a problem." He pushed against her back, entwining his fingers with hers. With little effort, he brought her hands above her head and spun her around.

She looked up into his hungry eyes. If they told a story in that moment, it would end with him devouring her.

Literally.

He leaned in, and Emery retreated until her back hit the wall. She was trapped between drywall and the most delicious vampire she'd ever seen. Which, to that day, only numbered at two.

Conditioned from the tender age of three to be repulsed by the very notion of vampires, she was supposed to hate him and everything that made him who he was. Her traitorous body had a mind of its own though.

August brought his face to hers, and she stiffened as his breath caressed her lips. If she moved a half inch, she'd know what his lips felt like on hers. And as much as she shouldn't, she wanted to know what they felt like.

August had other plans, though. Instead, he drew his breath across her cheek and down toward her throat. Her heart raced, hands clammed up, and her cheeks flushed in response to the unfamiliar attention.

"You smell absolutely intoxicating. Do you know that?"

He was one to talk. August smelled of sandalwood and fresh forest air. It surrounded her in an impossible way, filling her with the need to be close to him. The breath from his words fanned her skin, heightening her body's response tenfold. It was an intimate gesture, and for a split second, she'd forgotten what he was.

What *she* was.

She swallowed the lump clogging her throat. "I wasn't aware."

He sucked in a breath as his lips grazed her collarbone and, as if to confirm his words, let it out on a soft, breathless moan from his otherwise firm demeanor.

Emery's ragged breathing confirmed everything she wanted to deny. His lips continued exploring her skin. She shifted her weight, desperate to ignore the growing heat pooling between her thighs. August's hand gripped her hip, holding her in place, then he pulled away piercing her with his gaze.

"You're going to be my undoing, woman," he whispered, and before she could respond, his lips crashed against hers.

Every inch of her came to life, vibrating from the inside out. Emery gasped, and he took advantage. His tongue speared against hers, tangling with it at a slow, hungry pace that strung her body tight with need. Her back arched, needing more physical connection. When he tightened his grip on her hip, halting her movement, Emery hooked one of her legs around his hips and pulled him in.

August stumbled into her, and Emery moaned, as her hardened nipples brushed against him. He sucked her lower lip between his teeth and pulled back, sending a jolt of the most pleasurable pain through her as his fangs dragged over it. Never in her life did she expect to be fully and completely immersed in the feel of a vampire's fangs, enjoying them on her body. Wanting them to explore other parts of her body.

Still holding her against the wall with one hand, he stepped away raking the other through his hair. A soft moan fell from her lips, the distance he'd created too much for Emery's heightened senses. It didn't make sense, but she didn't need it to. All she needed was for him to continue what he'd started.

"Bloody hell," August whispered through panted breaths.

Emery opened her mouth to speak but froze when August whipped his head around. His eyes met hers and dilated.

"Go into the bathroom and get ready. You will forget everything that just happened."

Emery stood against the wall frozen and unable to breathe. She gave a slight nod and scooted into the bathroom.

Like she could forget what happened in a million years.

He'd kissed her. If she could even call it a kiss. More like he set every inch of her on fire and left her in a heightened state of sexual frenzy. It effectively gave her a pair of blue balls to go along with her already pulsing lady boner. She instantly regretted every time she'd lead a guy on.

Then, he compelled her to forget.

She'd never not wanted to be a witch more than she did in that moment. To sink into the reality where his body was never pressed up against hers and she didn't capture his deliciously innocent moans between her lips. Only she couldn't, and now was forced to live with the memory of August's lips on hers and face the reality that she wanted more than just his lips.

Emery inhaled a shaky breath and gazed into the bathroom mirror. Reaching up, she ran her fingers over her lips, committing August's fire inducing touch to memory. At least she was herself for the kiss. She'd remember forever that he kissed Emery, not Sloane.

She studied the face that stared back at her. Emery had

only just learned to see herself as beautiful after Ada died. The old bat had a penchant for tearing Emery down whenever she got the chance. She zeroed in on the tiny scar just under her eyelid she got after falling off her bike when she was six. The small freckle on her lip that no one even noticed but her. The tiny imperfections that made her Emery and told her story.

She was reminded last night that the face staring back at her also lived another life completely. A life she knew nothing about. That face belonged to a girl who'd been taken from her family and raised in a castle. Whose amber eyes had witnessed things most people could only imagine. A face that no longer lived but still survived, like a broken mirror.

She stood staring at a reflection that would never look back at her. A face that would no longer belong to Emery if she did what the prince demanded of her last night.

It would be Sloane's.

Not that she had a choice.

No matter what, she'd be going to the castle. She could stomach doing what August asked of her, if only to find justice for a sister she didn't even know. She'd always had a connection to Sloane, despite only being together five short years. They shared a womb, and yet it was so much more. It was a bond not even death could sever. An inexplicable need to know her.

Something was holding her back, though. A sadness she struggled to understand. Emery had only just started to feel comfortable in her own skin. After spending nearly a year traveling with Wren, she felt ready to live the life she was meant to lead. A life on her own terms, not one micromanaged by Ada.

Then, the mark showed up on her wrist, and all that confidence went out the window. Her life was going to be micromanaged again. And to make it worse, by overbearing vampires.

Emery hurried through her morning routine, shaking off the downward spiral of her life, and slipped into a fresh pair of black leggings and an oversized gray sweatshirt. Pulling her brown and pink tresses up into a messy bun, she stood before the bathroom door. It'd be easy to just hide out in the bathroom for the rest of the day. It was safe in there, and she could be herself.

But that wasn't what she was told to do.

Emery knew she'd have to become someone else as soon as she left the bathroom. She held her head high, not giving herself another moment to mourn the loss of her identity, and pulled the door open to her new normal.

Her jaw dropped when she stepped out. Carts full of silver domes sat in the middle of the room, and August gave her a satisfied smile.

"I ordered one of everything on the breakfast menu, plus some medicine for the headache I'm sure you have." He moved to the cart that held two silver pitchers on it. "I also ordered a pitcher each of Bloody Mary and Irish coffee, just in case the hair of the dog was more your style."

Shocked by his personality shift, her mouth dropped open, and she had to remind herself to close it before she caught flies. The man was dangerous, and she needed to remember that. "Thank you."

She peeked under a few silver domes, finding pancakes and eggs benedict. The third had a breakfast burrito. She needed to look no further. Emery grabbed the burrito off the plate, grabbed the pills, and poured herself an Irish coffee before plopping down at the head of the soft bed.

August watched her from the seat by the window, his gaze heavy. He propped his elbow on the arm of the burgundy chair and placed his hand over his mouth. Hiding the lips she desperately wanted to forget. Damn, he was hot as hell, all calm and relaxed like that. He didn't even need to try. All the while, she sat there looking like the hot mess express pulling into a station she had no business stopping at.

"Are you just going to stare at me or what? You can have some, you know. I'm not going to eat all this." Emery paused and cocked her head to the side. "Do vampires even eat real food?" She realized for all the warnings Ada had given her about how terrible vampires were, she never told her any useful facts. It was always, if you see one, run the opposite direction.

Fast.

That advice was null and void the moment the mark appeared on her wrist. Couldn't run away when you were shackled to a vampire. Emery didn't know if she would burn from the inside of her wrist out or if they'd send someone to kill her, but finding out was not on the top of her to-do list.

August chuckled in the deep sexy way that made heat pool in her belly. He sauntered to the bed and placed a binder in front of her she hadn't noticed while she'd been ogling his relaxed grace. The bed dipped, and he picked up Copper, examining her beloved stuffed dragon. "Yes, royal vampires eat food. Our turned counterparts less so. I've already eaten this morning, thank you."

"What's the difference?" She spoke with her mouth full, only realizing halfway through her question that she probably wasn't acting as ladylike as she should in the presence of royalty.

If August noticed, he chose not to comment on it. "Royal vampires are the product of a male vampire and a human female. A turned vampire is a human that was bitten by a vampire and made to be one of us. Like Malcolm."

"And they are sensitive to sunlight too."

"That's correct. They won't burst into flames, as history would have you believe. But they must stay covered or suffer severe burns. The castle's windows are treated so it's not a problem for Malcolm, the Queen, or any visiting courtiers."

"Wait, I understand how the Queen would be turned, but Malcolm isn't a royal vampire? How is that possible?"

"He is, technically. He was born first, but unfortunately, was the one-in-a-million child born human. He was turned on his twenty-seventh birthday but will never hold the title of crown prince because he can't produce an heir."

"That sucks." Emery couldn't believe the smallest part of her sympathized with Malcolm. He might be an asshole, but she would be too if her birthright was taken from her because of an anomaly. She knew all too well what it was like to be born flawed.

"It does."

"So, just one bite and I'd turn into a vampire?" The hand not holding her burrito instinctively went to her neck.

"No. You'd have to die with venom in your system."

"Noted. Don't die with vampire venom in my system."

"That would be wise. I don't think you would enjoy being like me."

"You have no idea," she whispered. Not only could she not stomach the idea of drinking blood, but her ancestors would turn in their graves if she betrayed her kind like that. Even if being a witch was the smallest part, it was still part of her.

August cocked a brow but didn't acknowledge her comment. "Any other questions?"

Her eyes dropped to the mattress, the culmination of everything she'd learned from August settling all at once. "Why me?"

"Why you, what?"

"Why me? Why my sister? Why the women that are at the castle? What is so special about us that we are forced to audition to be your bride?" There was something special about the family lines that required them to provide their oldest daughter, should the mark appear, but Ada hadn't ever explained to Emery why. Despite the number of times she cried for her sister's return, she was given nothing.

"You aren't special, Emery. You're cursed. As am I." He spat the words, as if they tasted like sour milk. "Our families' fates forever intertwined by bloody witches who thought to play God."

"Witches?" She swallowed the hard lump in her throat and tried to keep her heartbeat from skyrocketing.

"Yes. Witches are real and are the bane of my existence. They've been our enemy from the moment they created us. They killed us, controlled us, and they still do it to this very day, dictating our future with the same magic they used to create us. They're the reason we can only mate with certain human females. Hence, the Culling. In a very real sense Emery, you, your sister, and all the other women in my Culling are just players in a game masterminded by them from the start."

Her mind reeled. Vampires were created by witches. Ada

never told her that. Never let on that there was even a sound reason for the hatred between their two factions. She was in far more trouble than she realized. One wrong move and she'd be at the mercy of a witch hating vampire. It didn't matter that Malcolm seemed all too willing to keep her ancestry secret. August's hatred was palpable.

She wiped a stray tear before he saw it rolling down her cheek. "That sounds awful."

"It is. Now, on to business." He pushed the binder toward her. "Given the number of drinks you consumed last night upon my request for you to become Sloane, I take it you are less than amicable to the idea. I'm here to tell you, you've no choice in the matter."

Ah, there was his dickish nature. Emery rolled her eyes as she swallowed the last bite of her burrito and took a long sip of coffee. She got comfortable and sat crossed legged on the bed facing him. "First of all, it's a perfectly reasonable reaction for someone to get drunk and enjoy themselves on their last night with the only identity they've ever known. Second, why do you have to be a gentleman one minute and a complete asshole the next?"

"Enjoy yourself is an understatement. You ran up a thousand-dollar tab under my name."

Holy shit. A smile etched across her face. "You can afford it."

"I hope the 'best whiskey in the joint' was worth it."

"It was," she lied, though the joke was on her, she didn't remember taking shots of top shelf whiskey but wished she did. "I've thought about your so-called demand, and I'll go along with your plan. But on two conditions."

"You think to give me an ultimatum? I could just compel you to comply."

"Yes, you could." It wasn't the time to inform him otherwise. "But then you would have to explain to the castle why Sloane all of a sudden has zombie-like tendencies."

August glared at her, and she knew she had him.

"What are your conditions?"

"I want to know what happened to my sister."

He sighed deep and looked away from her. "We don't know. Her death is still under investigation."

"Then, I want to be kept in the loop and help with the investigation."

"Absolutely not. You'll get in the way, not to mention it's dangerous, and we don't need another human getting killed on our watch."

Emery shrugged and tried to appear nonchalant. "Then, introduce me as Emery when I arrive at the castle. Better yet, release me and let me go home. Either way, you can figure out how to explain away my sister's murder."

August's expression hardened. "What's your second condition?"

"Once we figure out what happened to my sister, and it's safe to do so, I want you to send me home. I have no intention of being your bride or bearing your heir."

Besides, you'd likely kill me if you ever found out what I am.

He sat silently staring at her and a sardonic smile formed at his lips. "Are you sure? I can smell your arousal, Emery."

Heat flooded her cheeks. Of course, he could smell her. That was just her luck. It wasn't like she wanted to be attracted to a vampire. Her traitorous body just hadn't gotten the memo that there were fangs behind his straight white smile.

She inhaled deeply, trying to steady her nerves. "Forgive me for saying this, but that's not going to happen. Your family has already taken too much from me. I have a life, and I want to get back to it as soon as possible."

August tilted his head, though his eyes didn't leave hers. "Alright."

"So, that's a yes to both of my requests?" She gave him a sweet smile and hoped her charms worked on him.

"I don't like what you're asking." His growl sent a warm wave through her body, even as her stomach churned when he hesitated. "But we need you if we want the upper hand in figuring out what happened to Sloane. To investigate and strike our enemies without them knowing they succeeded." He clenched his jaw and spoke through gritted teeth. "I agree to your terms."

"Then, it's settled." Emery bounced a little on the bed and fell back on the mountain of feather pillows. She could relax a little now that her demands had been met. "What's next?"

Chapter Four

AUGUST

August had no idea how he was going to keep up his end of the bargain.

Everything inside him screamed to push her down on the bed and wreck her. Forego reason and fuck her, claim her, and then fuck her again. In all his years, he'd never been drawn to a woman with such visceral need. It was as though she'd infiltrated his mind and body. She dominated his thoughts since their eyes met across the club.

Both her blood and her body called to him. Not in the way blood usually called to him, but to the dark, twisted, lust-filled part of his mind. He didn't care if the stakes were too high or that she was identical in nearly every way to a woman who'd just died in his care.

He wanted her.

Needed her.

He should care she was part of his Culling and off limits

by his own stupid code. He knew better than to shit where he ate. Still, he'd throw his bloody code out the window for the opportunity to explore Emery.

To make it worse, she wanted him, too. She may hide behind her innocent doe eyes, but the smell of her arousal didn't lie. Her need was so palpable it hung thick in the air. If it weren't essential for her to play the part, he would take her hard and fast right then.

Then, he could release her from her duty to him, forever.

That was a lie.

She was damn near the most intoxicating being he'd ever encountered. Something her sister wasn't, even if she looked like Sloane from afar. It took every ounce of self-control to walk away from Emery last night, and he hadn't even tasted her. He had no idea why he indulged in her terms.

He wasn't going to let her go.

She wasn't like the other women in his Culling either. No, Emery's eyes were curious and wild. Muting her spirit and her mouth to emulate her sister would be a challenge. Not only for her, but for him too. It was her mouth that fueled his libido.

Her exhilarating scent lingered on him, teasing him. She was different, though he couldn't place exactly what made her so. He did know the bloodlust that plagued him all his life ceased when she was near. Instead, his body hummed in response to her and drove him to the brink of insanity with the need to claim her. Even the mere thought of her caused him to shift in his seat.

She was it.

He didn't know how he knew, but she was it.

None of it mattered, though. His desires rarely did when it came to his Culling. His father had a plan, and he was expected to follow it. A plan that didn't include taking a no-name woman from California as his bride.

The entire Culling was a joke.

It was a horse and pony show every vampire crown prince had to endure to find his bride, to secure the family legacy. Bloody witches. Despite the few exceptions to the rule, the woman who became queen was chosen for who her family was and what they could bring to the crown, not love.

His father already had a few women selected as favorites.

Sloane never had a chance at winning his hand. Neither did Emery. The magic of the Culling deemed her responsible for her familial duty and nothing more. She had to play the game. Just like him.

It was a shame he'd already promised his father he'd bring her to the castle as Sloane.

He cleared his head of the idea that he could keep her as she was. He'd ultimately do as his father wished, just as soon as he got every image of her, real and fantasy, out of his mind.

Pressing her up against the wall like he did less than an hour ago. How he imagined she would take his entire length within her. Then, there was the glorious image of her from last night.

She'd been too drunk to remember dancing with him. When the first few beats of the song came on, she'd lost it, dragging him out against his will, telling him it was her favorite. He remembered, though. He remembered every moment with her in his arms. They were memories August would hold on to for the rest of his long life.

But why her?
What made her special?

"August?" Her sweet voice pulled him from his thoughts. "I said, what comes next?"

Her big whiskey eyes widened ever so slightly, and she smiled at him with those kissable lips. Lips he most definitely wanted to taste again.

He fought the urge to lean in. He couldn't let her distract him, whatever it was about her that captivated him and caused his nerves to fray. She may be in his world, but she didn't want him. Something she made exceptionally clear with her words. Even if her body said otherwise.

And he shouldn't want her. He was the bloody crown prince, and he didn't fawn over a simple woman. There were more important things to worry about than plunging into her pussy. There were plenty of women he could sample if he couldn't get a grip on his dick.

"First, sit up straight. Sloane had impeccable posture. If you're going to be her, then you'll have to act as though you've grown up in the castle." He picked up the binder that sat between them and placed it in her lap. "Then, you study."

"Study? Are you serious?" The hostile look in her eye and the way she cocked her brow had him wanting to fuck the smugness out of her.

He could count on one hand the number of people who could look at him like that and survive. Yet there she sat, as if he weren't the crown prince of vampires to one of the biggest territories in the world. As if he were just an average person who'd walked into her hotel room and sat down. That would be another thing he'd fuck into her.

Respect.

"You have twenty-four hours to become Sloane Montgomery, the most favored Culling woman of Augustine

Nicholson. That means you need to know everything she knew about the castle and the people who live there." He opened the first page of the binder. "In here, you will find a biography on each of the women of the Culling, photos of the royal family, advisors, and servants Sloane came into contact with regularly. In addition, there is a map of the castle for your convenience. Learn it."

He knew it was a daunting task, but she could do it. At least he had hope she could. Otherwise, it wouldn't be long before a court member or castle staff knew they had a death on their hands.

She flipped through a few pages of the binder. When her eyes returned to his, something darkened within them. "Do I have to be her, August?" Her full lip jutted out ever so slightly, begging to be nipped. She locked in on his gaze, and he could see every emotion she was feeling in them. Anger. Sorrow. Maybe even a touch of fear. Being as old as he was, he'd learned to read others easily but that didn't mean he enjoyed reading them on her face. "I've already agreed, but help me understand why I can't just be me."

Fuck, why did she have to look at him like that? Like he had all the answers she needed, when he didn't. She was putting her trust in him, but he hadn't earned it. He wished she could be herself, wanted nothing more than for her to go to the castle and wreck everything those pampered women thought they knew. He could imagine it: her hair in that same messy bun, the same ratty sweatshirt. Sitting cross legged on a three-hundred-year-old chaise lounge with Cooper eating a breakfast burrito with her face buried in an old tome.

Emery would have brought in a breath of fresh air to an otherwise stuffy life, but Emery wouldn't exist in the castle.

She was about to be stripped away and not in the fun, for his eyes only, kind of way.

All the things that made her unique would be taken from her, and he wished he wasn't the one responsible for asking that of her. He wished his world would get the opportunity to know the woman with the pink hair. The woman comfortable in her own skin, not afraid to be herself. The woman with the tiny little freckle on her lip that he wanted to taste again so badly his fangs ached.

No.

"Do you remember nothing I told you last night?" He spoke with a level tone, keeping a distance between them while continuing to berate himself internally.

She rolled her eyes and ungracefully shifted off the bed to grab the pitcher of Irish coffee. She sipped directly from the pitcher. Damn, she was adorable as hell. He didn't even know cavegirl-with-no-class was his type until just then.

"You and I both know, at a certain point last night, all coherent retainment went out the window."

He huffed a frustrated sigh. She had been a feisty, yet charming, drunk. "Right now, there is unease in the supernatural world. The truce between the three factions has never been so thin, and a death in the castle could tip the scales. I believe Sloane's death was intentional, to expose an inability to protect what's mine. To make me look weak in the eyes of the witches and the wolves. As I said before, having you become Sloane allows us to have the leg up. Let the murderers believe they didn't succeed in whatever plot they're trying to execute. We have the upper hand while we figure out what they are trying to accomplish."

"Did you fail to protect her?"

August rubbed the back of his neck. It would be easier

for him if she didn't ask questions. He could compel her to be silent, but he refused to be responsible for Emery losing her fire. "Yes."

She furrowed her brow, her face a picture of judgement. His judgement. "Do you think she was targeted specifically?"

"Yes."

"Why?"

He held his ground at her verbal challenge. It had been too long since a woman had the guts to spar with him, and damn if it didn't make him want to keep her more. "Because she was considered the front runner in the Culling."

"She was?" Her brows raised along with her voice.

Wrong answer. Telling the woman he wanted that her sister was the frontrunner in a game for his heart wasn't his smartest move. She'd thrown him off kilter with her questions, and he'd slipped up.

Then again, maybe this was the answer to his problem. If Emery believed he loved her sister, maybe she'd stay away from him. Make both of their lives a hell of a lot easier.

"Because we appeared to spend a lot of time together."

Emery slammed the binder down on the bed and glared daggers at him. "Did you or did you not have a thing with my sister?"

He shrugged nonchalantly. "I have a thing with a lot of women. But even if I did, it wouldn't be any of your business." That was a lie, and he bloody knew it.

Emery's eyes watered, on the verge of tears.

"Emery, I didn't—"

"Fuck you." Emery stood and effectively cut him off. She barely set the pitcher down on the cart before she turned on him, heat in her eyes. "I've taken every bit of this situation in stride. I could whine and complain about how unfair the whole thing is, but I'm a realist and can see that a pity party isn't going to do a damn thing for me. However, knowledge about my sister is sure as hell my business, and you know it. I'm going to be her, for fuck's sake, August. I have to know these things otherwise I'm flying blind. Otherwise..." she trailed off and put her hand delicately over her mouth.

"Otherwise what, Emery?"

She stared at him, her jaw clenched, eyes searching for something in his, but he didn't know what. Her internal battle waged silently with no guts to tell him the thoughts that plagued her. He wouldn't pretend to know what she was thinking. That was a dangerous game to play when it came to someone who made him feel the way she did. The things she didn't say could be more dangerous. So, he asked her again, this time lower, asserting his dominance. "Otherwise what, Emery?"

"Otherwise, I could be next."

An unsolicited growl formed deep in his chest. It'd been centuries since anything brought that sound from him, and she'd done so before the sun reached its apex. "I will not allow that to happen. You are mine."

"Because being yours worked out so well for Sloane? And I am not yours in any capacity." The words delivered a slow, cold slice to his ego.

His hands fisted at his sides, her accusation fanning his anger. He wanted to pin her down until she understood it wasn't his fault.

At least he kept telling himself it wasn't.

A single tear fell down her cheek. He wanted to look away, but he couldn't manage to pry his gaze off her. Her sorrow tugged at his heart, and he didn't like her effect on him. With most women, he'd walk away and allow them to wallow in their useless emotions. But with Emery, he wanted to do something he'd never done with another Culling woman.

He wanted to comfort her.

It should disgust him...but it didn't.

August steadied his voice, knowing she was not going to understand what he was about to say. Though, he hoped one day, when the time was right, she would. "It's not my story to tell."

If looks could kill, he would have a dagger through his chest. "It was my sister's life that was taken, August. I don't care whose story it is."

"I know, and I'm sorry she's gone." Her eyes narrowed on him.

Damn. He wasn't fooling her with his halfhearted answer. But he would do whatever it took to protect his family, and it wasn't his secret to tell.

Emery sank back onto the bed and rested her elbows on her knees. She raked her hands through her pink-streaked hair, lacing them at the base of her neck. "You don't know who they are, do you? The ones that killed her."

"No. I don't. Which is why you shouldn't be involved. As you said, you could be next."

"I'm only here to find out what happened to my sister. I'll keep my head down."

He wasn't sure if she was trying to convince him of that fact or herself?

August reached out and cupped her face, despite all logical instincts telling him not to. His skin hummed the moment he touched her, and her eyes widened. He leaned in, holding her gaze. "Emery, I'm only going to say this once.

From this moment on, you are mine. Until I deem it safe to release you from your duty. You. Are. Mine. I am a man of my word and will keep you up to date on the investigation of your sister's death. But make no mistake, I protect what's mine. You will be safe in my care." He closed the small distance between them and brushed his lips lightly against hers.

Emery closed her eyes, shutting him out from whatever emotions she was feeling. She spoke quietly against his lips. "I'll never be yours." With that, she pulled away.

August reluctantly let her go. He forced himself to steady his breath. They were just words, the words of a woman he barely knew. And yet, they inexplicably cut deeper than any sword his greatest enemy could wield.

When Emery opened her eyes, the fire in her gaze that shone when she went toe-to-toe with him had returned.

Good. She was going to need to be strong to succeed at the castle.

She didn't acknowledge his actions, instead her attention went to the binder in her lap. She thumbed through the first couple pages, stopping on a photo that was taken the month before. "Who's this?"

"That's Thea." A smile tugged at his lips as he studied the little girl with pigtails. "She's my younger sister. She looks innocent enough, but be warned, that girl is a hellion."

Her shoulders relaxed as he spoke of his sibling. The Culling women knew about his family, having been raised in the castle. It was rare someone new came, and he found it nice to talk about them with someone who had no knowledge.

She smiled, and he ached to pounce.

Her brows furrowed and she tilted her head. "I thought

vampires could only produce male heirs? Something about dominant genes."

"That's correct. Thea is adopted. My mother volunteers at one of the orphanages on the south side of Chicago. She met Thea there and instantly knew she was something special. Unable to leave her there, she brought her home to be a part of our family."

"She's human?"

"Yes, she is, and deaf."

"Wow," Emery paused, her mouth hanging open. "I wasn't expecting that."

"Why? Because a vampire family couldn't possibly do something nice for another living being?"

With the flip of a switch, August's need to protect his family took over. He was on the edge once more, needing to make her understand, but also keep her at arm's length. Welcome her, yet still be detached of any emotions that tethered him to her.

"You know, Emery, we aren't all bad." He tried to keep his composure, but a growl escaped him.

"I know that." Her voice was firm and direct. A show of falsities. "It's just interesting that a vampire family would take in a human girl. Human blood is your main food source. It's like a lion raising a lamb."

Her words pushed him over the edge. He had no idea who she learned of vampires from, but she clearly did not understand them or their motives. His motives. She may be the only woman to ever consume his mind and body, but she was still human. And in his experience, every human outside the castle was the same.

Discriminatory of that which they didn't understand.

"I'm sure you think you have us all figured out. We're the

vampires that prey on weak human children. The vampires that *took* your sister." His hackles were raised, and there was no backing down from the fight now. "You think you know us, but you're going to need to check that attitude at the hotel door. Whether you want to believe it or not, your sister loved living at the castle. She found love, passion, and friendship within its walls. Do remember that when you show up tomorrow."

Emery's jaw tightened, and her lips drew into a line. "I'm sure you know all about the love and passion Sloane found during her stay at the castle, *Your Highness*. She was your favorite, after all. Oh wait, I'm sorry. *I* was your favorite." Her eyes narrowed on his. "I won't be sloppy seconds, August. Especially not to my sister."

His hands balled into fists in his lap. He needed to leave before he said something stupid. Well, more stupid. Emery could think whatever she wanted about him. About his family. Everything would come to light in the end, and he couldn't wait to see the shock on her face when it did.

He stood from the bed and grabbed his coat off the chair before storming toward the door. He was blowing everything out of proportion, but he didn't care. He wouldn't admit the root of his problem, the reason he needed to get the hell out of that hotel room, was not her lack of knowledge about vampires or her accusations of her sister's role at the castle.

No, it was her tenacity. Her personality. The way she spoke to him with little regard for his station. She spoke her mind, and it drove him wild with need. Needs he couldn't explore with her if he were to keep his promise to let her go.

Emery continuously showed him she wasn't looking for his attention. Wasn't kissing his ass so she could be his next queen. She was honest to a fault and couldn't keep that damn mouth of hers shut. He could find plenty of ways to shut it for her. Ones he would thoroughly enjoy.

He liked that she talked back. Damn it, he hated that he liked it so much.

He needed to shake that woman from his system, needed to forget about Emery and every bit of her intoxicating personality. Because the next time August saw her, she'd be a distant memory.

The next time he saw her, she'd be Sloane.

Chapter Five

EMERY

Emery closed the binder in front of her and peered out the window at the beautiful sunset over the Chicago skyline. She'd finished her studying and knew everything from the difference between Victoria I. and Victoria M. to which fork she should use first when dining with the royal family.

She'd spent all fucking day in her luxurious hotel room reading that damn binder.

All day.

She should have raided the mini bar, ordered room service, and watched every pay-per-view as a big middle finger to August and his attitude, but that wouldn't solve any of her problems.

She'd still have to show up at the castle and play the part she'd agreed to. It was the only way she'd be kept in the loop on the investigation of Sloane's death. And once the investigation was over, she could leave and get back to her life in California.

Still, she had to admit, August wasn't what she expected the crown prince of vampires to be.

Left to her own devices, and the knowledge Ada had ingrained within her from the age of five, Emery imagined he'd be more like Dracula with a touch more supervillain. While his dominance reeked of villainous tendencies, there was more to him than he let on. He was an artist and a prince. A brother and a ruler. Two sides of a coin she desperately wanted to add to her piggy bank.

She may not know much about her heritage, but she knew it was dangerous for a witch to want a vampire. August confirmed it. Even led her to believe it may be more of a grey area than the black and white explanation Ada gave her.

Emery had always been grateful to have been born second. Her life may not have been sunshine and rainbows, but she always believed it was better than being raised by vampires. It was why she struggled to believe Sloane could be happy living at the castle.

But she was.

The binder had proved that with pictures of Sloane at events with the other Culling women, smiling and laughing. It didn't seem to be the fate worse than death like Ada tried to make her believe. And while August was an asshole, he didn't seem to be anything like the awful creatures Ada described.

Emery ordered room service for dinner. She wished she hadn't lost her phone the night before at the club so she could scroll social media one last time as Emery Montgomery. Before she could pick another movie to watch, a knock came at the door. Her heart dropped into her stomach as her hands trembled. Had he come back? She wanted to apologize for how she'd acted earlier. Not that she felt she was completely out of place, but she could have been more kind with her words and not lost her temper with him.

She opened the door, and her shoulders drooped. Instead of August, a man stood outside her door holding the same formal picture of Sloane she'd seen in the binder. "I'm Lenny. Mr. Nicholson sent me here to make you look like her."

Emery slid to the wall inside the door and allowed Lenny to enter. She watched from the corner as he set up a workstation in a robotic manner.

When she tried to ask him questions, he didn't respond. It was then she guessed the poor guy was under a compulsion. He'd likely forget her the moment he left the room.

When it was time to begin, Lenny gestured for Emery to sit in the chair he'd set up in front of the window, giving her a beautiful view of the city. As he swung the beauty cape around her, Emery's heart constricted. It was really happening. She was becoming Sloane.

Just one more look in the mirror. One more glance to memorize who she was.

Tears silently fell down her face as Lenny mixed the natural ash blonde dye to match the rest of her hair. Emery realized then she hadn't allowed herself to fully come to terms with what she'd agreed to. Learning facts was easy, she'd always loved to learn. But this? This made it real. It was losing her pink locks, a seemingly insignificant part of herself, that threatened to break her.

They'd been an impulse decision. A way to say 'fuck you'

to a life micromanaged by Ada. Not to say her life had been terrible with her. She had many happy memories to outweigh the dark ones. Wren and Miles made sure of it, helping her to escape the endless negativity Ada could weave into the tightest blanket of happiness.

When Ada died suddenly her freshman year of college, Emery vowed that her degree would be the last thing she did that was expected of her by another person.

As soon as she graduated, she dyed her hair pink and started working at the club with Miles to save for an epic trip around the world.

Emery winced as Lenny's brush lathered on the dye that matched her natural hair color. Sloane's hair color. So much for being herself. There she was, once again, becoming a woman who went along with what she was told to do.

That wasn't fair, though. This time, she wasn't doing it out of fear. Well, mostly not out of fear. Going along with August's plan was her choosing. She willingly agreed to lose herself. All she could do was hope it wasn't all for nothing.

Tense at first, Emery eventually relaxed and maybe even enjoyed herself. Lenny took his time making her hair just right. He polished her nails and sculpted her brows. The man even gave her a bikini wax, something she would never forget. Still, she'd never felt so pampered in all her life.

Lenny wasn't much of a conversationalist, which didn't bother her too much. At least, it didn't until her thoughts drifted back to a certain vampire. One who confused the shit out of her. His hot and cold demeanor, in addition to the secrets he kept, left her suspicious and unsettled. And yet, as much as she didn't want to be a vampire's bride, she couldn't deny the magnetic pull between them. The connection she would likely forever struggle to ignore.

The battle within her raged on until Lenny finished up her transformation and left without a word.

Compulsion was no joke.

Emery stood and made her way to the mirror atop the dresser. She closed her eyes, as if doing so could possibly bring back her old look. After a deep inhale, she steadied her nerves and mentally counted down.

Three…

Two…

One…

She opened her eyes, and a soft gasp escaped her. Lenny was a magician. She could have fooled herself. It was no longer Emery staring at her.

It was Sloane.

"Holy shit. You look just like her."

Too busy admiring herself, Emery didn't hear the door open, or the dark haired vampire sneak up on her.

In the reflection, she met the obsidian eyes of Malcolm standing behind her. They held each other's gaze, neither saying anything more. His eyes clearly searched hers for something, but she didn't know what, her mind too unsure of the moment to help her formulate any sort of thought. He wasn't the brother she wanted to come through the door, but he stood behind her, nonetheless.

Malcolm reached up and pulled the front strands of her hair back, then grabbed two bobby pins from the dresser and delicately braided the hair out of her face. "She wore it like this nearly every day."

"Thank you," she managed to whisper.

When he finished securing the braids, he gently finger combed the rest forward to frame her face. He continued trailing his fingers out to her arms, eliciting a shiver. She tucked her chin and looked down at his hands as they softly touched the silver mark of the Culling.

She slowly turned around, not realizing how close he stood to her until she was face to chest. Emery braved a look and met Malcolm's smoldering eyes.

He licked his lips, his teeth catching the lower between them. In every romance she'd ever seen, that was the signal. The moment just before the couple would inevitably kiss. But that didn't make sense. Malcolm shouldn't want to kiss her. She was no one. Even if he saw her as Sloane, her sister belonged to August.

She searched his eyes for any indication of what he was thinking but found only the same entranced gaze he'd had since walking in.

"You're so damn beautiful."

Before she could respond, his lips crashed against hers, and his hands tangled in the hair he'd just fixed to perfection.

Chapter Six

EMERY

MALCOLM WAS KISSING HER.

She parted her lips to question him, but he took advantage and delved his tongue inside. He was quite the kisser. Passionate. Frenzied. Skilled.

One thing she knew for sure was his kiss didn't cause her stomach to drop or make her skin vibrate. It wasn't a bad kiss, it just didn't feel right.

Not like August's had.

She deepened the kiss, if only to ensure that there was nothing between them. There wasn't. It felt wrong. Slimy even.

Emery gripped Malcolm's shoulders and pushed him away. "This isn't right."

He stumbled back from her and brought his hands to his lips, dumbfounded.

"Are you going to say something?"

"I...I'm sorry. I thought..." His voice was soft, almost defeated. He turned away from her toward the window.

She wanted to comfort him, but that wasn't right. He shouldn't have kissed her. She was a part of August's Culling. "Thought what? You can't just kiss me like that." Which was a load of shit, and she knew it. He was a prince and likely thought he could do whatever he wanted. Even if he shouldn't. His brother did, after all. Maybe it was a family trait. The difference was, she liked August's lips on her.

Malcolm rolled his shoulders back, straightening his stance. When he turned to look at her, his eyes had lost the softness that had been there moments before and were replaced with a cold stare.

"Pack your things." His words were clipped short. "August decided it would be better if we brought you to the castle tonight under the cover of darkness. Showing up in the morning might cause more questions than we want."

"Are we not going to talk about what just happened?"

"No."

Figured. Fucking blood-sucking men and their inability to take responsibility for their actions.

Emery held Malcolm's gaze for a moment longer, trying to understand the moment that passed between them. She usually would push until he talked, but castle educated Sloane wouldn't, and that's who she was now. "Let me grab my things."

Malcolm didn't offer to help, instead he carefully watched Emery as she packed. Pacing the length of the window impatiently. Every few moments, he would sigh and shake his head, lost in whatever was eating at him.

His attitude didn't improve much once they made it

down to the car, a black BMW convertible of all things. He couldn't keep his eyes off her, but always looked away when she caught him staring. He was quiet for most of the drive, only mentioning it would take upwards of an hour to reach the castle.

When the silence had reached the point of grating her nerves, she spoke. "What's going on with you?"

"Nothing."

"Liar."

"Just leave it alone, Emery." His words came out as a deep growl, and he white knuckled the steering wheel.

"Don't you mean Sloane?"

He didn't answer, but she was afraid if he gripped much harder, the wheel would snap under his strength.

"Fine. If you won't tell me why you're acting like kissing me was the worst thing in the world, will you at least test me on the people at the castle? I think I have them all, but I'm worried I'm going to fuck it up."

"You already have. Sloane would never talk like that."

She rolled her eyes. "Please, Malcolm? I'm trying here. We're going to have to be around each other, the least we can do is be cordial."

"No. It will be so much more fun to watch you figure it out on your own."

"There he is," she threw her hands in the air. "I knew the asshole tendencies of the Nicholson princes were lurking just below the surface. I was worried you'd gone soft on me."

"Still here, and very much hard."

Emery tried to keep her mind out of the gutter, but failed, her eyes dropping to Malcolm's crotch. "Do you really want to see me make a fool of myself? Doesn't this affect your family too? August mentioned how the situation was a personal slight."

"You have no idea," he muttered, flexing his tense fingers. "Honestly, I think this is a fucking terrible idea, but once we learned of your presence and the magic's transference to a twin, my father thought it was needed. So, of course, August went along with the plan."

"You didn't know about me?" She tried to hide the hurt in her voice. The fact Sloane never mentioned her twin hurt like a knife to the chest.

"No." He pressed the accelerator, propelling the car in sync with the growing tension between them. "You'll never be her, Emery. You're crass and impulsive and don't think beyond the moment. All things Sloane was not."

"Look, asshole, I may not have grown up in a castle, but I can be snooty and uptight like the rest of you." She took a sip of her water bottle, making a show of sticking her pinky up in the air as she did. "I may struggle at first to become the tame, timid girl Sloane was, but it can't be that hard. She grew up in a castle where she was kept away from the rest of the world. Her life couldn't be that complicated."

He shook his head, and his body went rigid once again. "If only you knew."

"Knew what, Malcolm?"

"Nothing."

"No, it's not nothing." Her anger became a tangible part of the air around them. It had already been an emotional day, and her nerves were fraying more with every passing moment. "I know you felt something when you saw me earlier, otherwise you wouldn't have kissed me."

Malcolm stayed silent.

Emery hit her fist against the window. "Damn it, Malcolm, just tell me what is going on! How am I supposed to believably become Sloane if you guys won't tell me everything?" She turned as best she could to face the older prince.

Malcolm jerked the wheel to the right, and Emery braced herself, nearly cracking her head on the window. When he hit the shoulder, he slammed on the brakes, thrusting her forward.

"What the fuck, Malcolm?"

He turned on her, his brows furrowed and mouth in a straight line. "You want to know what August didn't tell you? What I keep trying to forget but can't every time I look at your stupid, beautiful face? Sloane was my everything. She was my reason for existing. She was kind, and patient, and, for God knows what reasons, she loved me, too." He gazed out the front window. "August had been sneaking Sloane out so no one would know one of his Culling women was seeing another man, which is strictly forbidden. Punishable-by-death, kind of forbidden."

Malcolm sighed, he turned, his eyes locking with hers.

"In reality, he was bringing her to see me. We had a plan." He choked on his words, and she could see the pain behind his gaze. That powerful vampire was figuratively on his knees as he spoke of her twin. "We were going to tell my parents and make a show of August sending her home. She was going to ask to be turned so we could be together forever, but we never got that chance. She called it off between us and then was found dead the next morning. The morning we had planned to tell everyone of our decision. My very reason for living stopped breathing, and not in the fun vampire way." He paused and took a deep breath.

"Now, I get to see you every day as a reminder I can never have her back."

Emery sat, shocked, staring at Malcolm, unsure of what to say. She was on her way to pretend to be her dead twin, only to find out her dead twin's boyfriend was driving her there to do it. The situation was so much more fucked up than she originally thought, and she wasn't the only one having to endure. Malcolm was going to have to live through his own personal hell. It was no wonder he kissed her earlier.

"I'm sorry, Malcolm," she could only manage a whisper. "I didn't know."

"Yeah, well, now you do." He spat his words and put the car in gear before getting back on the highway.

The minutes flew by in silence. With each one, Emery felt like total and utter shit. She wanted to speak, to ask questions, but she knew Malcolm wouldn't answer.

Finally, when she spoke, she chose her words carefully. "Did you know I felt her the moment she died?"

She initially thought maybe he hadn't heard her, but after a moment, he broke his silence. "You did?"

Emery nodded, instantly pulled back to the moment it happened. "It was early in the morning. Three a.m., I think. I was in Madrid. I had just left a bar with Wren and some friends we made while traveling."

She thought back to how she'd stopped abruptly in the middle of the busy city street, clutching her chest while the group kept walking and making plans for the following day, none the wiser. "It felt as though my heart was being ripped in two. I thought I was dying. And then it was as if a piece of my soul was just gone. Vanished. People say twins have a bond. I always knew I shared something with Sloane, but never put much thought into it until that moment. I know now it's very real and how lucky I was to have that for twenty-five years, even if I didn't truly know her. Then, as if on cue, my wrist burned hot."

Emery looked down at her wrist, remembering the way the vines appeared, each one etched as if someone had taken a hot piece of steel to her skin. "The moment the mark of the Culling finished branding me, the pull began. All I wanted was to mourn the loss of my sister, but I couldn't ignore the pull, despite how hard I tried."

She wiped a tear from her eye. "I may not understand your connection with Sloane, but I know what it's like to lose a piece of yourself."

Malcolm stayed quiet, giving her nothing of how he felt about her admission.

They entered the castle grounds via a long gravel driveway, and Emery got her first glimpse of her new home. Even only lit by the moon, the stone castle was magnificent. A well-manicured lawn led to a circular drive at the base of a grand staircase that led to the main entrance. The castle itself looked to be plucked right from a fairy tale, with turrets and spires to complete the medieval feel.

It was breathtaking.

She wished Malcolm would slow down so she could admire every minor detail, but she wasn't about to ask him to. He passed the circular drive and pulled around to a secluded entrance on the side of the castle.

The car stopped, and the visage of August appeared in the doorway. He stepped out slightly and rested against the frame. He might as well have been a gargoyle with the stoneface glare he gave her.

Emery reached for the door, wishing she could clear the

air between her and Malcolm before facing her new life in the castle. He was literally trying his best to keep it together, and for losing the love of his life just days ago, he was doing a damn good job.

As she opened the door, Malcolm grabbed her hand and looked her in the eyes. "Thank you, Emery," he whispered.

A low growl from behind her broke the moment. Emery swung her head to see August. She glared daggers into his thick skull before looking back to Malcolm. With a squeeze of his hand, she stepped out of the car and into the cool air.

"How was the drive?" August's voice was no longer as warm as it was that morning.

Emery's heart sank. "Uneventful."

"I'm sure." He nodded toward his brother.

"Jealous?" Emery teased the beast like an idiot. She needed to learn to hold her tongue. Sloane would not have said that.

"Why would I be jealous? I know you don't want to be with a vampire." He retorted with no emotion whatsoever. "Nor do you want to be your sister's sloppy seconds. At least, that's the gist of what you said."

Ouch. Yeah, she'd said that.

What she should have said was she didn't want to be with a vampire unless it was August. But she hadn't known that at the time. It took a kiss from another vampire to realize he was the only one she'd consider.

Not that she should be considering any vampires. It was still a death sentence if they found out she was a witch.

August stilled and tilted his head, looking along the castle wall. His brow furrowed before he abruptly pulled her against him into a hug and dipped his mouth to her ear. "We aren't alone. Follow me."

Fear crept up her spine.

"Take my arm, let's get you inside." His tone was warm, even friendly. "I'm happy you're back."

She took his rigid arm, and he led her through the stone entrance. Up two stories via a narrow stairway and a hallway over. After that, she was completely lost. It didn't matter that she'd reviewed the map a dozen times at the hotel. Her emotions were running too high for her brain to catch up.

When they reached the dormitory wing, everything suddenly became real. Holding it together became impossible. She'd reached her breaking point, the day taxing her both mentally and physically. She ached to sleep or cry. Maybe both.

If only August would say something, anything to give her a foothold in her new surroundings. A word of confidence. A hint as to where they stood. But want in one hand and shit in the other, she knew which one would fill up first.

August stopped in front of a door and dropped her arm. "I'm glad you're feeling better. I'll leave you to get reacquainted with your room."

She nodded, unsure of what else to say or do. She hated the charade between them, wishing they could go back to how they'd been at the hotel. Before she'd put her foot in her mouth and fucked things up. Before she became her sister.

"I'm sorry, August, for what I said earlier." She took a step toward him, though she wasn't sure what she meant to accomplish by closing their physical distance. She couldn't take back what she said at the hotel room when her anger was high. With her apology, the ball was in his court.

August stepped back. "Think nothing of it, Sloane." He replied as eloquently as a prince should.

The name was a slap in the face.

She bit back tears as she tried to remember that's who she'd be for the foreseeable future. Emery never left that hotel room, and she wouldn't exist again until August released her from the Culling.

Emery turned to the thick, wooden door with intricate metal work like she'd never seen and opened it, resisting the urge to look back at the man who made her entire body go up in flames. She hoped he'd release her soon because being Sloane was quickly becoming too much for her to handle.

Being in that castle, around vampires who hated witches, with a murderer in the shadows, was going to test every part of her.

Chapter Seven

AUGUST

Her heart beat erratically on the other side of the door. It called to him, demanding he settle it or give it a very different reason to beat so quickly.

After a silent moment, the faintest rush of water came from the room, and it was all he could do not to break the door down and join her in what he knew would be the fuck of his life. And if he did that, he'd never have the chance to convince her to be his. He'd be exactly the kind of man she already thought him to be.

August ignored the pull and reached for his phone to text Malcolm.

Find me. We weren't alone.

He stared at the screen until the light went out, willing his feet to move away from the thick, wood door separating him from the woman he wanted to ruin. He needed to walk away, investigate the noise he heard off the back of the castle. But his body wouldn't obey.

Every part of him wanted to ignore everything else in the world and demand Emery open the door so they could explore the unexplainable chemistry between them. The feelings that made it impossible to think straight and licked at his skin when they got too close, making his dick painfully hard.

He leaned back against the cold stone wall, the shadows of the dimly lit hallway clinging to him as he slid to the floor. A sigh escaped his lips as he wrapped his arms around his knees and rested his head between them. There wasn't a single instance in his history where he felt as weak as he did then, sitting outside her door like an abandoned puppy. He didn't even know the woman, yet couldn't stomach walking away.

Get a bloody grip.

As the crown prince, no woman came before his kingdom. Never had he given such attention to a woman of his Culling, but never had they drawn his attention in the first place. They merely existed for when he decided to take a bride. Which he had no intention of doing. At least, not any time soon. They had another ten more good breeding years left in them, and August had every intention to wait until their last eggs dropped to take his bride.

That was, until two days ago. Sloane's murder landed him with a phone call from his father with a direct order to take his Culling more seriously and handle the situation in his absence.

He'd suspected the order would have been delivered regardless of her death. The king had grown tired of August's antics long ago. Taking women as he pleased from the club and never glancing at his Culling could only be tolerated for so long. They'd lived there for twenty years, and he could scarcely remember all their names.

Sloane's death slapped him in the face and brought him back to a painful reality. The women were his responsibility, and because of his indifference, he failed at keeping them safe. Eventually, he would have taken his Culling more seriously, without the king's order. It was only an heir his father cared about, after all. He could pick any one of them and make that happen.

August would never admit it, but he'd hoped over the years one of the women would hold his attention. That maybe he could have something his parents didn't.

Love.

When all twenty women in his Culling came of age, he'd tried to get to know them. Watching them from afar, making small conversations at events to see if any of them held his eye. None had. All the women had been brainwashed to want two things: a crown and his seed in their womb.

After those few attempts to get closer to the women, he resigned himself to having the same kind of marriage as his parents. Calculated and loveless. While his mother ensured August and his siblings were loved beyond measure, it never extended to their father. The king and queen could barely stand being in the same room together, let alone the same bed.

How they managed to have two children, he didn't know.

A half smile tipped his lips. If his father forced him to

choose his bride upon the order, August would have shuffled a deck of the women's photos and plucked one out to be his wife. But everything changed the moment Sloane died and Emery entered the bar. He'd stack the deck to ensure she ended up at his side.

August scoffed at the thought. Who the hell did he think he was? It wasn't some bloody romance novel he was living in. There was no such thing as instant-love, and he wasn't the hero of the story that got the girl. Sure, he would get a girl, but it wouldn't be Emery. She didn't want him, and he sure as hell didn't need the mouth that came with her.

But he wanted it.

God, he fucking wanted it.

Fast approaching footfalls echoed down the hall. Vampire. He tensed, not wanting to be caught and having to explain why he was sitting in the Culling women's hallway, but relaxed when his older brother slowed and towered over him.

"What the fuck are you doing up here? I've been looking everywhere for you."

"Relaxing, what does it look like?"

Malcolm raised his eyebrows before looking at whose door he sat outside of. He visibly winced, his eyes narrowing on August. "Why are you sitting outside *her* room? Do you enjoy punishing me?"

"No, Malcolm. Of course not. It's just—"

"It's not enough you agreed to bring her here as my dead ex-lover," his brother continued, his face twisting into an emotion August had never seen before, "but now you taunt me by sitting outside her room? The same room I would bring her back to in the early morning light and kiss her goodbye, knowing the moment I walked away she'd be your

Culling woman for another day. Just so I could call her mine for a few short hours. I've been avoiding this hallway for days, and you had to wait for me here of all places? You really are a fucking prick."

"I'm sorry, Malcolm. I didn't think. It wasn't my intention to hurt you. I just got lost in the...she calms it." His words were barely a whisper, as if admitting that fact out loud might negate the inexplicable effect she had on him. "I don't know how, or why, but she calms the urge to tear the throat open of the nearest human. Her mere presence soothes the ache I have been plagued with my entire existence." August raked his fingers through his hair. "I know it doesn't add up. She's just another human, but from the moment I locked eyes with her in the club, it's like something clicked, and I don't know what it is."

"You don't feel it at all?" Malcolm's eyes widened as his voice trailed upward.

Where Malcolm was the anomaly born human, August was born with the opposite problem. His vampire traits were more prominent, resulting in an unusually high penchant for blood from the vein. Bagged blood sated the urges well enough but didn't consume his every thought like tearing into a vein.

Malcolm was the only one who'd taken the time to understand August's addiction. He was more than just his older brother, he was his best friend, only friend. He knew August better than anyone else in the castle and had been there when the blood lust became too much to contain. He was the only one able to bring August back from the brink of insanity.

They knew what made the other tick and the best way to piss each other off. Which they did often. When Malcolm came to him about his feelings for Sloane, August had done whatever it took to make it work for his brother. Even committing treason.

If there was anyone he wanted to share his revelations with about Emery, it was his brother. Under different circumstances. Now the only thing he wanted to do was spare his brother's heart.

Malcolm was right, August was a fucking prick.

"We don't have to talk about it. About her."

Malcolm reached up and scrubbed his face with his hand. "It's fine. Explain the bloodlust."

It wasn't fine. It was fucked up. The entire situation was a train wreck of massive proportions, and there was no getting off at the last stop. "It's as if the thirst settles within me, content with having her nearby. The moment I leave her proximity it comes back with a vengeance. I was sitting here outside her door for a momentary reprieve."

Malcolm swallowed hard. He opened his mouth to speak, then closed it, as if he thought better. When he did speak, his voice cracked. "Did you feel that way about Sloane?"

"No, brother."

"Will you choose her to be your bride then?"

"That's the kicker. She doesn't want me or the crown. I was given an ultimatum I couldn't turn down. She wants to find out what happened to her sister and then be sent home." His stomach tightened as the bitter words left his mouth. As it stood, he couldn't handle her leaving. Not now. Not after he'd experienced so little of what she had to offer.

There was too much more to explore.

"Maybe it's for the best."

"You just don't want to stare at your dead lover's face for

the rest of your life." His knee jerk reaction to the thought of losing her hit his brother below the belt.

Malcolm's lips curled, revealing elongated fangs. "Fuck you, August. She hasn't even been dead a week. I know you weren't her biggest fan, but I loved her. I'd do anything to see you happy, you know that. But you couldn't, for even one minute, consider that I'm barely keeping it together." Malcolm gave August his back, his fists clenched in anger. "I don't have time for this shit. You're on your own tonight."

Regret hit like a ton of bricks as his brother started down the hallway. Malcolm's broken heart didn't deserve August's misplaced frustration.

"Wait." August called after him. "I'm sorry."

Malcolm paused mid stride. "August, you know, if she was the one for you, I'd stomach her for an eternity. But you and I both know you won't break her. She's different, I'll give you that, but she doesn't want to be here. She'd hate you with every fiber of her being if you forced her to stay, and based on what she has already made you feel, you wouldn't be able to handle sending her home. You want more than that, and she deserves more."

Malcolm was right. August fucking hated it, but he was right. If he made her stay against her will, she would hate him. They both deserved better than that fate.

With a deep sigh, he stood. Hanging his head, he admitted what his heart knew to be true, though he would never say it out loud again in case the universe held him to it. "I won't keep her against her will, brother. I am a monster, and she is the treasure I wish to hoard. Have you ever noticed in fairy tales the monster never gets to keep his treasure? Instead, he is slain by a white knight and forgotten while the hero gains the favor of the maiden. I wouldn't want to be forgotten by her. I want her to want to be my treasure. One I would cherish every day, body and soul, for the rest of eternity, if she'd allow me to. I can already see she has the makings of a queen, but I would rather let her go than cage her."

Malcolm entwined his hands and brought them over his heart, tilting his head, he batted his eyes. "I won't ever call you a heartless prick again, brother. You're just a big softy who wants love too."

August's knuckles met the soft flesh of Malcolm's stomach faster than he could react, and his brother doubled over. "Shut the fuck up. You tell no one of this. I may want her, but I haven't decided if she's worth the time or not." *Lie.* "Either way, I think I'll take my time choosing my wife, maybe woo a few and see how *my* little twin reacts."

Malcolm chuckled. "I'll ignore the lie I sense in your words. More importantly, you don't woo."

"I can woo."

"No, your dick can woo. You, on the other hand, are a prickly pear."

"And what's the problem with allowing my dick to woo? It's always served me well."

Malcolm raised his eyebrows, and August knew the moment he was silently recalling.

"It was one time, Malcolm. And how was I supposed to know she was the wife of Dracula?"

Malcolm covered his mouth, trying to hide his laugh, though failed miserably. It was a wonder his roar didn't wake the entire floor. "Come on, lover boy, let's go solve the mystery of who dared defy your curfew to catch a glimpse of our twin."

"*My* twin," August whispered possessively, though if Malcolm heard him, he didn't react.

They walked down the hall, away from Emery and the comfort she gave him. With every step, August felt the pangs of hunger clawing their way to the surface, reminding him of the monster he truly was.

Chapter Eight

AUGUST

August and Malcolm stepped into the brisk night air. Summer was trying it's best to push out the cool spring breeze that drifted off Lake Michigan, but it hadn't taken hold yet. August inhaled to pick up the scent of anything out of place. Nothing jumped out at him.

"I thought you did a perimeter check before we arrived?" Malcolm did little to hide the frustration in his voice.

"I did, not two minutes before you arrived. I wouldn't leave her open to a possible attack. Whoever I heard was not there when I checked."

"So, they appeared out of thin air?" Malcolm scoffed.

August narrowed his eyes, not justifying him with a retort. After all the heartbreak last week, he felt bad for his brother, but it wasn't the right moment to dissect Malcolm's headspace. They needed to figure out who was outside when it should have been clear. Then, he needed to address the need to feed that held him on a razor thin edge after walking away from Emery. He could just return to the hallway outside her door, claiming he was standing guard to keep his women safe.

What the hell was he thinking? He couldn't sit outside her door all hours of the night. He'd known the woman for one day and already she'd become his weakness. The one who could calm his soul with just her presence. But it was more than that. She'd slipped her way into his life, and he didn't want to know what it would be like without her. He wanted to know what every season of life was like with her. And that scared the shit out of him.

The wind whipped around the castle, bringing the scent of lemon and lavender to his senses. He kept to the shadows and led the way toward the unusual combination.

When he made it to the spot the rustling had come from, he knelt behind the rose bush and found evidence he'd been looking for. August touched the footprint left in the soft dirt. The indentation was small and narrow, obviously female by the shape and heel.

"My women were all instructed to stay inside, correct?"

"Yes," Malcolm huffed. "Before I left, I made certain Yessenia instructed them."

"So, these prints either belong to a female intruder or a staff member."

"The staff wouldn't disobey a direct order from the crown." Malcolm looked over his shoulder at the prints. "Plus, you don't know they are female. They could belong to a man wearing a tasteful pair of heels. You know what they say about making assumptions, brother." A smile pulled at Malcolm's lips.

"Indeed, but you're the only ass here, Malcolm." August

stood, his gaze following the tracks to the tree line of the forest that surrounded most of the castle.

Malcolm chuckled and followed the tracks with his own eyes before looking at August. "It looks like we are going on a moonlit stroll through the forest."

Whoever the prints belonged to had run and unfortunately was long gone. He should have gone after the person when he'd heard them initially. He should have had Malcolm escort Emery to her room. But after witnessing their intimate exchange in the car, jealousy got the best of him. He nearly pummeled his brother for touching her.

After that display, every primal instinct within him raged to claim her as his own. While she may not be his yet, she most certainly did not belong to Malcolm either. Blinded by her presence, he'd put the safety of all his Culling women second to Emery.

August chewed his lip and shook his head. He needed to get his head out of his ass and focus on the task at hand.

In silence, the brothers headed toward the tree line, following the tracks. The air was crisp, and the forest silent. Though summer started soon, it was rare to find animals in their territory. They kept a natural distance from the predators that lived within the castle walls.

Two hundred yards into the dense wood, Malcolm broke the silence between them. "I told her about my past with Sloane."

August clenched his fists, struggling to allow his common sense to peek through the need to bleed his brother. "That explains her apology." And further explained the moment he'd witnessed between the two of them in the car.

"August, wait. I have to tell you something." Malcolm

paused, and when August turned to look at him, his eyes were everywhere but on his.

"Is everything okay?"

"Yes. No. I'm not okay, and I need you to know I didn't do what I'm about to tell you to hurt you." Malcolm's eyes finally met August's, and sadness clouded his features. "She's not like Sloane. I selfishly wanted her to be. Thought it would be easier to accept it all if she had been. But she isn't."

"No. She's not." Thank the gods for small miracles.

"I know that now. But I had to be sure. When I picked her up at the hotel, I kissed her."

Before he could rein in his rage, August's fist met flesh. Malcolm flew back into a tree, splitting the bark with his impact. His fangs elongated and he gnashed his teeth, the bloodlust didn't help him to fight the urge to rip his brother's throat out for touching what was his.

Malcolm reached up and wiped the blood from the corner of his lip. "I'm sorry, August. She looks so much like Sloane. I fell into the moment."

"Oh, you just tripped and fell into her lips? She's new to our world, Malcolm, she doesn't need you confusing her. Did you at least have the decency to compel her to forget?"

"No."

August turned away from his brother, the soul shattering kiss he'd stolen from Emery's still fresh in his mind. He'd broken his own rule, compelling one of his women, to keep Emery from finding out how much he wanted her.

He clenched his fists at his sides. There wouldn't be any letting it go. If Malcolm was anyone else, he'd dismember them limb by limb, then set their body aflame ensuring they wouldn't return. But he wasn't anyone else. He was his brother, and there were other, more immediate things to handle than thinking of ripping his brother apart for kissing Emery. It was best to walk away and let cooler heads prevail. If he didn't, Malcolm wouldn't make it out of those woods until August felt better. And it would take more than one punch to make him feel better.

He spun to face his brother, eyes narrowed. "Do not touch her again."

"I won't." August didn't miss the dejected tone in his brother's voice. "She's not Sloane. I know that with unwavering certainty now."

Fuck. Once again, August was the asshole. Emery might heighten his emotions to an unnatural level, but Malcolm was his brother, and he should be able to see past a woman for him. Should being the operative word. He couldn't get the image of Malcolm and Emery out of his mind, and it wasn't something he would soon forget.

He crossed the distance and placed a hand on his shoulder. "I'm sorry she's gone. I know you loved her."

If he was a lesser man, he'd tell Malcolm what he really thought of that little snake he called a lover. Breaking off their relationship just before their plan to tell everyone put her right at the top of August's shit list. And she would have stayed there too. If she hadn't died, of course.

It was a cruel trick of fate that August was falling for the woman with the same face as his brother's late lover.

He clapped Malcolm on the back and stepped away. It'd been a shit day and an even worse week. They both needed a moment to cut loose and let go of everything that happened at the castle before they had to dive back in. "Want to go for a run?"

A lopsided grin formed on his brother's face. "First to the end of those tracks is the winner."

"What do I get when I win?"

"Not a damn thing. Because there is no chance in hell you are winning." He jumped up and down, like a runner before a track meet, as if he needed to. "But, just to make things interesting, let's put a wager on it."

"What do you have in mind?"

"What do you say the winner gets to pick your first official date of the Culling?" It was no secret Malcolm enjoyed poking fun at August's misery surrounding his Culling.

"Deal." August already knew who he would award the honor to, and the thought of her smart mouth made his dick hard.

"You better get ready to wine and dine Father's favorite Culling woman."

August looked to the starless sky and groaned. He knew exactly who Malcolm would torture him with.

Jessi.

The resident Culling bitch. If he could send her home, he would. However, her family came from money and influence, and thus his father ensured she remained the frontrunner.

August focused on the footprints ahead. The path to victory. There was no way in hell he would lose the race. "You ready?"

Malcolm didn't answer before he took off.

"Fuck." August exploded forward. The trees blurred alongside him as he gracefully navigated the forest. He loved to move that fast, breaking through wind like fangs through flesh. The cool air filled his half dead lungs, breathing life into them. With each pump of his legs, he felt more power and freedom than he had in days.

He caught up to Malcolm with ease. They'd trained together for centuries and were evenly matched. As he made a move to pass him, August grabbed a branch of a tree and planned his sabotage. He waited for the perfect moment, until he was a foot behind his brother. Falling into step with him, he shoved the branch between Malcolm's legs with precision.

Malcolm tumbled across the mossy forest floor and into the dense brush along the path, cursing with every roll. August took the lead and continued to follow the footprints deeper into the forest, a shit-eating grin plastered on his face. It wasn't long before he could no longer hear Malcolm behind him.

August slowed as he approached the river crossing their path, his brain already planning his victory date with Emery.

Dinner. Maybe a trip to the lake. Did she like long walks on the beach since she was from California? Was that too cliche?

He followed the footprints around a small bend in the path, only to find Malcolm, sitting on a large boulder, wearing the same shit-eating grin August had moments before. The trait that proclaimed their kinship beyond doubt.

"Bloody fucking hell." August threw up his hands in frustration. "How did you get here before me?"

Malcolm's smile never faded, only enraging August more. "Now I can't have you knowing all my tricks, baby brother."

Shit.

That's what he got for counting his eggs before they hatched. Karma was a bitch, and he was destined for a first date with Jessi. Something he'd managed to put off for years, not for her lack of asking every time she saw him.

"Does it have to be Jessi?"

"Oh, you know it does. But that's not our biggest problem right now." Malcolm pointed to the edge of the river. "The tracks end here. They don't pick up on the other side. The person who made them either swam downstream or, and this is my most morbid hypothesis, they disappeared completely."

August knelt and studied the tracks, considering the possible exit strategies. Swim or disappear. Humans didn't just disappear. That narrowed the options to something supernatural, which didn't sit well. As much as he would love to go toe-to-toe with the witches, now was not the time. It also potentially supported the theory Sloane's death was an attack made by another faction.

His money was on the witches. There was no way it was the wolves. They were the supernatural version of Switzerland.

He looked up to find Malcolm still lounging on the rock. "Seriously?" His eyes narrowed on him. "Are you not going to help me investigate?"

"I wasn't planning on it." Malcolm picked up a stick lodged between the boulder and fast running water. "Let's be honest, I'm only here to make sure the prince doesn't drop his gilded crown."

August rolled his eyes and hit him where he knew it would make the most impact. "This could be related to her death."

Malcolm stilled, then threw the stick in the river. "Fine." August didn't miss the glare thrown his direction.

The two of them spent the next ten minutes searching the

area for any clue that would point them in the direction of the mystery person. Just when he was about to hang up and head back to the castle, a glimmer of white caught August's peripheral.

He moved with calculated care, so as not to jostle the branches it was lodged in causing the paper to fall in the water. He reached out and grabbed it between two fingers. Unfolding it, he read the words elegantly scrawled upon it.

Bring me the witch in the castle.

"Fuck." August nearly crushed the paper in his fist.

"What is that? What does it say?" Malcolm sauntered over and snatched the paper from August's hand. He read the words, and his formerly lackadaisical expression distorted with the tightening of his jaw. He looked up, eyes meeting August's. "Fuck is right."

Not good. His father and the witch's high priestess had been at odds for centuries, with bad blood on both sides. The witches were a cancer that needed to be stopped, a threat to vampires unlike any other in the world. The pretense of peace between the rival factions was thin at best, and at worst…August didn't want to consider what at worst would look like. There was no line the witches wouldn't cross. If vampires didn't outnumber them, they'd be a force to be reckoned with.

Thankfully, they did.

There was one, though. One witch that'd been around

since before even Malcolm's birth. One witch even his father could stomach. "It could be Lilyana they want."

Malcolm shifted, suddenly rigid in his movements. "Does she even reside on the grounds? I didn't know she'd made the journey from Scotland."

August nodded. There were perks to being the heir. His father thought it pertinent he be aware their resident witch did indeed cross the Atlantic with them nearly three centuries prior. She'd been granted a small plot of land just outside the castle perimeter which was spelled so only those who knew where to look might find it.

It was his father's dirty little secret, and August couldn't blame him for wanting to keep her out of his court. The witches had taken more from him than any man should have to experience.

"Regardless if Lilyana is involved, we officially have a witch problem." He spat, his chest tightening.

The witches were responsible for more deaths than he could count, the most important being the king's first family. The family he wanted. The deaths subsequently killed any hope of happiness for any member of the royal family after that. His family now was only the replacement. He never wanted them to be his forever. His survival of the attack was solely because of Lilyana, which is why she was the only witch permitted on castle grounds.

If there was a witch in the castle, there was a chance they were involved in Sloane's death. And if that were true, the treaty would be null and void.

August's stomach flipped.

He looked up at Malcolm who continued to shift his weight from side to side. What had gotten into him?

"I need to head back to the castle. Let me know if you

find any other cryptic notes." Without another word, Malcolm disappeared through the dense trees.

Between Malcolm's strange behavior and the possibility of a witch mole in the castle, how he was going to focus on anything he needed to was beyond him.

His father would return from Canada in two days' time. He had that long to figure out as much as he could to brief the king and strategize what a war with the witches would look like.

And how to keep everyone he cared about safe.

Chapter Nine

EMERY

"Sloane?"

Emery shook the hand off her shoulder and rolled over, her brain demanding more sleep, but the woman persisted.

"Sloane, wake up. You can't be late today."

"Five more minutes," Emery groaned and tugged the covers back over her head.

"You've been sleeping the last two days in the infirmary. You've had plenty of sleep. Now wake up!" The soft down comforter was yanked from Emery's body, exposing her to the cold morning air.

"Fuck, was that necessary?" Emery's eyes flew open and met those of her sister's handmaid, Dahlia. She realized in that split second where she was, and her hand flew to her mouth. "I'm sorry, Dahlia. I was deep in a dream, and I don't know what came over me. I shouldn't have snapped at you like that."

If she didn't get a grip on her cursing, the entire castle would know Sloane was gone before breakfast.

Dahlia placed a silver tray filled with toast and an array of berries on the bed beside her, and Emery could have sworn she saw her fighting back a smile. "It's fine, Miss. Here's your breakfast."

Emery stretched, the feeling hitting the tips of her toes, and propped herself up in bed. Plopping a blueberry in her mouth, she watched in awe as Dahlia went about a seamlessly choreographed morning routine. It was strange to have another human taking care of her.

Dahlia disappeared momentarily into the closet and returned with a dress draped across her arms, beaming with pride. "You always look so radiant in blue, and it's the prince's favorite color. Plus, I'm told he has a big announcement to make to the Culling women today. You'll want to look your best."

Emery rolled her eyes, but she had to admit the dress was gorgeous. It was deep navy at the neckline, then transitioned as it flared to the lightest of blues, and tiny stars littered the skirt of the dress.

It reminded her of the eastern sky in the moments where day became night. She'd never worn anything so beautiful. Ada never considered appearances to be worth the investment, and once she was on her own, Emery never cared.

"Now, up with you. We need to get you ready."

Dahlia placed the dress on the bed and helped Emery up, swiftly pulling her nightgown over her head. Emery gasped and fought the urge to hide her breasts. She'd never been undressed by someone else before and had to remind herself it was something normal for Sloane. Emery plastered a fake smile on her face and tried to act like she was okay with standing in her bra and panties.

If Dahlia noticed Emery's hesitation, she didn't mention it. Instead, she continued with small talk about the gossip in the castle. Apparently, the fact the prince was taking any notice of the Culling women was a big deal. Before then, Sloane and Jessi were the only two he spoke to on a regular basis.

Emery recalled the pretty blonde's photo from the binder. Jessi had the look of royalty. Even in her picture, she looked like a proper queen. There was no way Emery could compete with that. She was a simple California girl, even if Sloane wasn't.

She shook the momentary doubts from her head. It didn't matter. She wasn't there to compete for him, or to be his bride, and needed to remember that. And she most definitely wasn't there to find out what made him tick, even if his voice caused her core to clench with need.

She was there to find out who killed Sloane. And survive long enough to go back to her old life.

That was it.

Dahlia zipped up the back of her dress and ushered her into the powder room. Emery's mouth fell open when she saw the vanity set up with every type of makeup and hair tool imaginable. It put Lenny's bag of tricks to shame, and he'd made her into the spitting image of her sister. Emery had no doubt Dahlia could make her into a woman worthy of a prince.

If she hadn't watched Dahlia transform her with her own eyes, Emery wouldn't have believed her face lurked beneath the hair and makeup. Even if it was Sloane that looked back at her in the mirror, she couldn't deny she was stunning. There was no going back now.

Dahlia placed a simple set of silver flats in front of her and took a step back, her eyes looking over Emery head to toe, admiring her work. "Yes, the prince will have a hard time keeping his eyes off you."

She imagined August's unwavering gaze raking over her, and traitorous butterflies erupted in her stomach. A small part of her hoped that was the case, and she hated herself for it.

Thankfully, a knock sounded at the door before she fell too deeply into thoughts concerning the vampire prince.

Feeling every bit the princess she wasn't, Emery slipped on the flats and entered the main bedroom to see who'd arrived.

Next to Dahlia stood a woman with dark hair and eyes that were fixed in a tight glare. Even though she hid behind the glasses and power suit, the woman commanded the room. Emery instantly recognized her from the binder as Yessenia, the liaison between the Culling women and the royal family.

"Miss Yessenia is here to discuss what you've missed the last few days while you were sick." Dahlia left the woman's side and gathered the breakfast tray from the bed. "Is there anything else you need from me before I go?"

"No, thank you for your help this morning."

"You're welcome, miss." Dahlia gave a small curtsey and stepped out.

Yessenia stood deathly still, looking over Emery from head to toe. "Well, you definitely *look* like her."

So, she knew who Emery was even if she didn't sound impressed with the idea.

"I would hope so. I'm her twin."

"Hmm. Yes, you are." Yessenia's nose scrunched as she silently continued to scrutinize everything about Emery. "You were given the binder, correct?"

Emery nodded.

"The answer is 'Yes, ma'am' when asked a question."

Emery rolled her eyes but swallowed the smartass retort on the tip of her tongue. "Yes, ma'am."

"Better." Yessenia produced a folded piece of paper. "Here is a list of your schedule for the rest of the week. Each day you will attend the refresher Scottish etiquette training with the rest of the Culling women. It's meant to prepare you for the Gala that is to be held upon the arrival of the Scottish delegation."

Great. More studying.

"It has also been brought to my attention that you have no knowledge of vampire culture or history. Therefore, in the evenings, after lights out, you will be attending history lessons until you are well versed in both."

"Wait, seriously?" She didn't sign up for more studying, and loss of sleep, to keep up this charade.

"Yes, seriously," Yessenia mocked with a tilt of her head. "You are already late, so if you don't have any questions, you need to make your way to the women's common room."

"Nope, I think I can figure out how to play princess for a few weeks."

Yessenia gave her a fake smile and turned for the door, muttering to herself, "If you last that long."

Emery cocked a brow but didn't say anything. With a murderer on the loose, Yessenia may not be far off.

The large oak door slammed shut.

Everyone seemed to underestimate Emery's ability to fake it till she made it, but she didn't survive life with Ada without perfecting the skill. She'd fool them all until she found out who killed her sister. And then she'd get the hell out of there.

Chapter Ten

EMERY

At the end of the hallway, large double doors marked the entrance to the women's common room. Relishing in her newfound confidence, she took a deep breath, opened the giant oak door, and stepped through.

Or tried to.

Instead, her foot caught on the lip of the door jamb, and she tumbled directly into the back of the man just inside the door. As she ricocheted back toward the ground, two arms swept her up, saving her from a complete fall from grace.

Her body came alive, humming from within and, she hesitantly opened one eye to peek at her savior. She had no doubt who held her.

Only one man made her body feel that way.

Shit.

It couldn't have been anyone else because that would mean fate was on her side.

Two cold blue eyes captured hers with a hint of a smile pulling at his full lips.

"I'm sorry for interrupting, August," Emery whispered the apology, acutely aware of every curious glance trained on them.

He leaned in close and pressed his lips to her temple, keeping his voice low. "*Prince August.*" The harsh correction was a cold reminder of where she stood with him, but the heat of his breath on her skin sent an unwanted shiver through her. "But I rather like the way you made an entrance. I could get used to holding you like this."

Her mouth dropped open slightly. Was he flirting with her? It was a stark contrast from the distant prince she'd encountered the night before.

Emery felt his smug smile against her cheek and hated the effect he had on her. "Sorry, *Prince August.*" She choked out as he released her legs and let them fall to the ground. "It won't happen again."

When she tried to step away, August kept a firm arm around her waist and raised his voice. "How nice of you to join us, Sloane."

His attempt to humiliate her was met with a few giggles, dousing any romantic feelings she'd had the moment before.

Emery looked out at the nineteen sets of eyes glaring in her direction, and heat flooded her cheeks. Fantastic. Not only was she late, but she'd made an embarrassing entrance, and it was now obvious how much every woman there disliked her. Or Sloane, rather. Who knew a simple touch from the same man they were all trying to marry would send daggers her way?

She gave the women a sheepish smile as she forced more distance between her and the *prince*. Her footsteps echoed through the silent room, calling more attention to herself as she searched for a place to sit. By the time she settled into the empty bay window seat, all eyes were back on August.

Including her own.

He held her gaze but gave away nothing as to what he was feeling. She had no idea where they stood. Prior to arriving that morning, Emery thought it safe to assume Sloane was not August's favorite Culling woman, but then he'd gone and flirted with her in front of the others, leaving her thoroughly confused.

August shifted his attention back to the ladies showering him with doe-eyed looks of adoration. Each sat at the edge of their seat, hanging on every word that came out of his mouth, as if it would save their lives. It was pathetic. It didn't save her sister's life.

A short redhead slid onto the bench next to Emery. Chelsea Raston, Sloane's best friend.

She leaned over and whispered in Emery's ear like they'd known each other their entire lives. "I was worried you weren't coming today." Chelsea's hand gripped Emery's and gave it a squeeze as she continued without taking a breath. "I'm so glad you're feeling better. They wouldn't allow me to come see you in the infirmary. Not for lack of trying. The bitch nurse, you know, the one who wouldn't give me more than Tylenol when I broke my arm, she was adamant about the fact you needed your rest, even though I assured her you'd want to see your best friend. But you are here now, which is great because Prince August was just about to tell us some big news."

Emery raised her brows at Chelsea, mouth open slightly. Did that woman never breathe? She talked faster than anyone Emery ever met, and damn, she was intense.

She gave Chelsea's hand a squeeze and forced a smile. The fact that there was someone who cared enough to check in on her sister was a relief. "I'm okay. Feeling much better, actually. Still getting my wits about me. What have I missed?"

"Oh, the usual. Boring etiquette lessons on things we already know and Jessi thinking she's God's gift to the castle."

"Quiet!" Scarlett Edison hissed and reached up to smooth a hand down her makeup-caked cheek.

The bitchy woman sat next to the queen bee herself, Jessi Reynolds. Also plastered with makeup.

The other woman in August's life apparently.

Her fists clenched at her side. August was not hers, but she didn't want him to be Jessi's either. The second most favored Culling woman. The thought of him being anyone else's had her heart rate soaring.

She inhaled a shaky breath and fought the scowl pulling at her lips. Instead, Emery smiled sweetly and mouthed "sorry" to Scarlett. She hated being her sister already. Sloane kept her head down and didn't show emotion. Her sister had to have feelings about the women around her, but she, according to the princes, never let them show. In contrast, all Emery wanted to do was tell Scarlett to fuck off.

With each breath, the anger flaring within her calmed. She glanced around the room, noticing the way each of the women balanced on the end of their chairs listening to August speak. Each of them was a pawn in a game they couldn't see. They were in it for the long run, and he was their prize.

Emery looked August over while he spoke charismatically to his adoring fans, and the pesky butterflies returned to her stomach. The other women saw a prize, but she saw something entirely different.

She saw an impossibility.

The vampire of her childhood nightmares housed within a man who was so much more than his title it took her breath away. She'd bet August never granted the other women the opportunity to see that side of him. Hell, he'd made it clear at the club she wasn't supposed to either. But she had. Then again, he'd given her a glimpse at the hotel. And it changed everything.

It shouldn't matter. He was still the vampire that took her sister from her. But that wasn't even the biggest hurdle between them. Her witch blood was. It didn't matter he was the vampire that made her skin hum and her stomach drop. The one who made her wet with a single look and wicked grin.

As she shook the thoughts from her head, a slumped figure caught her eye. Behind the sea of excited women sat one unlike the rest. Emery scooted to the edge of her seat to get a better view.

Flora Valentine sat hunched over with her arms crossed over her chest. Her eyes were not set on August like the rest of the room, instead they bore holes in the ground at her feet.

"What's wrong with Flora?" Emery whispered to Chelsea, attracting more wrath from Scarlett.

Chelsea's eyes never left August as she shrugged. "No one knows. She started acting strange the same time you got sick. We thought maybe she had the same thing you did, even though the castle nurses assured her she was healthy as a horse. But to be honest, she's always been a little weird and quiet."

Emery nodded, committing to memory the information

her 'best friend' provided. She wanted to believe it was a coincidence Flora's personality change happened the same time Sloane died, but her gut wouldn't let her. Ada once told her that a coincidence was the universe's way of sending answers to the questions held dear.

Flora turned her head toward the window where Emery sat. When their eyes connected, Flora's widened and her face paled. They awkwardly stared at one another, but instead of looking away, Flora's eyes softened. She bit her lip, looking Emery over head to toe. Tilting her head, she raised her brows.

Emery gave her a slight nod and mouthed, "Later."

She had no idea what the woman was trying to play at, but it was clear Flora knew something. And all the signs pointed to it being something to do with her sister.

Fear flashed in Flora's eyes as she shook her head and faced toward the front once more, all but confirming she knew something.

"And now for the big announcement." August raised his voice, demanding Emery's, and everyone's, attention. "As you all may have noticed, I have not taken my duties to you, my Culling women, seriously thus far. For that I apologize." He gave a slight bow, eliciting nauseating giggles and sighs.

Emery cocked a brow in his direction. *Was* he sorry? She may not know him well, but crown princes didn't seem the type who were sorry for anything.

He gave her a sinfully wicked grin before turning toward the rest of the room, allowing it to slide into a full smile. He looked damn good focusing on her like that. Even his half smile was enough to make her go weak at the knees.

"Well, that ends today," he stated and smoothed down

his shirt, sliding his hands into his pockets. "I vow to take my duty to you, and the kingdom, more seriously."

The women applauded, and Emery followed suit, giving her best golf clap.

Gag me.

She understood the blind attraction the women had to him. He was every woman's wet dream, including hers. Still, there was no way they possibly believed he was sincere. Right?

She glanced around the room and saw they were still hanging on his every word. Every movement. They ate up his bows and downed his smiles like shots on a twenty-first birthday. Guess she was wrong.

Emery leaned over to Chelsea. "Next thing he's going to say is he'll offer us a rose to stay."

"What?" Chelsea cocked her head to the side and stared at Emery like she had no idea what she was talking about.

Shit. She forgot the sheltered women had likely never seen an episode of *The Bachelor*. She shook her head until she was sure it'd pop right off. "Never mind."

Her eyes snapped to the front of the room once more where they met August's ice cold stare, his lips pulled into a sneer.

Of course, you heard me.

She shrugged at him with a wicked smile of her own. It was funny, even if no one else understood the reference. Though, it did strike as odd that he'd known what she was referring to. Was the impossibly old vampire prince into primetime television? Just the thought of him on an overly plush couch with a bowl of popcorn in his lap, feet propped up on a coffee table, tuning into the latest episode of *The Bachelor* had Emery biting back a laugh.

August continued, dropping his sneer and returning to his prince charming act once more. "Moving forward, you may be asked to leave if I feel as though you do not have what it takes to be queen. I want you to know we have loved having you grow up here." He made a point to look at every woman as he spoke. He was smooth, she'd give him that.

Emery suspected every contender felt like they were important to him. Maybe they were, but she highly doubted it. She also doubted they had any idea there was a different side to August that wasn't only suave and political. Personally, she didn't think they were getting the upgraded version. She much preferred the jazz-singing artist or the banter-wielding August from the hotel.

"When asked to leave, you will be given two options. You may return to your biological families, or you may request to be turned and join one of the courts of our kingdom. Either way, we will do everything to ensure your transition is as smooth as possible."

How nice. We only kept you hostage here your entire life, but now that I know you aren't "The One" you can either become a vampire like us or hit the road. But don't worry, you'll be okay.

Emery was astounded by this archaic, fucked up system they had going on. Even if it was brought on by the witches. There had to be a better way to find a mate for the crowned prince than lining up twenty women and handing them over to be brainwashed and groomed at such a traumatic age. They probably had no idea the years of therapy they were causing for the family members and the women that were cast aside. They probably didn't care either. This is how it's always been done. And would likely be impossible to elicit change from both vampire and witch.

She struggled to keep her face blank as she listened to August.

His eyes narrowed on her, and his lips tipped in a half smile. "With all that said, I would like to formally ask one of you out on the first date of this new journey we are embarking on together."

Fuck.

All the women sat up a little straighter as August left the raised foyer and made his way through the room. Each smiled at him, hoping he would stop in front of them and reinforce their dreams of becoming a queen.

He made his way toward the window where Emery was sitting.

No.

Veer right.

Don't come over here.

August's eyes swept over her, and heat burned her cheeks. She refused to look away. He knew she wasn't here for him. And what was worse, if he asked, she would have no choice but to accept. She'd pretend it was because she was playing the part of Sloane, but in reality, despite everything she knew to be true, she wanted to explore the fucked up attraction between them.

As if he could read her thoughts, a glimmer of laughter lit his eyes, and his kissable lips upturned at the corners.

He sucked his bottom lip between his teeth and raked his eyes down her body. Then, he winked and turned down the aisle of women adjacent to Emery.

She released a heated sigh and ignored the way her stomach dropped right along with her heart.

The game he played was dangerous, and she had yet to learn the rules. She imagined the stakes were too high for her pockets, but it didn't change the fact she needed to be all in. Emery only hoped she'd be able to walk away when needed because his predatory smile had her too worked up for her own good.

August stopped in front of Jessi Reynolds who tossed her golden curls over her shoulder, dramatically batting her eyelashes at him.

Shocker.

August's knee hit the floor, and every woman in the room sucked in a collective gasp. He took Jessi's hand and smiled. "Jessi, would you do me the honor of joining me for—?"

"Yes." Jessi exclaimed, interrupting him completely. "Of course, yes, I would be honored to be your *first* date of the Culling."

Every woman wanted to be Jessi right now. Including her.

"Well then, that's settled." August stood, giving a slight bow to Jessi. "I'll pick you up from the common room tonight."

Jessi curtsied low, giving August a peek of the cleavage popping out of her low-cut emerald dress. "I can't wait," she cooed.

The moment August left the room, the volume rose, and the majority of the Culling women crowded around Jessi, loudly gossiping about her upcoming date.

Chelsea scoffed. "Figures she got the first date. It should have been you, though. We all know there are two vastly different frontrunners, the crown favorite and the prince's favorite. Only an idiot would believe Jessi was chosen out of favoritism and not politics. Her family sponsors every charity in the royal family's name. You have her beat in every aspect that counts, though."

Interesting.

"Yeah, that figures." Emery agreed. She knew Sloane was a frontrunner and that Jessi was also favored, but it came as a complete and utter shock to Emery that it was due to family involvement. She was under the impression families didn't have contact with their daughters. At least, she never did. Ada told her writing letters was useless because the vampires kept Sloane secluded from the world.

That was just one more thing to add to the pile of shit Ada told her that more than likely wasn't true. At the moment, she wasn't sure if the reason she didn't have contact with Sloane over the years was because of Ada, or Sloane herself. One version seemed more and more plausible the longer she submersed herself in her new life. Would Emery's view of vampires be different if she'd stayed in contact with Sloane all these years? No. That would have never happened under Ada's watch. In her eyes, vampires would always be evil and witches forever superior.

More and more, Emery wasn't so sure.

Jessi strutted to Chelsea and Emery, stopping before them in a top-to-bottom power stance. "I guess you aren't the favorite after all, Sloane. The prince knows where his real future is." She turned to the women standing behind her, and they all laughed on cue.

She'd just been handed the opportunity of a lifetime with a mean girl she didn't give two fucks about, and she couldn't let it go to waste.

"Yeah, he does know where his future is. In my bed after he drops you off at your room. Well done, though, securing the first date. I'm glad he'll be able to see who to send home first." Emery winked with a satisfied smile.

Sloane wouldn't have said that, but Emery was barely holding it together where August was concerned, and Jessi had gone and poked the bear. Shit. Well, it was out there, nothing she could do about it except own it. She held Jessi's gaze, emitting solid confidence.

The queen of the lemmings deserved to be put in her place. She preyed on the weak, keeping them down purely for her own satisfaction. Emery had once been a weak girl. Not anymore. She worked too hard to pull herself out of the shell where she once lived under Ada's thumb. It was about time Sloane grew a bit of a backbone.

Jessi and her posse stared at her, mouths gaping. Emery didn't know all the history between the women, but it was clear no one stood up to the over-manicured blonde bombshell.

That was going to change. She may be there to find her sister's murderer, but she'd be damned if she was going to let them walk all over her during the process.

"It's clear your sickness affected your thinking if you'd ever believe the prince would choose you over me." Jessi's voice was thick with disgust.

Emery shrugged with a smile. "We'll see."

With her chin held high, she stood and made her way toward the door on the opposite side of the room that would lead her to the lower levels of the castle. She ensured she did her best model walk, swinging her hips, showing off her best assets. Hopefully, the interaction would knock Jessi down a peg.

Her hands were shaking by the time she made it through the door and into the hallway. In her first hour as a Culling woman, she'd made an enemy. Not that Jessi's opinion mattered. They shook because she'd failed in her first hour as Sloane. And because she knew what fueled her outburst.

August.

He was her kryptonite, and she needed to figure out how to rectify that before she found herself too deep to get out. Weakness got people killed.

She needed fresh air. To breathe deeply and calm her frayed nerves. There were still a few hours until afternoon lessons, and she planned to spend every minute of them away from the Culling women. In fact, she planned to spend every minute of every day at the castle as far from them as she possibly could.

Emery took the steps of the winding staircases, only glancing at the ancient royal paintings that lined the walls instead of studying them like they demanded. The last thing she needed was to look into the eyes of stuffy old vampires.

As she reached the foyer leading to the back courtyard, an arm wrapped around her waist and lifted her off her feet. Emery screamed as a hand covered her mouth, and she was pulled into darkness.

Chapter Eleven

EMERY

Her eyes struggled to adjust to the pitch black room, but that didn't stop Emery from kicking and punching at her assailant. There was no way she was going down easily.

The hand left her mouth, and strong arms wrapped around her, pulling her against a brick wall of a chest. "Fuck, knock it off, it's me."

The husky voice was the last one she expected.

"Malcolm?" Emery spun in his arms. "What the fuck are you thinking pulling me into—where are we, a utility closet? Last time we were alone, you kissed me, and I don't want an encore, thank you."

She pushed his chest to create as much space between them as she could, which was hard given they were in a storage closet. The smell of cleaning products and the heady scent of vampire was enough to make her head spin.

"I value my life, and while I may not be the most perfectly trained lap dog like the others, I don't think your brother would appreciate it if he caught us together in a fucking closet." Emery tried to maneuver to the door.

"I'm not sorry." Malcolm blocked her exit. "I needed to talk to you away from prying eyes and ears."

"And *this* was the best solution you could come up with?"

He stepped closer, challenging her question. "Yes, it was. You try finding a place in the castle where no one is following you or listening in. This is actually quite genius, if I do say so myself."

"You would think so because it was *you* following *me* around." Emery huffed, rolling her eyes in the darkness as she considered at least five better meeting places. Men, even vampires apparently, really lacked the finesse to be sneaky. "Well, you got me here, what's so important you needed to drag me into a closet?"

"Last night there was someone outside the castle when you arrived. There shouldn't have been anyone. As you can imagine, we went through great lengths to keep your arrival a secret. After you were safely inside, August and I followed their tracks. We didn't find the person, but we did find a note we believed they dropped." He paused, and even in the darkness, Emery could sense the change in his demeanor. The weight of his impending words hanging in the air. "The note stated: Bring me the witch in the castle."

Panic rose in her throat as she considered the ramifications of the note. No one at the castle was supposed to know she had witch blood besides Malcolm, and he only knew because of his history with her sister.

Emery didn't even consider her or her sister to be witches — the only thing they could do was resist compulsion— but defective or not, it would be damning enough in the eyes of any other vampire.

It would definitely be enough for whoever was seeking out witches in the castle. Which could be anyone.

Her chest tightened more. There was no one to protect her, except maybe the princes, and even then, she expected their loyalty to be with their family. As much as she hated growing up under Ada's strict rules, they kept her safe from finding herself under the fangs of a vampire. At the castle, she wasn't just prey. She was the enemy.

Her breathing became erratic, and the walls of the closet closed in. Sloane had already been killed. *If* it was because of her blood, Emery had no doubt they would be coming for her next. Even if it was only to rectify their mistake in properly killing Sloane. Coming to the castle had been a mistake, not that she had a choice. The binding on her wrist robbed her of any other option.

Malcolm ran his fingertips up and down her arms, leaning in and whispering against her skin. "Breathe. You're safe. We won't let anything happen to you."

His voice sounded far away, even though he was inches from her.

We.

Malcolm and August couldn't keep Sloane safe. Why should she be any different? Malcolm loved Sloane. Emery was just a stranger with her face. And August. Well, he was off finding his wife. He'd be no help to her.

Even if she didn't believe a word he said, he was her only potential ally, which left little to no wiggle room when it came to accepting his help. She leaned into him. Physical touch calmed the rising panic. She half chuckled at the irony.

Years of anxiety caused by the mythical being before her, and there he was, calming her.

"What's so funny?"

She took a deep breath in and slowly exhaled. "My life."

After a half of a dozen breaths against Malcolm's steady chest, the anxiety released her from its chilling grip. She looked up, her nose hitting Malcolm's chin. Her breath hitched, knowing even though she couldn't see him, his eyes were studying her for any movement. Any indication of permission for him to move.

Emery backed herself against the shelving, giving him as much space as she could.

Neither of them spoke, and an increasingly awkward silence grew between them.

"Thank you. For trying to help me calm down. The idea that my heritage has something to do with all this spooked me. I could be next."

"I won't let that happen," Malcolm growled. "And you're welcome. Your sister suffered from them too. The anxiety attacks."

"Really?"

"Yes, the only way to calm her down was to hold her."

Emery hugged herself and latched on to the knowledge she and Sloane shared such a unique trait. She wanted to demand Malcolm tell her more about her twin, but the distance in his voice spoke volumes, so she channeled her sister and bit her tongue.

Malcolm sighed. "I'm afraid heritage may have played a part in Sloane's death. Which is why I have something to ask of you."

It was never a simple exchange of information with the princes, always demands disguised as favors. If she could scoff without coming off pretentious, she would. "Okay, what is it?"

"I need you to find Sloane's journal. She mentioned she kept one, but when I looked in her room, I couldn't find it."

"I'll see if I can find them." Emery's heart raced at the opportunity to do more than look through a window into Sloane's life. If she found the journals, Emery would be able to get to know her sister better, and if she was lucky, they could potentially point her in the direction of Sloane's killer. "Any tips on where to start looking? If anyone should be able to find them, it's you. She was your girlfriend. Didn't you guys tell each other everything?"

"We did." Malcolm stuttered over his words. "Well. I thought we did. Sloane became distant in the last month before…" his voice trailed off for a moment, "before she died." He struggled to get the words out. "I was beginning to feel as though she was hiding things from me. And then she called off our plans to run away. Told me I wasn't good enough for her."

She didn't need to be able to see him to hear the hurt in his voice. He'd already been seen as less than by his family. To have Sloane slap him across the face with not being good enough must have broken more than just his heart.

More than ever, Emery wanted to find the journals. To understand Sloane's motives.

"Does August know about all this?"

"Not the journals."

The secrets and lies were building up like a primetime drama, and in her experiences, the truth generally came out at the most inopportune times.

"If Sloane wrote more than our relationship woes in her journal, then there is no way I could keep you safe from the wrath of the crown. What if she wrote about her heritage in those pages? Vampires and witches hate each other. And you would be no different in the eyes of my family."

He was right. August had blatantly stated his feelings concerning her bloodline. There was no wiggle room for a witch. What she didn't understand was why. Straight through her dying breath, Ada avoided speaking of her witch heritage or their history with vampires. She only mentioned them to make sure Emery stayed away from anything supernatural.

If only Ada could see me now.

"Emery?"

"Hmm?"

"I asked if you had any contact with the coven prior to coming to the castle."

"No. Without magic, I wasn't deemed witch enough to be taught anything about my heritage. I was hidden away from the supernatural world."

"I see now why Yessenia asked me to be your tutor in all things supernatural history."

"Wait, you're my teacher? Why didn't you wait until tonight to have this discussion then? It certainly seems like the safer option."

They were screwed. Malcolm could barely stand to be around her on a good day.

"I needed to talk to you now. Not later. No one knows who you are, so the choices for instructors were slim. And August," Malcolm hesitated like he wasn't sure how much shit to talk about his brother. "Let's just say as much as August wants to be in the same room as you, he didn't think it was smart for the two of you to be alone."

"Oh." Emery hoped she didn't sound as dejected as she felt.

"I'll explain as much as I can of the supernatural world later. For now, all you need to know is our father loathes witches, and August, while not as vocal, buys into the same train of thought. While I have evolved and can see beyond the past transgressions of our bloodlines, I don't intend to use you as bait to see if they can too."

"You're only saying that because I look like Sloane. You really don't care what August thinks of me, or my heritage."

"You're right. And you're wrong. I was at the back of the room when you put Jessi in her place. You may not be Sloane, but you are a force to be reckoned with. Still, it doesn't matter what I think. The factions barely tolerate one another on a good day. As future king, August is going to inherit the existing issues and likely the same distaste for witches as our father. Would you like the disgust to start with you?"

Emery's heart sank. August would hate her for what she was. The undeniable pull between them wouldn't mean shit. It couldn't fix their places on opposite sides of a supernatural feud. A feud that had started well before she was born.

"Okay. So, we won't tell August, and I'll find the journals. Anything else I need to be wary of?"

"Everything, Emery. Everyone" Malcolm moved toward the door and whispered just loud enough for her to hear. "I'm going to do everything I can to keep you safe. I won't fail you too."

"Thank you." Maybe he wasn't the moody prick she'd first thought he was. At least, not all the time.

"Wait." She grabbed his arm and halted his exit. "What

do you know about Flora? Small, blonde, one of the Culling women."

"She's quiet. Kind of a loner. Really sweet once you get to know her, though. At least, that's what I've heard. She's easy prey and has been put through the ringer by Jessi over the years. Why?"

Emery clenched her fists. She felt bad for the girl. To constantly be on the receiving end of Jessi would be miserable. It only fueled the disdain Emery felt toward the blonde.

"Nothing. She just acted strange when she saw me. I'm sure it's nothing."

"I'll question her."

"No, don't." The poor girl already had enough dealing with Jessi, she didn't need Malcolm adding to it. "What I mean is, let me talk to her. She might be more willing to talk if it comes from me."

"Fine. But if she isn't forthcoming, I'll be questioning her myself."

Emery nodded, unsure if he could see her in the darkness.

"Wait here before you leave. We wouldn't want anyone thinking you're sleeping with the wrong brother. I know you value your life," Malcolm chuckled. "See you tonight at your first lesson." He opened the door and strolled out, leaving Emery to recompose herself in the darkness.

She sat in the closet for five minutes trying to process everything Malcolm had said. Her sister had a diary. Journal. Whatever.

She stepped into the hallway and gave the courtyard door a longing stare. She'd been so close to enjoying a small slice of freedom. Even though the sunshine still called to her, there was more to do than ever before. Malcolm gave her a lead, an edge on the investigation August didn't have access to. She needed to find it and fast.

Winding back the way she came, Emery made it to the room she shared with Sloane.

Emery started with the dresser, pulling out every drawer and dumping the contents on the floor. Malcolm swore the journal was hidden in her room, but all she'd been able to find was an unhealthy amount of thongs. Emery shuddered, holding up a pair of the barely-there undies. She couldn't get behind butt floss, preferring lace booty shorts when it came to her intimates. Agreeing to become Sloane did not come with fine print regarding thongs, and she was not about to share underwear. Not even with her sister.

She moved methodically through the room, tearing apart any place she could think to hide a journal. The bookshelf was the next obvious choice, but instead of a journal, she learned Sloane was a monster who exclusively read non-fiction. Who didn't enjoy a good romance novel where the hero was hot and the sex was bordering on illegal?

Her search continued to reveal there was more that separated Emery and her twin than united them. The nightstand held no trinkets, unlike Emery's at home. Where Emery would shove anything and everything under the bed, Sloane's had no stray shoes or mismatched socks. The vanity contained no pictures of happy memories, and for as drafty as the old castle was, the hope chest at the end of the bed held no cozy blankets.

The closet had at least been fun to tear apart. It held a fantastic collection of leggings that looked to be untouched. Apparently, Sloane was a dress girl. Emery was not.

After searching all the obvious spots, she began to check

off the ones no one would think of to look for the journal. Behind the mirrors. The bathroom drawers. Even the toilet tank. She could thank her favorite detective show for that genius idea.

Still, the damn journal was nowhere to be found. She questioned if Malcolm made it up just to fuck with her.

In a mere two hours, she'd managed to wreck the entire suite. She'd have to triage the mess eventually, but all she wanted to do was crash on the soft pillow top.

She trudged from the bathroom through the piles of clothes and books, and flopped face-down on the bed.

Where the hell could Sloane have hidden the journal? It would help if she knew anything about her sister or had anything to go on. But all she had was the word of a shifty vampire with a broken heart that the damn thing even existed.

She slowly released a long breath and sat up, not ready to admit defeat. A second wind hit her, and she was ready to continue the search when there was a knock at the door, followed by the high pitched voice of Chelsea.

"Sloane?" Another incessant knock echoed. "Sloane, hurry up, we're going to be late and you know how Yessenia gets."

Emery raced to the door. She couldn't remember if she locked it, and since she didn't know dick about dick yet, didn't want to find out the hard way Sloane and Chelsea had an open door policy.

She opened it just enough to talk to Chelsea. "Hi!" That probably came out too friendly. "Uh, give me a second."

Chelsea looked beyond her into the disaster that was Sloane's room. "Wow, I like what you've done with the place."

Emery reached up and fiddled with her ear. "Yeah, I lost my favorite set of earrings and went a little nuts trying to find them."

"Oh, the one's your aunt sent you?"

She must have been having a stroke because she swore Chelsea just said Ada sent something to Sloane. After all those years of telling Emery the letters she wrote wouldn't make it to Sloane, Ada was sending things all along. And nice things. Emery was lucky if she got a card for her birthday.

She swallowed hard, biting back unexpected tears. "Um, yeah, those ones. Still didn't find them, but I'm sure they'll turn up."

"Okay, well, let's go. Dahlia will have this cleared up before you are back, I'm sure. Maybe she knows where they are. June always seems to know where my lost things are."

Emery nodded. She hoped that wasn't the case. She didn't like the idea of Dahlia cleaning up her mess. Really anyone cleaning up her mess. And what a fucking mess she was in.

She slipped on her flats and gave the room one last glance over before following Chelsea into the hall. She'd much rather continue her search, but instead, she put on her best princess smile and prepared herself for what was sure to be a boring afternoon of learning all there was to know about how not to piss off the Scottish snobs.

Chapter Twelve

AUGUST

The dusty brown steed kept a steady pace on the narrow trail. Jack wasn't as agile as his warhorse, but the stablehand insisted he allow Shadowfell a few more days' rest after his injuries. August tried not to let it bother him, even though there was no doubt he'd reached his patience level for the day. Putting on a show for the women was exhausting, no matter how long it was. One that resulted in him downing two blood bags after the fact just to right himself.

They were excited, having prepared for that moment their entire lives, and part of him didn't want to let them down. The other part, though, dreaded every moment of having to be the prince charming he wasn't.

Running would have been faster, but traveling by horseback brought him back to a simpler time, and he appreciated the momentary reprieve. August tipped his head back, allowing the summer sun to heat his face as it peeked through the green canopy.

No one visited Lilyana, with the exception of his father, and even that was few and far between.

The overgrown path flared into a clearing with a single story cottage complete with a thatched roof. It looked stolen right from the pages of a children's story.

Jack hesitated, pulling against the reins with every step as August forced him closer. The horse's intuition wasn't off. Witches deserved every bit of caution. His father reminded him of that every chance he got.

Never forget a witch wields magic that could end you. Or worse.

They could take everything you hold dear.

The last part his father would silently omit, unaware August knew the king's most treasured secret.

August gripped the reins tighter, keeping Jack on the course. It was during his first and only visit to the cottage that August learned of his father's past and the role Lilyana played. He hoped, given their fragile alliance, the witch would provide him with answers. Though, he hated he had to rely on the enemy for anything.

After tying Jack to a tree, August rolled his shoulders back and stood before the door. He inhaled deep and fully prepared to fight for the information he sought. The information that could keep Emery safe.

The last thought slipped in without consent. The feisty woman tended to do that, but now was not the time to consider the way she felt in his arms. Or the way her eyes lit up when she thought, for a split moment, he was about to choose her for the first date.

He shook his head and moved his fist toward the door,

but before he could knock, it swung open on its own. August stepped back, leery when the entrance remained empty. His eyes scanned the threshold, waiting for something to happen. Examining it, it looked like an ordinary doorway, except for the thin green shimmering outline.

Magic.

A moment later, a soft voice called from within. "Come in, Augustine."

He bit back the cringe his first name evoked. It reminded him of the vampire he was. The one he fought against every moment of every day, and still failed at most the time.

"Is it safe for me to enter?" he called out. "I distinctly remember this magic not being forgiving."

Lilyana chuckled. "Learned your lesson, didn't you?"

"Yeah, don't meddle with magic," he mumbled under his breath. As much as it fascinated him, magic was deadly.

Lilyana appeared in the doorway, and August sucked in a breath. She looked to be in her late twenties, maybe early thirties, but he knew her to be older than the dirt the cottage sat on.

"Feasgar mhath." Lilyana curtsied before him. "I wasn't expecting you, but I'm happy you're here, nonetheless. Come in. The house will not harm ye."

The Scotts Gaelic that fell from her tongue pulled at his heart, reminding him of times long past. Times that were carefree and didn't ask too much of him. Her voice was as much a relic as he was. No one spoke like that anymore. Not even he, who had allowed himself to lose much of his accent when adapting to his home in America.

"Thank you. It was a last minute decision to come today." He kept his voice steady. Holding his breath, he crossed the threshold.

The cottage was larger inside than it seemed. He hadn't seen the interior the last time he'd visited, but he appreciated its simplicity. Lilyana's home hadn't changed a bit. It was warm and inviting with copious amounts of natural light. All of which, the exact opposite of what he imagined a witch's home looking like.

A cozy sitting area sat adjacent to a kitchen with a large island for prep. Off to the side was a hallway he assumed led to a bedroom and bathroom. Definitely not the stuffy, dark, cauldron filled homes he remembered from their homeland.

"No worry. To what do I owe this pleasantry? 'Tis been some time since your last visit." Her words were formal, but August didn't miss the hint of disdain in her voice.

Fifty years, to be exact. August absentmindedly rubbed his shoulder. "Yes, my last visit ended with me being catapulted from your door and dislocating my shoulder."

A smile tugged at Lilyana's lips, and her eyes narrowed on him. "You should not have been listenin' in on my conversation with your father."

But he had. He'd been angry with his father for shutting him out of the meeting, so he'd concealed himself outside the open window and listened to their dealings.

August hadn't known about Lilyana until that day. Vampires and witches didn't associate with one another, and the allure of such a meeting was irresistible. His snooping paid off, and he learned how his family acquired Lilyana as their resident witch.

That and so much more.

He learned about the life debt forcing his father to provide sanctuary to the woman who caused the death of his beloved first wife and son.

"Please, sit." Lilyana gestured to the oversized armchairs

by the fireplace. She waved her hand and summoned a tray with two mugs filled to the brim. "Tea?"

"No, thank you."

"Suit yourself." She set the extra mug on the kitchen island. "How can I help you then, Your Highness."

"I have a few questions you can answer for me." August sank into the plush cushions. They'd be the perfect chairs to add to his library. The antiquated upholstery was much better suited to gothic architecture than the humble abode they currently resided in. Emery completed the picture, knees to her chest on a chair across from him, absorbed in a book while he worked out lyrics to a new song.

He shook his head, trying to keep her out of his mind but failing once again. He wanted her there, just on the edge of waking thought, where he could visit her smile. The curve of her hips begging to be grabbed. Bloody hell. He sounded like a prepubescent teen who couldn't keep his dick in check.

Lilyana sat across from him, her eyes never leaving him as a slight smile tipped her lips upward, as if she knew exactly what he was thinking. Could witches read minds? No. At least, he'd never heard of it being a power they possessed.

August returned her smile, and used the unguarded moment to assess the adversary across from him. Her petite frame sat poised and regal, her long brown hair falling in natural curls over her shoulders. The glow from the window highlighted her hazel eyes, which invited him in, giving a sense of security. It was a false sense. She was deadly. Of that, he had no doubt.

"We have reason to believe there are spies within the castle." He watched her, searching for the slightest reaction.

"I don't think I could help you with such a problem, nor do I believe you came all this way to tell me such."

"Sorry, I should have been more precise with my meaning. We suspect there to be witches in the castle." The words were ground out, betraying his own rising emotions.

"That's unfortunate, given your father's dislike of my kind." Her eyes twitched like she was fighting back a smile. "What does this have to do with me?"

He bit his cheek in order to keep his frustration in check. "I'm only going to ask you this once, so think carefully before you answer. Do you have *any* involvement with these witches?"

"No." The answer was immediate and adamant, her eyes meeting his, unblinking, as she issued the denial. "Before you showed up here unannounced, I had no knowledge of any witches infiltrating the castle. I am an ally of your father's and have had no contact with the coven since..."

"Since what, Lilyana?" Playing dumb was a strategic move. He wanted to see what she'd reveal on her own.

She stared at the embers, which flickered more intensely under her gaze. Sparks popped as if trying to ignite, a few escaping onto the fur rug between them. As quickly as they began, they stopped, and Lilyana continued, her voice low. "It doesn't matter. All you need to know is I am an ally of the crown. I live here peacefully and alone. Neither side wants me, and I am okay with that."

"That's where you're wrong. If my father didn't want you here, you wouldn't be. I know what happened all those years ago."

She slipped him a curious glance. "You know what I allowed you to know."

His jaw dropped, shock igniting before he reined in his emotions. "You knew I was listening?"

"I did. Your father has been successful in erasing history, but I needed you to know what happened. Immortals don't live forever, a fact I am all too familiar with. If history is erased, it's bound to repeat itself."

"Why did you do it?"

"What? Fall in love or save your father?"

"Both. You hate our kind," he scoffed. "What could possibly have been in it for you?"

"I think you will soon come to realize the heart does not care about misplaced hatred. Finding love, especially an epic love, is limitless. It's not bound by the prejudices we are taught. It removes us from the cage we've been shacked in by society and can set us free. Why would I not want that?" Tears shone in her eyes before she blinked them away. "As for your father, I wanted to live outside the realms of witches. The only way I could do that was if I was protected. I gave him an ultimatum as he lay there dying. If I saved him, he would protect me. He agreed, knowing the price for the magic it would take to cure him. The selfish bastard did it knowing it would kill his wife."

August's jaw clenched and his hands balled into fists. "No."

"Yes. Your precious father threw away his great love to save his own life. And I have no doubts he would do it again and again. Don't underestimate him, Augustine. Your father is a lot of things. A good man and a good king are not on that list."

Wasn't that the truth. While August didn't believe his father would kill his own wife, he knew all too well love wasn't something the king valued.

"You say you're our ally. Will you help me find the witches then?"

"No." Lilyana finished her tea, then stood and walked to place it on the kitchen island. Turned her back on the enemy. Stupidity wasn't among the attributes he'd have listed for her before then.

August cocked a brow. "You'd refuse a request made by the crown prince?"

Her shoulders tensed, spine straightened. "I do not answer to you, princeling. I am not a member of your court, nor am I a subject of the crown. I do not wish to ever be involved in supernatural politics again, and I'll see to it I will not again."

Refusal wasn't an option. She had the ability to help, and he would do whatever it took to keep his women of his Culling safe. "Lilyana, I do not wish to go to war. You know as well as I, if my father finds out about witches in the castle, he will not hesitate to raise arms against the coven."

Lilyana spun on him, eyes flashing with the first honest emotion she'd displayed. "I find it hard to believe you don't want war. From what I've been told, you have quite the appetite for blood." The accusation hit its mark as she drove home for the kill. "Like your father."

"I have my reasons to keep war far from the walls of our castle."

"Tell me your reasons, and I shall consider it. You are, after all, still a vampire, and I am still a witch."

August pushed up from his chair, rage simmering just beneath the surface. The conversation was not going as anticipated. He ran his fingers through his hair, hoping his next move would play to her heart. "I need to protect my Culling women. I fear they are the target."

Lilyana stilled, and fear flashed across her face. "Your Culling has begun? What does this have to do with the women?"

He'd hit his intended mark. There was no way she'd turn her back on his women, having been a member of a Culling herself. "Yes. They arrived twenty-five years ago and are now of breeding age. I need to know I can trust you before I tell you more."

Silence filled the distance between them. Neither looking away, and neither backing down. He'd put himself in a precarious situation. One that gave her the advantage. Handing power to the enemy never sat well, but it was a necessary evil given the direness of the circumstances.

A pit formed in his stomach as the silence grew to a dull roar. Lilyana was the only lead he had; without her, he'd be looking for a needle in a haystack.

Lilyana stuck her hand out to him. "I give you my word I will protect the secrets of the Culling women." The moment she finished the vow, purple tendrils of glowing magic crackled and snaked down her arm.

August's brows rose, and his mouth parted slightly. He'd only heard about a witch's vow in stories. The vow was sealed with magic, binding its will to the individuals involved. If broken, it was said the offender would writhe in agony for the rest of their days, wishing for death. Never did he believe he'd witness a vow, let alone participate in one.

He reached his hand out and placed it in Lilyana's. The tendrils danced their way toward him, nipping at his skin as if tasting his essence. Once satisfied, they twined around his hand and wrist. Pulsating warmth settled over his skin, then suddenly stopped. The purple glow seeped deep within them until all that was left was his hand in hers.

August looked up, meeting Lilyana's solemn gaze. "It's done," she whispered. "I will not be able to speak any secrets revealed to me pertaining to the women of your Culling."

He hesitated, in awe not only of the magic within him, but in the sacrifice Lilyana made for her enemy for the sake of his women. "Thank you." It was all he could think to say.

August pulled his hand from hers and stepped back to lean against the armchair. "Four days ago, one of my Culling women was found dead in the stables. We believe she was murdered. The moment she died, her mark transferred to another. Her twin." August paused, gauging Lilyana's reaction. Her mouth fell slightly in surprise, but she continued to listen intently. "As you know, the balance within the supernatural world is fragile at best. We didn't want the killers to believe they'd succeeded, so instead of reporting the death, we asked the twin to participate in the Culling, under the guise of her sister, until we could discover who was responsible."

"Gòrach píos de cac!"

August stared at the ground to hide the upturned corners of his lips at her outburst calling him a piece of shit. Lilyana surprised him with the fire she held within her. Fire he could work with.

Lilyana muttered under her breath in a language he didn't understand before narrowing her eyes on him. "There are a million ways this could backfire on you, you know that?"

"I didn't ask for your opinion. I was merely getting you up to speed."

"How are witches involved?"

"We found this outside the castle after the twin arrived."

He reached in his pocket and pulled out the note, handing it to Lilyana.

She studied it carefully, then raised her eyes to his. "So, you believe these witches had something to do with the lass's death?"

"We aren't sure, but the timing is coincidental, don't you think?"

"Aye. What do you need from me?"

"Can you tell a witch from a human by looking at them?"

When she nodded, a weight lifted from his shoulders. He'd hoped the plan he made would work, but it banked too much on the woman before him. At the very least, he'd assumed correctly. "The Scottish delegation arrives in two weeks. I'd like for you to attend the planned events and scan the crowd for witches."

"I knew you were stubborn, but I didn't peg you for stupid. I cannae attend court events. Your father would have my head, not to mention there is no love between the King of Scots and myself."

"What they don't know won't hurt you. I'll ensure you're hidden."

"You would deceive your father?"

"There are a lot of things I would do if it meant the women were safe. They are my responsibility, and I've already failed them once." What he really meant to say was, if it kept one woman safe, but that wasn't something Lilyana needed to know. The fewer people that knew about his obsession with the twin, the better.

"Does he know you are here now?"

"No."

Lilyana fingered one of her curls silently. "I will disguise myself and attend two events of your choosing."

"You can do that?"

She smirked and with the flick of her wrist, changed her appearance. Before him stood a young blonde with piercing blue eyes.

August raised a brow. "Impressive."

"You have no idea, princeling." With another quick flick, she reverted back to herself. "I will attend your events, but if anyone catches wind of my presence, I'm holding you personally responsible."

"Deal. You will attend the reception of the Scottish delegation, as well as the Gala. Both events should be attended by the majority of the castle, as well as the court."

He could see the unease in her gaze, but still she nodded in agreement.

"Tapadh leibh, Lilyana." After thanking her, August walked toward the door, and Lilyana followed.

She clutched the door frame as August untied and mounted Jack.

He looked over his shoulder and gave her a final nod before giving Jack a swift kick and riding toward the castle. Lilyana wasn't what he'd expected. Aside from her unfortunate birth as a witch, she was everything he wanted in an ally.

He still didn't trust her, but she'd earned his respect for putting the Culling women's safety above their differences.

As the castle came into view, he was sobered by the prospect of his impending date with Jessi. Protecting Emery had trumped devising his own torture, but it couldn't be put off any longer. Like his destiny as the future king, Jessi wasn't going to vanish no matter how much he willed it, and it was past time he stopped living as though they would.

Chapter Thirteen

EMERY

An uneasy feeling formed in Emery's stomach as Daphne spun her around, any sense of direction completely lost behind the dark blindfold.

"Alright. Ready?"

She nodded.

"Go!"

Daphne released her, and bare feet shuffled across the rug covering the stone floor. Emery widened her stance, trying to get her bearings. Placing her hands out in front of her, she listened before taking a timid step. The room was deathly quiet.

"Marco!"

"Polo!" a sea of feminine voices replied.

Emery's internal giggles matched those surrounding her. She couldn't believe she was playing Marco Polo in a centuries old castle with nineteen other women. Women who should be enemies as they fought for a future with the same man. More astounding, she was having fun.

Emery didn't have many friends growing up. Ada made sure of that. Which meant her evenings were either spent working at the club or curled up on the couch alone at home watching primetime television.

Warmth spread through her. This was what it was like to have siblings. Tears welled, and she was thankful for the blindfold that hid her eyes. She didn't know if Sloane would cry, but Emery was teetering on the edge of an emotional downpour.

Careful not to run into any of the ornate couches and chairs scattered throughout the room, she channeled her emotions into enjoying the moments she could with the normally uptight women. She wouldn't be there forever and wanted to hold onto the feeling of family for as long as possible.

One by one, she tagged each of the women, and they retreated to the couches, cat calling to distract her as she sought out the remaining players. The room grew quiet as the numbers dwindled. When the last woman remained, she smiled and opened up her senses. "Maaarcoo."

"Pooolllooooo." She didn't recognize the voice but knew it came from the far corner to her left.

With confident strides, she made for the voice only to be stopped by a misplaced couch. Emery cursed under her breath as the unmistakable giggle of Jessi sounded beside her. "Oops. Sorry, I moved the couch. Better vantage point of the door to see when August arrives."

Bitch.

She reached down and rubbed where her knee hit the corner. It would definitely bruise. With a bit more caution, she followed the sound of footsteps padding swiftly away from her.

When her hand hit the wall, she turned and leapt toward them, hoping no stray furniture *accidently* got in her way again. At full speed, she ran into what felt like a brick wall, bouncing off and tumbling back.

She was caught before she hit the floor.

Instantly, her skin hummed, and her stomach dropped. Not from the sensation of falling, but because there was no getting away from that feeling he gave her. No matter how much she wanted to feel absolutely nothing, to be able to walk away when it was all over and forget he existed at all, something inside her told her that would never happen.

"Marco," she whispered.

"Polo." His deep voice was no more than a whisper. "This is the second time I've found you falling into my arms. One might think you actually want to be here."

Emery reached up to tug off the blindfold, ready to remind him exactly where she stood on the matter.

"Oh, no, you don't." August chuckled, loud enough for the rest of the room to hear. "That's cheating."

Giggles erupted around the room, and he set her down, trailing his fingers down her spine as he did. She shivered under his touch, involuntarily leaning into his hand when it came to rest at the small of her back, steadying her.

He didn't move from Emery's side, nor did he drop his hand. "I'm sorry for interrupting your evening games, ladies. I'm here for Jessi." Charm dripped from his every word.

Still blindfolded, she stood helpless beside August. Heat filled her cheeks, but at least she was spared the embarrassment of seeing every set of eyes trained on her and her clumsiness.

The click of heels signaled an approach, echoing off the walls and perfectly preserved wood floor. "Let's go, August. I am so excited to spend the entire evening with you."

"As you wish." August gave her hip a squeeze, and as he leaned in, his lips brushed her ear. "She's right behind you." He spoke so low she almost missed it.

Emery waited until the door clicked behind her and then turned to tag the last player in their epic game of Marco Polo. After pulling off the blindfold, Chelsea's cheeky grin stared back at her. She threw the cloth at her and smiled. "I thought you were supposed to be my best friend."

"Who me?" Chelsea brought her hands to her chest as she mocked. "I am. But have you forgotten I'm also the most competitive person you will ever meet?" She wrapped her arm around Emery, and the two of them laughed their way to the nearest couch.

A rematch was out of the question as the room buzzed with speculations over Jessi's date with August. Was that really all the women did for the last twenty odd years? Lessons and games and gossip? If every day was like that, it was easy to see how out of touch they really were with the outside world.

"What do you think they're doing?" Chelsea flopped down on the sofa.

Emery shrugged, still burning from the caress of August's lips over her ear. Damn him. She wanted to hate him. Wanted to ignore the butterflies in her stomach. But she couldn't. Not when his mere presence made her come alive.

She shouldn't care what he was doing with Jessi. And yet, jealousy flared at the thought of any woman on his arm.

"You've spent the most time with him, Sloane. What's he like?" Amelia's question elicited an echo from the others sitting before her like puppies waiting for their owner to drop scraps from the dinner table. If they only knew how much time she'd really spent with him.

"He's something else, that's for sure." Beyond that half assed response, she had nothing. Everything she could say about August would be Emery talking. Not Sloane. She didn't know many details about the relationship her twin held with the prince. Either one for that matter. She only had two days' worth of memories with him, which wasn't much to go on.

Still, with all eyes on her, she had to say something. They adored him, and she decided to keep their dreams of Prince Charming alive. She only hoped August lived up to her description.

With a deep breath, she closed her eyes and pictured August. His piercing blue eyes. Broad chest. The way the corner of his mouth turned upward when he found something she said amusing, but not quite funny.

"He's masculine in every sense of the word. So much so that when he holds you, it's impossible not to feel safe. When he speaks, it's laced in the truth, even if a bit brutish. I think it's because, even though he has a reputation to uphold, he ultimately cares very deeply about the wellbeing of his court and his kingdom. He puts others above himself, but not for recognition. He does it because it's the right thing to do. If you entrust him with a secret, he will carry it with him without a single thought of betraying you."

"What if you give him your heart?"

Emery opened her eyes, not entirely sure who asked the question. She pressed her lips together and swallowed.

"Your heart? If you truly give him every part of your heart, and accept his in return," her voice trailed off while she chewed on the thought. How would August love? Her voice, no longer steady, came out barely above a whisper. "I think he would cherish the gift of true love. Though I can't say from experience. My heart is still mine."

Eighteen faces stared back at her silently, wide-eyed and filled with wonder. In that moment, for the first time since the mark appeared on her wrist, Emery wished she could experience the Culling from their point of view. Brainwashed to believe they had a shot with a prince, and wholeheartedly wanting it. Then, maybe her view of him wouldn't be so jaded by Ada's teachings and her own admittedly prejudiced views. But that would require her to unlearn everything she'd been taught, and she wasn't sure that was possible.

Even for the man she'd just described.

Suddenly uncomfortable with the attention, Emery slid from the couch. "It's getting late. I think I am going to turn in for the night."

The rest of the women began to talk quietly amongst themselves once more, some following suit and heading to their rooms.

Emery left the common room and gave the last door on the left a look of longing as she passed it. It'd be great to do as she said and turn in for the night. After the day she'd had already, sleep would take her as soon as she hit the pillow.

But it wasn't over yet. She took her time winding through the castle halls toward the Crystal Parlor, where she was supposed to meet Malcolm for her nightly history lesson.

As she traveled down the stone hallway adjacent to the

parlor, she realized her footsteps were not the only sound reverberating. The sound of people talking echoed around her.

Curiosity got the better of her as she approached the open door where shadows danced into the hall. A few yards from the door, Emery heard a distinct moan from a woman. And then another. They were not just any moans, and her cheeks flushed with realization. These were the moans of a woman being well and truly fucked. The kind of breathy moans that hit right before a woman reached—

"Oh, August. Yes. Please, don't stop."

Emery's thoughts were interrupted by the moan. The blood that flowed beneath her skin boiled at the thought of August with Jessi.

She shook her head. He was dating twenty women at once, what did she expect? Him to remain celibate while he did?

It doesn't matter.

She shouldn't care. Forced to be there and playing a game that could get her killed, she needed to focus on finding her sister's killer and getting the hell out of there. And yet she couldn't deny a part of her heart that sank at the vision playing in her head of August fucking another woman. She'd almost allowed herself to imagine him as the man she described earlier.

Almost.

A glutton for punishment, Emery pushed open the slightly ajar door. Her stomach rolled, and she forced herself to swallow the fear that bubbled in her throat.

There before her in what seemed to be a private study with wall-to-wall bookcases, was August with a big boobed blonde draped across him where he sat on the large desk.

One arm expertly wrapped around the shoulders of Jessi, while the other gripped her hip as if his life depended on it.

Maybe it did. His fangs would say it did. They were currently plunged deep in her neck, sucking her blood as sustenance for his very existence.

Jessi raked her fingers through August's dusty blonde hair, tugging as he continued to feed. Moaning loudly, her hips gyrated trying to make contact with something, anything, to fulfill the need she had.

Mine.

Whoa, where had that thought come from? The prince was not hers to claim. The voice inside her was way off base. She didn't want this fairytale life of pomp and circumstance. More importantly, no reasonable part of her wanted to take Jessi's place below his fangs. She shuddered to think of how it would feel to be at the mercy of a vampire. Her mission needed to stay in the forefront of her mind.

Sloane.

Find her killer and get out.

Emery sighed, casting her eyes downward as she tried to make herself believe any of that was true.

If she was so certain of her purpose, why was she raging at the sight before her? Convincing herself not to barge into the study and string Jessi up by her blonde mane? Why did her nipples tighten and heat pool in her belly at the thought of taking Jessi's place? Of sustaining August in the most intimate way possible?

She was exhausted. There was no other explanation.

Emery straightened her spine, determined not to give into her newly possessive nature or traitorous libido. August wasn't worth the heartache. Emery would never be his queen.

One final look was all she needed to seal her resolve. Only when she looked, his cold steel blue eyes were staring directly into hers.

They were glossed over, as if high off the feeding. "Are you going to join us? If not, Sloane, I suggest you wait for me elsewhere." He smiled at her, his fangs fully descended.

Her sister's name on his lips slapped her back to reality, giving freedom to her previously rooted feet and sending her fleeing from the room.

If he'd said her name, she'd have stayed. And Emery wasn't sure if his vampire nature or that knowledge scared her more.

Chapter Fourteen

EMERY

Running was pointless. Still, Emery continued pumping her legs as fast as she could, knowing full well August could catch her if he wished. Her only hope rested in him being too busy with Jessi to care about her or where she was going. Fire tore through her lungs, and her legs felt like they would give out at any moment. Stopping wasn't an option, though.

She pushed open the doors to the garden, her mind rapidly trying to make sense of what she'd witnessed. She needed to get away from August. Away from this castle. Knowing they were vampires and seeing their vampire nature were two completely different things.

He was drinking Jessi.

Emery's head spun. She'd moved from shock to trying to rationalize what she'd seen. It didn't matter the sounds Jessi made clearly indicated she was enjoying herself. Or that Emery had been turned on by the thought.

It was wrong on so many levels.

Was this a regular activity on his *dates*? Did he expect that of all his culling women? Just when she was beginning to warm up to the idea of being attracted to the insanely gorgeous vampire prince, life bitch slapped her with a stark reminder of who and what he was.

She couldn't afford to forget that fact.

Emery ran across the courtyard and prayed to which ever god was listening to provide an exit on the other side of the garden maze. Hedges spread in every direction and all Emery could do was hold onto the hope there was a way out.

An open wrought iron gate caught her eyes, with the promise of freedom. She was nearly there when the blurred figure of a man slammed into her at breakneck speed.

A solid grip on her shoulders caught her before she fell to the ground. She looked up into the dark eyes of her rescuer and saboteur. "Whoa. Where are you going in such a hurry?" Malcolm's mouth tilted upward at one side. "Ditching your first lesson is highly frowned upon, you know. Usually, I wouldn't blame you, but I happen to know I'm a fantastic teacher."

She averted her gaze and tried to shrug him off. Panic and adrenaline still coursed through her veins, urging her to keep moving.

Malcolm gripped her chin and tugged it upward, forcing her to meet his gaze. He studied her expression, and his own hardened. "What's wrong?"

"N-n-nothing. I just need some fresh air. I'll b-be in shortly."

His hand on her arm tightened. "Don't lie to me. What happened? You're shaking."

Was she?

Clenching and unclenching her fists in a manic attempt to steady herself, Emery took a deep breath. "It's nothing, Malcolm. Just— I need a moment. Please go. I'll be right up." She tried once more to pull herself from his grasp.

The doors to the castle slammed open, and a terrifying growl filled the courtyard. Even though they were hidden within the hedges of the maze, both Malcolm and Emery jerked to see what had made that horrible sound.

It wasn't a what, but a who. A disheveled August stood before them. His shirt untucked, and his hair tousled, no doubt from Jessi combing her boney fingers through it. Even with several feet separating them, Emery could see his eyes were not his normal ice blue. They were darker, his pupils dilated so only a faint blue line remained. His gaze roamed over her face, then shifted to where Malcolm still held her. "Release her. Now."

Emery zeroed in on tiny blood droplets that stained his collar and swallowed hard.

Malcolm released her arms, but kept hold of her hand as he tucked her behind him. "No. She's clearly scared out of her mind. What did you do?"

"Nevermind, Malcolm. I need to speak with Em."

Did he just use her name? Was he fucking crazy? Anyone could hear them out here, and the cover he insisted on her using would be blown.

"I don't think so, August." Malcolm puffed his shoulders out slightly. "Have you been drinking?"

"I'm not drunk if that's what you're asking," August replied sarcastically, and Emery made a mental note to ask if vampires could get drunk.

"You know what I'm asking, brother"

Emery peeked from around Malcolm in time to see August straighten his stance and rake his fingers through his hair. Releasing a sigh, his eyes met hers, and his scowl softened. "Please, I just want to explain what you saw."

Emery shook her head. "You really don't need to, Your Highness. It was pretty self-explanatory."

Malcolm squeezed her hand and swiveled his gaze toward her. "Wait. What did you see?" When she didn't answer immediately, he turned back to August. "What did she see?"

"She saw me feeding from Jessi."

"Almost fucking her is more like it." Emery huffed under her breath, forgetting they could both hear her perfectly.

"Fuck, August, seriously?"

August didn't respond. Instead, he continued to stare at Emery like she was the juiciest steak available. Hunger still evident in his eyes.

Malcolm dropped her hand and hooked his arm around Emery, attempting to press her into his back. "Are you sated, brother?"

"Yes," August spat through clenched teeth.

Emery brows drew together and tried to slip from Malcolm's grasp. "You expect me to believe that while you're staring at me like a piece of meat?"

"Yes." August took a step toward her but stopped when she flinched back behind Malcolm. "You know I'd never hurt her. The urge is gone."

Malcolm sighed and turned, steadying her once more with his hands. "Let him explain. While Jessi is the most vile creature, it's likely not what you think. It's a part of who we are. If you're going to survive here, you'll need to understand."

"Really? You're going to leave me with him? He's practically feral right now."

"He's harmless. And I'll keep an ear out. If he hurts you, just scream. I'll be back before you can blink."

"What about our lesson?" She gripped his arms, desperate to avoid being alone with August. Not only because he might take a bite out of her, but she didn't entirely trust herself not to enjoy it.

"View this as lesson one. Vampire feeding tactics. Honestly, no one could teach this lesson better than August."

August growled. "What's that supposed to mean?"

Malcolm shrugged out of her grasp and spun toward the door. "I'm sure you're smart enough to figure it out."

Emery's mouth hung open momentarily before she found her voice. "Seriously, Malcolm? You're going to leave me here to die?"

She knew she was being overdramatic, but her instincts told her nothing good could come of her and August being alone. Now or ever.

As Malcolm disappeared, August approached her slowly, like a predator approaching their prey, and she took a large step back.

"I'm not going to hurt you, Em."

"Don't call me that. Anyone could hear you."

"And I would tell them it's perfectly natural to call you by the initial of your last name."

For every step August moved forward, Emery took one back until she found herself pressed into an alcove hidden within the garden wall.

She sucked in a deep breath, her body still shaking. How could Malcolm have left her with him? Didn't he know what could happen?

With nowhere to run, Emery clamped her eyes shut and tried to imagine she was anywhere other than a deserted maze with a dangerous and hungry vampire stalking toward her.

As hard as she tried, she couldn't picture herself anywhere else. She was as helpless as she'd been all day. It didn't matter how hard she tried, she kept finding herself in situations she was not at all prepared for.

She flinched as the tips of his fingers caressed her face and tucked her fallen hair behind her ear. His touch was gentle, but she knew what he was capable of. Emery squeezed her eyes tighter, not yet ready to face the vampire before her. The vampire she couldn't resist in more ways than one.

"Open your eyes, Emery."

She inhaled a shallow breath and instantly regretted it when the scent of sandalwood and fresh pine hit her nose. Why did he have to smell so damn good?

"I'd rather not."

"Please." He cupped her cheek, brushing his fingers through her hair.

Feeling the familiar hum across her skin, Emery peeked through her lashes. August stood before her, his eyes now returned to their icy blue state. Her fear subsided, but only slightly. At least, he didn't look as though he wanted to tear into her neck anymore. Instead, he'd traded his feral predator stare for his I'm-fuckable-and—know-it stare.

Which wasn't any better at calming her fear.

His gaze trained on her mouth, and he wiped the pad of his thumb across her lower lip. Shifting his weight, he released her cheek and caged her within the alcove. August leaned in and nestled his nose against the curve of her neck, inhaling deeply. She tensed waiting to feel the graze of his teeth against the erratic pulsing of her artery. His tongue traced her life source, and Emery's breath hitched. Her traitorous body reacted to his touch, and she clenched her legs together to dull the ache between them.

"Are you here for dessert?" she whispered, her voice coming out light and airy.

August pulled away enough for her to see his coy smile and raised brow. "Are you offering?"

Looking anywhere but at his eyes, she made the mistake of settling her gaze on his lips. "You wouldn't like my brand of vampire hating blood," she spat defensively, though she didn't believe the words she spoke and knew he wouldn't either. She hated herself just a tiny bit for not being able to speak those words with more conviction. Witches everywhere would roll over in their graves if they knew how much she desired the man before her.

"I can smell your arousal. You don't hate me, you are angry at my actions, and possibly confused about what you saw. But you don't hate me, Em." August leaned every inch of his muscular frame against her "And for the record, I believe I would love the brand of blood you have to offer, if you ever chose to let me have a taste."

"Are you saying Jessi gave her blood to you willingly?" She paused and then chuckled. "Who am I kidding? Of course, she gave it to you willingly."

"She did. It was the only way I could get her to shut up about you promising her that I was heading to your bed after my date."

Emery's cheeks reddened. "She told you about that?"

"She did." A mischievous smirk tugged at his lips. "And I'll have you know I'm not totally opposed to that option."

Arrogant prick.

She glared at him. He may have only done what he did to pacify Jessi, but he still did it. "Explain whatever it is you wanted to explain, otherwise I have a lesson with Malcolm."

A low growl escaped his lips. "I will be your teacher tonight."

Damn if that growl didn't make her panties wet. He was a wildcard, and with the way her body reacted around him, she wasn't sure she could be trusted to be alone with him.

"Look, I'm sorry I interrupted your meal." Emery ducked under his arm and darted toward the castle. "While you would be the sexiest teacher I've ever had, I am sure Malcolm could teach me about your eating habits. He's a vampire too."

August reached out and grabbed her hand. The world spun, and she found herself pinned to his chest. "You think I'm sexy?"

Her eyes found his. Damn those baby blues. "That's all you picked up from that statement?" She tried to wiggle from his embrace, but there was no way she could escape him. "Please let me go."

"Let me explain and then if you would like to go, you may. Malcolm was right in saying you need to understand vampires if you're going to live here."

Emery chewed her lip. She hated that he wasn't wrong. "Fine."

August dropped the arm that held her to him but surprised her when he didn't release her hand. He led her down the moonlit garden path, maze hedges on each side, to the fountain in the center. It reminded her of the elaborate fountains she'd seen in Europe. This one had a marble statue of a man rising from the center pool with a woman draped in his arms.

Gently tugging on her hand, August urged her to sit next to him on the edge of the fountain.

He cocked a brow. "Do you trust me?"

"No." There was no hesitation on her part. He may make her body come alive, but he was still a vampire.

"Why not?"

"Well, let's see. I hardly know you. Your family took my sister from us and then she died in your care. And last but not least, I just saw you with your fangs deep in Jessi's neck while she basically had an orgasm in your lap."

"I didn't think you cared."

"I don't."

"You're jealous." His delicious smirk was back, making it impossible for her not to swoon.

"You have the most selective hearing of anyone I've ever met."

August laughed. "It's one of my more charming traits." His fingers gently rubbed over her palm. "I can't control most of the reasons you distrust me. They're in the past. What I can do is assure you that you have no reason to be jealous of Jessi."

Butterflies erupted in her stomach. Try as she might, she couldn't deny the jealousy that ripped through her body when she saw them together. She'd wanted to rip her from his arms and claim him, but that wasn't something he needed to know. It was something she needed to ignore.

"Jessi is one of your Culling women. What you do with her is your business. She could be your queen someday."

"As could you."

Emery snapped her head toward him. "We had a deal, August."

"And if I want to renegotiate?"

"Not up for discussion."

"I'm the crown prince. Everything is up for discussion."

"Not this, August. I can't and won't be your queen." She held his gaze, silently pleading for him to let it go. She couldn't tell him why. It would likely be a death sentence.

"We'll see." He turned from her and focused on the ground in front of him. "I'm sorry you had to see me that way."

Emery's eyes widened. He gave her emotional whiplash.

"I should have known better than to feed where anyone could see us. Moreover, I should have explained the process to you at the hotel."

"Maybe if you hadn't stormed out so quickly, we would have had a chance to talk."

"I'm sorry about that too. But I won't apologize for what I am. I'm a vampire, Emery. Blood is our sustenance."

"But did it have to be her? She's quite possibly the worst person I've ever met."

"She didn't taste awful."

If her eyes could shoot wooden stakes, the prince would be dead.

Well, she assumed he would be. She didn't actually know if there was any truth to that myth, and she didn't think August would confirm it if there were.

"I see. So, the real problem is that it was Jessi. Not that I was drinking from a human." August's lips turned upward in a playful smile. "For someone who's not jealous, you sure as hell sound like it."

"Well, she's a bitch," she bit back, not entirely sure what

she expected from him. He needed blood to survive, yes. But what she had seen had been intimate. Emery may not have had much experience with men, but it didn't mean she didn't know what foreplay looked like. Maybe feeding was supposed to be sexual. "Is it always that way? I mean, Jessi looked as though she was on her way to riding out the best orgasm of her life."

August bellowed a deep guttural laugh that echoed through the gardens. Emery felt it in her bones as it radiated through her. She loved his laugh. It didn't even matter it was at her expense.

"No, it's not always like that. Usually, I drink from blood bags, it's easier with my schedule. Tonight, though, I fed from Jessi in order to sate her vicious appetite and give her something to gloat about tomorrow. I didn't need her trying to take things further."

"What does that mean?"

"When a vampire feeds, trace amounts of our venom enter the bloodstream of the person we are feeding from. Our intent determines how the human will react. Inherently, our venom provides a high, but that mixed with the vampire's intent can change what the human experiences."

Emery's lips twisted in disgust, "So, you gave her an orgasm? Of all the things you could've given her?"

"She didn't complain," he replied smugly. "And I didn't have to actually do any of the sexual acts she wanted."

That was the most man-logic explanation she'd ever heard.

Pushing the picture of Jessi's orgasm out of her head, she continued, trying to understand the mechanics. "So, intent is what made it sexual. It's not inherently a sexual act?"

"It can be, but no, that is not generally the route most vampires go. It really depends on what the human wants."

"But I thought it was the vampire's intent that determined how it goes."

"It is. Think of it this way, every human has a preference when it comes to sex, right?"

She wasn't sure where this was going, nor did she have any experience with the topic, but she nodded slowly.

"Some prefer very traditional means while another's palette may be a bit more eccentric. There are those that get off on being dominated, while others like pain mixed in with their sexual endeavors. Your partner would help you meet your needs."

They would if she'd ever had a partner. Growing up isolated ensured she never had the opportunity. Would August be inherently domineering as his vampire side tended to be, or would he be the gentle and passionate lover she imagined his artistic side brought out?

"We take into consideration the needs of the human we feed from. Those who need a good orgasm shall receive. While those who like the element of fear have only to ask. Intent can be anything they want it to be."

"Wow. That's oddly beautiful and completely terrifying."

"Would you like me to show you?"

"Feed from me?" Emery jerked away from him. There were some lines she was not willing to cross. Not even for him. "Hell no. Why would I want you to do that? My blood is fine right where it is, thank you very much."

August chuckled. "No, that's not what I mean." Sliding from the fountain, he knelt in front of her. "I can take a tiny bit of my venom and place it on your lip. It will seep into your bloodstream, and you will experience the effects of my intent for a short time."

"Will it hurt? No, wait, you're not going to make me orgasm out in the open, right?" Not that a part of her didn't want him to. The sexually frustrated female inside her very much wanted this man's hands all over her, but she knew that was a terrible idea. Emery was already treading a thin line when it came to her feelings for the dark prince.

"That depends on my intent," he replied with a hint of promise laced in his words, and

Emery narrowed her eyes. "Em, I promise my intent will not hurt you or give you the sexual desires you know you want from me. Trust me, I would do a whole lot more than give you venom for that."

Despite rolling her eyes, she believed him. Even if common sense told her not to.

"Okay." The words left her mouth before her brain could protest. She could do this. She was going to be living in the castle for the foreseeable future, and it would help to learn about the vampires who called it home. Which would be useful, especially if one of them turned out to be her sister's killer.

Had Sloane let Malcolm feed from her? They loved each other, so it would make sense she would help feed him.

August inched forward, nudging her knees apart. He didn't touch her with his hands as he settled between her thighs. Her dress inched up her thighs, and his closeness was enough to cause a flurry of drunk bees to stir within her belly.

Emery gasped when he reached up to his mouth, flashing her his elongated fang. He pricked his finger and a tiny drop of crimson formed at the tip. This was a terrible idea. And yet her heart raced at the thought of tasting a part of him.

August used his free hand to push her hair from her face and cupped her cheek. Emery leaned into his touch, relishing in it. He gently rubbed his thumb over her lip, pulling it down and eliciting a shiver that ran down her spine and settled between her legs.

Keep it together, Emery.

August's ice blue eyes left her mouth and connected with hers. She gave a small nod, reassuring him she was okay. He didn't hesitate and smoothed the crimson drop along the soft exposed flesh of her inner lip.

Emery shuddered at his tender touch. The venom absorbed into her lip at an alarming rate, and a light fog tickled the edge of her mind.

August removed his finger, but still held her face in his hand, staring at her with an unreadable expression. She should be scared, fight the effects, but with him so close, nothing bad could possibly happen.

Emery closed her mouth and ran her tongue over the inside of her lip, grazing the spot where he wiped the venom. Initially, it tasted metallic, similar to blood, but it transformed on her palette into a sweet caramel. Her favorite. Was venom specific to each person, or was this the prince's personal flavor?

An intense calm trickled over her. It started at her head and worked its way downward, each muscle group it passed tensed momentarily, then relaxed like she had a full body massage. She sank into herself, even though her body never physically moved from the spot on the fountain's edge.

Emery's gaze held August's, and she yearned to convey what she was feeling, but no words would come out.

Usually that would cause panic, but none came. In that moment, she was lost in the calmness of August's oceanic eyes, completely content to be there with him for the first time since they met.

August smiled, and unlike all his other smiles since she reached the castle, that one reached his eyes. Emery nearly melted. It was the same smile he wore the night he'd been singing at the club. The smile that shone through when he thought no one of importance was looking. She was no one of importance, which made her love all the more that she got to bask in it. That smile was a rarity.

Her core clenched with need, her body responding to the carnal desires August elicited. She'd never felt so empty.

She wanted him. Every part of him. It didn't matter what he was, and she struggled to see a reason why they couldn't act on the connection between them. Nothing ever felt more right.

Emery slid from her seat and straddled August. He stilled and raised his brows as she shrugged off her cardigan in one fluid movement. She whipped her hair behind her and gave the prince her best bedroom eyes.

He swallowed hard, and his jaw tightened. "What are you doing?" he asked, his voice laced with tension. "You're playing a dangerous game, Sloane, because I won't stop if you keep going."

Hearing her sister's name was a hard slap against her heightened emotions. Emery paused, fighting the need within her. He would regret implying she was anything other than herself. She wasn't Sloane, and he damn well knew it.

She wanted this.

Him.

Deep down, she knew she'd wanted this from the moment she met him.

She embraced the sudden confidence, forgetting the perpetual worry she was in over her head. Gone was the hatred she felt toward those who took her twin from her all those years ago. Only her and August mattered.

Emery allowed herself, for the first time since she'd met him, to dive deep into the untapped emotions she felt for the blond haired, blue eyed prince. She ground her hips against him, and a soft moan fell from her lips when his length grew beneath her needy sex.

A deep growl rumbled from August's chest.

Her lips turned upward at his reaction, and she leaned forward, hovering her lips above his. "Then, don't stop."

His hands were on her ass, pulling her closer to him as his lips took hers. Her breath hitched with excitement and anticipation. August nipped at her lower lip, demanding she open. Emery obliged, and August swept his tongue into her mouth. He tasted of the sweetest caramel mixed with the salty sea, and Emery could not get enough of him.

She wanted more.

Needed more.

August was a puzzle she desperately wanted to solve. He was more than what he let everyone see, but to her, he inexplicably felt like home. Something she had never known but always longed for.

Reaching between them, Emery fiddled with the top buttons of his dress shirt. They were the death of her, refusing to be undone, keeping her from the prize beneath. She longed to run her hands over his muscular chest.

With each button she undid, August deepened his kiss, exploring every facet of her mouth, making it impossible to concentrate. When she finally managed to push open his shirt, Emery broke their kiss and gave August a devilish grin. She traced her eyes downward, admiring the perfect specimen of a man before her.

Sex on a stick was much too tame to describe him. He was a freaking god among men.

Emery brought her lips to his chest, trailing kisses across it while her hands traced the ridges between his washboard abs. She pushed him back, closed her mouth over his perfectly erect nipple, and flicked the tip of her tongue across it.

August moaned and shifted beneath her. It was the only encouragement she needed to rake his nipple with her teeth and suck it into her mouth while grinding her hips along the ridge of his hardened cock.

"Fuck," he hissed and she smiled against his chest.

His hands moved from her ass, tracing the length of her spine upward until they fingered her hair. Entwining it with his fist, August pulled her head back and forced her to meet his gaze. "My turn," he whispered with a devilish smile.

He released her hair, and his hands found the top of her dress. With one swift tug, he popped the buttons that held it together.

Hot damn.

August's hands found her hips, and he lifted her with ease. He laid her back across the wide lip of the fountain, shoulders hanging just over the edge. Her hair draped behind her, the ends trailing into the water, and she strained to hold her head upright to see August. He placed her feet on the ground and knelt between them. Emery panted as his eyes roamed over her body, taking in every inch of her now exposed skin.

"You are fucking gorgeous, Em."

Before she could respond, he was invading her space, feeding the fire within her. Supporting her head, his lips found hers, and he coaxed her mouth open, invading it with his skilled tongue. Emery moaned against him. Fisting her hands in his hair, she gently tugged him closer, urging him on. She'd found heaven in the last place she expected.

August trailed kisses along her neck, tracing her artery to her collar bone. In one swift motion, he ripped the seam of her bra, exposing her breasts with their tightened peaks to the cool night air. He teased her left nipple with his mouth, softly raking his teeth over the sensitive bud while rolling the other between this thumb and forefinger.

Her body hummed with pleasure. Each subtle movement pushing her further toward the edge she longed for. She arched her back searching for more and pushed her hips against him, grinding herself on his hardened length.

August was unreal.

He settled between her thighs and pulled her hips toward him, draping her legs over his shoulders. Leaning forward, he placed light kisses on the inside of her thigh, working his way down one, then the other. Pushing aside the scraps of dress that lightly covered her, he brought his mouth to her hip and ripped the thin lace fabric of her panties. Trailing his tongue from her hip bone, his mouth found the sensitive bundle of nerves between her legs. She jumped at the sudden presence of his tongue across her clit. It sent a jolt through her like nothing she'd ever felt before, sating the ache in her core while simultaneously fueling her need. He swirled his tongue around her sensitive flesh and clamped down on the tender bud, sucking it between his lips.

"August," Emery moaned, her hands tangling in his hair. She arched her back, dipping her head toward the water below her, its coolness a refreshing sensation in comparison to the heat growing.

He moaned against her, and the vibrations nearly sent her over the edge. When the sensations became overwhelming, she tried to slam her legs closed, but August's grip on her thighs held them open.

Her body felt like it was ready to explode from the inside out and all ability to think ceased. The muscles in her core seized, and when she couldn't hold on any longer, Emery let go. Waves of ecstasy rolled through her. She bit her lip, trying to muffle the echo of her cries as she arched under August's skilled mouth. He teased her with light caresses, riding the swells of her climax.

August released her thighs and climbed up her body. He cupped her face and pulled her mouth to his, effectively silencing her moans. She tasted herself on his lips and was surprised to find it only stoked the flame of desire.

The desire that had only grown since August touched her.

Emery closed her eyes, trying to regain some semblance of composure, though her thoughts focused on the growing ache between her thighs. She thought one good orgasm would have been enough, but she wanted more. Hell, she was confident they could go all night and it wouldn't be enough for her.

August broke the kiss and groaned. She opened her eyes and stared at him. His expression was dark, almost wild. His breathing as erratic as hers.

"I need you to say yes, Em. I need to be inside you."

"Yes." The word was out of her mouth before she could think twice. She wanted him to be her first.

Her only.

Tears pricked at her eyes. It was impossible for them to remain together, but for one night it could be her reality.

August swiftly freed his erection from the strain of his pants, and Emery's mouth fell open. She hadn't seen many, but it wasn't necessary to know August was well endowed.

He moved forward, sliding his thick length through the wetness of her slit but did not take her immediately. Leaning over, he kissed her thoroughly, exploring every delicious inch of her mouth. It was more than a kiss. It was a claim, raw and possessive.

August dragged his mouth from hers, raining kisses down her neck and the swell of her breasts. He dragged his teeth back and forth across her nipples while methodically rubbing his cock through her slick folds and over her clit. Her stomach tightened, and Emery nearly came when August ceased all movement.

"Please, August," she whimpered.

"Please what, Princess." She could have sworn she felt his lips widen in a smile against her skin.

She shivered with desire before whispering words she never thought she'd say to him. "Be my first."

August stopped. Positioned at her entrance a growl vibrated against her skin.

His wide eyes found hers, though she wasn't sure if it was fear or surprise that filled them.

"Just push. I know it's going to hurt."

August stared at her blankly as if he couldn't register her words. "You're a virgin?"

Emery stared at him, her jaw open in disbelief. Did it matter if she was? She wanted this, and clearly, so did he.

"Aren't all your women?" She wiggled beneath him, needing him to either move or vacate the area.

"Yes, but they grew up here." August bit his swollen lip and raked his fingers through his hair. "You didn't. I just thought you would be—"

It was as if he'd smacked her in the face. "You thought I would be more experienced."

"It's not that. It's just..." His voice trailed off and she watched an array of emotions play across his face while still halfway inside her.

She shook her head. He didn't need to answer. It was clear August thought she was more loose with her legs. An easy fuck. Not someone he would have to teach.

"Get off me." Emery pushed against his chest and dislodged him from between her legs. Pulling up the sides of her ripped dress, she covered as much of her body as she could. "I'm going back to the castle. You taught me my lesson and then some. We're done for the night."

August stood and pulled up his pants, shoving his dick inside.

Emery narrowed her gaze, trying to read August's thoughts. His eyes softened, and she recognized the expression. It was the same expression Ada had given her each time she complained how unfair it was that her sister was taken from her.

Pity.

"Here, take my shirt, it will help cover you."

Tears welled in her eyes as she watched him shrug off the still blood stained shirt. Jessi's blood. How could she have been so stupid?

"No, thank you. I don't need anything from someone who doesn't want anything to do with me."

"Is that what you think?"

"No, I get it, August. You get me all sexed up on your venom, which I might add is exactly what you said you wouldn't do. But then you back out when you realize you weren't quite getting the easy lay you expected."

"Me? This wasn't my fault. My intent had nothing to—."

"Oh, yeah sure, you expect me to believe that? You know, just because I'm a virgin doesn't mean I want you to put a fucking ring on it."

"Would you shut the hell up, woman, for five seconds and let me speak?"

Emery's spine straightened at his harsh tone. "I'm sorry, *Your Highness*. Go right ahead."

"Oh, so we're back to formalities, are we?" He turned his back on her and took a few steps away, his hands fisted at his sides. "Well, Miss Montgomery, I'll have you know—"

The moment he stepped away a wave of crippling nausea washed over her, and a ringing sounded in her ears. Doubling over to hold her stomach, she rode out the uneasy feeling. When it passed, she sat up, and as she did, it was as if she had been doused with cold water and a dense fog cloud had been lifted from around her.

When she'd righted herself, August was in front of her once more on his knees, his hands grasping her shoulders. "Em? Emery, are you alright? What happened?"

She didn't know what happened. Only that she had given into every wanton desire she had for the man in front of her. She'd almost let him fuck her, something she hadn't let anyone do. And as much as she wanted to claim it was the venom that made her do it, she knew that would be a lie.

Emery had wanted all of August.

It was him that didn't want her.

"I'm so sorry, August. I don't— I don't know what just happened. That wasn't me. I mean it was but—" Her cheeks warmed, and she knew they were the brightest shade of pink. "I can't believe I just threw myself at you. And you clearly didn't want me. Now I feel sick to my stomach and like a haze lifted, and I want to forget this ever happened." She buried her flamed cheeks in her hands. "Can you just go please?"

"Emery, look at me."

"No. Please just go."

Gentle hands caressed hers, and he pulled them away from her face. "Emery, this isn't your fault. What you just described is the effects of coming down from the venom. I don't know what happened, but having you seduce me was not my intent. My intentions were for you to be relaxed. For a calm to wash over you, so you may sleep soundly tonight and forget the stresses of your day."

Emery considered his words and the queasy feeling returning to her stomach. She distinctly remembered feeling those things as the venom took hold. Then, she got one look at August's authentic smile and she'd wanted to— She gasped. "Oh shit."

August arched a brow. "What?"

"Is it possible for someone to override your intent?"

"I've never heard of such a thing. Why?"

She whispered, afraid that what she said was the truth. "Because I think it was my intent. Not yours."

A smile grew on August's lips. "That means deep down you do want me."

Emery rolled her eyes. "Again, with the selective hearing."

"Do you?"

"Any woman would want you, August. You are a wealthy immortal prince. You must know that. Look at the plethora of women you have throwing themselves at your feet to marry you."

"I'm not asking them. I'm asking you."

"It doesn't matter. You had your chance, and clearly, virgin blood is not what you want. Let's just pretend this didn't happen."

"Oh, sweet Emery. That's where you are mistaken. I want you. I want every inch of you and every inch of me inside you. And now that I know where your heart's desires lie, I'll patiently wait for your mind to catch up. You're torn by what I am. You want to hate me, but clearly, that's not all you want. I am the monster you fear, but I'm also the man you want. I'm living for the day you realize I can be both those things in your heart and in your bed. And when that day comes, I am going to wreck you so fucking sweetly. You deserve to be wooed, and your first time will not happen on the ledge of a fountain. When I take your virginity, it's going to be in my bed, upon the softest blankets the world has ever known. I am going to adore you and then I'm going to ruin that beautiful pussy for any. Other. Man."

Stunned by his words, Emery silently stared at him.

A million thoughts ran through her head, the most prominent being he'd just promised to be the one who took her virginity. She should protest, should say anything to deter August's claim, and yet she couldn't force a single coherent word from her lips.

He looked down at her. "You don't need to say anything,

Princess. You can even try to pretend tonight didn't happen. But it did, and it will again." He leaned into her ear and with a sharp intake of breath sucked her lobe between his lips. "I'll be seeing you soon, Emery."

She watched as August strode toward the castle. His fabulous ass left as much of an impression as his words had.

A single tear stained her cheek. She was in way over her head. She needed to put on her big girl panties and remember August would never accept her once he found out she had witch blood running through her veins. But that wasn't what her heart wanted.

Not anymore.

Emery stood from the fountain and wrapped her arms around herself, securing her tattered dress. She looked to the sky at the precise moment a star fell. Quickly squeezing her eyes shut, she played the part of the princess in the castle and wished for her heart's desire, knowing full well it could never become reality. And while it hurt, she would always have tonight in the garden.

That would have to be enough.

Chapter Fifteen

AUGUST

He needed a cold shower and a bottle of whiskey.

Scratch that.

He needed something stronger than whiskey. Something smooth and velvety that would quench his thirst. The moment he crossed the invisible barrier surrounding Emery, his bloodlust returned with a vengeance. Each heartbeat of the humans working in the castle taunted him on the walk back to his chambers.

August struggled to remain in control. Not weak enough to give into the bloodlust, but too stubborn to seek out the one woman who calmed it.

He should drink.

If not only to satisfy his hunger but to distract him from the perpetual hard-on he sported and the sweet minx who caused it.

Who was he kidding?

Not even feeding could get her out of his head. The image of her splayed before him under the summer moonlight with his cock at her entrance would forever be his favorite memory. She was incredible. Divine even. He knew he was in trouble the moment her lips touched his.

To top it all off, she was a bloody virgin.

August fought the urge to simultaneously punch something and rejoice. He couldn't believe Emery considered giving herself to him right there in the middle of the garden. Where anyone could have walked in on them. She hadn't told him it was her first time, and for that, he wanted nothing more than to punish her pretty porcelain ass.

Like hell would her first time be on a fountain bench. While he found exhibitionism to be a turn on, she deserved so much more.

She would get so much more.

What infuriated him most was she thought he saw her as an easy fuck. That couldn't be further from the truth. The only reason he stopped himself from plunging deep inside of her was because she was more than any other woman. She deserved the world. She deserved everything. He would be the one to give it to her. So much had already been taken from her, and he couldn't fathom cheapening her first time. It deserved to be as special as she was.

Thinking about the ways he wanted to please her with his touch kept his cock rigid in his pants. The way he wanted more than anything to keep his promise. To ensure every inch of her beautiful skin knew his touch. Then, he'd wreck her until she screamed his name and begged him for more.

She wouldn't even be able to look at another man once he was done.

All of which would be done in the privacy of his bed where he could ensure she was taken care of so thoroughly. And without prying eyes. After that, all bets were off. He'd take her anywhere he could get her. Likely, all over the castle.

God, did he want to make that pretty pink pussy his.

But if he was honest with himself, he wanted more than that. Needed more. More of her. More than just her body. August was drawn to Emery's entire being. He wanted all of her.

She thought for herself and didn't let the fact he was a prince sway her. She was smart, and most importantly, she stood up for herself. Emery was charming, yet snarky. And God help him, he loved that curse laden mouth of hers. The fact she was attractive was icing on the cake. A cake he would very much like to eat in his bedroom right now.

If he wasn't a noble man, he'd charge into her room and demand she tell him what he needed to do to win her heart. To convince her the venom only worked to enhance her true feelings and that the connection between them was the realest thing he'd felt in his long life. He'd beg if need be. Plead. Get down on his knees again and again. A lesser man wouldn't have thought twice to go to her if it meant he got to feel the way she made him feel.

Like nothing else mattered.

Her kiss.

Her touch.

It melted away the bullshit, setting him free of his responsibilities, wrapping him only in the moment, with her.

But life wasn't simple, and August wasn't a lesser man.

He may not have strict morals, but he would never force a woman to be with him.

August paced the length of his suite while considering the situation. It wasn't a habit so much as an indicator he was walking the fine line between in and out of control. The line he straddled between being the monster he was and the man he desired to be for Emery. He needed to get his head on straight and start thinking logically, but with what happened in the garden and the fact he could still smell her on his lips, it was nearly impossible.

He was spiraling.

The signs were there, and if he didn't get a grip soon, he would find himself fang deep in an unsuspecting maid. He'd already fucked up by feeding from Jessi, and he couldn't afford to go on a bender. At the very least he found comfort in knowing Emery was safe from him.

It was still surprising she calmed the bloodlust. He could go to her, sit outside her door like he had before.

August stopped pacing and glared at the door. He took a step toward it, ready to go to her and throw caution to the wind. Then, he thought better of it. The last thing he needed was her stumbling outside her door to find him sitting there. She'd question him and inevitably find out about his unusually high lust for blood from the vein.

If he hadn't already scared her with his venom and by seeing him feed from Jessi, he had no doubt his addiction would cause her to run. And run fast.

He turned his back on the door and stalked to the small fridge in the corner. His grip nearly tore off the small door when he yanked it open and grabbed a blood bag. Downing its contents helped take the edge off. But it wasn't enough.

August cursed under his breath and headed for the

bathroom to shower, hoping his initial plan would calm his mind. He quickly stripped and stepped under the hot water, allowing the steady stream to caress his skin.

He reached up and pushed the button to dispense his favorite soap. The blue glob fell into his hand, and he hesitated, staring at it. What had moments ago felt like the answer to his problem now posed a new one. He didn't want to wash Emery away. He wanted to relish in her scent as it clung to his body. Bask in what they shared.

Visions of Emery pressed their way to the forefront of his mind.

She looked up at him, a smile playing on her lips, as she toyed with her breasts. Her tight curves begged to be gripped by his hands, and his hands alone. The soft brown curls on her mound drew him in, framed her perfect pussy.

A pussy drenched for him.

The scent of Emery's arousal wrapped around him. Calmed him and fueled his monster's desires in the same breath as he longed to drive into her.

His breath quickened as he stroked his dick, moving his hand along its full length, and groaned. The pleasure soothed not only his need for blood, but his need for Emery.

To fill her with his cock. Fuck her hard and fast to fill his own desire.

And hers.

Emery stood before him, bare and beautiful. Perfect. Water droplets hit her skin and cascaded over her breasts. She threw her head back and moaned as his hands roamed freely over every precious curve of her body. Teasing her. Caressing her. Bringing her to the brink of orgasm with the simplest of touches.

He stepped forward, pushing her against the wall, and fell to his knees. Burying his face between her legs, he sucked her clit into his mouth and swept his tongue over the sensitive nub. With a growl that solidified him as every bit of the monster he knew he was, he slid his finger within her and fucked her hard and fast, bringing her to a swift climax. Emery cried out his name as she clenched around him, and he rewarded her with continuous violent orgasms, one right after the other, until she begged him to fill her with his cock.

August groaned and pumped his cock faster. His pleasure grew, his balls tightening before he threw his head back. His orgasm crested and stole possession of his entire body, as each wave of his climax rippled through him. He pressed his forehead to the cold tile and focused on controlling his breaths. If he could feel this good from merely a fantasy, he couldn't imagine what she would feel like in the flesh.

He needed to know.

Needed to be inside her.

More than ever, he wanted to claim her as his own.

He'd made it known he wanted her, and she stared at him like he'd grown a second head. She claimed it was the venom that made her act as she had, but it wasn't possible. Venom didn't work that way. He couldn't explain why she didn't react the way he'd intended or how her intent played a role in what happened.

But she changed it, of that he was sure.

He should have at least a small ounce of regret, but he didn't. It only proved that she felt for him as he did for her.

Still, Emery made it clear from the start she didn't want to be his queen. That she had no desire to rule beside him. Regardless of the obvious attraction between them, his gut told him she would not easily be swayed to change her mind. He didn't think anything short of abdicating his throne and forsaking his family would ensure she was by his side when all was said and done.

It was a dark thought.

One that had only crossed August's mind once before, a hundred or so years ago in the throes of a blood bender. But ultimately, he realized his fate was predetermined and nothing he did would change that. His mother couldn't have more children, and neither of his siblings could produce an heir.

Everything rested on his shoulders.

His and his alone.

A knock on the bathroom door pulled him from his thoughts. His footman, Clovis, peeked his head in the door. "I'm sorry to disturb you, Your Highness, but your father requests your presence in the throne room immediately."

"Fuck," he exhaled and muttered under his breath. "Thank you, Clovis. I'll finish up and be right there."

His father wasn't supposed to be back until the following morning. Early arrivals and urgent meetings in the throne room never amounted to anything good.

August washed and rinsed while trying to mentally prepare himself for what his father inevitably had planned.

Looking down, he smirked.

On the upside, he'd managed to rectify the erection problem.

Chapter Sixteen

AUGUST

August inhaled a slow breath as he stood outside the ornate floor to ceiling double doors. The second blood bag he'd consumed before heading to the meeting with his father helped to settle his nerves.

He hated the throne room.

It held the chair that was his future, but as it was currently occupied, it was nothing but a constant reminder that nothing he did would ever be seen as good enough for his father. He'd come to terms with it long ago, vowing if he couldn't please the king, he'd strive to be a better version of him.

With confidence, August pushed open the doors and glided across the polished floors toward the dais. Sitting in an intricately carved high back throne surrounded by draped purple tapestries was his father, King Lewyn Nicholson. The king known for settling the Americas and maintaining vampire order within his realm. A great, albeit strict, king and absent father. At least, he had been, until it came time to train August. Then, he'd become an overbearing asshole, dead set on controlling every aspect of August's life.

And he fucking hated it.

"You called for me? I wasn't expecting you home until the morning." He met his father's cold stare. "How was your trip to Vancouver? I suspect Lord Gerald was happy to have you."

"Ah yes, well you know the Canadians, ever the welcoming hosts. They sure do know how to throw a party." The King's eyes narrowed. "What I am more interested in is the progress you've made here, Augustine. I hear there was a development?"

August winced. Of course, his mother had told him. Ever the dutiful wife. Something he never understood.

"Is it safe to speak here?"

The King nodded, and August proceeded to recount the happenings of the last few days, minimizing any details pertaining Emery as well as his visit to Lilyana as promised.

The king mulled over the information as he picked up a small bell from the table beside his throne. With a flick of his wrist, he chimed it three times, and a busty redhead, dressed in little more than a shift appeared from his father's attached study. Her eyes were glazed over, compulsion evident in her lax expression. She approached his father and took his outstretched hand, allowing him to drape her across his lap.

His father sank his fangs into her neck, and August struggled to hide his wince. He should have been sated after drinking from Jessi and the two blood bags in his room, but he wasn't. He never was, and he'd opened pandora's box with that one taste of the vein.

"Would you like some?" his father offered.

August clenched his fists. *Yes.* "No, I already fed, thank you."

"Ah, did you now?" The king raised a brow. "I'm so glad you've finally come to your senses and embraced your true nature."

"Yes, well, it was a means to an end. You know I prefer the glass to the vein."

"A sentiment I will never understand." The king leaned down and sank his fangs once more into the feeder.

His father wouldn't understand. He'd never believed August had a problem in the first place.

For most vampires, blood was a means to an end. A necessary part of life. For August, it was so much more. Hovering over an artery with the throbbing of a human's life force beneath his fangs. The way they twisted to his every whim, always coming back for more but never quite understanding why they yearned for him. It was euphoric. But what really got him was the way their bodies pumped the velvety crimson liquid into his waiting mouth, as if they were made to do so.

It was enough to send him over the edge and into a bender every time.

Once August had one vein, he wanted them all. He lost all rational thought and didn't understand why a vampire would only feed once every few days. Older vampires didn't need to feed often, but why wouldn't they want to? With walking blood donors easily accessible, why wait to sink their fangs into a warm body?

He'd played a dangerous game feeding from Jessi

tonight, like an addict taking just one bump in the bathroom of a night club, hoping and praying it didn't send them back into the throes of their spiraling addiction.

While he hadn't worried about being around Emery so soon after feeding, being around the other women would be a challenge for the next few days. He would either need to keep Emery close or ensure he was stocked up on an ample supply of blood bags.

He knew which he preferred.

August hadn't realized his father stopped feeding until his voice pulled him from his thoughts. "Based on the events, I agree the witches are somehow involved, although I don't know that it has anything to do with the replacement girl."

August shook his head. "It's too much of a coincidence to have a death and now possibly a witch within the castle."

"Maybe so. I'll reach out to my contacts in New Orleans and Tennessee and see if there have been any rumblings from the witches or wolves. Detestable beings, the witches. If one of theirs has penetrated the castle, you will find them, do I make myself clear?"

"Yes, father." He would do more than find them. He would string them up and make them wish they'd never stepped foot within the castle walls. He'd do whatever it took to find out if they were responsible for Sloane's murder, and if they were, he'd make them beg for death.

"They will be met with swift justice," the King added, as if he'd read August's mind. He looked down and softly added, "The witches have taken too much from me already."

"What do you mean?" He played dumb, knowing full well about his father's first family.

"Never you mind," the King chided. "All you need to know is the witches aren't to be trusted."

"Something we agree on."

"Good." Shaking off his melancholy tone, the King changed the subject. "In the meantime, have there been any other leads on the girl's death?"

August didn't think his father knew Sloane's name. Nor did he care to learn it.

"No, but Malcolm and I are working on it."

"And what of your Culling?"

"I informed the women of my intent to take it more seriously. They are thrilled with the prospect."

"That's fantastic. Which is why I expect you to eliminate three tonight, and three more before the Scottish delegation arrives."

"But I only just told them today I would be taking it more seriously. It's only fair I give each woman a date before I eliminate any of them."

"Come now, son, there must be a few terrible looking ones you know don't have a chance in hell at being your bride. We want to show our court you are serious about finding your future queen. It sets a precedent. Our people are watching, and now it would seem the witches are as well."

August gaped at his father. He didn't know why he'd expected his father to be supportive of his Culling, allowing him to find the right girl and fall in love. If anyone should understand what he was going through it would be him, having been through the process twice in his lifetime. But wishful thinking wouldn't change his father's ways. This was, after all, the man who'd allegedly sacrificed his true love to save himself.

"The women will be here in five minutes, so I suggest you think about your decision quickly." He licked his lips and dipped his head to the woman he'd designated his personal blood bag. He took his time, pulling as much as he could before she teetered on the edge of consciousness. When he finished, he helped her from his lap and swatted her ass. "Thanks, dear."

She stood wobbly on her feet, gave a small curtsey, then walked toward the study from which she came.

August wished he could offer her another option, a better life than a walking blood bag. The irony was not lost on him that a vampire addicted to blood wanted to save the very thing he craved. Still, no human deserved to be treated like they were nothing more than property. She may have volunteered for the position, likely an addict herself, in it for the venom high, but that didn't make it acceptable. The only one he'd possibly bend that rule for was the witch in the castle. He'd consider letting them be a personal blood bag as part of their punishment. Then again, a witch's taste likely matched their vile nature. It would be easier to just take their head.

His father stroked the corner of his lips with his fingers, wiping away the stray blood. "Also, I need you to give extra consideration to Jessi Reynolds, Chelsea Raston, and Sutton Ashberry. They all come from wealthy families that support us and our charities. It would behoove you to choose one of them."

"With all due respect, father, I had hoped to marry for love. Not for advantageous gain."

"Love isn't everything, my son. You will be king someday, a fact you would do well to remember. Your mother was a strategic move. One that paid off. I now have an heir and a kingdom of my own."

That's not the life August wanted, though. He didn't see why anyone would willingly choose to live in a loveless marriage. Not when one could have a partner. Someone who supported them. He'd seen it over the years in other royal families and longed for it with his own. The strongest kingdoms were built on family. While his father dictated the kingdom, his people did not unify behind him. Not in the same way those with a unified king and queen did. How did his father not see, with the witches plotting against them, they needed their kingdom behind them?

If August followed in his father's footsteps and chose to live in a loveless marriage, he feared he would turn off the emotions tethering him to his humanity. The night's events already had him teetering close to the line. His father may not need emotion to rule, but for August it was essential.

What's worse, he loathed to admit, his father was right. There were girls within his Culling that weren't memorable, and there would be no love lost if they were gone from the castle. A tiny part of his half dead heart felt bad for them. They hadn't asked for this life. Then again, neither had he. They'd all been born pawns in a cruel game with someone else moving the pieces.

A low knock at the door pulled him from his thoughts, and he turned just in time to see the twenty women of his culling ushered into the throne room.

As much as he would have loved a moment to consider his choices, fate was a conniving bitch. Instead ,he'd be forced to break the hearts of three women, ending their chances to the only life they'd ever prepared for.

He tried to ignore each of their erratic heartbeats as they shuffled forward, each in various states of dress. It was clear they were not given time to prepare themselves either. Some still wore their dresses while others who'd already been ready for bed now clutched their robes to their chest. The one uniformity was the frightened unease etched on each of their faces as they gripped the hand of the woman next to them. They were sisters, bonded through the same terrifying experience.

All except one.

Emery.

He knew the instant she entered the room. A calm washed over him, and he no longer had the urge to tear into the vein of every woman before him. She walked in with her head held high, like she believed she had no stake in the culling. Little did she know, she held the highest stake. One that would cripple him should she shove it through his heart.

August's eyes roamed over her. She'd changed from the dress he'd torn apart into an oversized sweater paired with leggings that hugged every curve of her delectable ass.

It wasn't until her amber eyes pierced his that he realized they were puffy, as if she'd been crying. He had to stifle the urge to pull her aside and demand to know who hurt her, worried he was the culprit. She gave him a half smile, and his heart swelled. Even though she was hurting, she'd still put on a brave face, still played the game he'd demanded she play.

She didn't even know she had all the makings of a queen.

Her eyes never left his as she curtsied before the dais and made her way to her seat. He wondered what was going through her pretty little head. She would no doubt have an opinion on being called here last minute for an impromptu elimination.

August didn't want to give her the satisfaction of looking away first, but when his father sat on his throne silent, he had to concede.

The fucking coward. This was his idea, and of course, he would leave it to August to be the bad guy.

Clearing his throat, August began what was sure to be a shitshow. "Thank you all for coming down so late. I'm sorry you were not given more notice." He placed his hands behind his back and looked down the line of women. "Tonight, under the King's advisement, I have decided to eliminate three of you from the Culling."

His words were met with gasps and whispers. One woman, he believed her name was Beth, audibly sobbed.

After the initial shock, they fell into an unnerving silence. "If your name is called please step forward. You will be given the choice to leave the castle and return to your human family, or you may opt to join our kingdom as an immortal. As such, you will be given a place at court and may choose any one of our North American embassies to call home." August paused, he didn't want to do this, if only because his father demanded it. "Beth." *Because you cry way too much.* "Gianna." *You are sweet, maybe too sweet for the life of a queen.* "Sutton." *Mostly because it's going to infuriate my father. Also, you're a bitch.* "I'm sorry to say your time here at the castle has ended."

"Are you fucking serious?" Sutton erupted. "Do you know who I am?"

August was on her in a matter of seconds, his motions a blur across the throne room. Nose to nose with the ungrateful excuse for a woman, he growled, "I honestly don't give a shit who you are, or who your parents are. You would do well to remember who the fuck I am."

Sutton tensed beneath his narrowed gaze, cowering back from him. He loathed the thought he could potentially run into her for all of eternity if she opted to be turned. Maybe he could just ensure it wasn't an option for her, or that her turning didn't take. He was the crown prince after all. That had its perks.

Nothing but silence filled the room. Turning to the other two women, August softened, "Say your goodbye's tonight. We will need your decision by tomorrow morning as to where you would like to go from here."

With that, he dismissed the women to their rooms, knowing none of them would sleep well after this ordeal. They were resilient, though. They had to be if they wanted to survive the Culling. At least, that's what he told himself.

Amber eyes found his as they shuffled toward the door. They held sympathy and maybe even pity. Neither of which he deserved. Not from Emery. Not from any of the women.

He turned to his father and met the king's irritated stare. "Are we done here?"

His father's jaw tightened. "We will have words later."

Fan-fucking-tastic.

"Then, I'll take my leave. I have club business to attend to."

The king rolled his eyes. "Yes, go ahead and play business owner, but as you are making moves to ascend into your rule, consider investing in a real business. That bar brings nothing to your kingdom."

He bit his tongue and bowed low. August's happiness couldn't possibly be considered a worthy addition to his rule. "Yes, father," he ground out, unable to hide the irritation in his voice.

The king had a knack of shitting on everything good in his life.

Tonight was no different.

Chapter Seventeen

EMERY

Well, wasn't that the frosting on a bullshit cupcake. Emery hadn't known what to expect when they were summoned from their rooms, but it wasn't an elimination. While she had no stakes here at the castle except to solve the mystery of her sister's death, these women did. They were distraught upon leaving the throne room, tears staining every cheek. Each woman took their turn hugging those that had been eliminated. The petty walls they'd built between themselves had fallen, even if only for tonight.

Watching them comfort one another left Emery feeling like the imposter she was. While she played her part as Sloane, she couldn't imagine the loss these women were feeling. Well, almost. She had an inkling of what those who were eliminated were feeling, being pulled from the only life they had known and thrust into something completely new.

For Emery and the remaining women, the Culling had

just become real. Well, not so much for her, but for the sixteen women still competing for the ring on their left hand. Emery was determined to keep hers unmistakably naked.

The women shuffled toward the common room to commiserate together, but Emery made a swift exit, heading for her room. She no longer wanted to pretend.

Halfway down the hall, a hand slid into hers, taking her by surprise.

"Can you believe it?" Chelsea bounced beside her. "I just can't believe Prince August would send anyone home that quickly. And Sutton of all people, I thought for sure she had a chance at being a contender."

"It wasn't the prince. Didn't you hear him say it was at his father's request?"

"Well, yes, but you know he was only saying that to save face with the rest of us."

Was he? Emery didn't think that sounded like August. Not that she knew him all that well. Only well enough to almost give him her virginity. As much as she'd like to blame the venom, she wanted him to be her first from the moment she laid eyes on him in the club.

Before he was the vampire prince.

Chelsea continued to talk about the elimination the rest of the way to their rooms. Pausing outside Emery's door, the talkative bestie grew quiet.

"Is everything okay?"

Chelsea's eyes darted from the door to the ground, and if Emery had to guess, she'd say Chelsea was shaken up by the elimination but was overcompensating to try and make it seem as though nothing was amiss.

"Yeah, of course it is," she bubbled. "It's just, could I maybe stay with you tonight?"

Fuck. Emery rolled her eyes internally. She had a duty to keep up the charade of being her sister, but all she wanted was for her head to hit the pillow and sleep away her first day at the castle.

"Of course, you can stay!" she cooed, trying to convince both herself and Chelsea it was a great idea. "We'll have a sleepover!"

Chelsea rapidly clapped her hands. "Perfect! I'll just run to my room and get a few things." She turned and took off down the hallway.

Emery released a sigh. The last thing she wanted was to entertain Chelsea with girly sleepover shenanigans. She was nice enough, but she didn't even come close to Emery's best friend. Where Chelsea would be the perfect person to take with you to shop for a prom dress, Wren was the woman who would hold your hand as you got your nose pierced, then sit down in the chair after you. Chelsea would have scoffed at her pink hair as it wasn't worthy of a queen, whereas Wren bought the dye when Emery second guessed herself. There was nothing wrong with Chelsea, they were just from different worlds, and it was hard to genuinely connect.

She closed the door, but it was stopped before it shut by a stray hand. When she opened it back up, she found a wide-eyed Flora standing in the doorway.

Logic told her Flora couldn't be more than a year or two younger than her, but she looked as though she could easily be ten years her junior. She was petite with platinum blonde ringlets. "May I come in? It's urgent I speak with you."

"Of course, come in." Flora looked as though she was going to vomit, and Emery didn't need that outside her bedroom door. "Is everything okay?"

Between the prince's magic tongue and the sudden elimination, she didn't have any more fucks to give at the moment. But what was one more person's problems when it came to keeping up the Sloane charade?

Taking a step forward, Flora closed the door behind her and unsheathed a dagger from the folds of her dress. "No, everything's not okay." She held the dagger out in front of her, pointing it directly at Emery. Her hand shook as she swallowed hard. "I saw you die. Like never come back die."

Emery took a step back. The night just kept getting better and better.

Flora thrust the dagger, finding more courage with every word she spoke. "So, you better tell me who you are, I'll not let you harm the prince or his family."

"You saw me die?" Then, it clicked. "Oh shit. You saw Sloane's death." She took two steps toward Flora, feeling an instant connection. It didn't matter her motives, she was the key to finding out what happened to Sloane. "What happened? Tell me everything, now!"

Preferably before Chelsea returned.

Flora met her movements, keeping distance between them, and thrust the dagger again. "No, you tell me who you are first. How do you look just like her?"

"I can see how my appearance could be terrifying." Emery chuckled softly. She admired Flora for her willingness to seek the truth and stand up for August and his family, even with the pointy end of a dagger tipped in her direction. Emery put her hands up in surrender. "Please put down the dagger. I'm Emery, Sloane's twin." Emery took a step forward but hesitated when Flora raised a brow, almost as if she didn't believe her. "Wait, she never mentioned me, did she?"

"No."

Shoving down the sting of Sloane's silence, Emery twisted her wrist showing Flora the silver vines. "After Sloane died, the family debt transferred to me, and August ordered me to take her place. He said no one could know Sloane died."

"Why?" Flora hadn't moved a muscle, the knife still pointed at Emery.

Shrugging her shoulders, Emery stepped back and sat on the chest at the end of the bed. She fidgeted with her hands in her lap. "I'm still not one hundred percent sure. He said something about vampire politics and it being better if no one knew Sloane died. It gave them a leg up. I had to come anyways, so I agreed to be my sister as long as I could go home as soon as we found out what happened to her." Meeting Flora's eyes, Emery went silent, realization striking her like lightning. "You can tell me what happened."

Chelsea knocked on the door and pushed it open and Flora nodded, concealing the dagger.

"I was thinking we could send for popcorn from the kitchen, and maybe some of that chocolate cake from dessert if they have any left over." Finally looking up, she took notice of Flora and quieted. "Oh. Hi, Flora. I didn't know you would be joining us."

"I'm not. Actually, I was just leaving. Sloane and I can talk later."

"No, you should stay Flora. Truly. It would be nice to have another friendly face right now," Emery offered. Also, she was not letting Flora out of her sight. Not when she had information pertaining to Sloane's death and knew who she really was.

"Really?"

"Yes, absolutely. Let's go grab some clothes from your room while Chelsea sends for supplies."

Following Flora toward the door, Chelsea mouthed at Emery, "What are you doing?"

"Don't worry. I'll be right back," was all Emery could offer with a smile. "Have them bring up the popcorn and cake. Maybe some of the jello from dinner if there's any left over."

Chelsea's brows pulled together. "But you hate jello."

Damn it.

"But I don't." Flora chimed in, saving Emery from having to explain. "I was just telling Sloane how much I loved it."

"Okay. Jello it is then."

Emery followed Flora six doors down to her room. Upon entering, Emery noticed her room had a much more vintage feel compared to the modern décor of Sloane's. It was warm and comforting instead of cold.

Flora's demeanor changed from smiling to solemn as she sat on the identical hope chest at the foot of her bed.

Cautiously, Emery made her way to sit next to her. "Will you tell me what happened to my sister?"

"I was in the stalls with my favorite horse, Shadowfell. He'd gotten a pretty nasty cut on our last ride and needed to have the wound cleaned regularly. While I was in the stall, I heard voices up in the loft. Recognizing Sloane's, I almost called out. Although, now I'm glad I didn't."

"Do you know who she was talking to?" Emery interrupted, determined to commit to memory as many details as possible.

Flora shook her head. "No. They sounded female, but I could be wrong. I never saw the person's face. I could only hear every couple of words. They talked about a plan being put into motion. After that, there was a shuffle and hushed whispers. Something about a promise of power. There was a struggle and then a loud crack. After that, it was silent until a hooded figure carried Sloane's body from the loft wrapped in a blanket. They made a phone call and told the person on the other end that Sloane was dead. Ultimately, the hooded figure said they would deal with the repercussions accordingly. They unrolled her body on the stable floor, took the blanket, and left."

Why would they leave her body?

Unless it was indeed a message, as August had thought.

"Did you recognize the person? Their voice?"

Flora looked at the ground and shook her head. "They were tall but that's about all I noticed. They spoke low and in whispers. I was hidden in the stall. I couldn't see very well."

"Why didn't you tell anyone?"

"I was scared. What if the hooded person was someone in the castle?" Flora inhaled sharply as she recounted. "Then, the next morning when I'd worked up the courage to say something, Yessenia told us Sloane was sick and would be returning in a few days. Something didn't sit right with me about any of it. So, I kept my mouth shut for fear I'd be next."

"Then, I showed up."

Flora nodded. "Yes. I've been trying to work up the courage to talk to you all day, but I didn't know if you were one of them or not. I didn't know what to think. Once eliminations started, I became worried I would be sent home at a moment's notice, and the truth might never have been found out if I didn't speak up."

"Thank you, Flora. You have no idea what this means to

me. But you know you could have gone to August or even Malcolm."

She shrugged, unconvinced. "I supposed I could have, but they wouldn't have believed me. No one believes the quiet girl in the corner. Also, they are super intimidating. Telling you was a way I could be the hero for once."

Emery reached out and took Flora's hand in hers. "Thank you for being the kind of woman who is daring enough to seek out the truth. We're incredibly lucky to have you in our corner."

"It's not a bad last act of humanity."

Emery stilled as she comprehended her statement. "If you're eliminated, you're going to take their offer then?"

Flora nodded. "I think I am."

Emery pulled Flora in for a hug, wishing she had even an ounce of her bravery. "I hope someday, once I am out of the castle, we can still be friends. I have no doubt you are going to make an amazing vampire."

"Thank you." She gave Emery a squeeze before pulling away. "I wish it had been you that came here instead of Sloane. I think we would have been friends."

"Well, we're both still here for the time being. Let's go back to my room and enjoy cake and popcorn and make the best of tonight."

Emery tucked away all the information she'd learned and tried to have a good night with Chelsea and Flora. Things were tense at first between the three of them, but as soon as Emery and Flora let Chelsea take the reins, it was nonstop entertainment for the rest of the evening. She was every bit as extra as Emery had imagined, and then some. But it worked for their little trio.

They stayed up late and ate way too much chocolate.

Chelsea recounted each of the women's screw ups from their Scottish etiquette practice with amazing accuracy. Even Flora joined in on the fun, poking fun at Emery's epic butchering of the Scottish language. Emery laughed at the way the two women put August's binder to shame. If he thought his information was thorough, he was greatly mistaken. Chelsea and Flora had given her enough gossip filled truths to fill at least two more.

The trio didn't settle into the comfy queen size bed until the wee hours of the morning.

"Thanks for letting us stay. I don't think I could have slept alone tonight." Chelsea yawned, fighting her eyelids to stay awake. "It was fun."

"I can't remember the last time I had this much fun," Flora chimed.

"Me too. We should do it again." She meant it. Even if Chelsea was a bit high strung and not entirely her cup of tea, Emery was happy to have her as a friend. Flora wasn't what she expected, but Emery could see why people underestimated her. That was a grave mistake because the tiny blonde had a fire within her just waiting to be tapped. Emery was happy to have her as a confidant within the castle. It felt good to have someone other than the princes to share her secret with.

Girls night had been exactly what she needed to unwind and even become comfortable in her new surroundings. Mostly it was what she needed to avoid thinking about what had happened in the garden.

She was torn between her heart and her brain. She couldn't be his. Witches, even defective ones, were as good as dead in the hands of a vampire. Her mission to find out what happened to her sister was almost complete since

Flora's admission. A few more details needed to slide into place, like why on earth someone would want a young woman dead in the first place, and she'd be on her way out of the castle.

A pang shot through her heart. It forgot what August was, choosing to see the man and not the monster. Believed he was different than his family, and clung to the notion that the intense attraction between them could defy the logic of history.

Her eyes welled and tears began to silently fall. She bit her lip, failing to hold back the sobs.

From the middle of the bed, Flora stirred and scooted closer to her. Wrapping an arm around her, she held Emery.

When she stiffened, Flora gave her a squeeze and whispered softly. "I knew you were different from the moment you arrived because of your strength. Well, that and your sarcasm. But it's okay to not be okay sometimes."

Emery released a chuckle laced sob. "Thank you." *But you're wrong*. She only knew how to fend for herself, fake it till she made it and only allowed herself to fall apart when she was alone.

One full day in the castle had reduced her to tears multiple times and made her question everything she thought she'd known about herself and the world she lived in. She'd given up so much of herself to be there, only to realize she'd have to give up so much more in order to leave.

Chapter Eighteen

EMERY

Sleep evaded her. And not just because she shared the bed with two of the worst blanket hogs.

Emery tossed and turned, and when sleep finally came, it brought with it nightmares of August. They'd started off as a replay of their time at the fountain. Just thinking about it made her stomach drop and tighten with need.

She'd been fine with those images. It was the way her subconscious twisted the events after that caused her chest to constrict in fear.

Instead of melting her core with his promise to ruin her for any other man, he'd taken her then and there with anger in his eyes. He thrusted into her, again and again, his hands tightly woven around her neck, restricting her breath. Even still she couldn't shake the sound of his voice calling her a dirty whore witch and a deceitful liar who didn't deserve his time or his love. He reveled in taking her virginity, ensuring she couldn't be used against him by the witches in one of their sacrificial spells. Emery wasn't even sure that was a thing, but coming from August's mouth, it hurt, nonetheless.

After the third time Emery woke gasping for air, she'd gotten up, leaving Chelsea and Flora in her bed and headed to the women's dining room to wait until breakfast.

The silence of the castle in the early morning embraced her. While she hadn't found Sloane's journals yet, she did find an empty notebook in her room. She'd brought it with her hoping to find clarity through writing.

Snuggling into the window seat of the dining room, Emery followed in her sister's footsteps, pouring her feelings onto its pages.

It was cathartic. Still, she found she could step back and view her emotions with fresh eyes. Even if she wasn't any closer to understanding them. Of course, she'd left out any indication of being a witch. The last thing she needed was someone finding the notebook and outing her to the royal family.

"While I am in complete agreement, my eyes are quite sexy, I am disappointed you still find me terrifying. We'll have to work on that."

Emery jumped at the sound of August's smooth voice. Pushing up from the window, she found herself under the full weight of his gaze.

"You scared the crap out of me. You can't just sneak up on people like that. Also, this is private. You have no right to read this."

His eyes narrowed on her, and his voice lowered to an octave she found downright sexy. "I'm the crown prince and you are a member of my Culling. I have every right."

Emery hated what his voice did to her. The way it

slithered down her spine and sent electric shocks through her lower belly.

"On second thought, I think I like that you are a little terrified of me. Especially if you keep looking at me the way you are right now."

Behind August, a few of the other Culling women trickled in for breakfast, their eyes on the prince.

Emery smiled and played her part, happy to no longer be alone with him. "How can I help you, Your Highness?"

His lips parted slightly and tipped upward. "You can join me on a date today."

"Nope." The word flew out of her, and she shook her head. "I don't think that's a good idea."

"Interesting. I detect truth in your words, but the sweet arousal surrounding you tells a completely different story."

Her cheeks reddened.

"Your Highness?" One of the footmen approached with a folded sheet of paper. August snatched the note, and his brows furrowed as he read it.

"Excuse me. I'll return in a moment." His eyes narrowed on Emery. "We're not done discussing this."

That's what you think.

Emery clutched the pen and notebook to her chest and scanned the room to see who else had arrived. Amelia filled her plate while Annie and Marigold giggled in the corner. Odds were good when August returned, she could pawn one of them off on the prince. There was no way she would have it out with him in the middle of the dining room.

Before she could finish formulating a plan, Jessi stepped into her sight.

"What was that about with the prince?" She popped her hip and rested her hand on it in a classic power stance. Her fire engine red body con dress dipped between her breasts, leaving little to the imagination.

Emery blinked, her eyes widening slightly at the onslaught of bitchiness so early in the morning. "Oh, our conversation? Not that it's any of your business, but he asked me on a date."

Just because she didn't plan on attending said date didn't mean she'd pass up the opportunity to rub it in Jessi's face. Even if it's not what Sloane would have done.

Her face scrunched in disgust. "Are you serious? That's not even fair."

Emery shrugged. "Yup." She emphasized her answer with an exaggerated lip pop and side stepped around Jessi, ready to be done with the conversation and get the hell out of there.

"You know he only asked you out this morning because you're nothing but a whore."

There were a few audible gasps, and the room went silent, all eyes on them.

Emery stopped and slowly turned to face Jessi. "What did you say?"

"I saw you in the gardens last night seducing Prince August." Jessi pulled a scrap of fabric from her pocket and threw it at Emery. "I'm sure he just wants to sample the goods before he sends you on your way. After all, he has no use for a slut as his queen."

Emery didn't need to unravel the scraps to know it was the underwear August had torn from her body the night before. Tears welled in her eyes, as Jessi unknowingly twisted the knife embedded in her heart by the August of her nightmares. She waited for Jessi to continue and call her a deceitful lying witch, even though she knew there was no way for her to know what she was.

Emery looked around her, all of the Culling women present waited to see how she would respond. The heat of their judgmental stares were almost too much for her to handle.

Her throat tightened, and she struggled to find words. "W-what happens between the Prince and me is just that. Between us." The image of Jessi under August reignited the fire within her. "It's not my fault he'd rather use me for my body than only for my blood, like he does you."

"At least he sees me for the queen I could be and is saving taking my virginity for our wedding night."

Blinking back her tears, Emery tried to come up with a witty retort, but nothing came.

Appearing from out of nowhere, August stepped between them with a sigh. "What's going on here?"

Jessi, responded in her sickly sweet tone. "Nothing, Your Highness. Sloane was just offering to let me have her date slot today seeing as she interrupted our time together last night."

August snapped his head toward Emery, his eyes locked on hers, and she didn't need words to know he was pissed.

"Is this true? Did you give up your time with me, Sloane?"

She could say no. Could unravel Jessi's ploy for attention and call her bluff. But that's not what came out of her mouth.

"Yes, Your Highness." Emery averted her eyes. She didn't want to spend time with August right then, but that didn't make the hurt and anger in his stare less of a heavy weight on her chest.

"We'll discuss this later." He looked around the room at each of the women. "There has been a change of plans for today. As a reward for all your hard work during etiquette training in preparation for the Scottish delegation's arrival, today there will be none." Applause, giggles, and sighs of relief filled the room. "There will be no individual dates today. Instead, throughout the day, I'll be going on a walk with each of you through the gardens to get to know you a little better."

Excited whispers erupted, each of the women likely excited to spend their time with the prince. Meanwhile, she stood there wishing the ground would open up and swallow her whole.

Using the excitement and commotion of the women as a distraction, Emery slipped out.

Once more, she fled, knowing August could find her if he wanted to. She needed space. Primarily from the all consuming gaze that made her stomach drop and stirred up feelings she didn't think were possible in the short time she'd known him.

Yet they were real, so very fucking real, and she couldn't stand it.

Running with no destination in mind, the castle walls blurred as she sped by. She needed to retreat and restore the walls she barely managed to keep up.

What was it about him? He was just another man. No, not a man, a vampire. She should hate him. How many times could she talk herself in circles before she spiraled out of control? She couldn't afford to lose it. Not in a castle where she was his enemy.

Emery stopped running and clutched her chest, the beginnings of a panic attack threatening to constrict her lungs. Her eyes darted around. Nothing looked familiar.

Shit.

Of course, when she needed stability the most, she'd managed to get lost.

She forced air into her lungs and closed her eyes. Wrapping her arms around herself, she ran her hands up and down her upper arms, trying to bring her from the edges of panic.

Breathe in. *I'm safe. Well, relatively.*

Breathe out. *They don't know what I am.*

Breathe in. *I will survive this.*

Breathe out, *I'm stronger than my circumstances.*

When she'd finally calmed herself enough to keep moving, Emery opened her eyes and noticed an open door ahead of her. She moved toward it and hoped someone was there who could point her in the right direction.

The contents of the room sent an unexpected jolt of excitement coursing through her, instantly replacing the previous moments of panic with joy.

It was a room dedicated to music. Well-lit from skylights above, each of the walls were insulated and designed for premium music creation. Where there weren't acoustic panels, breathtaking art of musicians throughout the ages lined the walls. To the left was a sound booth and recording area Emery could see August making full use of.

Emery barely kept herself from running to the grand piano. Instead, she slowly walked into the room allowing herself to absorb every detail.

She'd just discovered her new favorite room in the castle.

Shifting her focus back to the object that drew her in, Emery made her way to the piano. She ran her hands over the sleek black exterior admiring the craftsmanship. She'd always wanted a grand piano. They had an upright at her uncle's club that sparked her joy of playing music. While she always had a love for music, creating music was different than listening. Even as a young child, Emery was able to create melodies where words failed her. Learning the way notes worked together became a way to voice the emotions she was forced to keep hidden away. It became the one thing no one could take away from her.

She took a seat at the bench and closed her eyes, allowing her hands to roam over the weighted ivory. When they found their home, she played the first chord.

The notes were chaotic at first, tapping into the emotions lurking just beneath the surface. The melodies slowed as she weaved them from within herself, reaching the place where she kept her secrets. Her wants. Her desires. Haunting refrains gave way to hopeful choruses only to find their way back to a melancholy verse. Each note a reflection of her journey to that moment.

Lost in the notes, Emery's heart swelled as the music she created grew. No longer echoing the journey in the castle, but instead the notes pulled from her imagination, painting images of her future. It was fueled with passion even she didn't understand, only realizing it was locked within her, begging for release. Longing for her embrace.

Emotions swelled with the crescendo of her melody as she slammed the keys. Tears streamed down her face as feelings pulled from deep within her and the same vibrating sensation that came when August was near overtook her.

Only that time, it was different. It wasn't in reaction to him—it was as if the music entwined itself with her soul, pushing from within, begging to reach the surface.

Emery breathed heavy as she reached the end of her heart's song. As quickly as the vibrations started, they halted with the music. She leaned forward, resting her head on the top of the piano. The release was the equivalent of an emotional marathon, and damn, if it wasn't liberating.

She wanted to stay in the realm of music just a little longer, but a little girl with beautiful blonde ringlet pigtails appeared beside the piano, startling her from the peaceful interlude.

Thea, August's sister, ran her fingers along the piano's body with a broad smile on her face.

Emery smiled and pointed at herself, then signed love and twirled her own hair within her fingers, hoping Thea would understand what she was attempting to communicate.

Thea's face brightened and she smiled as signed, "*Thank you*."

Emery patted the piano bench and the tiny royal jumped up to join her. Thea played as any six-year-old would, which was more of a free for all banging on the keys.

When she was satisfied with her melody, Thea reached out and took Emery's hand and placed them on the keys. Emery played the first few notes of one of her favorite jazz tunes, and Thea's eyes widened, locked on Emery's fingers as they danced over the back and white keys.

Her heart clenched and she wished this sweet little girl could hear music the way she did.

The memory of something Emery's uncle used to do when she was a child gave her an idea. She stood and closed the cover, then reached out to Thea. The princess hesitantly extended her arms, and allowed Emery to pick her up. She placed the smallest royal , and objectively the most loveable, on the top of the piano. When she was safely seated, Emery smiled and placed her ear, and the palms of her hands, on the cover. Thea mimicked her action.

When Emery began to play again, Thea's face lit up. She pressed her little hands more firmly onto the top of the piano as Emery played lilting triplets. Thea tapped her fingers to the beat and smiled each time Emery would play a fast-moving phrase.

"There you are," a woman gasped from the door, ending the first sweet moment Emery had since she'd arrived. *"I have been looking for you everywhere."*

The moment Emery realized who stepped in, she stood abruptly and curtseyed. "Your Majesty, I'm sorry I didn't know Thea was missing, I would have brought her back to you immediately."

The Queen's concern eased when she caught sight of Thea smiling on top of the piano. Emery's heart swelled, then sank to the pit of her stomach at the Queen's maternal display of worry. She'd never had anyone look at her like that.

Blinking back tears, Emery did her best to explain why she'd put a priceless young royal on top of a piano. "She likes the vibrations."

The Queen smiled and Emery was struck by her beauty. Her soft green eyes were welcoming but seemed to hide an air of mischief. "Well then, by all means don't stop on my account." She turned and made her way across the room to the seating area near the recording studio.

Emery played through a montage of her favorite piano pieces ranging from jazz ballads to modern melodies.

When she'd finished, the Queen walked over to the piano and leaned over, pulling Thea across the top with a giggle. "That was beautiful. Where did you learn to play?"

"Thank you." Emery slid the lid over the keys with delicate care. "My uncle taught me. It was love the first time I sat down in front of the piano."

"Come sit with me." The Queen lifted Thea from the piano and carried her to the oversized armchairs, tucking her into her lap as she sat. Emery followed, her hands fidgeting nervously. The Queen was dressed in an elaborate blue gown with her chestnut brown hair piled on top of her head. It looked as if she was going to an important meeting with dignitaries or other royals. Even though she was dressed in a beautiful tea dress, Emery was out of her element under the watchful gaze of the Queen, without the piano to hide behind.

"I wish my boys had stuck with the piano. I have tried to get them to learn over the years but neither took to it. There is just something about the way the strings reverberate within a piano that evokes such emotion."

"I couldn't agree more." Emery took the seat next to the Queen, her nerves thrusting her heart into her throat. "But your sons are quite talented. Well, I can only speak for August. I don't know about Malcolm."

"That boy could never sit still enough to hone any kind of musical skill. August, though, his passion has always been his voice."

Emery smiled, surprised at how easy it was to talk with the Queen. She thought, based on some of the rumors fed by the Culling women, that she was quite a bitch. But she didn't get that vibe at all. It further proved the point that she couldn't judge vampires by the rumors women or witches spread.

"He speaks highly of you, you know." The Queen grinned at Emery as she ran her fingers through Thea's tangled pigtail. "You seem to have caught his eye. Which honestly is a breath of fresh air. I love my son, but he puts too much thought into what his father wants. I yearn for him to be his own man. His own king. You have him thinking as he should."

Her stomach sank. What had August told his mom?

"With all due respect, Your Highness, you know who I am. I'm only here to find out what happened to my sister. August has only known me a few days. I assure you, I am not important to your son."

The Queen looked into her eyes and furrowed her brow. "You are so much prettier than her," she whispered.

"We're twins, how could that be?"

"Her soul, sweet girl." She lilted, as if it was obvious. "Her soul was dark."

Emery gasped at the comment. Could she see her soul, or was this a general observation? It was clear the Queen saw something more in Sloane than those around her had. What had her twin been up to? Had she done something unforgivable that lead to her death?

"I don't know much about my sister, Your Highness. As for me, well, I'm just that…me. That's all I want to be." Ironic, since she could be anything but.

"You are so much more, my dear. So much more." She placed Thea on the ground. "And please, when it's just us, call me Cosmina."

Thinking it was one thing, but the informality of saying it out loud was something else entirely. Still, she'd do as requested. "Cosmina." Emery nodded, "What do you mean by that?"

"I think with some time, and some patience, you'll find yourself on the edge of your greatest adventure yet." The queen stood, and Emery followed suit. She leaned over and rubbed Thea's back, signing to her as she spoke, "Come, Thea, we should be getting to your lessons, and I believe Emery has to be getting ready for some time with your brother."

Emery stilled. Yeah, that wasn't happening. He was the very person she was avoiding.

The princess's hands moved quickly, signing something to her mother. Cosmina tilted her head and glanced to Emery. "My daughter is quite taken with you. She's requested to have music lessons with you again."

Emery offered a smile. "I would be honored." She got down on one knee and worked with her limited knowledge of sign language, "*I will see you soon.*"

"*Thank you,*" Thea signed and leapt into Emery's arms.

Cosmina made for the door, and Thea ran to catch up. She paused before exiting. "Emery?"

Her real name spoken on kind lips had her choking back a sob. To be seen. To be heard. To be recognized as herself was all together a moment she would cherish. "Yes?" she finally choked out.

"Beware of my husband, would you? You remind me of myself before I came into this world. He would have you broken if he knew how special you are. He has a habit of crushing such sweet things."

Emery nodded and suppressed the urge to react. Yessenia would have been perfectly pleased at her utter lack of emotion. One thing was clear, while the King ran the castle, the Queen was the one who saw all. With knowledge came power.

And she was willing to bet the King, like all men, often underestimated his wife.

She waited a moment before exiting the music room, taking mental notes on her way back to her wing of the castle, so she'd know exactly how to get back in the future. Meeting Thea and the Queen had turned an otherwise mortifying and dramatic morning into something that gave her hope. Emery smiled to herself, relieved to have found something to give her a renewed sense of purpose while indentured inside the castle walls.

Chapter Nineteen

AUGUST

The gardens were a terrible spot for speed dating. Not that they weren't beautiful, but each time August walked one of the women back to the castle he had to pass the fountain. Each time he did, visions of Emery's beautiful body splayed across it, open and bared completely to him, flooded his mind. She'd given herself to him, and he treasured every minute of it. Until the second the venom wore off, and she retreated back into that pretty head of hers.

He scoffed quietly when Jessi's high-pitched voice yanked him from his visions of Emery. "She's just a whore trying to sleep her way to the top. We've been involved for years now, and I've never tried to seduce you like that. I know the value of a queen."

August raised a brow. He grew tired of Jessi, but given his father's order to keep her around, there was little he could do. That's not true, he could think of a million ways to make her life miserable, and he should for the way she treated Emery.

He halted their walk and narrowed his eyes on Jessi. "Do you? I don't find such gossip becoming of a queen. It's reminiscent of a little girl with too much time on her hands. How do you know it wasn't I who seduced her?"

"But—"

"I wanted to be there with her last night." Her eyes widened at his proclamation. If anyone could get away with putting her in her place it was him. He should have taken the time to put her in her place years ago, but it wasn't until then he cared to do so. "We are done with the extra curriculars until you can learn to act like a queen. I don't like the taste of gossip mongering socialite in my blood." He dropped her hand from the crook of his arm, happy to be rid of her for the day. Their entire date had been about her and why she should be chosen over Emery. Not once had she asked about him or what his thoughts for the future were. "Leave me."

Before Jessi could retort, Flora pushed out of the castle's double doors, right on time for her date with him. He'd almost eliminated her, but Malcolm said Emery questioned him about the small blonde. It may have been for superficial reasons, but her interest in Flora is what kept the woman from being sent away.

"Your Highness." Flora curtseyed.

Jessi reached for his arm in one last ditch effort to gain his attention, but August easily sidestepped her to move toward Flora. He could easily turn off his humanity and give her what she wanted, only this time an orgasm wouldn't be the result of his venom. Unbridled fear might do the bully some good.

August whipped his head toward Jessi, eyes narrowed in a murderous glare. Jessi flinched away from him and, with an unhappy huff, spun and headed for the castle doors.

Flora stood with her mouth hung open. He softened his eyes and offered his arm. "Good afternoon, Flora. How are you?"

She looked down at the ground, but August saw a smirk tug at her lips. "I'm well, Your Highness."

"Look at me, Flora." She pulled her gaze to meet his, her eyes a mix of fear and amusement. "I'm sorry if I frightened you. Jessi—"

"She had it coming," she interrupted. "But remind me not to get on your bad side. That look could've killed."

August laughed, something he was doing with more frequency the past few days. "I doubt you'd end up on the receiving end of one of those looks." He placed her arm in his and led her toward the garden. "Walk with me. I am looking forward to learning about you."

"Yes. About that."

August led Flora through the gardens making small talk. She was pleasant and surprisingly funny with a hint of sass. Too often she was the quiet woman in the back of the crowd that didn't talk or participate beyond what was expected of her.

He actually enjoyed spending time with her in an unfamiliar platonic way. He enjoyed her company and the ease with which conversation flowed. It was clear why Emery took an interest in her. She was a breath of fresh air in an otherwise stuffy castle. Flora wasn't after his crown, unlike Jessi and the other savage women.

"I've enjoyed our time together today, Flora. Thank you for allowing me to get to know you a little bit better."

"You're welcome, Your Highness." Flora's hands fidgeted in front of her. "Um, before we head back, may I speak freely?"

"Of course, what is it?"

"Well. I mean." Flora stumbled over her words, and damn, if it wasn't adorable. "I don't even know where to start."

"The beginning is a good place."

"I was in the stable when Sloane was killed, and I know about Emery." Her words rushed out of her faster than August had ever heard anyone speak followed by her face scrunching up like she was preparing for someone to hit her.

An involuntary growl reverberated from within him.

She threw her hands up in surrender and quickly sputtered. "I mean her no harm. Actually, I quite like her."

He narrowed his eyes on her, a protective feeling washing over him as his body stiffened and fangs elongated.

"Having now accomplished being on the receiving end of that look, I can confirm it's intimidating. It's just…Emery told me I could speak to you about it."

Had she now? Emery trusted him enough to send Flora with valuable information. He was leery of someone outside the royal family knowing Emery's true identity, especially if Emery was the one with loose lips. "Explain," August ground out. His fists clenched at his sides. The only indication he was barely keeping his emotions in check, and within him, the need to protect Emery had grown strong enough he was liable to rip Flora's throat out if she didn't explain herself quickly.

Flora swallowed, but much to August's surprise, her voice exuded confidence. "I mean no harm to Emery." Her heartbeat was steady as she spoke.

Truth.

She recounted Sloane's last moments, and he listened intently for any holes in Flora's story. With any luck, something she said would point him to the murderer.

She stared at him with tear-rimmed eyes as she concluded the story, waiting for his reaction.

August mentally tallied the pertinent information. Sloane met with someone who wanted her dead. Someone who wanted his family to know she'd been murdered.

"Have you shared all this with Emery?"

Flora nodded. "Last night."

"Thank you for sharing honestly with me. I should go ensure Emery is okay."

"Of course." Flora's hands returned to fidgeting with her dress.

"Was there something else?"

"No. I mean, yes, Your Highness." She smoothed her dress and clasped her hands in front of her waist. "I know that I am not high on your list of women to stay and become your wife, and I am mostly okay with that fact. No disrespect to you, but I don't think I would make much of a queen."

"Would you like me to send you home, Flora?"

"Oh, no." She shook her head, instant fear in her eyes. "Please no, that's not what I want. In fact, I think I'd possibly like to take the opportunity to be turned."

"Really?"

"Yes. Only, I'm not sure where I would like to go. I'd really like to remain friends with Emery."

"Emery may not be at the castle long." A fact he loathed.

Flora tipped her head at him with raised brows. "Come, Your Highness. We both know you're interested in her. You may have liked Sloane, but you didn't attempt to sleep with her on a fountain. You've shown her more interest than you ever have to anyone."

August winced. Jessi ensured everyone knew about his tryst with Emery. It had been brought up more than once on his dates that day.

Though she was quiet, Flora was perceptive.

August leaned in toward her and grinned. "I hope you will keep my little secret."

Flora returned a playful smile. "I don't know that it's a secret, but I promise not to fuel the rumors."

"Thank you. And I will see what I can do when the time comes to ensure that you are placed in the right court, should that be what you want."

"Thank you, Your Highness." Flora curtsied. Upon rising, she added, "I'm happy for you. A genuine smile looks good on you, and Emery is an amazing woman."

"Thank you."

Flora strolled toward the castle. She was definitely not what he expected.

He didn't need to check the schedule to know Emery should have already arrived for their scheduled date. She'd been last on the lineup, and he'd been looking forward to their conversation since she stormed out that morning.

He waited at the wrought iron gates to the garden for another ten minutes. It was possible she was running late. She'd been late the previous morning too. Something he would need to rectify if she were to be his queen. Royalty could be late, and it would be considered on time, but he wouldn't permit her to be late for him.

Time ticked by, and it was looking more and more like he would need to go and find his date.

August stopped by the kitchen to grab a few pastries before continuing to Emery's room. She'd missed breakfast and knowing her, likely skipped lunch in the hopes of avoiding everyone.

Especially him.

While in the kitchen, he heard tell-tale giggles heading in his direction.

When Thea rounded the corner, he was ready for her. The moment she saw him, her eyes lit up, and she took off in a full sprint. Wrapping her up in his arms, he swung her in a circle before settling her on his hip. She smiled and signed how much she'd missed him.

That sweet girl had every bit of his heart. Being the youngest of the royal vampires, he didn't know what joy a younger sibling could bring. The innocence of a child was contagious. Thea brought unconditional love to their family and didn't let being deaf smother her happiness or love of life. The way she persevered and took on every challenge life threw her was admirable. At six years old, she'd taught him more about life than he'd learned in the centuries he'd walked the earth.

Setting her down, he knelt before her and signed while speaking, "I have missed you too, little princess."

"I met Emery this morning," Thea relayed, her hands and arms signing wildly.

"Did you now? You know we call her Sloane though, correct?" He signed without speaking. Most of the residents in the castle hadn't taken the time to pick up American Sign Language.

She huffed and rolled her eyes. *"Yes. I remember."*

His mother joined them in the kitchen, worry etched in her features. Thea kept her on her toes, often running away and getting into trouble. She relaxed when she August.

"*Have you been running wild this morning, Thea?*" August chided playfully.

"*No.*" The small princess lowered her eyes. "*I just wanted to play on the piano. That's where I found Emery. She said she'd give me music lessons.*" Thea bounced with excitement.

"*Is that so?*" August looked up, silently questioning his mother. She gave him a knowing smile and a nod, and he returned his attention to Thea. "*You know you could have asked me for music lessons.*"

"*You're busy, August.*"

He'd been sucker punched. He never wanted to be too busy for his little sister. Pulling her into his lap for a hug, he reassured her. "*You've got me there. I'm sorry. I will make sure to open my schedule up for proper Thea time.*"

She beamed, then wrapped her arms around him. Thea settled and looked up at him. "*Emery is really pretty.*"

"*She is beautiful, isn't she?*"

"*Will you pick her?*" His little sister hummed with excitement.

"*I don't know, Thea. I'm not sure she likes me very much.*"

"*Why not?*"

"*This life is all very new to her, and I'm not sure I have done the best job helping her to adjust.*"

"*You are an idiot then.*"

"Thea!" the Queen gasped and stepped beside August so she could get her point across. "*You know better than to use such language. Where did you learn that?*"

Thea shrugged, then signed lazily. "*Playing video games with Malcolm.*"

August failed to suppress his laughter. Malcolm was definitely going to receive a talking to.

"*Thea, why don't you go look in the cookie jar? Jenkins said he just finished making a fresh batch.*"

Sufficiently distracted by the promise of sweets, Thea skipped across the kitchen, leaving August to speak with his mother. "What did you think of Sloane?"

"She's too good for you."

Ouch.

August winced as he stood. That was harsh, and accurate.

"Do you even know anything about her past?"

Leaning against the kitchen island, he considered her question. No, he didn't know anything beyond a run of the mill background check.

"I didn't think so. Son, while she would make an excellent queen, I am not sure she is up for a life on your arm. You'll be king, and she'll need to be comfortable with the life she'll be expected to lead. I don't think you realize the time and strain that will be put on your future wife."

"But it would have been okay for Sloane and Malcolm?"

"No. I may have been privileged to that information, but I was not in agreement." Her lips twisted in disgust. "Malcolm was too good for *her*."

August chuckled. "Tell me how you *really* feel about it."

"It's too early for me to drink enough to address that subject."

He loved his mother. She was a warm contrast to his father, especially when she was far from his side. How she ended up a queen to an unforgiving king baffled him. "It's amazing how different Emery is from Sloane."

"Indeed." She pulled him into a rare hug. "You would be wise to remember that."

Thea joined them, hugging their legs. His mother pulled away and signed. *"Come, Thea. It's time for your lessons."*

Sweetly, she looked up at August. *"Can't I stay with you?"*

"Not this time, sweet girl."

Emery might not want to be his queen, but she was capable. She not only exhibited the qualities needed for the job, but she called to him on a visceral level. She saw him as more than just the crown.

He covered the pastries and closed the picnic basket. *"I need to go find a lost woman and convince her she belongs here."*

Chapter Twenty

EMERY

An angry grunt escaped her lips, as Emery threw the shoe from inside the closet. Who knew chucking shoes was an effective way to channel frustration? That particular shoe had been fueled by her anger at a certain vampire prince. The heel currently stuck in the drywall of the closet was the result of her feelings toward Jessi. She'd have to see about getting that fixed before anyone noticed.

Focused on the pile of shoes around her, she didn't notice Dahlia's presence in the doorway. "What are you doing, Miss Sloane?"

Emery startled, dropping the shoe she'd picked up. She didn't have a good explanation for why she was sitting in the pile of shoes. She couldn't tell her she initially yanked each pair out with increasing desperation to find her sister's hidden journals, then when she'd come up empty handed it had turned into a therapy session.

She hated that the lies were coming easier each time she was forced to tell one. "I couldn't find my boots. I was planning to go down to the stables."

Dahlia raised a brow. "You mean the boots that are by the door where you left them last week after going to the stables? You decided they were too dirty to keep in the closet."

Shit.

"Oh yeah." Emery stood, picking up the shoes closest to her and replacing them in each of their cubbies. "I completely forgot I said that."

How was she supposed to know what Sloane said that one time on a Tuesday a few weeks ago? This whole impersonating her sister was supposed to get easier, but each day brought new challenges she hadn't considered.

Dahlia slid next to her and put the shoes back in their cubbies. Reaching behind them she pulled the heel out of the wall and raised a brow.

She shrugged and silently helped put the shoes in their designated spots.

When the floor of the closet was once again clear, Dahlia released a long, heavy sigh.

"I'm sorry I made a mess of the closet."

Dahlia pressed her lips into a line, her face contorting into expressions conveying a multitude of emotions before settling on wary determination. "May I speak candidly, Miss?"

"Always."

"I have been Sloane's lady's maid since she was a little girl, we have shared many details of our lives with one another, and I considered her to be family."

Emery stilled, taking notice of the way Dahlia spoke of Sloane in the past tense.

"She does not have a cut above her lip as you do, nor did she practice sarcasm with so little effort. Most of all, she was not kind unless it was earned. Growing up here hardened her in ways you're not." Dahlia placed her hands on Emery's shoulders. "I know you're not her, Emery. I assume she is dead, otherwise you would not be here."

And there it was. She knew she wasn't Sloane.

Emery remained silent, searching Dahlia's eyes for any indication of her intentions now that her identity hung between them.

Dahlia sighed and tears rimmed her eyes. "It's okay, child. I'm not going to tell anyone in the castle what I know. I just wanted you and I to have an understanding, and maybe help you adjust better to life here."

"How do you know my name. Why tell me you know my secret? You could have just outed me?"

"What good would that do?" She raised an eyebrow, and Emery realized she was missing a piece to this puzzle. "I assume the royal family knows who you are since you haven't been detained thus far."

Emery nodded in agreement and waited anxiously for the other shoe to drop.

"I knew Sloane had a twin named Emery, but you are much more than I expected. She didn't talk much about her life beyond the castle, never confiding in anyone. It took a long time before she trusted me, even though I was sent to keep her safe."

"You were sent to keep her safe? Why? From whom?"

"I think you know the answer to that, dear."

Vampires.

If Dahlia was sent to keep Sloane safe, that would mean she knew that she needed to be kept safe. It could support Emery's theory Sloane was killed for being a witch. Which would mean—

Emery gasped when she made the connection.

"Yes. I know what you are. I'm one too."

And there was the other shoe. Except it wasn't just a shoe. It was an entire department store. Emery tried her best to keep her expression indifferent, but she failed.

She fisted her hands, angry Dahlia had been sent to protect Sloane and somehow failed. Jealous she'd gotten to spend all the years with her twin that should have been Emery's.

"Slowdown that mind of yours, dear, I'm not going to harm you or use the knowledge against you. Incriminating you would lead to incriminating myself. I want to help you."

Emery narrowed her eyes and tilted her head. "The same way you helped Sloane?" she spat angrily. "I'm sorry if I find that hard to believe considering my sister's death in your care. Why didn't you help her?"

"I tried." Dahlia's shoulders slumped, and her chin fell to her chest. Her voice, once steady, was now quiet and shaky. "But I failed her. She wanted more out of life than to be a spy for the coven. She wanted power I couldn't help her obtain. A few months ago, she stopped confiding in me. I knew something was different, but I figured it had to do with her relationship with Malcolm not playing out how she'd hoped. I had no idea she was in contact with the coven."

"Wait what? She was spying on the vampires? And in contact with the coven?" Emery had grown up in the outside world and she'd never been given the opportunity to meet the witches she'd descended from. According to Ada, she was defective and therefore not worth anything to the coven. Maybe only she was defective and Sloane had more magic in her as the older twin.

"Yes. I didn't know until after she died, but she was trying to get them to help her out of the castle." Reaching for Emery's hands, Dahlia led her out of the closet and sat with her on the hope chest. "I suppose I should start from the beginning. I was sent to find work in the castle the moment the mark of the Culling appeared on Sloane's wrist. Knowing she would be taken, the coven determined they would need someone on the inside to watch over her and help her once her magic appeared. They knew it would be minimal magic, as you and Sloane's powers were bound before birth."

Emery's mouth hung open. "They were?"

"Ada didn't tell you? I was assigned to your sister, and Ada to you. Our powers were bound so we would appear human."

"Ada didn't tell me anything but lies, apparently." Emery did little to hide the disdain that grew within her. "But why were ours bound?"

"No one knows. We assumed it had something to do with your family line. Your mother's powers were bound as well."

"You knew my mother?" Hope filled Emery's voice. Maybe Dahlia could tell her more about her mother. Ada would not discuss her, and Emery had been smacked more than a few times for asking.

"No, I'm sorry, dear."

Her shoulders slumped forward. "Oh."

Dahlia ran her fingers over Emery's. "Sloane often asked

about her too. I wish I had more answers for you in that regard."

"It's okay. Tell me more about my sister."

"Sloane grew up as all the Culling women did. They were educated to be prim and proper, biding their time until they came of age and the prince was ready to take a bride. None thought it would take so long for Prince August to decide to take it seriously. From what I've learned, many take their bride while the women are young. It provides them with more time to produce heirs before the woman is turned."

A cold shiver crept down Emery's spine. She couldn't imagine becoming a vampire. It was easy for her to forget what would become of the woman chosen to stand at August's side, but the other women of the Culling were raised to be prepared for that outcome. They relished in it. For Emery, it was one more thing to add to the list of why she could never be August's queen.

"The coven didn't ask much of us, the occasional report about what the royal family was doing. Sloane was happy here. Until she wasn't. She wasn't getting any younger and her chances of winning the affections of the crown prince were slim to none. He certainly didn't exactly give off any affectionate feelings toward the Culling women."

Dahlia shifted her wait, an uneasy smile etched across her face.

"Unbeknownst to me, Sloane reached out to my contact at the coven and began trying to convince them to help her find a way out. Of course, the coven didn't want to give up their access to the vampire royal family. While I see much as a maid, Sloane had the opportunity to see more. They continuously denied her request for help, and that's when she took matters into her own hands."

"How so?"

"She went after Prince Malcolm. Sloane decided if the coven wouldn't help her leave, and she likely wouldn't be chosen to marry Prince August, Malcolm was the next best choice to amass some power within her situation. She thought if she married one of the princes, the coven would see her as more of an asset. And maybe they would consider unbinding her magic. She knew vampires were the coven's enemy, what she didn't realize was it's forbidden by law for a witch to be with a vampire."

Emery's heart broke at the knowledge Malcolm was nothing more than a pawn to Sloane. He was in love with her, loved her with his entire being. She may not have known her sister, but she couldn't believe Sloane was capable of that level of deceit. Only a monster would do that to another being.

Unwilling to believe Sloane was a monster, Emery focused on something else Dahlia had shared, and a glimmer of hope surged within her. "It's possible to unbind our magic?"

Dahlia's eyes softened. "Yes, though highly unlikely for you, just as it was for Sloane. Magic must be unbound by those who bound it. It's likely a curse was placed on your family many generations ago. It's why no one in your family has wielded magic for centuries. That level of magic can only be practiced by an original witch. Of which, there are only four remaining. Two of them haven't been seen for hundreds of years."

"Hundreds? How is that even possible?"

"Did Ada teach you nothing?"

"Only that I was defective and would amass to nothing."

Dahlia pulled her into her arms. "I'm so sorry. Here I thought you received a better upbringing outside these walls. I'll do what I can to teach you. I don't know much about your family history, but I do know about being a witch."

Curiosity bubbled within Emery. She'd never spoken so candidly with someone about being a witch. She should be focusing on finding the journals, but she couldn't pass up the opportunity to learn more.

"What does magic feel like?"

A light sparked in the woman's eyes. "It's the most incredible thing I have ever experienced, and I didn't appreciate it until I no longer had access to it. It radiates from you, vibrating from within your soul."

Emery stilled, slowly pulling herself from Dahlia's embrace. Was what she felt within her magic? "Dahlia, when you say vibrate what do you mean?"

"Quite literally magic swells and vibrates within a witch. It's part of the very of our beings."

The vibrations she'd felt in the music room. It was her magic. The thought felt right, and she knew without question it was the cause of the vibrations.

"I think I can feel it."

Dahlia froze. "What do you mean?"

"There are times where it feels like my body is humming from within. Like it's a part of me, woven into my soul, and fighting its way to the surface."

"I've never heard of magic surging within a bound witch, but what you are describing is how our magic manifests when we're young. It's the first indication a witchling is coming into their magic."

"Did Sloane ever mention it?"

"No. But I fear she wouldn't have told me even if it did."

"Oh." Emery didn't know how to feel about the fact her magic decided to make an appearance now, after all these years. She didn't want to consider why, especially since the only thing that changed was her move to the castle. Hoping Dahlia wouldn't pry, she changed her line of questioning. "Do you miss your magic?"

"Some days yes. I was chosen for this task because of my past indiscretions. It was considered a punishment. Although, it wasn't the punishment they'd hoped it would be. I've enjoyed slowing down and just being me. It's reminded me how important it is to remember who I am beyond my abilities."

"What did you do to deserve that punishment?"

Her eyes glistened, and she patted Emery's hand. "That's a sad story for another day. Today is about you and Sloane."

Emery nodded. She'd leave it alone for now, but her intuitions told her Dahlia's story was just as important as her own. "There is one thing that doesn't add up. If Sloane's contact with the coven was done without your knowledge, how did you find all this out?"

"I read her journals after she didn't return for days. I was worried the worst had happened."

Emery jumped from her seat. "You know where her journals are? I've torn this room apart looking for them."

"That explains the shoes." Dahlia chuckled lightly. "Yes. Count five bricks above the center of the nightstand and push inward."

Emery ran across the room and followed Dahlia's instructions. Pushing the rough red brick inward, Emery heard a click and it popped back out, revealing a hidden storage compartment within. Inside sat three leather bound journals. Her heart swelled in her chest, threatening to choke her. She pulled each of them out and ran her fingers over the buttery soft leather and brass buckles. She'd expected notebooks, but instead found journals worthy of the dusty castle they were hidden in. Hugging them to her chest she brought them back to where Dahlia sat.

"You have no idea what these mean to me. They are only piece of my sister I have left. Thank you."

"Oh, honey. Please don't read them."

Emery clutched the journals tighter. "Why? What's hidden in them you don't want me to see?"

"It's just—" Dahlia hesitated, her voice conveying the same regret behind her eyes. "Those journals are a recollection of her feelings during her journey here at the castle. They detail her triumphs but also her spiral into the clutches of desperation. They also share her feelings toward you, the sister who wasn't sent away. The fantasy of Sloane is likely far better than the reality of her. Preserve your positive feelings toward your sister, and leave the journals be."

Emery never considered the possibility of Sloane being the woman Dahlia described. She'd always anxiously awaited the day Sloane would be free of the Culling, and they could be together again. She'd always assumed Sloane felt the same way.

These journals potentially held the answers to who murdered her, and even if her sister hated her, she still deserved justice. Solving her murder was the key to her own freedom, and she needed to get out of here before she made any stupid rash decisions due to her attraction to August.

"I need to know my twin. Need to know what happened to her."

"You don't need to read them to know what happened to her. I believe it was the witches who killed her. As you know, vampires and witches are enemies, but the highest of all crimes within the coven is mating with a vampire. Sloane didn't listen when I cautioned her about Malcolm. I have no doubt when they found out about her relationship, they ensured she would never follow through with her intentions to marry him."

Emery's heart was being squeezed while it threatened to beat out of her chest. "Our own people killed her? But they asked her to stay here for a chance to marry August. Isn't that the same thing?"

"Relationships with a vampire are considered treason, Emery. The coven allowed Sloane to remain part of the Culling as a spy. Not so she could woo a prince and live happily ever after. It's only been a few days, but I imagine they will expect the same of you once they realize you've taken her place."

All at once, her body went numb. She knew she was a pawn in the royal family's game, but she hadn't considered the witches would also use her. They hadn't given two shits about her when she was a child, but now that she was of use to them, they'd want her to spy on August and his family. She prayed Miles never figured out where she went and didn't relay any information back to the coven.

Emery wasn't sure she could do that to August's family. The thought of doing anything to harm sweet Thea made her sick.

She swallowed hard, considering how much a hatred of vampires had been ingrained into her from the moment she was born. Yet in the almost forty-eight hours she had been in their care, the princes had protected her, the queen offered her warmth and confidence, and Thea charmed her way into Emery's heart with their mutual love of music.

Her eyes watered. It was more than the coven had ever done for her.

"Dahlia, how is it possible everything I was taught about vampires is wrong?"

"It's not wrong, dear. It's just not all right." She wiped a stray tear from Emery's face as she continued. "I must get going, I have things to prepare before dinner. I'll be back to help you get ready."

"Thank you, Dahlia."

She nodded and stood, but before she opened the door, she turned back to look at Emery. "Please be careful." The silent, I-can't-lose-you-too evident in her grim expression.

"I will."

With that, she left Emery sitting alone with her thoughts. Thoughts too big for her to consider in that moment. Instead, Emery thumbed through the journals, savoring the sight of her sister's neat handwriting. The lies revealed by Dahlia were suffocating and the room seemed to close in around her.

Emery slipped on her boots, shoved the journals in her satchel and left Sloane's room, needing the change of scenery.

It was time her and Sloane got acquainted, and what better place to do so than the last place she was seen alive.

Chapter Twenty One

AUGUST

Emery wasn't in the music room where his mother and Thea had seen her, nor was she in her room. Not only had she stood him up for their date, but she decided they'd be playing hide and seek.

Thankfully, he planned for her to be his last date of the day with the intention of spending more time with her. Good thing hunting prey was a favorite pastime of his.

He slipped into Malcolm's study in the hopes his brother had seen her.

Malcolm ignored his entrance and kept focus on the video game he was playing.

"Oh, come on, you guys were supposed to cover me!" he yelled into the headset.

How long had it been since he'd sat down and played video games with his brother? Weeks? No, months. So long he nearly forgot his study was equipped with the same TV hidden within the wood panels. They used to play frequently, and at times he forgot he was a royal, he was just a man vying for bragging rights over who had the most kill shots. The memories brough a rare smile to his lips that fell as quickly as it had come.

They weren't just men. A fact shoved down his throat by his father. If he wasn't looking for Emery, he'd join his brother and go a few rounds like old times.

But he was on a mission.

"Have you seen Emery?"

Malcolm pulled the headset off his ear. "Huh? Can this wait? This thirteen-year-old asshole has picked me off three times, and I'm finally going to make them pay."

"He's thirteen, Malcolm, you're how old?"

"She. And that's not the point."

"Getting your ass kicked by a little girl?"

"Shut up." He turned back toward the television, but kept one side of the headset off his ear. "What do you need?"

"Have you seen Emery?"

"Uh, yeah, I passed her in the hall a bit ago. I think she said she was going to the stables."

"And you let her go alone?"

Malcolm's fingers stilled on the controller, pain cutting into his features. "I told Emery to check back in with me when she came back to the castle, and if she wasn't back in two hours, I'd send you looking for her. Seemed like a sufficient threat. You know I can't bear to go there."

August raked his fingers through his hair. He understood why his brother couldn't go to the stables, but it was overridden with the all consuming need to protect Emery. "Yeah, I'm sure it was. Don't bother going to look. I'll find her."

"She looked pretty upset. I don't know what you did, but you might want to fix it."

"I didn't do anything but give her what she wanted." Images of the night before danced through his mind. Yes, he had most definitely given her what she wanted, and then some.

"I don't know what that means, and I don't think I want to." His character fell to the ground after an epic headshot. "Oh, for fuck's sake, come on!!"

"Have fun losing to a teenage girl." August slipped out the door, barely missing the controller that hit the wall right where his head had been. He had better things to do than banter with his brother, and at the top of the list was finding Emery.

Which meant a trip to the stables.

When he arrived, there was no evidence of Emery's presence. Shadowfell poked his head from his stall, stopping August before he could go deeper. "Hello, boy."

He stroked the stallion's neck gently. "Are you feeling up for a ride soon?"

Shadowfell whinnied and nuzzled into him, coaxing a second smile in under an hour. For being a magnificent warhorse, he had a gentle soul. Then again, it's not like August was riding him into battle. Shadowfell was definitely more for show than for war.

"Have you seen my girl?" Shadowfell nuzzled his palm looking for treats, which was an entirely unhelpful response.

"I'm not your girl." Emery's voice echoed softly from the hayloft.

August crossed the barn and climbed the ladder. Emery

sat against a bale of hay on the exterior wall. Legs against her chest, with a leather-bound journal propped open on her knees. She didn't need to look up for him to see the tears that stained her cheeks.

The need to rip apart whoever caused those tears to fall coursed through him, and he longed to pull her into his arms.

"Emery, what's wrong?" His voice was low, deadly even.

"I'm fine." Her hands ran over the leather of the journal before she gripped the sides tightly.

"Am I just to ignore the tears then?"

She sniffed, "Yes."

No way in hell that was going to happen.

"Is this your first time down here since you've arrived?"

She nodded, still avoiding his gaze. "Can you tell me what happened to her?" Her voice cracked.

August scrubbed his face with his hand, he didn't want to cause her more pain, but she had a right to know. "Sloane was found on the ground below. By the time we found her, she was already gone."

"She didn't fall from the loft. I know what happened before she was killed."

"I do too."

"Flora," she stated more than questioned.

He nodded, though she still hadn't looked up at him, her gaze focused on the leather in her hands. "Yes. She told me on our date."

"Do you have any suspects in mind?"

"No. Do you?"

Her heart rate picked up. "No."

Lie.

"Are you sure?" He didn't think it was possible, but it beat faster.

"None."

Lie.

August closed the distance between them and knelt in front of her. He itched to take her hands in his, but refrained. "Emery, I'm hundreds of years old, I can tell when someone is lying."

"Leave it, August," she snapped, her hands balling into fists on the journal. "Nothing I know will help you figure out what happened."

Lie.

She was hiding something she must think damning, otherwise she wouldn't need to hide it. His mother was right, he knew little about her and had done nothing to earn her trust.

He reached up and fingered the edge of the journal, letting her keep her secret for the moment. "What are you reading?"

Emery's eyes darted to where his finger touched the leather. "Her journals."

"Sloane's? Have you found any good information?"

"She thought you were a complete asshat."

He chuckled. For as much as he'd helped Sloane be with Malcolm, she'd never grown fond of him. "Pretentious jerk, maybe. I'm not sure about asshat. I don't think I even know exactly what that means."

For the first time since he'd entered the barn, her eyes met his. The beautiful whiskey color somehow more vibrant after being wet with tears. A hint of a grin played on her lips.

It was a start. If he had to call himself every four letter word in the world to break her out of the shell she was in, he would. "Aside from her clever word choices for me, what else did she say?"

Emery sucked in a breath like she was about to spill the thoughts that plagued her, but instead she paused. Her face contorted, a multitude of emotions playing across her face, before her shoulders racked with a sob. "She hated me."

Without thinking, August pulled her into his lap and against his chest, landing into a soft pile of hay. Emery leaned into him, fisting his shirt. As her body shook in his arms, he rested his chin on her head and methodically rubbed circles into her back.

"She didn't even know you," he whispered against her hair. "How could she possibly hate you?"

Her sobs quieted, and she spoke through hiccupped breaths. "Being born second was enough."

"That wasn't a choice you ever had a say in. It was fate. It wasn't fair for her to hold that against you."

"It was enough for Sloane. I got the life she always wanted." Emery laughed through a sob. "Jokes on her, though, she got the better end of the deal. Life in the castle is far better than anything I ever knew."

"What do you mean?"

"I didn't have any real family, no one to help me along my way. At least Sloane had the other Culling women to spend her days with. She had friends. People who were there for her. I had a stuffy old woman that on her best days remembered I existed enough to ensure there was food on the table. And trust me, that didn't happen every day."

August held her tighter, he wanted to take away her pain. Erase the life she came from and give her one full of comfort. Why couldn't she have been born first? No, he already knew he wouldn't have wanted that either. Life experiences made a person, and she wouldn't be the woman he held in his arms if she hadn't been through those things. She was awe-inspiring, possessing strength, ferocity and the most wonderful tenacity of life. He only wanted to show her, that if she'd let him, he'd be the one to help her carry her burdens. He'd be the one to help her along her way.

Emery tipped her head back, meeting his gaze, and he smiled to reassure her he was not going anywhere.

She parted her lips, and a soft sigh escaped.

He leaned forward, resting his forehead against hers. "Emery."

"Don't." Her head shook against his, but she didn't pull away. "Don't say another word, August."

Instead, he softly pressed his lips to hers. Emery leaned into him, tugging his shirt, pulling him closer. He restrained himself, not allowing the kiss any deeper. It was about gaining her trust, not getting her naked.

She broke away and slowly let out a breath. "Are you kissing all the other Culling women and letting them cry on your freshly pressed shirts?"

"No."

She looked away from him and sighed, flattening her hands on his chest. "I didn't think so."

August didn't let her push away from him. Not that time. He threaded his fingers through the hair at the nape of her neck, cupped her chin with his thumbs, and tipped it up so she met his eyes once again. "You're different, Em."

"No. I'm a new shiny toy, August."

The tears that welled in her eyes were like a punch to the gut. "That's not true."

"Isn't it, though?"

"If you were a shiny new toy to be played with, I

wouldn't have walked away last night. I'd have fucked you where everyone could see, and I sure as hell wouldn't have tried to find you today. Why play with the same toy twice when there are plenty of new ones to try?"

Emery shoved his chest, falling back toward the hay bale. "You don't have to be disgusting. I'm not an object to play with."

"I'm not playing with you as a toy. You're a collector's item, Em. You turn me on in a way no other woman has. You intrigue me. Make me want to think beyond sinking my teeth into your neck while my cock is inside you. Which believe me, I've considered often since meeting you. You can't tell me you don't feel it too. The pull that happens every time we're near. I want you by my side, Emery." He narrowed his gaze, ensuring her eyes met his. "And I always get what I want."

"I can't ever be yours, August."

"Can't? Or won't?"

Emery shook her head and pressed her back further against the hay, creating more space between them. "I won't bow to you. Not if you were the last man on earth. You aren't my prince, and you won't be my king. You may think every girl on this planet wants to kneel at your feet by day and worship in your bed each night, but I am not that girl. You're a fucking vampire. A parasite. You need me to live, not the other way around. Why would I agree to marry something I've feared my whole life?

"I'm here because I was forced by the damn mark. Not to be another whore you stick your dick into while you find your wife. It will never be me. I will not be a pawn in anyone's game and that includes your little bachelor wannabe competition. If you don't like it, send me home."

He leaned away from her and his jaw dropped momentarily before he reigned in his shock and hardened his features. He should have expected those words from her mouth, but he didn't. Usually he controlled a situation, calculated the moves of those around him far before they were put into play, but where Emery was concerned, he continuously flew blind.

Maybe she needed a little time to work through her feelings. They'd made progress the night before. He knew the pull wasn't one sided. Hell, it was her intent that fueled their tryst in the garden, and he could smell the faint traces of her arousal when he kissed her just then. Something changed in the last twenty-four hours that had her fortifying the walls keeping him out of her heart.

The journal.

Whatever Sloane wrote within those pages, whatever Emery was hiding from him, had her on the defensive.

August eyed the journal she clutched to her chest. He needed to find out what was written in those pages, but there was no way he could tear them from her. Not when she clung to them as the only thing left of her twin.

He allowed his eyes to roam over her as he considered his next moves. He shouldn't allow her to get away with speaking to him that way. He was still the crown prince and she a member of his Culling. What he should do was call her bluff and send her packing. He'd be well within his rights to do so.

A sick feeling rolled through his stomach. No, he couldn't send her home. Not only because he craved her, but because she was hiding information regarding Sloane's death.

Information he needed.

August stalked away, leaving her to believe she'd won

the battle. He needed to get away from her before he said or did something that would jeopardize him winning the war. When he reached the edge of the loft, he didn't bother with the ladder, and instead jumped to the level below.

As soon as he left the stables, he nearly doubled over as the need to tear into a vein hit him. It was getting worse each time he left her presence.

Stronger.

He would put up with the pain if it meant Emery would reason with him. Place her trust in him and give him a chance.

She'd just declared she'd do no such thing.

What drove him mad was Emery wanted him as much as he wanted her, but continued pushing him away. If that's what she wanted, so be it. He wasn't going to waste his time trying to change the misconceptions she had regarding him or vampires as a whole. She wanted him to search for a wife? She could watch him make every other woman happy for the rest of her stay. A little jealousy would do her some good. She thought he was a monster, and he had no problem proving just how right she was.

August's spine straightened as he remembered he was the bloody crown prince of vampires.

He bowed to no one except his king.

And the king expected him to secure the safety of his castle and find his queen. He would do what it took to ensure his kingdom remained strong in his reign.

Let the Culling officially begin.

Chapter Twenty Two

EMERY

Ballroom dancing was not for the faint of heart.

Emery thought she'd be able to pick it up fairly easy. After all, dancing was in her blood. She'd been doing it since she could walk.

The crap Malcolm had her learning was nothing like that.

With the blues, she felt the music, moved with it, and as long as her partner had a firm hand, could generally anticipate what came next.

This was nothing like that. There was no improv. No adding personal touches. The dances were choreographed, and each told a fucked up story where the man seduced his woman and everyone celebrated. To make things worse, there were five different ones she needed to have memorized by the time the Scottish delegation arrived.

Emery missed a step, and Malcolm caught her before her face hit the floor.

"How is it you grew up around music and have two left feet? Can you not keep a beat in your head?"

"It has nothing to do with the beat, Malcolm," she snapped, ready to take off one of the ridiculously high heels she wore and throw it at his head. "It's all the useless knee raises and hand flourishes that are killing me. Why do I have to learn these? It's not like I'm going to be chosen for the Culling. I can just stand on the sidelines and let the actual contenders participate in these archaic dances."

Malcolm pulled her into position with a hand gripping her waist. "You'd like that, but tradition dictates *all* of the Culling women must participate in the dances with the members of the court. You're the only one who doesn't know them. The other women have had years to learn and perfect these dances. You have two weeks."

"Good for them. They can impress the members of the court. I don't give a shit." It was a lie, and she knew Malcolm could see right through it.

At the heart of it all, Emery didn't want to fall flat on her ass in front of a room full of people, even if she didn't care what the court thought of her.

That wasn't the reason she kept practicing night after night with Malcolm, though. The truth was she didn't want to fall flat on her ass in front of August. Because even though he had been an absolute prick since their argument in the stables a week ago, he hadn't been wrong about the undeniable electricity between them. One she fought to ignore every damn day she watched him with the other women.

She was positive she'd get stuck dancing with some crusty old vampire while Jessi danced the night away with

August. And that thought pissed her off way more than it should.

Life wasn't fair.

She knew that.

She just had to be a fucking witch. A witch with a hard-on for the one creature she wasn't allowed to go near for fear of losing her damn head. If the vampires didn't kill her first, the witches would.

Malcolm released her from his hold. "Are you sure it's the dances that are bothering you? We've been at this for a week, and between your snarky remarks on vampire history, your apparent hate of dancing, and the fact that you look like you're about to punch something, I'm inclined to think there's more going on."

"Nope. I'm right as rain. Unless you count being stuck here against my will."

Malcolm cocked a brow. "I hate to be the one to remind you, but you agreed to this."

"I did no such thing, Malcolm." Emery raised her wrist, making a show of the visual reminder that kept her within the castle. "My sister died, and I inherited her fucked up duty."

He winced, and his words came out softer than they'd been before. "It's not like she did it on purpose."

Fuck, she'd hurt his feelings. She'd forgotten he didn't know Sloane was a conniving bitch that never truly cared for him. That wasn't his fault, and Malcolm had been nothing but nice to her since they'd started lessons a week ago. Even though there was no way she wasn't a daily punch to his gut. "I'm sorry. That was a dick thing to say."

"That's your line?" Malcolm chuckled. "Talking shit about my dead girlfriend, who's also your sister is too far, but reminding me all week how vampires, the very essence of what I am, are the parasites of creation, wasn't insensitive?"

Emery shrugged and gave him a smile, thankful they weren't going to touch the sister topic. "Truth hurts, buddy."

Disbelief etched on his face. "Is that really what you think of us?"

She sighed deeply, trying to remember that Malcolm wasn't the enemy here. "No. But it hurts less if I tell myself that."

"You know he's as fucked up as you are."

Emery ignored Malcolm. She'd seen August over the last week, throwing himself into the arms of every other Culling women. They'd boasted each morning about their dates and how great the prince was. A few had proudly the hickeys he'd left behind as a souvenir. August had moved on. He wasn't as his brother put it, as fucked up as she was.

He was out on dates and partying each night, every moment within the castle was a struggle for her to forget him. And each day it seemed to get worse. She fought against her heart's wishes to be near him. Each night he plagued her dreams, and each morning she'd wake up more hot and bothered than the last. Her subconscious playing out every fantasy it could imagine, fulfilling his promise to wreck her.

She shook her head, trying to remove the images of a naked August. "It doesn't matter, Malcolm. You and I both know I have a genetic predisposition that prevents me from ever being with him. It's better if he hates me for turning him down."

"I was with Sloane, though."

Back to Slone, they'd come full circle.

She wished she could tell him Sloane played him like a fool, but she couldn't break Malcolm's heart. Better he lived with the happy memories than a harsh reality.

"You aren't the crown prince. August doesn't see things the way you do. Somehow, you saw past what we are. Past the hatred practiced by both witches and vampires."

He raised his shoulders in a halfhearted shrug. "It's not hard when you love someone."

Fuck, he was breaking her heart. Malcolm loved Sloane, and the bitch hadn't seen him as anything more than a steppingstone to power.

He shifted his weight. "Hear me out, I may not share the same penchant for witch hatred as my father, but I think August will surprise not only us but the vampire world. He has what it takes to bridge the gap between the factions. With you."

Emery took a step back and fingered a strand of hair that fell into her face. "I'm no one. I'm just a girl who drew the short straw and landed where she was never supposed to be. Contrary to every romance novel I've ever read, my vagina can't fix everything."

"With an attitude like that it can't."

"Tell me this, Malcolm, when you found out Sloane was a witch how did you react?"

Malcolm chuckled. "It's a funny story actually. I tried to compel her after she caught me siphoning gas from one of August's cars. When I couldn't, she panicked and tried to lie her ass off. Her compulsion act was worse than yours. When I called her out on it, she told me what she was and begged me not to kill her. That's when I first took an interest in her."

"So, you're telling me she told you she was a witch and your first reaction was to date her?"

Malcolm shrugged as if it was no big deal. "Much like you and your sister, I was the defective one of my family. I should have been the heir, but I wasn't born with the right genetics. I could relate to Sloane on that level."

She frowned. "I somehow don't think August's reaction would go over quite as well."

"You won't know unless you give him a chance."

That wasn't happening. Not when he had a predisposition for doing as his father, the witch hating King, told him to.

Emery's brow furrowed, and she tilted her head. "Why were you siphoning gas? You have like ten cars to choose from. Surely one of them was fueled up."

"Just because August is the crown prince doesn't mean I won't fuck with him. He's still my younger brother."

Laughter burst from her. "Touché. I wish I could've had a relationship with Sloane like that."

Malcolm smiled, and Emery couldn't miss the twinkle in his eye. "You would've liked her."

"I don't think I would have." She crossed her arms over her stomach, uneasy about where the conversation was headed.

"She was amazing, Emery. A bit of an acquired taste and rough around the edges."

"If you say so."

"No seriously, Emery." He paused and studied Emery's face. Malcolm was smart and she was shit at concealing her emotions, which meant he saw the anger and hurt tearing through her. His smile dropped, and the twinkle vanished from his eyes. "You found the journals."

Emery nodded slowly, hoping he wouldn't ask what Sloane had written.

"What did they say? Did they give any inkling as to who killed her?"

Wishful thinking.

"I—" Emery knew she should tell him, but how could she tell him the person he loved so wholeheartedly played him? She didn't want to break his heart, so used the same explanation she had with August. "She hated me. Really hated me. Being born second was a crime punishable by death in her eyes."

He took a step toward her, extending an arm to comfort her. "I'm sure it wasn't that bad."

She spun out of his grasp and took a few steps toward the window, needing to look anywhere other than his face. "It was, but it's fine. I've come to terms with the fact she wasn't who I expected. I don't know what I thought I was going to find, but it wasn't a sister who hated me."

"And her death?" he asked hopefully. "Do you know who?"

"No." She swallowed hard and tried to keep her breathing steady. Failing epically.

"Nice try, but I know you're lying."

"Fuck. I hate the way you guys can do that." She turned to face him, hating the way his eyes softened. He wanted justice for Sloane's death, but she'd gotten herself killed by playing a dangerous game with the witches. A game where Malcolm was just a pawn. "Please don't ask any more questions. I don't want to lie to you, but trust me, it's better if I do."

Malcolm's jaw tightened, and the veins in his forearms bulging as his fists clenched at his sides. "Who. Killed. Her."

The dense fog of his compulsion tickled her brain, but

like before it didn't take hold. She clamped her eyes shut and shook her head, hoping he would drop the subject.

"For fuck's sake, Emery just tell me." His voice boomed throughout the room, the pain within him evident.

She shouldn't tell him. It could end so badly. Like supernatural war badly. But Malcolm had been nothing but honest with her the last week, and she had no allegiance to the witches, whether she was one or not. "I think it was the witches."

He stepped back, and several emotions played across his face before settling on shock. "Why would her own people kill her?"

She took a step forward, reaching out to rest her hand on his arm. "Because she got too close to you."

Malcolm's face paled and he looked as though he was going to be sick. "I'm the reason she's dead," he choked out.

Emery took his shaky hands in hers. "I can't say for sure, but I believe the coven thought she was too close to you, and any relationship with a vampire is treason."

"How did they know?"

Fuck. This was spiraling fast. "She told them. Sloane was in contact with the coven. They wanted her to be their eyes and ears in the castle."

"She was the spy in the note."

Emery nodded silently.

Malcolm stood there, still as the dead. Which technically he was. She wasn't even sure he was breathing until he finally gave her hand a squeeze. "I know you aren't lying, but I find it hard to believe."

Emery winced. She should stop there, but the only way Malcolm would believe her was if he knew the whole truth. "There's more."

"Fuck." He dropped her hand and raked it through his hair. "How could there possibly be more? You just told me the love of my life died because she loved me, and there is still more to the story?"

"Yeah." She swallowed hard. "This next part is going to suck to hear."

"Out with it."

Emery took a step back, worried she might become the target of any potential rage. "She didn't love you."

At first, Malcolm didn't react. He just stared at her, his eyes glazed over. Then, his fist clenched at his sides, and his jaw tightened.

"I'm sorry, Malcolm. I—"

"What the fuck, Emery?" He interrupted her, his eyes blinking away the daze. "Why the fuck would you say something like that?"

"You didn't want to believe she was the spy. That she could have possibly deceived you."

"And you expected me to believe this? That she never loved me at all?"

"Did I lie?" She hated using his ability against him, but he wouldn't believe her otherwise.

Malcolm's eyes narrowed on her. "She played me. Then, got killed for it. Is that what you are saying?"

"Yes. She was playing a bigger game and it backfired on her."

Malcolm stuck his hand out, palm open. "I want to read it."

"Help yourself." Emery crossed the room and pulled the journals from her satchel.

She studied Malcolm as he read Sloane's words, his expressions a window to the emotions he felt as he did. They revealed the man within. The anguish and grief he felt as his image of Sloane shattered. She knew the moment he finished the passage about their relationship, not because he slammed the journal shut, but by the empty stare that filled his eyes.

"Do you want to talk about it?" she offered, unsure what else to say.

"Not particularly." He handed the journal back to her but wouldn't meet her gaze. "I have all the time in the world to deal with it."

And just like that he was no longer the grieving man, but a vampire. With a full immortal life to dwell on the transgressions of a woman that didn't deserve him.

She returned the journals to her satchel, worried everything had changed between them because of Sloane's motives.

"Do you hate me now?" She whispered the question, afraid of his answer.

Malcolm sighed and closed the distance between them, wrapping his arms around her. "No. This doesn't change my stance on fixing things between the factions, it's long overdue. Though, I'd be lying if I said I didn't particularly want to see your face right now."

"You felt that way before you knew about Sloane, so maybe that's not so bad."

He nodded, his chin hitting the top of her head. "It's events like this that have fueled the animosity between witches and vampires. I may have been a fool to believe a witch could love me, but I am still a fool who believes in love."

She hugged him tighter, wishing she could take away the pain Sloane had caused him. Malcolm was one of the good ones and deserved so much better than her cunt of a twin. "She fooled everyone. Not just you. Plus, I don't think the world is ready for that kind of radical thinking."

Especially not the witches. She really didn't know much about vampires except what she learned from Malcolm's lesson. Which only consisted of boring facts about the line of succession for each royal family.

Witches, on the other hand, believed all vampires should burn in the flames of a thousand suns. At least according to Sloane, which lined up with the snippets of bigotry she'd heard from Ada throughout the years.

Emery never truly cared about any of that. She hated vampires for taking her sister. That was reason enough for her. Beyond that, she was inclined to agree with Malcolm. Though, she was the first to admit she didn't fully understand the roots of the hatred. August gave her a brief run down at the hotel, but it wasn't the full story.

After untangling herself from Malcolm, she walked to the bar in the corner of the room. Usually, they waited until the end of her lessons, but after the Sloane conversation, she could really use a drink.

Malcolm moved to sit in the one of the plush chairs they'd moved out of the way before they started their dancing lessons.

After handing him his glass, she asked the question that had kept her up more than a few nights since her arrival at the castle. "Why do they hate each other so much? Witches and vampires, I mean. August told me a little bit, but I'd like to hear the full story."

Malcolm chuckled, and she was happy to see he hadn't lost his sense of humor. "Does everything I say just go in one ear and out the other?"

"I'm guessing you already told me this story."

"I did. But to be fair, it was the first night we had lessons after the fight you had with my brother, which you refused to talk about."

"Still not up for discussion. But you can't blame me for not listening that night, I was not in a good place." After the truth bombs Dahlia dropped on her, followed by the journals and then her talk with August, she was three for three and emotionally tapped out. She'd barely made it out of the stables and to her lessons. She knew the rest of the night had been a blur of vacant stares and half responses. Malcolm was handling the news a hell of a lot better than she did.

"I'm aware. Do try to pay attention this time."

"I'm all ears."

He took a long sip before starting. "The first witch, Celeste, created vampires to be an army for her husband. They were made impervious to time, as well as stronger and faster than any other beings. What she didn't account for was magic of that magnitude comes with a price. The price for this particular magic was our need for blood. This was fine during times of war, but what do you think happened when blood was no longer readily available as a casualty of war?"

"They turned to the humans that surrounded them."

"Precisely. Celeste became disgusted by her creation and sought to exterminate every last vampire, but her husband had other plans. He'd become attached to his warriors and went behind his wife's back and asked his sister-in-law to bind his life to the original vampires created. This gave him immortality and prevented his wife from destroying his warriors."

"I'm sure Celeste was thrilled."

"She was furious. The love she had for her husband was the only thing stopping her from destroying every vampire both created and turned. Unwilling to lose her husband, she cursed the created vampires. From then on, no more would be created, only turned, and those turned wouldn't be able to procreate."

"The original created vampires are those that make up the royal vampire lines."

"Correct."

"That doesn't explain why witches and vampires hate each other."

"Ahhh, but remember, all magic comes at a price. Witches paid the price, cursed with hypersexuality and low fertility outside of their own royal lines."

Emery was suddenly thankful her magic was bound. It would suck to be classified as hypersexual. Especially when the subject really didn't interest her much. Unless it was with a certain crown prince. She'd done little else during daily etiquette lessons than daydream about August finishing what they started in the gardens.

She swirled a sip of whiskey in her mouth. If it was because August was good looking, why wasn't she attracted to Malcolm? He was gorgeous and actually nice to her. But there was no tummy dip when she looked at him.

Emery shook her head. She didn't have time to go down the path leading to the depths of her attraction to August.

"You said there is witch royalty?"

Malcolm's eyes widened, and Emery wasn't sure what she missed. "You really know nothing about your people?"

"When you're deemed defective, you fall on the need-to-know basis. I didn't need to know anything."

"I'm sorry you went through life feeling that way."

"Don't feel sorry for me." She stood and walked toward the window, unable to stand the look of pity Malcolm gave her. She took another long sip and set her glass on the windowsill. "That doesn't seem like enough for the factions to hate each other to the degree they do. Vampires, maybe. They got the shit end of the deal. Witches, though, why do they hate you so much?"

"That grew over time. Vampires held a grudge against them and persecuted them over the years. Ever heard of Roanoke? Salem? Those are two of the more recent skirmishes between vampires and witches."

Emery whipped her head toward him. "Seriously?" She remembered learning about them from her history books, but Ada never let on they were historical events in witch heritage.

Malcolm nodded. "Both of those I can confirm personally."

"How old are you?"

"You know it's rude to ask those sorts of questions of royalty."

"Good thing I'm not a member of your court."

"Yet." He tipped his glass toward her and smiled.

"Never going to happen."

Laughter drifted up from outside and Emery turned her gaze to see who was out so late. It was well past curfew, unless—

All thoughts stopped when her eyes locked on August walking arm in arm with Willow through the courtyard, a toothy grin on his face and her head tipped back laughing at whatever he'd said.

Emery's fingers curled under the windowsill in an attempt to ground herself and fight off the jealousy that raged within her. The hum of what she now knew was her magic started deep within her chest

She inhaled deeply, reminding herself he was supposed to be with the other women, and his declaration of wanting her meant nothing. The minute she'd denied him, he'd gone to warm the other women's beds.

As he should.

He was the crown prince, she was nothing, and that's how it had to be.

Malcolm walked up and stood beside her. "He doesn't want her."

As if August knew the stakes of what Malcolm said, he twirled Willow, and pulled her into him.

Then, kissed her.

And he didn't just kiss her chastely. No, he plundered her mouth with his.

The vibrations started as a low hum in her chest then flooded every pore until her skin visibly tremored.

Eyes locked on the couple below, she spoke through gritted teeth. "Really? He has a funny way of showing it."

"Emery." Malcolm's usually steady voice was low and gravely. "Are you okay?"

Malcolm's use of her given name pulled her from the scene below. Emery whipped her head toward him with a manic laugh. "Do I look like I'm okay, Malcolm?"

"No. Your eyes are glowing, and I think maybe we need to get you away from the window."

He placed his hand on the small of her back as she adjusted her gaze to her own reflection in the glass. Her normally dull eyes were indeed glowing. They looked like the softest amber, back lit with the glow of a flickering fire. "Well, that's new."

"New?" A hint of panic laced Malcolm's question. "Are there other things happening to you?"

Emery sighed and gave her back to the window, unable to stomach any more of the show below. "I vibrate like a damn cell phone when I'm near him, or my emotions are heightened."

"Does August know this?"

"No. He'd think I'm a witch, which I am, and he'd kill me. You can't tell him anything. He needs to forget about me and move on. I don't know why I react to him this way or what it means, but he needs to believe there's nothing between us."

"Why?"

"Please, Malcolm. If you tell him how I feel, or the way my body reacts to him, he'll want to explore this thing between us." Her gaze dropped to the floor, and her voice fell right with it. "I don't know if I have the strength to push him away again."

"Okay. For now, this stays between us." He nodded, but Emery got the feeling he didn't agree with her.

"Thank you. You're a good friend." She went up on tip toes and placed a soft kiss on his cheek. "Did my sister ever vibrate or glow around you?"

He shook his head. "Never."

"So now, not only am I defective, I'm a freak."

"You aren't a freak." Malcolm chuckled and pulled her against his side. "We'll figure it out, but maybe you should try to control your emotions better until we can figure out what it means."

"Thanks," she huffed, shrugging him off her. "I'll get right on that."

Chapter Twenty-Three

EMERY

Birthdays were never a big deal.

There were no balloons. No tables filled with food. No three tier cakes topped with candles to make wishes on. Nothing like what the Culling women created in the common room.

Birthdays usually consisted of Ada cursing her existence and, if she was lucky, a new book from the secondhand store down the street. As she'd gotten older, Miles allowed her to celebrate at the club, but considering her sorely lacking friend department, she often ended up behind the bar helping Wren sling drinks.

She wasn't the help anymore, though.

Instead, she was an imposter. An outsider looking into the world of the Culling in awe. She sat on a sofa in the corner with Flora, grazing from a plate filled with Scarlett's favorite foods while trying to pull down the hem of the too short body con dress Chelsea insisted she wear. It was all she could do to stop herself from glaring at August across the room on a sofa, surrounded by the mean girls, Jessi, Scarlett, and their newest addition, Amelia. He laughed and carried on like they were the most interesting women in the world.

Maybe they were, but she didn't see the appeal.

They were the most self-absorbed bunch of bitches she'd ever met.

If she'd been given the choice, she wouldn't even be there, but Chelsea and Flora insisted Emery needed to have fun and shake the funk she'd been in. They'd also promised her August wouldn't be there.

They'd been wrong.

Her skin tingled the moment he walked into the party, mocking her attempts to ignore him as he socialized with every woman present, except her. The same thing he'd done all week. Picking up his dates from the common room, making sure to pass her on their way out, even choosing to eat in the Culling dining hall. All while going out of his way to ignore her.

She should be grateful. That was exactly what she asked him to do, wanted him to move on and find a wife. She pointed out on multiple occasions how it would never be her. But as the days went on, his absence from her life chipped at her resolve to keep him away. Jealousy became her best friend.

"This is unbelievable," Emery whispered the words, pulling her gaze from August and his groupies

"Birthdays weren't always like this," Flora answered softly, and Emery realized she thought she'd been referring to the party in Scarlett's honor. "Vampires don't see the need to celebrate the day they were born, or turned. But we're human, even if they like to pretend we aren't. Some years ago, we took it upon ourselves to start celebrating one another."

"The royal family didn't mind?"

"They did at first, but over time they started to look the other way and allow us to have this one thing. They even helped us acquire presents and supplies. The parties weren't always this ostentatious, but seeing as it's the only time we really get to embrace our humanity, they tend to get bigger each year."

Big was an understatement. The common room had been turned into a small scale club. All of the couches and tables were pushed up against the walls allowing for a dance floor in the center of the room where some of the women already danced. Waist height speakers filled each corner, and two light bars were secured overhead, casting colored beams throughout the otherwise dimmed room.

The music transitioned to a slow and sultry song Emery recognized from the millions of times it was over played on the radio.

It was overdone, like everything else in the room.

Scarlett jumped up and grabbed August's hand. "Oh, you have to dance with me! This is my favorite song, and it's my birthday. You can't say no."

He cocked a brow, and for one tense moment Emery thought he might refuse. But, a smile crept over his face, and he stood, giving Scarlett a slight bow. "It would be my honor."

Emery rolled her eyes, failing to tamp down the rising jealousy. He was supposed to be flirting with them. Getting to know them. Falling in love. They would be his future. A position she could never fill.

Everyone cleared the dance floor and watched as August swung Scarlett around, then pulled her against him.

Emery dug her nails into her palms as Scarlett ran her fingers through the hair at the nape of August's neck, giggling at something he said. August smiled at her as his hands settled just above her ass, and it almost reached his eyes. Almost. She should hold on to the memory of his full, carefree smile. The one that had been only for her. But the smile he currently beamed in Scarlett's direction was too close to a genuine smile. As if he wanted to be there, with her.

She clamped her eyes shut, needing to get the rising hurt and jealousy under control. If not, there was a good chance her eyes would help light the dancefloor, branding her as the witch she was.

Flora's hand slid into hers and gave it a squeeze as Emery took a few deep calming breaths.

The same moment she opened her eyes, a popular upbeat song filled the air and the dance floor flooded with excited women.

Emery turned to Flora, whose brow was furrowed.

"It's still hard for you to be around him, isn't it?"

"Yes."

"I don't understand. The way he talks about you, and how you look at him when you think no one is watching, it's clear there's something between you. Yet, both of you have your heads so far up your ass trying to make the other miserable you can't accept what's right in front of your faces."

Flora was blissfully unaware she was his mortal enemy, and she could hardly explain it. So, she'd have to suffer Flora's attempts at matchmaking. Every time Emery had a date with August, she could almost guarantee Flora would attempt to get them in a room together. Which often resulted in the two of them awkwardly staring at one another until one of them stormed out.

"It's not about accepting what's in front of us, it's about accepting we can never be together."

Flora opened her mouth to argue her point, but before she could, Chelsea appeared in front of them and grabbed their hands.

"Come on you two, tonight's supposed to be fun. You can contemplate life's mysteries in the corner another time." Chelsea danced circles around them. Literally. The complete lack of rhythm Chelsea displayed brought a rare laugh from Emery as the beat of the music seeped into her bones. She couldn't help but join in, dancing with the two women who'd become her closest friends.

The music blared from the speakers, the bass encouraging them to dance song after song, and Emery enjoyed the moment of carefree bliss. The urgency to find Sloane's killer slid to the back of her mind for a few blissful minutes. Even the low hum within her due to August's proximity couldn't dull her mood. He was where he was meant to be, and so was she. Coexisting in a false sense of harmony.

After half a dozen songs, Flora breathlessly begged for something to drink, and Emery's aching feet agreed with the reprieve. She'd nearly made it off the dance floor when someone grabbed her hand and pulled her back into the fray of tangled bodies.

She spun, trying to catch her balance, until she landed in the arms of the blue eyed prince she'd been avoiding. His heated gaze roamed over her face, and she leaned into him against her will.

"Did you need something, Your *Highness*?" She forced a nauseated amount of sweetness into the word, ignoring the way her arms tingled where he held her.

"Dance with me." August lifted her arms, draping them over his shoulders and replaced his hands on her hips. He pulled her closer, pressing her against his broad chest as he guided her hips with the beat of the music.

Emery tipped her head back, fully intent on telling him what a bad idea it was, but every ounce of resolve she had left vanished when her eyes met his. The heat in his gaze trapped her, stole every ounce of fight she had in her as her eyes fell to his lips. All she wanted in that moment was to close the distance between them and taste the sweet caramel of his lips.

A change in the music shook her from the trance she'd been in, and she spun herself to press her back to August's chest. She couldn't bring herself to walk away, not when being in his arms felt so damn right.

A new song began, its slow melody mixed with heavy bass. A song intended to ignite passion and lower inhibitions.

August's fingers dug into Emery's hips, sending a shiver through her when he pulled her hips flush with him. They moved as one with the music, and it was impossible not to notice his growing arousal against her back. He leaned over and whispered in her ear. "You've been avoiding me."

Emery arched her back and ground her ass into him. "It doesn't seem like you've lacked for company. I know for a fact Amelia enjoyed kissing you in the stables. And I might be mistaken, but I think Daphne was asking how to get rid of a hickey this morning. You wouldn't know anything about that ,would you?" she whispered, but a rumbled chuckle in her ear told her he'd heard every word.

"Jealous, are we? *You* told me to find my bride."

"Don't flatter yourself. But I suppose I should leave you to it." She needed to get away from him. Before she did something extremely stupid.

Like let him put his lips back on her.

As if he read her thoughts, August tightened his grip on her hips. "I didn't know dating the other woman meant we couldn't be friends."

She wished she had half the audacity he possessed. "Don't fool yourself, Your Highness. There is nothing friendly between us. We run from hot to scorching, with very little in between."

"You're right. But we have this moment. Can you give me that?"

In the short amount of time she'd been pressed against him on the dance floor, the emptiness she'd grown accustomed to in the last week disappeared. She should say no, but she lost the will to protect herself.

Emery nodded, promising herself she wouldn't let him take more than she was willing to give. "One song, then you forget about me."

"I could never forget about you." He pushed her away before catching her hand and spinning her, pulling her against his chest. When she looked up at him, the world around them fell away. The lights brushed his face the same way they had at the club, and a genuine smile crinkled his eyes.

He was a prince in every sense of the word, but not the one who would inherit the vampire throne. He was *her* prince. Her August. The passionate man who ignited her body. The intellectual who stimulated her brain. She'd take their last dance and hold on to the memory of it because it would have to last her a lifetime.

Emery placed her hands low on his chest and ran them upward over his pecs before lacing them behind his neck. She positioned herself, straddling one of his legs. The hem of her dress rose to her upper thigh, as lust tunneled through her veins and she ground her hips against him.

August's gaze raked down her body as he ran his palms down her sides, igniting an inferno and sending heat flooding through her veins. His thumbs grazed the sides of her breasts, a touch she felt so much lower than where contact was made. One hand came to rest at the small of her back while the other gripped her thigh, hiking up her leg and wrapping it around his torso. Nothing but thin cotton separated them, and the pressure in her chest increased tenfold. He ran his fingers up from her calf and up the length of her thigh, disappearing beneath the hem of her dress and brushing against her panties.

He certainly hadn't done this with anyone else, and her heart raced its way into her throat as she debated how far to let him go. It might do Jessi some good to see what real lust looked like, but she wasn't sure the lesson taught would be worth the price she'd pay.

Everywhere he touched sent a delicious tingle down her spine and fueled the growing ache between her legs. August pulled her up against him and leaned in close, his lips grazing her ear as he whispered. "Where would you say we are on that spectrum of yours?"

Emery turned to look at him, her lips a hairsbreadth from his. "Hot." She wanted to say more, but her throat was like the Sahara and the word she had managed barely escaped.

"Well, I'm not doing my job then."

He slid her down his leg and spun her into a dip, hovering over her. The warmth of his breath caressed the exposed skin of her breasts, the sensation slowly receding as he righted her, trailing the barest touch of his lips along her collarbone and up her neck.

He hesitated for a fraction of a second, hovering over the hollow in her neck, and Emery was half a breath away from offering it to him.

"And now?"

Emery opened her mouth to answer when the stillness of the room caught her attention. She pried her gaze from August and surveyed the room for the first time since she'd landed in his arms.

No one was dancing, and all eyes were on them. Most stared wide eyed, but she couldn't miss the glares from a handful of the Culling women.

Primarily the birthday girl and her bitch squad.

She brought her eyes back to meet August's. His brow was raised, waiting for her response.

Dancing with him had been a mistake. One moment would never be enough, even when it had to be.

"Nothing." She swallowed hard. "We're nothing."

She untangled herself from August's arms and turned from him, biting back tears, refusing to fall apart in front of not only him, but the entire Culling. Running for the exit, she didn't stop when he called her name. The walls were a blur as she tore down the hallway, ignoring the footsteps behind her, moving faster until she was down the hall and back in her room.

She slammed the door home, locked and fell against it, clutching her chest to ease the ache as tears streamed down her cheeks. She tried to hold back the sobs, but there was no stopping the well of pain surging within her. The cost was far too high for a single moment with August Nicholson. Yet, she continuously tortured herself to feel what she'd yearned for her entire life. Of course, it had to come with a price impossible to pay.

All she could do was hope when she left the castle, there would be enough of her heart to continue beating.

Chapter Twenty Four

AUGUST

THERE WAS SOMETHING ABOUT THE WAY WHISKEY HIT A GLASS that made August smile. It wasn't so much the whiskey itself as it was the promise of the buzz to follow.

The buzz he needed in order to get through the fucking party. He didn't understand why his father insisted on having a welcome reception for the Scottish delegation. They were family, not some foreign dignitary that needed to be impressed. But between his father and his Uncle Lachlan, everything was go big or go home.

The usually empty gardens had been turned into something out of a fairy tale, complete with floating lanterns, twinkling lights, intimate seating areas, and a walk up bar hidden in every corner. Usually, August could talk his way out events like these, but he was the star of the show. His Culling was the talk of the vampire community.

Playboy Prince August was finally settling down, and everyone wanted to know who would be chosen to stand by his side. Which meant he was expected to entertain the snooty courtiers and parade his women before them. The only upside to events like these was the excuse to drink.

Heavily.

His father strode up to him at the bar just inside the garden gates. "You're late."

August took his glass from the bartender and turned to face the garden, feigning interest in the members of their court as they mingled. "I was busy doing what you asked of me. Dating my Culling women." He wasn't, and his father probably knew that. Especially after that little display on the dancefloor with Emery. Which he still couldn't get out of his head, the women still hadn't stopped talking about, and he still didn't regret it. Even if it meant his blood lust had increased exponentially with each day away from Emery, and he'd been pathetic enough to sit outside her door in the middle of the night to ease the ache.

Twice.

But that had nothing to do with his absence the previous week. He'd been at the club dealing with a string of suspicious vampire deaths nearby. The details were still pouring in, but August didn't like where it was going. Additional deaths were the last thing he needed on his plate.

The King grabbed his drink and stepped away from the bar, not looking to see if August followed. "Your duty comes before your cock."

August scoffed and swirled his glass, watching the lights glint off the amber liquid, turning it different hues. "What duty is that? You've made it clear you won't be relinquishing your crown any time soon, even if I do marry."

"I've been thinking about that." His father swirled his glass of thick crimson liquid. "After talking with Lachlan, I think it's time you take more of a role in the politics of the kingdom. Callum seems to be doing well in his position, and you'd do well to take note from your cousin."

August brought his glass to his lips and took a long sip. He hated being compared to his cousin, and the King knew it. Callum grew up with Kipton, the true crown prince. That alone solidified his cousin as a pseudo son to his father. Especially after Kipton's death at the hand of the witches.

The King raised a brow, seemingly waiting for August to react. When he didn't, his father continued. "It's why I put you on your current investigation. Have there been any new developments?"

"I believe we're getting closer, but no suspects yet." Not for lack of trying. He'd retraced his steps, Sloane's steps, and poured over all the information they'd gathered, and he'd still come up empty handed. He needed a breakthrough, and the one person who might provide it was the same person who refused to talk to him.

Those bloody journals could be exactly what he needed, but she never let them out of her sight. Despite his best efforts, he hadn't been able to find them. He did, on the other hand, find some extremely sexy underwear he'd love to see her in, and if the stakes weren't so high, it would have been a damned good consolation prize. But he'd never see her in them. Not after Scarlett's party.

Making her jealous wasn't working, so he decided to go back to his original plan of seduction, which proved even more disastrous despite its promising start. No matter what he did, he pushed her away. Since he left her alone, she thrived in the castle. She'd found happiness and friendship with Flora and Chelsea and excelled in her courses with both Yessenia and Malcolm.

He'd grilled his brother about both Emery's feelings and the journals, hoping she may have confided in him, but Malcolm had become unusually tight-lipped with regards to the vexing woman. Which only served to piss August off more.

"Keep me posted." His father's voice pulled him from his thoughts, reminding him there was another line of business he'd meant to discuss with him.

A smile crept across August's face. "Only if you keep me posted on what is going on in the city. Ten vampire deaths in one week isn't likely to go unnoticed by the other factions. Not to mention they were sloppy in execution."

It wasn't uncommon for rival groups of vampires to war with one another for hunting territory in the city. As long as they were complying with the grounds set forth by the king, the castle tended to look the other way. From what his sources told him, the vampires weren't just killed. They were mutilated to the point they were almost unrecognizable.

His father side eyed him, raising a brow. "So, you are paying attention to more than your cock."

"Contrary to your beliefs, I can multitask."

August almost gasped when an actual smile formed on the king's lips. "We'll discuss the details later. For now, you need to play nice with the courtiers and prepare for your Culling to arrive."

He wouldn't be playing nice with anyone. He'd be

avoiding and dodging per usual. Still, he plastered on a fake smile and nodded at his father. The King took his leave, heading to where his Uncle Lachlan, the Scottish King, entertained a crowd of courtiers with one of his tall tales. August's father jumped at the chance to correct his brother's version of the story into something that made him the hero.

There were moments his father seemed like a normal person, reading the room and being what was needed. The storyteller. The confident leader. But in the blink of an eye, the King could become a merciless killer. One that struck fast, dismantling any threat to his reign.

Turning from the bar, August surveyed the members of his court. Most were scattered in small groups across the garden engaged in small talk, while others took advantage of the plush seating areas and openly fed from their personal feeders. He hoped Emery would be okay with the public display. While the other women had witnessed the courtiers at other parties over the years, she'd only ever seen him feed. His moment of stupidity with Jessi had backfired in so many more ways than one. Even if it did lead to an evening of stolen bliss. Though, that stolen bliss demanded its due, and it was a price he hadn't been willing to pay.

Emery.

It was no surprise she danced to the forefront of his thoughts, and when she did, it sliced his heart and comforted his soul. No matter how he tried, he couldn't help but relive the stolen kiss in the hotel room, her body open and ready for him on the garden fountain, or pressed up against him at Scarlett's party.

He tried to focus on his dates with the other women, but none of them carried the same fire as Emery. They didn't defy him at every turn or challenge his authority. They were nothing but the meek and docile women they assumed he wanted.

She'd be arriving at the party soon with the rest of the Culling women, and he found he was looking forward to seeing what she wore and if she wore her hair down as he liked it.

August downed the rest of his whiskey and left the bar, forcing her from his mind. Careful to avoid eye contact, he made his way through the crowd until he found the perfect viewing spot for the arrival of his Culling.

"Your Highness." A woman stepped out in front of him and curtseyed. Her floor length dress was a bit formal for a garden party, but it was possible he was out of the loop on fashion trends.

August gave her a curt nod and smiled. "How may I help you?"

The woman looked up at him, her long red hair falling away to reveal familiar hazel eyes. August paused, staring longer than was socially appropriate in a fruitless effort to place them.

"You asked me to be here."

He raised a brow in question. "I did?"

She nodded. "You did. You asked me to find someone."

"Lilyana?"

Her disguise was impressively thorough but knowing her true form helped him see through the ruse. Her height was the same, as were her eyes, though her face was a bit longer and her curves slightly rounder. The thick brogue should have been the give away, but as a good number of the attendees were from Scotland, she blended in well.

"Are you enjoying the party?"

"It's a party." Lilyana's eyes flitted around the garden as she gave a small shrug. "I haven't seen who I'm looking for, but the night is still young."

"I appreciate your help."

She looked up, her eyes narrowed. "You know why I'm doing this."

From the corner of his eye, he noticed the bulky frame of his cousin, head and shoulders above most of the courtiers, walking toward them. Every inch of him exuded Scottish royalty, from his tartan to the ceremonial sword strapped to his back.

Callum stopped beside Lilyana and tilted his head in her direction. "Cousin, who is this lovely lady you have in your company? Is this one of your Culling women?"

"No, they haven't arrived just yet. Callum this is—" he paused, unsure what name to use.

Without missing a beat, she offered Callum her hand. "I'm Kip. 'Tis a pleasure to meet you."

Callum paused, looking her over before he pulled Lilyana's hand to his lips and inhaled deeply. August stilled, and for a moment, he worried that Callum would be able to smell her deception. He inhaled himself, noticing nothing different about Lilyana's scent. When Callum pressed a gentle kiss to her hand and released her, August relaxed.

"You have the tongue of my people. Did you come with the delegation, lass? How did I miss seeing you before?"

"I'm an old acquaintance of Prince August's. From his time in our homeland."

"I see." Callum nodded. "Have we met before?"

Callum grew up with Kipton, so it stood to reason he'd also met Lilyana at some point. He hadn't thought to ensure she didn't have any contact with any member of the delegation.

"I'm new to this court," Lilyana replied, and once again August relaxed. She'd expertly crafted her answer so that no lie was told. A smile tipped his lips, thankful she held her own so well. If she wasn't a witch, he might employ her himself beyond their arrangement.

"Well," Callum brought his hand to his chest, puffing it out slightly, "should you need anything, or perhaps a tour, I should be glad to help."

"Thank you." She smiled demurely, playing the role to perfection. There wasn't a subdued bone in her body.

A low growl caught the attention of Callum and August.

Malcolm stalked toward them, eyes unwavering on Lilyana.

Callum wrapped an arm over Malcolm's shoulder. "Cousin, it's so good to see you."

"Yeah, you too." Malcolm didn't turn to look at Callum, instead his eyes flitted between Lilyana and August. "Who is this?"

The words were more of an accusation than a question, and Lilyana sucked in a harsh breath, her body going rigid. She opened her mouth to answer, but no words flowed.

"Kip," August offered. "She's an old friend."

Malcolm and Lilyana sized each other up, neither moving to engage in any sort of appropriate greeting. He'd never seen his brother react in such a way to a woman. He didn't think Sloane's death had hardened him so much he would be an absolute prick to a woman he'd never met. They'd been raised better than that.

August opened his mouth to chastise his brother when a

bagpipe sounded from across the garden, pulling the group from the increasing tension between them.

The steward announced the arrival of the Culling women, and everyone applauded as they moved to gain a better vantage point.

August's body warmed the moment Emery entered the space. Her scent engulfed him, sending a jolt of electricity through his body. For the first time since his last pathetic midnight stroll to her room, the thirst for blood eased. Calm engulfed him, and he felt almost serene. Though the demon lurking on the fringes of his mind may have been forced at bay, there were still plenty of tangible things keeping him on edge. He shifted uncomfortably, his eyes zeroing in on her.

She was beautiful as ever. The tea length dress she wore hugged every one of her curves perfectly. His hands fisted repeatedly at his sides, itching to grip them. To pull her against him and feel the way her body molded to his as if it was made to be there. The need to claim her intensified as time went on, and each time they were in the same room became a war with himself

Respect her wishes or keep on his path to seduction. Which usually drove him to wrap himself up around another woman.

Emery's eyes met his, daggers hitting their intended mark. She was nothing if not consistent in her reminders she wanted nothing to do with him. Unfortunately, her body didn't agree and betrayed its needs with the most delectable scent. The faint aroma of her sweet arousal filled his senses. It sliced through the air, seeking him out as if it knew who would fan its flames. His lips tilted into a knowing smile, and he arched a brow as he made direct eye contact.

Emery fidgeted under his heated stare, and he could

see her shift to clench her thighs together before she rolled her eyes and shifted her attention back to Flora and Chelsea.

"Are you okay?"

Callum's question tore him from Emery, and he turned to find his cousin's arm around Lilyana's waist, her hand white knuckled around his opposite forearm.

Immediately, August moved to her side. "What happened? Is she okay?"

Lilyana didn't answer, but August wasn't sure she could through her rapid breaths. Her eyes were wide, and her mouth slightly ajar. The death grip on Callum didn't abate, and her face had lost every ounce of color.

"I'm going to take her to get some water." Callum steadied Lilyana and steered her toward the bar.

Malcolm stepped in front of them, his chest puffed out. "I'll take her."

Just above a whisper, Lilyana objected. "If it's all the same, Your Highness, I'd like it if Callum accompanied me."

A tic appeared in Malcolm's jaw, and for a moment, August thought the two men were about to fight for the right to take Lilyana. Malcolm may have recently lost Sloane, but that didn't give him the right to act like a complete asshat.

He smiled internally at the use of the world Emery had taught him.

Malcolm sighed and backed down, stepping out of the way.

The brothers watched as Callum guided Lilyana away, but not before August heard her whisper to Callum. "I don't know what's wrong with me. My skin is vibrating."

Before August could consider what she meant, Malcolm

spun on him and gripped August's shoulder. His eyes narrowed and mouth set in a firm line. "Who is she?"

"That was Lilyana." August shrugged off Malcolm's hand. "You want to tell me what the hell that was about?"

Malcolm's eyes widened. "The—" he stopped, his words hanging in the air, probably thinking better than to mention Lilyana was a witch in a garden full of vampires.

"Yes, *that* Lilyana."

Malcolm lost all color in his face. He raked a hand through his hair, and when it rested on the back of his neck, he kneaded the muscles. "Fuck."

"You want to clue me into what the hell that was about?"

"No. Yes. I don't know." Malcolm's eyes trailed upward in the direction Lilyana had walked with Callum. "I gotta go."

"Wait—" But Malcolm had already walked away, leaving August standing alone.

August finished off the little remaining whiskey and cursed the bottom of the glass. He didn't know what the hell just happened, but either blood or whiskey was needed to process it. And as much as he'd love to start binging blood, whiskey was safer.

But the universe hated him.

Emery stood at the bar with Flora and a male member of the delegation. The male's lips were pulled back into an award-winning smile as he laughed at whatever the girls said.

Mine.

August's gums ached with the need to rip the male apart for staring at his woman like she was the most brilliant thing in the room.

For a brief moment, August considered walking the

opposite direction and avoiding her entirely when Emery caught him staring from the corner of her eye and gave a sly smile. She reached out and placed her hand on the male's forearm and gave it a squeeze.

Emery was playing him at his own game, and she was doing it better than he had for the past two weeks. He knew this was payback for every kiss he'd shared with other members of the Culling. It didn't matter that he imagined it was Emery each time he forced himself to play the game. She'd told him to find his bride, and he'd made sure she thought he was doing just that.

He'd fucked up.

It wasn't his game he was playing. It was hers. She held all the cards, and he'd pathetically bluffed his way through the round, thinking he could win with the shit hand he'd been dealt.

He'd wanted her jealous, but he couldn't handle the taste of his own medicine. She was his. Only his. And he was about to remind her of that.

Two steps into his mission to fix things with Emery, Victoria M. snaked her arm though his. "Join me for a drink?" she asked sweetly.

It was the last thing he wanted to do, but courtiers were staring, and he was playing more games than the one with Emery. "Sure." He offered Victoria his arm.

As they made their way to the bar, Victoria prattled on about her excitement for the ball in two days, but August wasn't paying attention. How could he with Emery inches away?

She spoke with the Scot, throwing her head back in laughter while stealing glances at him. Not affectionate ones, either. Glances that promised death at the wrong end of a broadsword. If her game wasn't at his expense, August would've been impressed. She'd fit right in at court.

Victoria attempted to wrap herself in August's arms, leaning into his chest, but he took a step back. He didn't want to keep playing the game, it wasn't working anyway.

August untangled himself from Victoria and reached for their drinks, purposefully allowing his arm to brush against Emery's. A jolt of electricity sparked where their skin touched, and both jumped. Their eyes met, each reflecting the same expression of surprise, laced with the heat she tried so hard to deny.

"I need to speak with you," August whispered low enough that only she would hear.

"We have nothing to discuss, Your Highness." She reached for her drink and gestured for the Scot to join her and Flora. "And it seems you're busy."

August reached out and grabbed her hand, stopping her, desperate in his need to keep her close. "What do you want from me? Tell me, and I'll do it."

"Let me go." She looked down at where his hand held hers and returned her fiery glare to him. Her lips were pressed into a firm line, but there was a sadness in her eyes she could do nothing to hide.

Anyone else might think she meant her hand, but August knew she meant for him to release her from the Culling. To let her walk away from him forever.

Without another word Emery shook her hand from his hand and stalked off toward the center of the garden, following Flora and the Scotsman.

August debated following her, but he knew it would only end in an argument and that was the last thing he needed in front of all the guests. He needed her alone so they could have an actual conversation.

"Why are we here?" Victoria's shrill voice jolted him back to where his attention was supposed to be.

"What?"

Her eyes narrowed on him and disgust twisted on her lips. "Why are we here? We all see the way you look at her."

August cocked a brow, hoping to appease her and not call attention to themselves any more than they already had. "I don't know what you mean."

"I may not ever be your queen, but I was educated to be one, so don't play stupid with me, Your Highness." Victoria looked around, then lowered her voice to a stern whisper. "We have given you our lives and watched you ignore us, sleeping around with every two-bit hussy that would spread her legs for you. We heard the rumors. And still, we pined for you. For the chance to be your queen. But you never gave us a second look.

"Now you proclaim to be taking us more seriously, only to give us weeks of halfhearted dates that end with kisses that are fueled by lust, but not for any of us. We can all see you're trying, but you aren't fooling anyone. You don't want this."

A glance around showed far too many sets of eyes on them and far too many fans raised to hide conversation. "Victoria, I—"

She gave no indication she'd heard him, continuing as she gestured toward where Emery had disappeared into the garden. "She's the one who's caught your eye, but for whatever reason, you refuse to act on it. We are not pawns in your game, we are humans. We deserve to find love. Any man, human or vampire, would be lucky to marry us. You're the crown prince, start acting like it."

Victoria spun to leave, but then turned back and pointed a finger at him.

"And while you're at it, please for the love of God, put Jessi in her place. If I have to hear one more time about how you fed from her and promised her the crown, I am going to vomit."

August chuckled. "She's truly that insufferable?"

Victoria's eyes softened toward him, the wind in her sail gone after speaking her piece. "Worse."

She leaned in and placed a kiss on his cheek. "I'm going to pack my things. I wish you every happiness, August, I do. But if you don't pull your head out of your ass, you'll lose a lot more than her." She walked away not giving him a chance to respond. He downed his whiskey and requested another, knowing he would need many to make it through the rest of this fucking party.

Everyone around him shuffled, pretending they hadn't heard every word she said, but it was a garden full of vampires. They heard everything.

Callum strolled up to him as August finished his third whiskey. His cousin leaned against the bar and raised a brow. "Would now be a bad time to ask if ye'd share your Culling women?"

"Seriously?" Callum lost his wife and son during childbirth some years ago, but August wasn't aware he was ready to get back on the horse and find another wife.

Wife. That's what he was to have as well. And yet the word left a foul taste in his mouth. All the games and the bullshit. He didn't want any of it.

"You can't blame a guy for asking. It would be so much

easier to find a woman of the correct bloodlines through you instead of having to go through another Culling."

"Isn't that the truth." August scoffed. He wouldn't wish the process on anyone, he couldn't imagine going through it twice.

Callum patted him on the back and ordered them another round. "That was pretty brutal with the lass. But she was a little spitfire. She up for grabs?"

"If she'll have you, she's yours. Speaking of women, where is Li— Kip?"

Callum sipped his drink. "She felt faint and decided to head back to her room."

Fantastic. He'd publicly gotten chastised by Victoria and now the witch bailed on her duties. The party was nothing short of a clusterfuck.

"What's the deal with that one over there? She's a pretty little thing."

August followed Callum's finger to Emery, who was laughing with her head bent close to Flora.

His voice lowered, and he made direct eye contact with Callum, ensuring he didn't get any off handed ideas. "She's off limits."

Callum laughed. "Why? Is she your front runner?"

"No, she's just not interested."

Callum cocked a brow, and August knew he didn't buy a single word from his mouth. But he'd say and do whatever it took to keep him away from Emery. She may not want him, but he sure as hell wasn't about to let someone move in before he made her see sense.

"Oh, she seems very interested, just not in you."

August bit the side of his cheek, trying to keep his emotions in check. "I mean it, Callum. Hands off."

She was his. At least, as long as she was in the castle. Which only served to prove Victoria's point. He couldn't very well serve his kingdom and have Emery under the same roof. The women of his Culling and the people of his court deserved a crown prince that took his duty seriously. All he'd been doing was playing a losing game with Emery while trying to solve a murder to keep her safe.

She'd become his world.

But she couldn't be anymore. Not if she continued to deny him and the crown.

He needed to build his future with someone who wanted to be there. Who wanted him.

"Excuse me." August left Callum standing at the bar and walked to the stage in the center of the garden.

"May I have everyone's attention?" Silence crept throughout the garden, all eyes on him. "Thank you all for coming today to welcome our family from Scotland. As many of you know, I am in the process of finding my future queen. The women of my Culling are extraordinary individuals. Each beautiful, smart, and kind. I would be fortunate to have any of them as my queen. However, only one can stand by my side."

Cheers sounded throughout the garden. When they had quieted, he continued. "Originally this weekend was to be an opportunity for the members of our court to meet these amazing women, which I still encourage you to do. However, what will be different is that at the ball on Saturday evening, I will be eliminating all but five women. These five women will then be in the forefront of the court. Attending meetings and entertaining as if they were my future queen.

"To my Culling," August scanned the crowd locating

where the majority of the women flocked together, speaking directly to them, "I want you to think long and hard if this is something you want. You have been trained for this your entire lives, but now I ask you if this is what you want." His eyes locked with Emery's, willing her to hear his words. "If you do, I invite you to attend Saturday's ball as my guest, ensuring your consideration for the night's elimination. Should you decide you want to forgo your eligibility, please either find me to remove your mark or refrain from attending and I will remove it the following day."

August gave a small bow to his women, and they all responded in kind with a curtsy. Even Emery. The sight of her forced demure gesture forced anger to flow through him. She would be the perfect queen if she'd just accept him. But she wouldn't, and he was done playing games.

"Thank you. I am looking forward to sharing this experience with our court and finding my future queen."

The garden erupted in cheers once more as he stepped down from the stage. He looked at the vampires surrounding him and saw something he hadn't seen in some time within the kingdom. Excitement. Happiness. The prospect of his union gave them that.

Receiving smiles and a few pats on the back, he made his way toward his mother and embraced her in a tight hug.

"Are you sure you're ready for this?" she whispered against his ear.

"No, but it's what's expected of me, and for once, father is right. My duty needs to come first."

She pulled away and placed her hands on his shoulders. "I'm proud of you, August. Go make her our future Queen."

He smiled and nodded. "It may not be her, Mother, the choice cannot be mine, but I will strive to make you proud."

"I know you will."

Amidst the cheers and hollers, August realized he meant what he told his mother. Not only did his duty need to come first, but he needed a woman who chose him. He wanted to do what was right for his kingdom, to fuel the happiness and excitement he saw in them as they celebrated his future. As much as it hurt to admit, that might mean watching the woman of his dreams walk away from him forever before the week's end.

Chapter Twenty Five

EMERY

THERE WAS SOMETHING ABOUT A BEAUTIFUL BALL GOWN THAT brought out the little girl in any woman. The way it had the ability to transform them into the princess in every story ever told was incredible.

Emery thought back to her childhood. There was a time where she wished she'd grown up in a castle like Sloane. Imagining she could be a princess. Once, when she was seven, she'd dressed up in one of the few dresses she'd owned and twirled around the house pretending she was going to a fancy ball like her twin. Ada found her and scolded her, reminding her Sloane's fate was worse than death.

She smiled to herself. Sloane may have been a witch in a vampire castle, but Ada's assessment was far from the truth. Her twin lived a life of royalty. Emery swished the bottom of the elegant navy gown she'd selected for the ball, imagining the horror filled look Ada would wear if she saw her.

"You won't be going home tonight, Sloane, not wearing that dress," Chelsea crooned from the next pedestal over.

Emery gave her a halfhearted smile, the ache at losing one of the few true friends in her life hitting already. "I don't know about that, but at least for one night I might get to feel like a proper princess."

That is, if she decided to go to the ball. She'd been warring with herself ever since the garden party the night before, and she was still torn.

She never imagined she'd be able to wear something so stunning. Her hands drifted over the curve of her hips, and she studied herself in the mirror while the handmaid tailored the velvet of her dress.

As she eyed her reflection, reality set in. She was no more a princess than her right high heel. She should have refused Chelsea and Flora when they insisted on getting their final alterations done together. There was no way she could attend the ball. Not after the speech August made. He was respecting her wishes. Giving her an out.

After the party, she'd gone back to her room, packed, and then unpacked, only to pack everything again. Each time she filled the suitcase and considered leaving, her skin would begin to vibrate in time with the pulsing burn of the vines on her wrist, and a pit of nerves would grow within her stomach until she felt like she'd be sick.

Her magic, if that's what it was, didn't understand she was nearing the moment she'd no longer be welcome within the castle walls. It fueled her urges to be near August, but she was fighting a losing battle. She already shouldn't be there. She'd found out what happened to Sloane, and that should've been her cue to leave. As much as Emery's body urged her to tell August the truth about her heritage, she couldn't damn herself in the process. She imagined the way his face would contort with disgust the moment he found out she was a witch. She'd rather leave with a broken heart and feeling wanted than with the reality of his blind hatred.

"Are you okay?" Flora asked from the opposite side. She looked magnificent in a soft emerald dress. The sheath design hugged her perfectly, but the real highlight was the draped back that hung low, exposing a wide expanse of her back, and a small silver chain dangled between her shoulder blades. She looked incredible.

"You aren't considering going home, are you?"

"No. Yes. I don't know. I don't feel like I belong here."

Flora's gaze held sympathy and maybe a dash of pity. She knew Emery's dilemma better than most.

"Are you kidding me?" Chelsea piped up, shooing the handmaid that tailored the full skirt of her princess-cut gown. She huffed toward Emery. "I totally understood Caroline and Annie bowing out. *They* never fit in here. But you can't leave, Sloane! We're in this together! Till the end, remember?"

Emery's eyes darted between Chelsea and Flora. Over the last few weeks, the three of them had become inseparable, often having sleep overs in each other's rooms. She didn't want to leave them, but she didn't see how she could stay. They were friends, her first real and true friends, and she regretted leaving them as much as she did August. Maybe more.

Chelsea grabbed Emery's hands and gave them a tight squeeze. "Plus, if by some miracle you aren't chosen for the top five, then we can choose which court we want to go to together."

Emery tilted her head at Chelsea, the implication of her

words hitting her like a Mack truck. "You decided you're going to become a vampire? I thought you were weighing your options?"

Chelsea shrugged, and a full smile curved her lips. "I was, but I made my decision. The two of you have practically become sisters to me. I can't imagine life without you in it. Flora has already decided she wants to join the realm of vampires, and let's face it, with the way August looks at you, it's likely you'll wear a crown on your head soon. I want to be part of that. Plus, did you see the vampires that came with the Scottish delegation? They are cake, and I for one, would like a big slice."

Despite the short amount of time she'd spent at the castle, Chelsea and Flora had become the sisters she never had. They'd become the ones she'd always hoped Sloane would be.

"Don't you start crying, Sloane, or I'll start, and we both know Flora is a lush, so she'll start too."

"I love you guys," Emery whispered. To her surprise, she actually meant it.

Flora wiped a tear from her cheek. "Seriously, it's supposed to be a happy time, why are we crying?"

"Because it could very well be our last night together." Emery wiped away a stray tear.

"Okay." Chelsea clapped her hands and made her way back to her pedestal. Patting down her dress, she looked between Emery and Flora. "Instead of dwelling on that, let's talk about how Sloane needs to attend the ball. What's going on with you and Prince August, anyway?"

"He loves her, she loves him, and both of them are too stubborn to do anything about it," Flora answered before Emery could deny there was anything between them.

"It's not that simple." Emery wished she could tell them the whole story. Confide in them every messy detail that kept her and August apart. That's what sisters did.

But she couldn't.

The only one she could confide in, and who somewhat understood, was Malcolm. Not that he was any help. He tried, but he was so deep into his own feelings over Sloane the two of them avoided talking about anything too far outside their lessons. In that sense, it was nice. She could just be herself for a few hours each night.

Her skin began to tingle moments before the one voice she both loved and hated filled the room. "What's not that simple?"

The three women whipped around to see August step into the room.

"Hey!" Chelsea exclaimed. "You can't see us before the ball! It's bad luck."

"I'm pretty sure that's only for weddings, but I'll play along." August made a show of covering his eyes with his hand. "Sloane, may I speak with you?"

She debated saying no but knew he'd just corner her later. Things changed the moment he declared he was sending all but his top five choices home. She'd hoped to slip out without having to hash it out with him, but it was never easy with August. "Can I have a minute to get out of this dress?"

"I'll wait outside."

The moment August stepped outside the door, Flora and Chelsea were a flurry of whispers.

"What do you think he wants?" Chelsea's whisper was more akin to a silent scream as she began to bounce on her pedestal.

"He's finally going to talk to you."

"Do you think he's going to ask you to stay?"

"What if he professes his love?" Flora clasped her hands together and mimicked an exaggerated swoon.

Emery laughed at their childlike enthusiasm as the seamstress helped her down. Their whispers helped to distract her from the nerves that took root in her stomach. "You do know he can hear every word you are saying, right?"

A muffled laugh sounded from outside the door confirming what she'd just said.

"Sorry, Your Highness," Chelsea loudly sang before she and Flora burst into a fit of giggles.

Emery slipped into her everyday dress and flats. "Let's meet in Flora's room when you're done for a girl's night."

"Deal," Flora confirmed.

"Then, you can fill us in on what the prince told you." Chelsea made an exaggerated kissy face at Emery, complete with lip smacking.

"You know I don't kiss and tell."

She shrugged. "A girl can hope."

Inhaling a breath to steel her nerves, Emery started towards the door. "Wish me luck." When she opened the door, August leaned against the opposite wall like the cool guy in a high school rom-com.

The white long sleeve t-shirt hugged every muscle, and his low-slung dark wash jeans made him look so damn good it should have been illegal.

Against her better judgement, she trailed her eyes over him, committing to memory the vision before her. He was casual, like the night she met him in the club. How she wanted to remember him.

Unfortunately, checking out the man who made her vagina go pitter patter and walking were not conducive to one another, and when the door clicked behind her, she tripped and found herself careening toward the floor.

With speed only a vampire could muster, August was there, catching her before her face made the floor's acquaintance. He pulled her against his chest, holding and steadying her. Just like that day in the common room.

The low hum grew deep within her, shattering any hope she'd held it wasn't August who caused it. Eyes closed, she took a handful of deep breaths against his chest in an attempt to steady her emotions. The last thing she needed was glowing eyes.

The ability to burn his scent, the feel of his arms around her, into her memory was just an added benefit. But all good things had to end, and that included her time with the prince. No matter how much it hurt. No matter how much is stung knowing this may be the last moment they ever had.

When she finally opened her eyes and tipped her chin up, identical pools of deep blue met hers. Emery shifted her gaze, unable to bear the weight of his stare, but hers landed on his perfectly kissable lips.

Her brain immediately calculated the distance between them and how easy it would be to close it.

August's tongue darted out, wetting his, and she nearly tested her theory on distance.

She needed to get away from him. The only way to survive this would be to walk away now, before she gave in to whatever is was that demanded they be together.

Still, she didn't move. Being in his arms was right. It kept the vibrations to a low hum instead of the all-out rage against her skin when she fought it.

August pressed his forehead to hers, a soft sigh escaping his lips. "Why is it whenever we're alone we end up here?"

"Because close proximity makes us stupid, and self-control isn't our strong suit."

August's deep chuckle filled the space between them, and a needy ache settled between her thighs. "We've done a good job pretending we don't want this."

"I suppose we are pretty good at it."

His hand lifted to cup her cheek, and he traced the pad of his thumb softly over her bottom lip. "And if I don't want to pretend anymore?"

"August I—"

"Em, don't lie to me. Not today. Not tomorrow. Not ever. I'm done with the lies. If you think I can't hear the way your heart is racing right now or smell the arousal between your legs, arousal that is only present when we're near, then you're greatly mistaken. I know you want me as much as I want you. I'm sorry for the part I've played the last few weeks. For all of it. I was wrong to make you jealous. Wrong to pretend every other woman was you because they're not. I'm done with this game we've been playing." He shifted one hand to cradle her cheek, his fingertips brushing lightly over her skin. "Tell me what I need to do to prove to you I'm not the monster you believe me to be. Whatever it is, I'll do it."

His words, so achingly sincere, were a sucker punch to her gut.

Emery wanted to correct him. To tell him she didn't believe him a monster. She wanted to confide in him, no matter how stupid and risky it was. If she was only a human woman, this wouldn't be a problem. She'd jump right into bed with August and show him all the ways she wanted him. But she wasn't human, and neither was he.

She tried to steady her breathing. "Can we go somewhere more private?"

"Why?" He grinned, his fangs flashing, and for the first time, they didn't scare her.

She wanted them in a way she couldn't articulate, the same way she wanted him. Everything about him. Even if it went against every single belief she'd once held.

As if he could sense her thoughts, his tongue traced the border as his smile deepened. "You don't like the idea of me showing you how much you mean to me right here? Pushing you up against one of these walls and kissing you senseless where anyone could see?"

"Well, there's that." She swallowed her lust down, not wanting him to see it the way he could sense it. "I'm also afraid of what you'll say next, and I guarantee Flora and Chelsea are on the other side of the door, fighting over who gets to look through the crack to see if you'll do just that."

"Well, we wouldn't want to disappoint them, would we?" His eyes flared, a carnal lust in them stronger than she'd ever seen. A true predator after his prey, and she was more than eager to be devoured.

His lips were on hers before she'd registered what he said. Her traitorous body leaned into his kiss, and August inhaled the moan that escaped her, taking advantage of her parted lips and plundering her mouth with his tongue. He dug his fingers through her hair, holding her still as he angled her mouth to allow him deeper, to drink more of her.

Refusing him, pushing him away, was well out of her abilities in that moment. All she could do was receive him, let him turn her until her back hit the wall, and welcome his pelvis as it pushed hard into hers. He may be able to smell her arousal, but she could sure as hell feel his, and there was no questioning how much he wanted her.

The moment he stepped away she gasped, forcing air into her lungs as the unmistakable sound of giggles echoed from behind the closed door.

A devilish smirk played on his lips. "My study is just up the hall, we can continue this conversation there."

Unable to formulate words after that kiss, Emery nodded and allowed him to lead her with a hand on her lower back.

She didn't know how they were supposed to have any sort of meaningful conversation after a kiss like that. Especially when all she wanted to do was press him up against the wall and beg him to finish what he started. But then, maybe that's what the study was for.

He opened the door for her and waited for her to enter.

The sight of it was just the bucket of ice she needed to calm her libido and regain some sense. She hated his study, could still see Jessi sprawled across his desk, August's fangs in her throat. The same thing she'd wanted just minutes ago, and the one thing she could never have.

Needing to take ownership of the room from Jessi, Emery strolled around the rich mahogany desk and sat in his chair. Kicking her feet up onto the top, she crossed her legs and reclined back.

August poured them each two fingers of whiskey before settling against the desk next to her. His eyes roamed the length of her body, only pausing slightly where the hem of her dress had slipped dangerously high on her thighs.

"Comfortable?"

"Quite." She brought the glass to her lips, savoring the

smokey flavor on her tongue. "So, what was it you came to talk to me about?"

August cocked a brow. "You may not know this, but you are an intoxicating blend of beauty and irritation."

"I may have heard something similar from Malcolm a time or two."

A low growl rumbled in his chest, but with his lips still closed, it came out as a very sexy hum.

August shifted his weight and took a long sip of the amber liquid. "I told you I'm done with the jealousy charade. You can't pretend there is nothing between us."

"There *is* nothing between us, Your Highness." She didn't need him to call her out to know she'd just lied to him. "I'm not pretending."

Her denial was met with a half smirk and cocked brow. "Really?"

August pushed off the desk and stood behind her. She could feel him hovering, and that caused every nerve to go on high alert with both excitement and fear.

A moment later, she felt his breath on her ear. "You're telling me you don't notice me the moment I step into a room?" Her breath hitched when he ran his hands down her arms, grazing the side of her breasts as he did. "You're telling me your skin doesn't tingle at my touch?" It did. God, it did. "Or that those perky nipples straining against your dress aren't a direct sign of your arousal?"

They were. And she didn't need him to tell her that if he were to touch the apex of her thighs, he'd find her slick with need.

He trailed one hand back up to her neck pulling aside the top of her dress and leaned in, tracing the length of her now exposed collar bone with his tongue. "I think you're lying not only to me, but to yourself, Emery."

"It doesn't matter." She tried to steady herself, but her words came out breathy and filled with need.

"Oh, but it does," he interrupted. August spun the chair so that she was facing him and gently tipped her chin, so her eyes met his. "What you don't realize is I don't need permission to pursue you as a member of my Culling. But the difference with you, Emery, is I want your permission. I want you to admit you want me, my dear princess, because I fucking want you."

August leaned in and placed a chaste kiss upon her lips.

"I want you more than I care to admit. I can't quite explain it because I have never experienced this sort of visceral reaction to a woman. Ever."

He tangled his hands in her hair, pulling at the nape of her neck to arc her neck, exposing it and tracing his lips over her pulse. Not for the first time, she wanted to experience what it would feel like to have his fangs break though her skin while his hands brought her to the brink of orgasm.

"It's more than just physical. I want to know you. Understand you. See what makes you tick. What brings the smile that touches your eyes. The one that makes me hard the moment I see it. I want to comfort you when the world is too much. To slay the demons that haunt you. I want to share my life with you. Expose the deepest parts of me. The parts that no one else gets to see. And honestly, that scares the shit out of me because I'm not a good man, but you make me want to be."

"You are a good man." The words were a soft whisper, echoing her deepest thoughts.

"I'm not, Emery. I am every bit the monster you think I

am. I crave blood in a way no other vampire does. I am addicted to blood from the vein." August spat the words, his face contorting to an expression that spoke of deep self loathing. "Remember when I told you I drink blood from a bag for convenience? That was a lie. I do it because when I drink from the vein, I can't stop at just one willing human. The more I give in to my need, the more I crave it. I go through double the number of bags as other vampires. I was born with the need to slaughter. A need I have given in to more than once over the years."

Emery turned her head, fully expecting his already elongated fangs. The expectation didn't dampen her reaction, and her stomach hit the floor as a shiver of fear crept down her spine. Fear he would tear into her exposed throat and turn her without her consent. But also a shiver of excitement at the sheer carnality of his need for her. She lifted her gaze from the sharpened points to look deep into his crystal blue eyes, searching for any explanation for why he was telling her this. Something that would serve to push her away.

August's eyes glistened, and remorse lurked in their depths. He closed his eyes and inhaled deeply, keeping her from going any deeper.

Every bit of fear left her body, replaced with compassion for the broken man in front of her. He wasn't trying to push her away. August was showing her he meant what he said about sharing the deepest parts of him, even what he saw as his most deadly flaw.

She lifted her hands to lay on either side of his face. His skin was cool beneath her fingers. "That doesn't make you a monster, August. You have a castle full of human staff and raised your Culling women here, which proves you are more than your craving. More powerful than your craving."

She trailed her finger over his lips and dipped it within to softly press against his fang. "I know you won't hurt me, August. You may see yourself as a monster, but I see you as so much more. A man who is worthy of his title. Worthy of his future queen."

"Just not good enough for it to be you." He shook her hands from his face and took a step back. Just far enough for her to miss the comfort his nearness brought.

Emery hung her head, the hurt she'd caused him slicing through her heart, leaving an open wound she wasn't sure could heal. "I didn't say that."

"You didn't have to."

Emery took his hands, not wanting him to walk away. To leave her. They couldn't have forever, but they could have that moment in his office. She'd just add it to every other stolen moment she had with him. She chose her words carefully, wanting to confide in him, to ease his pain, but needing to protect herself. Which meant not lying, which left her in a precarious place with regards to what she could and couldn't say.

"There is plenty about me you don't know, and if you did, you wouldn't want me as your queen. I wish I could tell you my story, but other people rely on me to keep their secrets. I want you more than I've ever wanted another man, but I cannot be what you need me to be."

Bile threatened to creep up her throat. Her excuse was weak, and she hated it when he gave it to her. She had nothing to say to make things better for either of them, but it was true. Her secrets didn't only belong to her. It would damn her sister, possibly get Dahlia killed, and start a war she hoped would never happen.

"Then, you need to go." August wrapped his hands around her wrist and whispered words in a language she'd never heard. He lifted the wrist with the mark of the Culling and placed his lips to the vines, kissing them softly, sending the low hum into an angry frenzy.

The instant his lips left her skin, Emery's heart beat erratically. Her lips trembled as she watched the silver vines, the ones that sent her life careening off the track she thought she wanted, break apart and evaporate from her wrist. When the last silver line vanished, she choked on a sob and pulled her hand from August's, clutching it to her chest. Wanting to demand he undo what he'd just done, hating the freedom she'd asked for since the minute she met him.

She clamped her eyes shut, fearing they would start to glow with the hole growing in her chest.

"You are free of my mark."

The words added a layer to her pain to cut deeper than she'd imagined possible. She was bleeding out before him, and he hadn't laid a fang on her. Everything she wanted since the second those vines appeared, everything she'd demanded, was now hers.

But she didn't want it. Any of it. Those vines were the only things keeping her there, the only things tying her to the man she wanted more than life itself. But now they were gone, and she had no reason to stay.

No reason she could risk indulging.

"I have a duty to my kingdom to find my queen. And if you refuse to be her, then I need you to leave because I can't even consider another woman when you're near." His voice was distant and cold. His pain palpable, electrifying the air between them. Nothing like the prince who, moments ago, declared his need to have her at his side.

The vibrations started, building slowly, each of his words sending them toward their crescendo. "When this is all over, I'll be engaged to my future queen, and neither of us can stop that. I won't force you, and I'm done fighting you. Go or stay, but you need to make your choice so I can make mine. It's your decision, and yours alone, whether or not the princess by my side at the end of this is you."

She heard his footsteps move toward the door, but she kept her eyes closed.

"But I want it to be."

The door clicked shut behind him and the dam holding back Emery's emotions came crashing down. Sobs wracked her body, and she gave into them until every muscle within her ached. But none more so than her heart. August let her go. Gave her everything she'd wanted from the moment she met him. Only, she didn't want it anymore. Not really. Nothing waited for her in California.

She wished with everything in her she could be his queen. That her veins weren't filled with the blood of his enemies.

But they were, and she could never be his.

Chapter Twenty Six

AUGUST

Stone shattered beneath his knuckles where August punched the wall outside his study.

She wouldn't even look at him after he removed the mark. His mark. If she had, she would've seen how much he regretted it the instant the vines faded from her delicate wrist. It was the right thing to do, giving her the choice to leave, but it was also the hardest thing he'd ever done.

Worse than watching Malcolm being turned, knowing there was nothing he could do to help him through the bloodlust. He was helpless then and even more so now. He'd confided in her, put his heart in her hands, and all he could do was wait to see if she'd walk away with it or give him hers in return.

Once again, he found himself on the opposite side of a door from Emery. Only this time, he'd given himself no assurances she'd be there when all was said and done.

He stormed away, the speed helping him ignore the pangs of hunger as the distance between him and Emery grew. At least, if she left, he wouldn't have any intense spikes in his need for blood. But he wouldn't have the reprieve she provided either. He managed his bloodlust before Emery arrived and would manage it again.

He needed to get back to who he was before she arrived, needed to focus on his duty to his kingdom. But the thought of her leaving twisted his gut, the knowledge he may never touch her again left a pit in his stomach.

Bile rose in his throat at the realization he may never again feel her lips beneath his, smell the distinctly sweet scent that was just Emery. Nausea plagued him as he contemplated an eternal life with someone other than Emery at his side.

August wanted to believe he could care for another, but that was a lie. Emery would always be there on the edge of his mind. And as long as she was, he'd never be able to give himself to his future bride.

Bride. The word was almost as bad as wife.

August threw open the door to the common room he shared with Malcolm in the royal wing and stopped dead in his tracks.

Callum and Malcolm sat on the chesterfield with their backs to him, two half empty bottles of whiskey on the coffee table. The wall in front of them had been transformed into a Culling command station. There was a photo of each woman taped to a white board with two numbers written underneath, one in blue and one in red.

Malcolm pointed at a photo of Emery labeled Sloane, a number one underneath in red. "My money is still on Sloane. She'll stick around, she's got it bad for him."

"No way" Callum disagreed, his speech slurring only slightly. "Did you see the hatred in her eyes at the garden party? I'm thinking he goes with the blonde with the big boobs. I would."

"Jessi? Of course, you would. Be warned, cousin, she's a bitch of the worst kind." Malcolm took a swig of whiskey straight from the bottle. "Besides, there is a fine line between hate and love."

"Well, if Sloane does decide to leave, I'd like a piece of her before she goes. She's something special tha' one."

A low growl echoed from August's chest, and both the drunkards spun toward him. "What the fuck are you two doing?"

"Cousin, come join us! We're arranging a lineup of who we believe has the best chance of becoming your future queen."

"Is my life a game to you two?" He skipped the bar cart and went straight to the mini fridge. Pulling out two bags of blood, he downed them simultaneously. He wiped his mouth and grabbed a bottle of scotch and took three long pulls before joining his brother and his cousin. There was no way he was going to deal with this idiocy, or Emery's rejection, sober.

"We're royals, cousin..." Callum lifted his bottle to August before bringing it to his lips. "We've been pawns in a game our whole lives. This just helps me get to know your women a little better, so when they're eliminated, I can swoop in with my devilish charm and find myself a wife."

"You have no shame, Callum."

"None," he said with a smile.

August took another long swig and studied how they'd ranked the women. Malcolm's lineup was more in line with his emotions, whereas Callum's was strategically chosen. His father would have been proud. "So, your pick is Sloane, and his is Jessi. Any other thoughts?"

"Amelia seems nice," Callum offered.

August shook his head. "She's a terrible kisser." Unlike Emery's intoxicating kisses that left his entire body tingling long after they'd parted.

Malcolm snickered from behind him. "We can't have you saddled to someone who doesn't know what to do with their lips, now can we."

It was the first time since Sloane's murder he'd heard his brother laugh. August had little doubt it was fueled by the empty bottles scattered throughout the room, but still, it was nice to see Malcolm finding his way back.

Maybe he would too, one day. He wondered if Malcolm was an accurate depiction of how long it took to come back from having your heart ripped out. Or if the timeline was different when suffering from a murdered love versus a lover who walked away.

Callum stood and joined him, pacing along the row of photos. "How about the Victorias?"

"Victoria M. is leaving, although I almost commend her for her candor at the party." August took another long swig. "And you can remove Caroline, Annie, and Samantha. They've asked me to remove their marks prior to the gala." He'd almost included Sloane's name in that list, but a part of him still foolishly held to the hope Emery would appear at the ball

August shrugged the thought away and took another pull from the bottle. "Victoria I. is wild once you get a few drinks in her. Though, I'm not sure I could handle her being liquored up at a formal event."

"Pity." Callum tore the five from beneath Victoria I.'s photo. "She was in my top five."

Throwing his feet up on the coffee table, Malcolm relaxed back into the sofa. "More importantly who are *your* top five, brother?"

August cocked a brow and a half smile tugged up one side of his mouth. "I guess you'll have to wait until tomorrow night to find out, won't you?"

Callum laughed openly. "Which means he hasn't decided yet."

"It's hard to decide when you're unsure who will be there to pick from." That and he really didn't want to pick any of them.

"Okay, then," Callum steepled his fingers in front of his mouth, as if he needed a moment to think about his next words. "Let me rephrase the question. Who do you *hope* to see there?"

"It doesn't matter what I want. What matters is who will be best for my kingdom."

Callum gave his best mock applause, joined by Malcolm. "What a diplomatic answer."

"You've been through this. You know how the game goes, Callum. It doesn't actually matter who I want. Each of these women is a good choice, but you know our fathers will make our lives hell if we don't choose from *their* pool of approved women."

"That's true, but you did something unheard of. You gave them the option to walk away. Not even your father can dispute that."

"Have you met my father?" He'd purposely avoided his father since the garden party so as not to have to answer for his actions, though rumor had it the King was furious. "Not to mention, I want my women here for the right reasons. Not only for me, but for my kingdom."

"Touché. Just remember, you have time to form any one of these women into the queen you want. We both know our fathers aren't going to hand over the reins any time soon."

"True." August looked over the photos, lingering on Emery's longer than the rest. "But I want more than just a queen I trained. I want someone to be my equal, and not all of them have that capability."

"You want a mate."

August turned and narrowed his eyes on Callum. "A what?"

"A mate. You know, like how wolves have mates and humans have soulmates. I'm sure there has to be a vampire equivalent."

"I think the thin air in the highlands has gone to your brain," Malcolm chortled.

"No, really. The kind of woman that makes your heart sing and your blood boil. The one you lie awake thinking about each night. The one you'd give it all up for."

"Mate," August tested the word out on his tongue. It felt good. Better than bride or wife.

Callum cracked his knuckles. "I may be the crazy one, but I'll still hold on to the hope there's a woman out there for me that'll be impossible to ignore. That will put up with my bullshite while inspiring me to be the best version of myself. And most importantly, a woman that will force my dick to full mast the moment she enters a room."

What Callum described was exactly what he was looking for. What he had with Emery. She met every one of the requirements Callum put forth for mate status, including making him rock hard when she was in his presence.

Malcolm chimed in from the couch, "Mate or not, August here has to narrow it down to five."

Callum stepped up next to August and placed a hand on his shoulder. "It's just something to think about."

"Yeah," August mumbled, his eyes trained on the photos of the women in his Culling. They all had good qualities, but only one stood out to him as queen material. Mate material.

Unfortunately, it was the one least likely to still be there the next morning.

"Well, this looks like a lively bunch o' lads." His Uncle Lachlan and father stepped into the common room. "What are you boys up to?"

Callum met his father halfway and offered him the bottle. "Just trying to help August decide who will be his queen."

Lachlan took the bottle and finished off half of what was left. "Any prospects?"

"A few," August answered, not wanting to give his father the option to weigh in.

"As long as my other choices, and additionally Amelia, are in the top five, you can have the other two slots," his father scolded, as he moved to stand behind the chesterfield. "But that's not why I came to find you boys."

Malcolm turned to look at their father. "Is everything okay?"

"We aren't sure, but for now, I don't want any of you going into the city without escorts."

"More deaths?" August hoped the answer was no. He'd yet to hear from his men in the city, but the last thing they needed was a vampire killer to worry about.

His father nodded. "Twenty in total. Same as the last bunch. All the victims are vampires and their deaths vampiric in nature. The bodies are drained of blood and eviscerated. The kills are poorly executed, sloppy."

Bloody hell.

"Has anyone witnessed the murders?"

"No. But they've all taken place in the district your club resides in."

August hoped it was a coincidence, but if there was anything he'd learned in his long life, it was true coincidences were rare. "Is it possible these deaths are the doings of rival vampires vying for the district in the city? Or do you think these are targeted attacks?"

"Initially, I thought the former, but every vampire in the city knows that district belongs to you. They aren't stupid enough to take on the crown. The kills aren't a rogue vampire or a casualty of rival clans, there is more to it. After the first round of bodies, our men noticed they had a faint glimmer of silver magic where the skin was flayed open. After a time, the magic seems to fade, though we're unsure where it goes. We've been unable to trace it thus far, but we're working on figuring it out."

"Fucking witches," his Uncle Lachlan muttered under his breath. "I don't know what they're up to, but I don't like it."

"Neither do I, not with your delegation visiting and August's Culling in full swing. They're up to something, and I intend to find out what it is. Even if I have to torture every witch left in the Chicago area to do so."

August knew damn well there weren't any witches left living in the Chicago area. At least not any that valued their life. His father either killed them or ran them out of town nearly a century ago. And rightly so. They'd made life difficult for their courtiers coming and going through the city. They'd fled to New Orleans, and most resided there still.

There had to be at least one residing in the city, otherwise there wouldn't be traces of magic left on the bodies. Interesting coincidence there was a witch in the castle, and vampires were showing up dead near his club.

August did not believe in coincidences.

"Enough of this talk of witches." Callum slid between the sofa and the kings with a tray of shot glasses poured to the rims. "We promise not to go to the city alone, Uncle Lewyn. Now let's drink to August and his top five."

"Here here!" Uncle Lachlan bellowed and helped his son hand out shots. Once they all had glasses in hand, he raised his toward August. "To August! May you have better luck than the rest of us in finding a woman to love."

"To August," the rest of the men chimed in.

August tossed back the alcohol, and it burned going down, but not as much as the nagging thought replaying over and over in his mind. Too much had happened in the last few weeks for any of it to be a coincidence. Sloane's death. The note. The vampire deaths. He had a sinking feeling they were all connected.

He only hoped they figured out how before another death came knocking on the castle door.

Chapter Twenty Seven

EMERY

Robert Frost wrote something about taking the road less traveled. The sentiment stuck with Emery over the years, even if she'd never been faced with a decision quite as pressing and pivotal as the one she faced now.

The visual representation of her choices sat before her. On one side of the bed, a gorgeous ball gown tailored to fit like a glove. It was delivered that afternoon along with a small box wrapped with a pink bow, which now sat atop the dress.

On the other side sat a packed suitcase. She didn't have much to take with her, since most of the clothes provided at the castle were Sloane's, but there were few sentimental items she'd stowed away to remind her of her time there.

It should've been an easy decision. Her life was worth more than her heart, and August deserved a queen able to rule beside him. One his kingdom would accept. Her blood promised she'd forever be vile in their eyes.

It wasn't that simple, though. Logic held no place when it came to her feelings for August. The thought of leaving ripped a hole in her heart, and if she followed through, there was no way she'd be leaving whole. Part of her belonged to August, and she'd never get it back again.

There was a soft knock at the door, and Dahlia let herself in and eyed the items on the bed before meeting Emery's gaze. "What have you decided?"

"I have no idea." Her vision blurred as tears streamed down her cheeks. "I thought I did." Her voice cracked, and she bit back a sob. She pulled at the sleeve of her shirt, lacking the strength to tell Dahlia about August removing her mark. She yearned to find him. To beg him to give back the mark she once hated, but now longed for.

"What are your reasons to stay?"

"I need him. He's part of me, and I'm not sure I can let him go." On a primitive level, her body reacted to him. Constantly aware of not just his presence, but his proximity. The thought of leaving made her sick, but Dahlia wouldn't understand. Hell, it didn't even make sense to her. She only knew she was inexplicably connected to the crown prince and every fiber of her being demanded she stay near him.

"And your reasons to go?"

"I'll never be what he needs. Love doesn't change a thing." Her hands whipped up to her mouth, as if covering it would allow her to take them back.

She loved him.

It was the first time she'd spoken the words out loud, though she suspected the emotions had taken root weeks ago. It was ludicrous, she'd known August less than a month. Emery always laughed when the heroine fell instantly in love with her hero, but there she was. She'd seen the man beneath the vampire exterior. The man who took care of those around him. Who loved his family above all. The prince who strived to put his kingdom first.

Being in his arms felt like home in a way her actual home never did.

And that's why she couldn't stay.

It was selfish to take away August's chances of finding a home with another woman. Someone who could give herself completely and not have to lie about who and what she was. Have to worry constantly about being found out and burned at the stake.

"Oh, my dear, the war between selfish and selfless is the hardest battle to be fought."

Emery hiccupped a sob, barely finding the edge of the bed before another tore through her.

Dahlia handed her Copper and joined her on the bed, cocooning her in a comforting embrace. Emery clung to the ratty stuffed dragon as she released her emotions like she'd never been able to before. Each tear that streamed down her face, landing on the soft fabric of Dahlia's dress, was either a reason to stay and have her happy ending or a reason to go and hurt forever.

When she'd purged every last argument she had within her, Emery righted herself and wiped away the last of her tears. "I can't stay," she whispered, trying to exude the confidence her words lacked. She looked to her wrist where the mark should have burned. A reminder she was free to leave. To do the right thing and never look back.

Dahlia nodded and pulled her suitcase from the bed. "I'll have this delivered to the footman and let them know you'll be needing a car. I suggest waiting until all the court guests are in the throne room."

Emery nodded her thanks. "What are you going to do? Will you stay here in the castle?"

"My job here is complete, but I'm at the service of the coven. I'll stay until they give me instructions to do otherwise."

"I wish you could come with me."

"Oh, I'll see you again, my dear. One way or another, I promise you that."

Emery crossed the room and pulled Dahlia into a hug. "Thank you for everything," she whispered into her ear.

Dahlia squeezed her tight before disappearing into the hall with Emery's suitcase in tow.

That was it. She was really leaving.

Emery took one last longing look at the gown on the bed and reached out to the tiny box on top. Before she could make contact, she pulled her hand back. Already she tread too closely to the line between staying and going. Whatever was in the box might push her to the other side.

She let her eyes travel over the room one last time and took a deep breath, the ache in her chest growing with each now familiar corner. It seemed like just yesterday she'd torn through it looking for journals, but just a few short weeks later, and she cherished every stone and crevice.

There was so much more to miss than just what was in her room. The women who'd become her sisters. Lessons with Malcolm. The prince who stole her heart. Teaching music to Thea. God, she hoped Thea would understand.

The life she built with the only family she'd ever known.

Bells tolled through the castle, signaling the start of the night's events.

One.

The first bell tolled, echoing throughout the castle, counting down to the start of the night's events.

Two.

Three.

Tears threatened to fall, but she bit them back.

Four.

Five.

Six.

That was her cue to leave.

The final two bells tolled as Emery grabbed a backpack she'd found in the closet and packed the few items she wanted to keep close: her sister's journals, the binder August gave her, a book on vampire history she'd received from Malcolm, a photo of her with Chelsea and Flora, and a picture Thea had drawn her. Such simple things, but they held so many memories and love unlike she'd ever experienced. She'd gone there hoping to find her sister's killer, but instead she'd found family.

It fit so well with her life that when she finally found the family she'd yearned her whole life for, she had no choice but to walk away.

With the pack slung over her shoulder, she fought against the last bit of temptation to stay and made her way toward the door.

She opened it, expecting the hallway to be empty, but found herself face to face with the broad frame of Prince Callum, hand raised as if he had been about to knock.

Emery froze for a moment before remembering she was supposed to curtsey.

The prince cocked a brow. "Aren't you supposed to be in the throne room?"

"Aren't you?"

"I noticed you were missing and thought it pertinent to ensure my cousin's favorite woman was safe." He looked her over, his eyes lingering on the backpack slung over her shoulder. "But it looks to me like you are in good health, so I can't fathom why you would be sneaking out while everyone is busy."

Emery swallowed hard and steadied her nerves. "I've decided to take August up on his offer and abstain from attending tonight. I don't belong here."

"How about my court? Would you belong there?"

"No." She tried to carefully choose her words, remembering vampires could sense a lie. "I don't belong in the world of vampires, Your Highness."

"Aye, I see. Yes, Emery, you do."

"Why? Because August wants me to?"

She attempted to sidestep the Scottish prince but should've known better. In a battle of human against vampire, the vampire would always win.

Callum stepped in front of her, and leaned in, his breath tickling her ear. "I can't let you leave. August may be a good man, but I promised to be no such thing." His voice sent shivers down her spine. "Sorry about this, lass, but he needs you. We need you."

Before Emery could ask what he meant, Callum sank his fangs deep in her neck.

She opened her mouth to scream, but nothing came out. Her body slumped against his torso as panic tightened like a vise around her chest. The same tingling sensation she had with August crept through her, except his tickled her mind, probing gently, whereas Callum's assaulted her senses. Emery searched for his intent but found nothing. That didn't mean it wouldn't come, and when it did, all she could do was hope Callum didn't have some nefarious intent.

Her heart slammed in her chest, and it was increasingly harder to breathe. The desire to fight, scream, clawed to break free, but she was helpless and frozen in his grasp.

She was alone. Dahlia would assume she was already gone. No one would come looking for her. Not even August, who'd assume she'd left.

Emery frantically tried to remember what she'd done to override August's intent in the garden, but nothing came. She'd wanted August. Needed him on a primal level. The same could not be said for Callum.

Her body jolted against him, and a wave of shivers wracked her body.

After several long gulps, the prince abruptly pushed her away and doubled over, gagging. Without him to keep her upright, Emery landed on the floor and scooted back against the edge of the bed, watching him fight for air.

When he caught his breath, his wide eyes snapped to hers, his voice mingled surprise and awe. "I was right. You're her, you're his."

"What does that even mean? What did you do to me?" She laid her hand over her neck, where he'd assaulted her both physically and mentally. No blood oozed, but the wound was no less real.

Callum stepped fully into her room and kicked the door closed. He sped to her, scooped her up from the floor and placed her on the bed. "It doesn't matter right now, princess." She hated August's term of endearment on his tongue. "I held off as long as I could in allowing my venom to enter your bloodstream, hurry and put on the ball gown before it takes hold completely."

Emery spoke through shivers, her teeth chattering. "I-I'm not going to the b-ball."

"Yes. You are." His eyes narrowed on hers, and a half smile tipped his lips. "You can dress yourself, or I can do it for you. I can tell you which I would prefer."

Emery stared him down, weighing her options. "F-fine. But you n-need to turn a-around."

He slowly raked his eyes over her before giving her his back and walking across the room. "I'll know if you try to leave. Just put the damn dress on."

The shivering slowed and warmth returned to her core, a sign she hoped didn't mean the venom was taking hold. With each second ticking by, the thought of getting to August seemed more and more appealing. The promise of protection while she succumbed to the venom temporarily overrode her sanity. She quickly slid into the navy dress, not wanting to be unclothed with Callum for more than a moment.

Heat continued to roll through her, becoming more unbearable by the moment. Each nerve was like a fuse sparking to life, lighting a path through her body only to settle low in her belly. She felt like she'd been set on fire, and a carnal need flamed within her.

Suddenly, putting on the dress was the last thing she wanted to do. She let it drop so it pooled at her feet and she raked her hands over her bare skin. Up her arms. Along the curves of her breasts. Over her belly.

A soft moan fell from her lips as her hands sought to soothe the need within her. Like soft petals, she traced circles up her abdomen until reaching her aching breasts. She ran them over the soft lace of her bra and her nipples pebbled beneath it, begging to be pinched. Anything to release the tension within her.

"Christ, lass, you're not going to make this easy on me, are you?"

Emery narrowed her eyes, appreciating just how handsome Callum was. The way his jet black hair fell perfectly, except for the one stray lock falling in the way of his deep emerald eyes. He had the body of every bodice ripping highlander she'd ever read about. Broad. Muscular.

And because of the ball, he even wore a tartan like the men in her fantasies. She suddenly wondered if what they said was true. What might wait for her beneath it.

Emery looked up at him with sultry eyes. "Easy is overrated."

"Bloody hell. Get your dress on, lass." He sped across the room and pulled the gown from the floor.

She slipped her arms through the thin straps, running her hands over his muscled forearms as she did. "You're no fun." She stuck out a pouty lip for good measure.

"I assure you, I'm plenty of fun. Just not with what's not mine."

"I could be." She looked up at him and chewed her lower lip. "Yours, I mean."

Callum gently turned her and zipped the back of her dress. Emery stuck her ass out, knowing he would have to run his hands over it to complete his task.

"You couldn't keep up with me."

"You wanna bet?" She looked over her shoulder and gave him a wink.

Callum pulled Emery so her back was flush against his chest. His earthy scent filled her nose and tiny warning bells went off in her head. It wasn't the smell of the man she wanted, but too focused on what she wanted, she ignored them. Right then, she wanted Callum. She ground her backside against the prince, needing more of his touch, more of his everything, to stop the growing ache within her. She grabbed his hands, resting them on her waist, digging her nails into his skin and moving his hands lower.

God, she wanted him, needed him to sate the growing pressure between her thighs. Preferably with the ample cock growing against her ass. She wiggled against him again, imagining what it would be like to be filled by him.

"Don't tempt me, little witch."

Emery froze at the whispered threat. It was important he didn't know about her bloodline, but she couldn't remember why.

Callum reached for the box on the bed and opened it to reveal a simple chain with a pink, teardrop diamond hanging from it. He slung his arms around her and fastened it at her neck, completing her ensemble.

"I ache. Please help me, Your Highness." She didn't recognize the sweet and sultry voice that came out of her. It was sexy. Something she wasn't.

"Someday you'll see that I am. Let's get you to your prince." He swept her up into his arms, placing her arms around his neck. "Hold on tight."

The prince took off, running through the castle at speeds only a vampire could achieve. Emery gripped his neck and buried her face in it. She wiggled against him, trying to relieve the ache within her, but it was useless.

After their mad dash through the castle, he set her down before the double doors of the throne room. At the loss of his touch, Emery groaned and nearly doubled over, her hands involuntarily roaming her body as she tried to relieve its need for physical contact.

"I hate you," she spat, glaring daggers at the Scottish prince refusing to sate her.

Callum shrugged and smiled. "I can live with that."

"Please. Don't make me go in there. Take me. I'll do anything." The need to take him between her legs was so great she'd moved straight to begging.

"You aren't mine, lass. Though, I can't say I don't wish you were. Those little mewling sounds you made on the way down here have me standing at attention."

Emery took a step forward and wrapped her arms around the prince's neck, pressing her body to his she whispered through a moan. "I could be yours."

"Sorry, lass. You're his problem now."

With those final words, Callum pulled open the door to the throne room and pushed her inside.

Chapter Twenty Eight

AUGUST

SHE LEFT.

She actually fucking left.

August worked his fists at his sides, trying to rein in the emotions fluctuating between rage and dejection.

She wasn't supposed to leave. He wanted her to have the choice, but she wasn't supposed to actually leave.

She wasn't supposed to. She was supposed to choose him. To walk into the ball with the other Culling women and smile when he called her name. Hell, he'd have picked only her if he thought Emery would allow it. He'd told her as much the day before.

"And who is the final woman to move on?" His father's tense voice pulled him from his wallowing. He should be focused on the task at hand, picking the top five women, any of whom could potentially be his wife, but all he could focus on was the hole in his chest.

The piece Emery took with her when she walked away.

The King's eyes narrowed on August, surely suspecting he was taking his sweet ass time announcing the final name. He was. Giving Emery every opportunity to change her mind. He'd even gone so far as choosing the four women his father asked him to, just to placate him while he stalled.

Jenni, Amelia, Jessi, and Chelsea stood beside him on the dais, each staring at him wide eyed, wondering which of their Culling mates would be joining them.

August's gaze drifted over the remaining women, each hopeful they'd be chosen. He scanned until he landed on the petite blonde. He'd keep Flora, if only for the fact he'd at least have one woman left in the Culling he could stand for more than ten minutes. Where Chelsea had become tolerable since Emery befriended her, he found Flora to be a true friend.

He opened his mouth to call Flora's name when a loud bang from the back of the room startled him. Every head turned to see what the commotion was, but August didn't need to.

Emery.

His skin hummed, and her intoxicating scent hit him before he saw her. It was the sweetest blend of lavender mixed with a mulled spice he only smelled when she was aroused.

She stood at the end of the center aisle. God, she was beautiful. The velvet gown in navy blue hugged her body to perfection. Even better than it looked the day before. It was conservative and sexy, exactly what a ruler should wear.

When he finally tore his eyes away from her beautiful figure, he noticed she wasn't wearing any make up, and her hair was a tangled mess of waves framing her face. She looked like herself, not the sister she was supposed to be portraying. Normally brilliant eyes were bloodshot, and the skin beneath her eyes puffy.

Something wasn't right. Emery wouldn't show up to the ball looking as she did.

The panicked smile stretched across her face confirmed his suspicion.

The need to run to her surged within him, but with a room full of courtiers, the royal game had to be played.

"Ah, and here she is, just in time, my final pick for the top five. Miss Sloane Montgomery."

August swore he heard his father curse beside him at the same time cheers erupted from the court.

The invisible string tied between them pulled tight, and August started toward her.

His patience wavered as he walked down the aisle, but if he ran to her like he yearned to, the court elders would question his concern. Until he knew what was going on, he needed to act as though nothing was wrong.

She was visibly shaking, and her eyes held a blank stare. August gave her the slightest nod, looking toward the floor as he did, to remind her where they were.

Emery scurried to gather her gown and curtsey. He bowed in return, getting a peek at the back of her dress. She offered him her hand and he brought it to his mouth. The second his lips touched her skin, a whimper fell from her lips and she stepped toward him. His body reacted in kind, every nerve stood on end and a low growl rumbled in his chest.

But something wasn't right.

This wasn't like her. Emery didn't advertise her feelings

publicly. Didn't allow them to be so plainly written on her face.

He turned and pulled her close to him, placing his free hand on the bare skin at the small of her back. Emery leaned into his touch, her grip tightening on his hand as if it were her only lifeline. She took his arm and brushed it over her breast, releasing a soft guttural moan.

If he didn't have a million questions concerning her wellbeing, he'd push her back out the door and see how many other ways he could make her moan like that.

"Are you okay?" he whispered against her ear.

"No. I ache. I-I need." She continued to babble, none of her words making sense except that she was hurt in some way.

August looked her over again, attempting to find any sign of injury. He would kill whoever hurt her. His eyes roamed until they landed on her neck, where two tiny holes marred her flesh.

His jaw clenched so tight it was a miracle he didn't crack teeth. Someone bit her. A vampire in his court bit what was his. Not only that, but they wanted him to know they'd done it. They hadn't even attempted to heal the puncture wounds.

Emery went up on her tiptoes, grinding her body against him to reach his ear. "Make it stop," she pleaded softly, her voice a sultry breath. "Please, help me."

August tensed, filled with both rage and the undeniable need to claim her. Let every vampire in the room know she was his and anyone who touched her would die by his hand. To hell with the fucking ball. Emery was the only woman he needed. And if the state of her arousal was any indication, she needed him too.

More importantly, she needed him to help her, and he'd be damned if he didn't.

His eyes skirted the crowd, trying to find a way to get her out of there without making a spectacle of the situation. Unfortunately, his father wouldn't allow him to interrupt the night. Not with the delegation and their entire court present. He'd sooner kick Emery out of the castle than let him choose her publicly.

August reached up and fingered a lock of her hair, moving it to hide the bite marks. He pressed a kiss to her temple. "Hold on, love, I've got you. Try to fight it just a little while longer."

She nodded, but the look in her eyes told him she was losing the battle.

With every eye in the room on them, he slowly led her to the dais. With each step, Emery's arousal wafted, and he was no longer the only one who noticed. Every male in the room, and even some of the females, stared at her like she was a feast to be shared.

Bloody hell. The last thing he needed was Emery to be the cause of turning the ball into an orgy.

He needed to get her out of there. More importantly, he needed to find out what happened and help Emery through the onslaught of lust brought on by the venom. He cursed the vampire who did this to her. They must have been older than dirt if she wasn't able to override the venom as she did his.

When they reached the dais, August turned toward his court, Emery still pressed against his side. "I would like to thank each of the Culling women who are not moving forward. It has been a pleasure knowing each of you and watching you grow into amazing young women. Any man would be lucky to have you on his arm. Enjoy the ball this evening, and by morning, let your maids know your decision for the future."

A few sniffles reached his ears, a sound that would typically bother him, but Emery was his sole focus at the moment. She needed him, and that was all that mattered.

"As for the rest of you," he addressed the courtiers. "Please make your way to the Grand Hall and let the festivities begin."

The crowd shuffled toward the exit as the musicians in the corner played a lively interlude.

August looked down into Emery's pleading stare. "Come with me. We have thirty minutes before we're expected for the first dance."

She nodded and allowed him to lead her out of the throne room.

Before they could cross the threshold, his least favorite Culling woman stepped in front of them.

"Why does *she* get to enter with you, shouldn't all of your top five?" Jessi spat, glaring daggers at Emery.

"I need to have a few words with Sloane about her tardiness. I'll find you inside."

Jessi stuck out a pouty lip, and August wanted nothing more than to rip it off her smug face and watch her jaw literally hit the floor. "Fine. But I expect to receive alone time with you tonight as well."

"You are in no place to make demands, Jessi. Now, get out of my way." August pushed past her, Emery in tow.

God, how he wished he could be rid of that woman. If she wasn't his father's favorite, she would have been gone long before the ball.

Once in the royal suite, August scooped Emery into his

arms. She shifted against him, burying her face in his neck, and placed soft kisses along his sensitive flesh.

His mother entered the room behind them, eyes full of concern. "What happened to her?"

"She's been bitten. It might be too late to remove the venom, but I need to try, or at the very least, dull her needs."

His mother nodded in understanding. "I'll distract your father. Take her to my study, it will be safer there."

"Thank you."

August ran to the study, then set Emery down gently and cupped her face in his hands.

"August, I need to feel you. To feel something. I'll combust if I don't touch me right now."

As much as he shared the sentiment, lust brought on by venom was not the way to take her virginity. Especially if it wasn't his venom. Once more murder crossed his mind, but he had more important things to attend to, and vengeance would have to wait. "Bloody hell, Em. Can you turn it off? Change the venom's intent like you did with me?"

"I've been trying. I don't know how I did it or what he did to me. It feels different. Your venom was nice. This…this isn't. I feel so out of control." Tears welled in her eyes as she clawed at every part of his body she could reach. "I'm sorry. I'm so sorry."

August dropped his hands, swallowing his rage at another man touching her. "Don't apologize. This isn't your fault." He reached up and wiped away a stray tear.

"Please, help me." Her lip quivered, and he could see she was hanging on by a thread.

"I'm going to, Princess. Give me just a minute." He shrugged off his coat before moving to lock the door. It was not the moment for an interruption. He inhaled deeply in an attempt to get his anger under control, but all it did was fuel it when the only thing he could smell was Emery's arousal.

Whoever did this to her was going to pay with their life.

He turned back around just in time to watch Emery's dress pool at her feet, leaving her standing before him in only a black lace set and the pink diamond necklace he'd chosen for her.

Holy hell. That escalated quickly.

"Emery, we don't have to do this. There are other ways to negate the venom that don't require you to get naked."

She reached behind her back and undid the clasp of her bra. She wiggled out of it with grace, allowing her perfectly round breasts to bounce free. "I want you, August."

Bloody hell, she was killing his will to say no with every step she took toward him. He wanted to take her so thoroughly she wouldn't be able to walk down the stairs in the Grand Hall, but Emery deserved better. She deserved her first time to be special. She deserved more than a rushed fuck.

"Let me attempt to suck the venom out. If it doesn't help, then I'll do whatever you need to take the edge off."

Emery stopped halfway to him, and a truly wicked smile formed on her face. "I know you want this to be special because it's my first time and under all your asshole tendencies you're a gentleman. But the reality is, I need to come. I *want* to come. And if you won't help me, I'll go find the vampire who did this to me. I'm sure with a little convincing Callum would be happy to use what he's got hiding under his kilt."

Ice flooded his veins, dampening his lust. There was no way he'd heard Emery correctly because it sounded as though she named Callum as her attacker.

If Callum so much as thought about taking Emery, he'd kill him. Fuck, he'd kill him anyway for what he'd already done. His fists clenched at his sides, and he took a deep breath. Then another.

When he snapped out his rage filled haze, Emery was standing chest to chest with him, her hardened nipples grazing his shirt as she loosened his tie.

Mine.

He palmed her ass and picked her up, her legs wrapping around him as he spun and slammed her up against the closed door.

"Did he touch you?" His growl betrayed the anger simmering just below the surface, threatening to break through. Emery was his and only his.

His to touch.

His to taste.

"No." Emery pushed her hips out to rub against his length, a soft mewling noise escaping her lips. "He left me where you'd find me."

The fucking prick. Callum's actions were planned and deliberate, and at Emery's expense. His cousin better be living it up because despite his seemingly immortal status, his days were numbered.

Emery moaned, and he looked down to find her head leaned against the door while her fingers pinched her nipples.

Callum was a problem for later. Much later. Now he needed to take care of Emery. If she wanted to come, he'd satisfy her in every way possible.

August tipped her chin to meet his gaze. "I'll help you, Emery. Then, you're going to tell me exactly what happened."

She reached up and unbuttoned his dress shirt, placing kisses along his chest as she did. "Deal. Now please fuck me."

"Oh no, little Princess, I'm not going to fuck you, but you are most definitely going to come. Fast and hard."

Before she could protest, August palmed one of her breasts while the other hand slid between them, under the soft lace of her thong to cup her mound, his fingers dancing along her soaked entrance.

She moaned as he leaned in and whispered against her lips. "I have wanted you from the moment I laid eyes on you in my club. I've thought of little else since tasting you in the garden, waiting for the day I'd get the chance to taste you again. Callum may have forced my hand, but it doesn't change the fact that you, Emery Montgomery, are *mine*."

"Yes." Her words were more plea than agreement.

It wouldn't take much to push her over the edge. At least, not the first time he helped her over. She was wound so tight, she'd likely come from the slightest touch, and damn, did he want to watch her fall over the edge.

August plunged a finger into her slick folds and pressed his thumb against her already swollen nub. He rubbed tiny circles around her clit while his other hand roamed her breast. A low growl escaped his lips as he tugged her already peaked nipple, rolling it between his fingers.

She arched her back against the door, thrusting against his hand, driving him to go faster. She whimpered against his lips, her body tightening around his finger, and he imagined what it would feel like rippling around his cock.

August released her breast to tangle his hand in Emery's hair, pulling her head to the side and exposing her neck. As she rode out the waves of her climax, he sank his fangs deep into the crook of her neck.

Emery cried out, but it quickly morphed from pain to ecstasy. She moaned and tilted her head back farther as August pulled her blood into his body.

He should have warned her. Should have told her what he'd planned to do. But there was no reasoning with her so long as the venom was in her system. She didn't realize she would only regain control if he removed the venom or fucked her senseless. As much as he wanted the latter, he'd made her a promise to make her first time something she'd never forget, and he intended to make good on it.

In a good way. This was not the unforgettable he'd meant.

The moment her blood passed his lips, something snapped into place, connecting her to him in a way he'd never experienced with anyone else. He could feel her. Every bit of emotion she felt hit him in tandem with the waves of her release. It caught him off guard, the rush nearly causing him to come himself.

He tightened his jaw and took a long pull, attempting to ground himself in what he knew best. Blood. Hers fulfilled him in a way like no other. It fueled a need for more, but it was unlike his usual bloodlust. He was in control of his need to consume Emery. Her mind. Her body. Her blood. All of it was his own personal brand of heroine.

On the next pull, he was hit with crippling lust. His dick flexed, and he groaned through his swallow, struggling again to keep his own release at bay as he savored the sweetness and mulled spice of her blood.

Emery bucked against his hand, his fingers still sheathed within her, and August nearly lost his resolve with the need to bury his cock as well as his fangs. She needed him. Needed his dick to fill her and sate her arousal, and bloody hell, he wanted to give it to her. If she thought he was going to let her walk away now, she was greatly mistaken. He would never let her go. Tasting her confirmed what he already knew to be true.

Emery belonged to him.

The next pull of blood snapped the connection. It was pungent, bitter like black licorice, and tasted foul on his tongue.

Callum.

It was his venom. A growl rumbled deep in August's chest, and he sucked frantically, attempting to rid her body of the foreign substance and restore her sweetness.

"August," Emery moaned, her nails digging into his shoulder blades. She leaned forward as much as she could and buried her face in his shoulder, muffling the sound of her cries against his flesh. Her body shuddered around his fingers once more and a jolt of pain hit him the same moment another wave of release captured her body.

August took one last pull from her neck, to ensure he'd gotten it all, before releasing her. He shifted to look down at Emery, panic flooding him when her head lolled back, revealing how close she was to unconsciousness.

Bloody hell.

He'd taken too much.

He cradled her and rushed her to the sofa across the office, settling her in his lap.

Emery's eyes fluttered open, groggy as they met his. "More," she murmured, just above a whisper. Her eyes widened and fell to his shoulder, and she licked her lips. "Please, I need more."

He twisted his head, and lowered it to where she stared. August gasped when he saw she'd bitten him. Her teeth had left tiny indents where she'd clamped down. There wasn't more than a little welling of blood, but she'd definitely broken the skin. Not good.

She pushed herself up, her eyes never leaving his shoulder. August remained silent, unsure of what she wanted more of. Him or his blood. Never before had he been bitten back.

"Are you okay, Em?"

Emery placed one hand on his chest while the other wiped the fresh wound on his shoulder. She traced her index finger through the remaining blood and brought it to her lips. August's dick twitched as she placed the finger in her mouth and sucked it clean, a moan escaping her as she did.

"You taste incredible. Why do you taste incredible? Why do I want to taste more of you? What the hell is wrong with me?"

"I don't know. I've never seen a human react this way to venom. Or blood."

"Can I have more? I can't explain it, I just— I need more of you."

"Yes," he replied shakily. He'd never allowed someone to take his blood before. It was considered taboo in anything but a life-or-death situation. But he'd give Emery anything she wanted. "Here, let me." August reached up and bit his wrist, offering her the open wound. "Your teeth don't exactly break the skin easily."

She shifted, straddling him as she grabbed his wrist and wrapped her lips around the wound. Closing her eyes, she took a long pull of his blood.

An unsolicited moan started in his chest at the same

moment his eyes rolled in the back of his head. He fisted his hand, struggling to stay in control. He wanted to take her.

To feel himself inside her. The need to bury himself in her growing with every pull she took.

To claim her.

To make her his.

To fill her with his seed and let everyone know she was his queen.

All that stood between him and what he wanted were two thin scraps of fabric. Emery reached between them and pulled his tartan out of the way, taking his cock in her hands. With every small pull at his wrist, she stroked his length, chipping away at what little control he had left. He was on the edge of becoming a barbarian.

"Em, you need to stop." His voice came out low and strained as he reached between them, covering her hand around his shaft. "If you don't, I will take you. I am hanging on by a thread, and if you keep drinking from me and touching me like that, I won't hesitate to take what's mine."

Emery smiled against his wrist before she pulled away, revealing plump lips stained with his blood. A shiver shot through him, going straight to his balls. She looked sexy as hell with her lips tinted red and he could only imagine how she would look with other parts of him between them.

"August, for once, I want it to be me and you without thinking of all the reasons we shouldn't. I know them by heart, and they will still be there when we walk out that door." She dropped his wrist and lifted herself onto her knees. Moving the thin scrap of black lace to the side, she rubbed the tip of his cock over her clit before positioning him at her entrance.

A soft moan escaped him, as she teased him with her

warmth. It called to him, and he struggled to keep himself from thrusting his hips into her.

"I don't need something special, not with you. Please, let's just have this moment for us. For you and me. Then, we can worry about the rest."

He didn't have time to think about what the rest was before Emery slid down his cock, stopping before she was fully seated.

"Fuck me," she pleaded. "Make good on your promise. Show me why no other cock will satisfy me the way yours will."

August leaned forward and whispered against her ear. "I'm going to do more than show you, Emery." He rocked his hips slowly, loving the way her tight passage cradled his cock. "I'm so fucking desperate to claim you. I'm going to try to be gentle, but I need to make you mine. You need to tell me if it's too much."

"I want to feel every inch of you deep inside me, August," she panted.

August grinned against her temple. It would be his pleasure.

He reached up and tangled one hand in the hair at the base of her neck while the other found her hip. He ripped the lace of her panties and tossed it to the side, wanting to feel her bare flesh beneath his hand. Tipping her head back, he captured her mouth with his, and at the same time, he thrust upward, claiming what no other man had. What no other man would.

"Yes," she screamed, and he drank her cry into his mouth, kissing her savagely, pushing both his tongue and cock deep within her.

August stilled his movements, allowing Emery to adjust

to his length. The last thing he wanted was to hurt her. He wanted her to enjoy her first time. He wanted her to be as desperate for him as he was for her.

He savored her mouth and her warmth as she clenched around his shaft. She rocked her body forward, and August met her rhythm, letting her set the pace at first. When her movements became more erratic, he gripped her hips and slammed into her. Impaling her on his cock.

He gave himself to her with an intensity he'd not given a woman, gliding in and out, claiming her with each thrust. His gums throbbed as his fangs elongated once more. Emery was a drug. His fucking drug. The only woman who'd ever robbed him of the control he sought to maintain. His entire world, his every breath was focused on the woman in his arms.

And nothing felt more right.

"August," Emery tossed her head back, her long hair tickling his thighs. He sucked her nipple as she continued to bounce on his cock, and when he felt her tremble around him, he clamped his teeth lightly on the bud and tugged. He drove himself into her hard, fast, and deep, over and over again until he was nearly mindless with the need to claim her. To sink his fangs into her soft flesh and once again taste her essence.

Her nails dug into his shoulders where she gripped them, using them as leverage to meet his eager thrusts. "I'm so close. Give me your wrist. I need to taste you."

August stilled inside her and met her gaze, his eyes widened as he gaped at her.

"Please," she whispered, rolling her hips. "I know it's weird, but I can't stop the need to claim you."

He understood completely. Without hesitating, he bit into his wrist and brought it to Emery's lips.

She held onto his wrist as if it was her lifeline. Her eyes met his and she swung her hair to the side, offering him her neck as he tunneled in and out of her once again. "Together. We go together."

Bloody hell, she was incredible.

Emery ground against him, meeting his erratic thrusts. August's balls tightened at the same moment Emery contracted around him. Her nails dug into his arm as she sucked hard, frantically pulling his blood into her as she came undone around him. He leaned forward and sank his fangs into the crook of her neck, emptying his seed into her womb. They peaked in perfect rhythm, each shuddering contraction in unison with the steady beat of blood coursing through them.

August promised to ruin her for any other man, but the truth was she ruined him. He was fucking destroyed. No other woman would ever compare.

Emery shivered as their hips stilled and she released his wrist, trailing her tongue along the length of his hand. August sealed the marks he'd made with his venom and rested his forehead against hers, their heavy breathing the only sound in the room.

She was so beautiful.

Everything he needed.

His queen.

He would worship her every day.

A knock at the door pulled their attention from each other, and Malcolm's muffled voice reached them. "You're expected in five minutes."

Damn it.

"Thank you," he answered.

Turning his attention back to Emery, he placed a soft kiss on her lips. "I'm sorry we can't stay here a bit longer. Are you okay?"

She clenched her pussy around him. "More than. That was amazing."

August gasped. "If you keep doing that, I'm going to show you again how amazing I can be." He placed another kiss on her lips, sucking her bottom lip between his teeth as he pulled away. "It's I who should be thanking you. How are you feeling?"

"I'm—" She grew silent for a moment, and August swore he felt every emotion she did, even though her face remained stoic.

Excitement.

Worry.

Fear.

Happiness.

He'd always felt her presence in the room, but this was different. It was as if the emotions radiated from her.

"I'm happy. I'm not sure exactly what happened tonight, but for the first time in a long time, I can breathe. And now I don't feel the need to have sex with everything in sight." She smiled. "I feel good enough to kill Callum myself for what he did."

"I'll let you get in a few punches before I decapitate him."

Emery laughed, causing her to clench around him again.

"I can't believe I'm saying this, but we need to get dressed. If I stay inside you a moment longer, I'm going to take you again."

She nodded, though he could have sworn he felt sadness. He wasn't sure if he was going crazy or if she felt it too.

August concentrated on what he was feeling, sending out the hope he felt at that very moment.

Emery tilted her head, and her eyes widened, roaming over him.

"You felt that, didn't you?"

She gasped. "Why can I feel you?"

"I have no idea, but I'm not upset about it. Are you?"

She smiled, but another wave of sadness radiated from her.

"Are you okay, Em?"

"Yeah." Her gaze fell to the floor as she climbed off him. "It's just, what happens now? This doesn't change anything."

August reached for the torn panties and knelt before her, using the scrap to clean the remnants of their love making from her thighs. He leaned in and kissed her mons, memorizing the scent of her before standing to cup her face. "It changes everything. Now, you'll accompany me to the ball. We'll dance, and I'll show you off to my court. Then, I'll whisk you away to my chambers, where I intend to make good on my promise over and over again.

"But next time, I'm in control. I'm going to take my time, exploring every inch of your perfect flesh, and then I'll remind you again why I'm the only man you'll take between your legs." He paused to take a breath. "And after we're both totally and completely ruined, we'll talk about what happened here tonight at length and what our future looks like. But for now, we enjoy the ball and each other's company."

He leaned down and kissed her chastely, knowing

anything more and he'd skip the ball entirely. As much as he'd like to ignore the world and get lost in Emery, he still had a duty to his kingdom. They expected the pomp and circumstance of his Culling to play out before them, and for the first time, he didn't mind. As long as Emery was at his side.

"Okay." Emery gave a halfhearted smile and nodded. "Will you help me get dressed?"

He knew she really didn't need his help with the zipper so low on her back, but he'd take any opportunity to have his hands on her. He ran his fingers down her bare back and cupped her ass before zipping the dress. "I should apologize about your panties, but I'm not sorry you're going to have the reminder all night of what we did."

She turned and placed her hands on his chest. "I don't need to go commando to remember this, August. I could never forget."

He didn't like the distance in her voice or the regret pouring off of her.

Malcolm opened the door behind them. "Let's go, August. We can't stall any longer."

He'd have to wait to question the thoughts that plagued her. They'd have plenty of time for that later.

August brought her hands to his lips and kissed each of them. "Let's go. You're much too beautiful in that dress to keep you locked away."

Chapter Twenty-Nine

EMERY

Emery looked up at August as they waited outside the door to the Grand Hall to be announced.

He looked straight ahead, a shit-eating grin on his face. Happiness radiated from him. Her eyes widened, still mesmerized by the notion they could feel one another. It was as if they'd become one soul in separate bodies. It was both freaky as hell and comforting at the same time.

The Emery from hours ago would be freaking out, yet all she felt was a calm confidence in the bond they now shared. It didn't matter that in the last hour she'd been bitten by a vampire, succumbed to lust by venom, been bitten a second time by a different vampire, drank blood, and lost her virginity.

Holy hell, she drank August's blood.

She was so lost to him in that moment, consumed with the need to claim him. And then she'd asked for more. Not to mention she'd drank from him as they climaxed together, heightening her orgasm beyond anything she could ever imagine.

Talk about never forgetting her first time.

August was right. He'd ruined her. She'd never feel a fraction of what she felt for him with anyone else.

Not that she wanted to.

Everything changed between them the moment he'd bitten her. And yet, nothing had changed at all. She was still a witch, and he was still the crown prince of vampires. Mortal enemies destined to be on opposing sides till the end of time.

The difference was, for the first time since they'd met, she had an inkling of hope they could figure it out. Maybe Malcolm was right, and they could be what he and Sloane didn't get the chance to be.

Even if it wasn't possible, she had no doubt August and she were meant to be together.

Especially after what they'd just done in his mother's study.

Oh shit. Emery's eyes widened. Would she know what they'd done in her study?

Panic coursed through her at the thought of having to face the Queen.

August gave her hand a squeeze. "You okay? I just felt a wave of anxiety from you."

Heat flooded her cheeks. "I was just worrying about your mother knowing what we did in her study."

His mouth tugged up into a smile. "I guarantee she'll know exactly what we did in her study, as will every vampire in the room. You forget we can smell arousal."

Her mouth hung open, and she tried to take a step away

from the door. "Are you saying they can smell what we just did on us?"

August nodded.

"I can't go in there."

"Why not? You are mine, Em. Who gives a bloody fuck what anyone else thinks?"

She was his.

He was hers.

He was right.

She gave him a shaky nod, and he pressed a gentle kiss to her forehead.

"Plus, more than anything, they'll be jealous I got to see you naked."

Emery snorted as the doors to the hall opened and the steward announced them. "Introducing, His Royal Highness, Prince August Nicholson, and Sloane Montgomery, a member of the Royal Culling.

All eyes swiveled toward them as they made their way down the grand staircase. Most of the courtiers smiled and curtsied as they walked past.

August was made for the spotlight. He smiled and nodded to the members of his court, personable and approachable, yet still emanated the grace and leadership expected of their future king.

She'd never realized the weight August carried every moment of the day. And he wanted her to help him shoulder the burden, he'd said as much when he removed her mark. A pit settled in her stomach and she worried she couldn't be what his people needed. Hell, she wasn't sure she could be what *August* needed.

He had so much faith in her.

When she tasted his blood, connecting them on a visceral

level, she'd tasted his love for her. Literally. He'd never told her as much, but he didn't need to. She'd felt it. When he said she was his, he meant it with every fiber of his being. She could only hope he felt the same way once he learned of her true heritage.

When they reached the dais, Emery curtsied low while August bowed before his parents. She straightened and turned toward the remaining Culling women standing to the left of the royal family. She took one step when August tugged her back, wrapping an arm around her and pulling her to his side.

He leaned down and whispered. "Remember when I said you were mine?"

The king coughed, and the two of them turned to look at August's father, who wore an unmistakable scowl.

"How nice of you to join us, August. *Sloane*." His voice spoke the pleasantries like a king, but his glare as he emphasized the false moniker revealed he was anything but glad she was at August's side. "Now that you're here, I'd like to invite the court to join us in a toast."

The king clapped his hands and stewards flooded the hall with trays of champagne flutes. Only they weren't filled with the golden liquid she expected, instead, they were filled with blood. Following behind were scantily clad women and men shuffling in and lining the walls. Members of the court came forward, claiming them, and guiding them back to where they'd stood.

Emery, despite her new taste for August's lifeforce, had to bite back a gasp as realization came over her. Living the vampire life with August in private was one thing, signing on for this to be her life was quite another. She glanced at the other Culling women, trying to figure out if they shared her sentiments, but their well trained placid faces betrayed nothing.

From the side of the dais, a steward brought two blood filled champagne flutes followed by two women. The flutes were handed to Malcolm and the Queen. One of the women stopped before the King and the other in front of August. The king gestured for August to take the woman before him, and Emery reacted at the same time she felt August's disgust.

Waves of apprehension rolled off him as several long seconds marched by.

The King's lips curled into a sardonic smile, and Emery sensed he planned the toast on purpose.

Rage flooded her. Only a cruel man would subject his son to the addiction that plagued him, and any doubts Emery had about his nature died a swift death.

August released the tension he'd been holding and sighed, then stepped forward and reached his hand out toward the woman, his mouth set in a tight line.

Bile rose in the back of her throat. There was no guarantee August could feed from another woman and stop himself. Without so much as a second thought, she stepped forward and placed her hand in August's.

His gaze traveled up her arm until it met hers. His eyebrows drew together, and his lips titled in a frown.

"Use me."

"You're sure?" His eyes widened, and she felt a mixture of hesitation and relief flood the bond they shared.

"I'm yours, remember? Me. Only me."

August smiled and brought her hand to his lips, brushing them over her knuckles. "Thank you." he whispered.

The king glared at the two of them but didn't

acknowledge August's blatant defiance. "A toast." He raised the hand of his feeder, and every member of the court did the same with their own or the champagne flute of blood. "To my son, may the gods guide him in his endeavor to claim his bride."

"To Prince August!"

Each of the members of the court downed their glasses, or sank their fangs into the neck of their willing donor.

August pulled her in close and dipped her, then leaned in and placed a kiss on her chest, just above her heart, and whispered in the same language he'd used to release her from his Culling. He trailed his lips along her skin and placed another kiss at the base of her throat, again whispering against her flesh. With one more chaste kiss on her lips, he pulled away and looked into her eyes, whispering a final sentiment in the beautiful language.

While she didn't understand the words, they resonated in her heart.

"What did you say?"

"Forever in my heart. Forever in my veins. Forever on my lips."

"Forever," the word barely whispered through her strangled breaths.

August leaned down and licked the crook of her neck, and she felt him position his fangs. "Forever mine."

He bit down, and Emery gasped at the same moment the crowd behind her cheered. The familiar sensation of venom flooding her system overcame her. Instead of lust or calming, this time she was filled with an overwhelming eruption of happiness, causing her to smile to the point her cheeks hurt. As the wave of emotion settled, lust creeped in behind it, filling the cracks and setting her skin on fire as it trickled over her, settling in the apex of her thighs.

August took another long pull and removed his fangs from her throat, licking her wound closed as he did. When he stood her upright and met her gaze, he had a smile stretched across his face.

"You don't play fair, Your Highness."

"That's only a fraction of what I feel when you're near, Em."

"I know."

Emery gave him a sly smile. She may not have the power of venom on her side, but the connection between them went both ways. She focused on what she felt for him in the study. When the venom's lust faded, and in its place, raw unabashed love consumed her. She pushed the emotions outward, hoping he'd feel everything she experienced in that moment.

August coughed and looked at her with a raised brow. "Now who's not playing fair, Princess? You keep projecting like that, and we'll leave right now."

Emery looked over the ballroom where his court lined the dancefloor, waiting for him to lead them in the first dance as was custom. "We could, but we wouldn't want to disappoint your adoring public."

"No, we wouldn't want to do that. Dance with me?"

"Only if you promise not to laugh."

"I make no promises."

August led her to the dance floor, and Emery silently thanked Malcolm for the endless practice. They glided through the traditional dances, joined by August's parents as well as the Scottish delegation. Even Jessi's glares and exaggerated whispers, which Emery could only guess were less than flattering toward her, couldn't dampen her mood in that moment.

Callum smiled at her as he joined the festivities, and Emery glared openly while silently promising to castrate him when the opportunity presented itself.

A low growl rumbled in August's chest, and she looked up to see he was also sending death threats in Callum's direction.

Emery patted his chest. "Calm down. Remember, you promised to let me get a few punches in, and we both agreed this wasn't the time."

"Hmmmm," Was August's only reply, and Emery wasn't convinced he wouldn't kill Callum before she'd gotten a word in with the manipulative bastard.

After the final dance dedicated to the delegation, August pulled her against his chest. She tipped her head back and met his gaze. Their joy permeated the air around them, and Emery pitied the world for not being able to experience it.

August smiled and pressed a kiss to her forehead before turning to look toward the musicians in the corner. The conductor met his gaze and gave him a nod. August returned one in kind before returning his attention to Emery.

"Dance with me for just one more song, then I promise to whisk you away."

"We can't leave. You're the crown prince, your court expects you to wine and dine them tonight."

"They also expect me to secure a bride."

She placed her hands flat on his chest. "August—" They had plenty to talk about before she'd agree to be his bride. That was, if he still wanted her after he found out about what she was. She opened her mouth to protest when the familiar tune of "When a Man Loves a Woman" filled the ballroom and words failed her.

Emery looked up at him. "The song from the club."

"From the moment I saw you, I knew you were mine."

Mine.

She'd never get tired of hearing him say that. "You didn't even know if I was coming tonight."

August cupped her face. "But I hoped you would. I hoped you'd choose me."

Emery prayed he couldn't feel the guilt cloaking her. She hadn't chosen him. Not in the way he thought. August hadn't forced her into a life she didn't want, he offered her freedom, chose to release her, even though it would have killed him inside. She'd never again deny she was his.

He'd forever be her prince.

Her hand had been forced by Callum, and as much as she hated him for it, she would forever be grateful for the push in the right direction.

August leaned in, and her entire body warmed as his breath tickled her ear. "Dance with me."

Emery clung to August, and they moved as one while members of his court danced around them, waltzing to the seductive melody. He sang the words in her ear, his voice melting away the fears she clung to. In his arms, the rest of the world fell away, just as it had when they danced together at the birthday party, leaving just the two of them. A stolen moment in time.

When their song finished, a manicured hand appeared on August's shoulder, pulling him away. Jessi stepped between them and wrapped her arms around his neck.

"Mind if I cut in? You've spent all your time with *her*. I think it's only fair the rest of us get a turn." The sugary sweetness of her voice did nothing to hide the venom of her words. A venom far more dangerous than a vampire's.

Emery inhaled deeply, biting back the urge to pull Jessi off him and bitchslap her. She'd been so wrapped up in August from the moment they'd arrived at the ball, she forgot she technically wasn't the only one left in the Culling. Her naked wrist where the mark no longer sat burned far more than it ever had while the silver vines proclaimed her as his. In the eyes of his court, she might be out of the running for his hand.

August's lips tightened into a grim line.

Emery opened her mouth to assure him it was fine if he danced with Jessi, when she followed his gaze to the King, standing with a group of advisors, wearing the same grim look that marred his son's face.

"I need to speak with my father, maybe later Jessi." He turned to Emery and gave her hand a squeeze. "Go say your goodbyes to Flora. Don't leave the ball. I'll come find you when I can."

Emery nodded and faked a confident smile while pushing feelings of calm and warmth in his direction.

"That's not fair," Jessi whined, but August had already stepped away from where they stood.

Emery turned to leave when nails dug into her arm and stopped her.

"You may have his attention now, but mark my words, Sloane, he'll be mine."

Emery glared at Jessi's hand, anger flaring within her. When Emery brought her gaze to meet Jessi's, the other woman's eyes widened, and she cowered away from Emery.

"Your eyes. They're… they're glowing."

Emery clamped her eyes shut and reined in the need to fight for August. Jessi would say or do whatever it took to be the last woman standing, but she'd never have August's heart. An unexpected laugh bubbled in her throat, and she barely managed to keep it from escaping. She opened her eyes, confident they were amber once again and shrugged. "It must be a trick of the lights."

Jessi took a step back, and her voice wavered. "I know what I saw."

"You saw August claim me in front of his entire court. At the end of the day, Jessi, you can tell yourself whatever you need to sleep at night. But August is a grown man, and he's already made his choice."

"We'll see who ends up at his side." She turned and stomped off to where Scarlett and Amelia stood.

Emery shrugged off Jessi's declaration, feeling nothing but pity for her. She only hoped Jessi wouldn't go blabbing to anyone who would listen about her glowing eyes. They were becoming harder to conceal, and she would be as good as dead if any vampire happened to turn her way during an episode. Even August wouldn't be able to save her.

The sight of Flora and Chelsea standing next to the buffet caught her eye. She took two steps toward them when Callum's looming figure blocked her path.

"Dance with me?"

"I'd rather gouge my eyes out."

"It would be an insult for the prince's favorite to refuse his cousin. And I promise to be on my best behavior."

Emery hesitated, but then placed her hand in Callum's and allowed him to lead her to the center of the room. The last thing she needed was to cause a scene. A scene that could likely end with August coming back and committing murder.

"You're lucky we aren't alone, or I'd kill you."

"I believe you'd try. Listen, I—" Callum pulled her closer and inhaled a deep breath.

"Did you just sniff me?" Maybe she needed to reconsider joining this family.

His eyes widened, and a half smile tugged at his lips. "You've had his blood."

Emery snapped her eyes to his. "How did you know that?"

"Your scent. It's different. It's yours, but now mingled with his. I didn't think you'd complete the bond so quickly."

"Bond?" Is that why she could feel August's emotions? Even from across the room, she could feel his anger on the edges of her mind. "You knew this would happen?"

"Why do you think I ensured your attendance? You and August are part of something bigger than yourselves." A passion filtered into his voice, and there was an edge to it that wasn't there before. "You'll change everything."

Before Emery could ask what he meant, Callum was torn from her and August held him by the collar.

"What the hell do you think you're doing with her?" August growled, and for a split-second, Emery feared for Callum's life.

"Nothing, cousin. I was just welcoming her to the family."

"Like you welcomed her earlier?"

Emery placed an arm on his bicep, willing him to calm down. Those dancing around them had stopped and were beginning to form a circle around the three of them. "You're causing a scene, *my* prince."

August shoved Callum back and immediately pulled Emery into his arms. "He didn't hurt you, did he?"

"No, I'm fine." Emery snuggled into him, her eyes narrowed on Callum. "What did you mean that we're part of something bigger?"

Callum shrugged. "You'll see. Tell him, though, he'll understand if you give him the chance."

"Tell me what?" August looked between her and Callum.

Emery gripped him tighter, her wish for Callum's death growing each time he opened his mouth. She had to tell August what she was, having a life with him meant being honest with him, but she was terrified of his reaction. What they shared was incredible. Something out of fairy tales. She wasn't afraid of the backlash from his kingdom as long as August was at her side. She wanted to believe Callum was right, and he'd see beyond her heritage, but she wasn't convinced he could look beyond his prejudice.

She turned to face August and looked up into his narrowed eyes. "We need to talk."

"We do," he nodded. "But right now, I need you to go with Malcolm and allow him to take you to my chambers. There's been an incident outside the castle perimeter. I need to go investigate, and I won't be able to concentrate unless I know you're safe."

Emery nodded. At least it would give her a moment to consider how to tell him.

He leaned down and placed a kiss on her forehead. "Mine."

"Yours." She whispered in return, inhaling deeply and filling herself with him before he left.

He turned toward Callum. "You're with me. You better hope I don't kill you on the way."

Callum chuckled. "I'm older than you, I'll take my chances."

August and Callum made their way out of the hall, and Malcolm appeared, offering Emery his arm. "Shall we?"

Emery placed her hand in the crook of his elbow and allowed him to lead her out of the grand ballroom. "You going to tell me what happened with Callum? Or why you arrived late to the ceremony smelling of a whore needing to get her fill?"

Emery winced, hating the echo in the stone hallways. "I'd rather not. August already wants to kill your cousin, I wouldn't want you jumping on that train as well." After her brief conversation with Callum, she didn't think he did it with the intention of harming her. That didn't mean she'd forgiven him, but he didn't deserve to die.

Maybe just get his fangs knocked out.

"Fine. Keep your secrets, August will just fill me in later. Speaking of my brother, I saw the little show you two put on. You seem to be on good terms again."

She shrugged and smiled, remembering the way he'd claimed her in the study, then again in front of his court. "I was forced to stop fighting what I thought I wanted and embrace what I needed."

"I've never seen him smile so much. Or blatantly disregard an order put forth by my father."

"I wasn't about to let him take the vein of a stranger, not when it would cause him to lose control."

"He told you?"

She nodded.

Malcolm leaned toward her and sniffed.

"What is it with everyone and sniffing me?"

His brow furrowed. "Em, why do you smell like him? It's more than just on your clothes. Your essence has changed."

"I... We..." Emery paused, unsure how much she should tell Malcolm. She didn't think he would judge her, but she didn't know the protocol on vampires and humans. She'd learned vampires sometimes shared blood during sex but giving blood to a human was another matter. "I bit him. I assume I smell like him because his blood is in my veins."

Malcolm stopped walking and stared at her with wide eyes. "Wow. Um." He stumbled over his words and then paused completely. "That's completely unheard of. It's an intimate act most vampires wouldn't partake in, especially with a human. Not even a human, a witch."

Heat flooded her cheeks, and she averted her eyes from Malcolm's questioning stare.

"Holy hell." He reached up and raked a hand through his hair. "Did you tell him?"

"Not yet. I tried, but he said he had to go, and I had to go with you."

"He claimed you in front of the entire court. *You* need to be the one to tell him before he finds out from someone else."

"He didn't claim me, but he definitely made it known I'm the front runner."

"No, Em, he did. The words he spoke when he kissed you on your chest, your lips, and your neck, those were the vows every vampire makes when they've found their bride. He may not have put a ring on your finger, but he made it known to our kingdom you're it."

Holy shit.

She knew that's how August felt, but she had no idea

he'd gone and told the entire court she was it. They hadn't talked yet. They'd agreed to talk. And have more mind blowing sex. But mostly, they needed to talk.

"I have to find him, Malcolm. I have to tell him." She turned to walk away when Malcolm's hand caught her.

"There is nothing you can do right now. He needs to know you're safe. He'll return when he's finished."

"What if he hates me when he finds out?" She whispered the words, afraid saying them too loud would give them life.

"He won't. He may fly off the handle at first, but ultimately, I see the love he has for you. He needs you."

Malcolm turned and walked down the hallway to the royal residence and, though Emery's feet moved to follow him, her thoughts were a million miles away.

"Here's August's suite. If you need anything, there's a phone in the sitting area. Clovis will get you whatever you need." He paused and took a deep breath. "Don't worry, Emery. It will all work out."

"Yeah." Emery slipped through the door to August's room, unable to focus on anything but finding the words to tell August she was a witch. When he returned, he'd either accept her for the witch she was, or he'd break her heart as well as her neck.

They both seemed equally likely.

Chapter Thirty

AUGUST

He should be inside the damn castle adoring every inch of Emery's perfect body, but instead he was trudging through a dense patch of forest toward a dead one.

Not at all how he wanted to spend his evening.

Memories of his night with Emery played through his mind. It wasn't what he expected. He'd have been happy if she'd just shown up, but she'd done so much more than that. Trusting him to help her through the venom, allowing him to claim her. Hell, she'd claimed him right back. Demanding his essence fill her as she drank him in. He never imagined he'd share something as intimate as his blood with a woman, but she wasn't just any woman. The connection they shared deepened to a point he'd never let her walk away. Hell, walking away from her moments ago had been—

He paused mid-thought, realization stopping him in his tracks. He walked away from her, and there were no pangs of hunger. No need to tear into a vein. He'd walked away, but still felt as though she was standing next to him, calming the monster within.

"You okay?" Callum stared at him from a few yards ahead.

"What?"

"You just stopped walking and got this stunned look on your face. Almost like you finally believed I wasn't trying to hurt Sloane and were reconsidering killing me."

Leave it to Callum to make everything about him. "The only thing I'm considering with regards to your death is the method."

If Emery hadn't stopped him in the ballroom, his cousin would likely have a chair leg through his heart, or at the very least a black eye. Or two. Probably a busted lip as well. There was no way he was letting Callum off easy after what he'd done.

Callum gave a shrug. "We'll see. Either way, I'm sorry you got pulled away for this."

August squared up with Callum. "That's what you're sorry for? That I had to leave a ball neither of us wanted to attend? Not that you attacked Sloane and sent her into a room full of vampires smelling like she was seconds away from climaxing."

His cousin huffed a laugh. "She showed up, though, didn't she? I found her with bags packed, and one foot out the door. Anyone can see the two of you are made for one another, she just needed a push to see it."

The image of Emery packed and ready to leave was a sucker punch to his gut, and all too easy to believe. Maybe she hadn't chosen him. Maybe it was the venom. "She was going to leave?"

"Looked like it to me. But the important thing is, she didn't. She chose you. Allowed you to claim her in front of your entire court. You'll do great things with her at your side. That is, if you stop playing your father's game."

August clenched his jaw. "I'm not *playing* his game."

"Aren't you?" Callum arched brow, and a smug smile tugged at his lips. "Three of the five women that remain in your Culling are because he chose them. You walked away from the woman you claimed tonight to do his bidding. I'd venture to say if he said jump, you'd answer with 'how high?'"

"It's my duty to protect my kingdom. That's why I'm out here. Not that you'd know a thing about that."

In the blink of an eye, Callum stood nose to nose with August, who puffed out his chest and refused to back down. "Hold your tongue, little cousin. There is so much you have yet to learn about the world around you. Lies that run deep. I'm doing more than you could ever imagine to ensure the future of our people. I'd give up everything. Can you say the same?"

"You know I would."

"Even Emery?"

Her true name on Callum's lips caused something inside August to snap. His fist met his cousin's face, knocking Callum to the ground. "How do you know her name? Did you have something to do with Sloane's death?"

Callum jumped to his feet and wiped away the blood at the corner of his lip. "It wounds me you think I'd kill a woman." He sprang forward tackling August to the ground.

He took two good punches to the gut before August was able to swing his legs up around Callum's shoulders. He used his calves as leverage around Callum's neck and brought his cousin crashing down into the dirt.

The two of them rolled through the mud, scrambling for the upper hand. August landed an elbow to Callum's ribs, followed by a punch to the stomach, which gave him the time to recover. He stood and readied himself for Callum to come at him again.

"It wouldn't be the first time," August huffed between panted breaths. "It's what we are, Callum, killers. They are our prey, and I have no doubts you'd do whatever it took to further your agenda."

"You're right." Callum stood, a sardonic smile twisted upon his lips. "There will always be casualties in war."

"We aren't at war. Sloane did not deserve to die."

"Yet, cousin. We aren't at war yet."

Silence hung between them as Callum's last words echoed in August's mind. He didn't want to go to war, but if that's what it took to ensure the safety of his kingdom, of Emery, then he would. He'd slaughter any enemy that threatened her.

A soft cough pulled their attention back to the direction they'd been traveling. "Are you two quite finished?"

Lilyana stood fifty yards away from them with her hands on her hips and eyes narrowed.

August stood, pushing Callum back to the ground as he did, and started toward Lilyana. She was standing over the body they'd been sent to investigate. He looked down, and his stomach dropped enough he almost had to look away.

It was one of the vampires that frequented his club. She showed up at the club years ago, looking for a safe place to hunt. Over time, she'd fallen in love with the music and even met her partner there. Her wife was going to be heartbroken.

If the wife was even alive.

He squatted next to the body, careful not to get too close. Her head was cocked at an awkward angle, exposing where her throat should have been. Only it had been torn out, leaving her spine visible. Her arms were placed over her abdomen, as if they could hide the gaping hole where her entrails hung outside her body. Absent was the blood that should have surrounded her corpse indicating she's been moved.

Moved to this exact spot. It all but proved this was a message to his family. He wasn't sure what the message was, but he doubted this would be the last body to make its way to the castle.

His father seemed to think it was the work of a vampire, but if it was, they'd either been sloppy or just plain sadistic with no regard for the code of secrecy they had to live by to be among humans.

It wouldn't be the first time in history.

And it likely wouldn't be the last.

August winced. He'd been that sadistic once. Lost in the rage brought on by bloodlust. Malcolm barely managed to keep his killing spree a secret, following him and cleaning up his victims. Though, he'd never taken it as far as their killer. August tore through throats with little regard for the bodies he left behind, but he didn't eviscerate them.

The other noticeable attribute that set the body apart from a typical vampire in the throes of bloodlust was glowing silver magic hovering along the wounds. It moved along the jagged flesh, shimmering like a diamond in sunlight. If he didn't know it was magic from a witch, August might say it was beautiful.

Callum released a breath as he moved to stand by August. "What are you doing here, Lilyana? This is no sight for a woman."

"You two know each other?" It made sense given they were connected through Kipton.

"We do." Lilyana nodded in his cousin's direction, a knowing smile on Callum's face. "As to why I'm here, the King sent for me, asking that I meet you here to ascertain the origins of the magic on the body."

"And?"

Lilyana knelt down beside the body and reached her hands over the wounds. Tilting her head toward the sky, she closed her eyes and whispered words he didn't understand.

Callum gasped and August took a step back, as the silver magic grew in brightness and shifted, pooling under her hands. It remained stagnant for a moment before it rose and wrapped itself around Lilyana's wrist, much like the magic from the witch's vow to August. It danced along her skin and then seeped within her and disappeared.

Lilyana bit her lip, muffling a cry as a single tear fell down her cheek. For a split-second, August's breath caught, and he warred with the need to help her. Then, he remembered that whatever Lily was doing could help him protect his kingdom. The pain of one witch was worth saving the lives of many.

Callum rushed to her side.

"Don't touch her," August cautioned. The last thing he needed was Callum falling prey to some sort of magical transfer.

"Lilyana, stop this," Callum pleaded. "If it pains you, don't take it within you."

August watched silently, his muscles tense, ready for whatever might happen next.

Once Lilyana absorbed the magic from the body, she slumped back on her knees and looked to Callum. "I'm fine."

"What just happened?"

"The magic needed somewhere to go, so I became it's vessel."

August took a step back, and his fangs elongated, ready to take Lilyana out if necessary. "Are you now filled with its evil?"

She huffed a laugh. "No. Magic doesn't work that way. It isn't inherently evil. The witches who wield it may be, but magic is pure. It's a living entity and will always seek a vessel to return to. If it doesn't find one, it returns to the earth."

That explained why the magic disappeared on the bodies found in the city before they could study it.

Lily rubbed her hands over her forearms where the magic had entered her. "Most witches will absorb their own magic residue after casting, allowing it to continue powering them. Whoever cast the spell on this body was either sloppy or they didn't have control of the magic used."

"Can you tell who cast it?"

Lilyana shook her head. "If I recognized the signature of the witch, yes, but this magic is different. It was cast by a witch, but at the same time not. I'll have to do some research, but I can tell you it's unlike anything I've ever seen before."

"Of course, it is." He was hoping for a win. For something to point him in the right direction, an answer, or at least a clue, for once. He was no closer to discovering who was murdering vampires than he was to finding Sloane's killer. August sighed and raked a hand through his hair. "Thank you for helping us, Lilyana."

She gave a small bow, her eyes never leaving August's. "I wasn't doing anything productive, and this gave me a chance to be useful."

Lie.

He was sure Callum could sense it too. Though, Callum didn't know Lilyana had been at the ball all evening with them, searching for a witch. Her words said she hadn't been successful, but her body told him otherwise.

He arched a brow. "We'll be in contact soon to discuss your research." She was hiding something, and he had no intention of letting her.

"Of course, Your Highness."

August turned to Callum. "Can you wait here until Malcolm arrives with a way to transport the body back to the castle?"

Callum nodded. "Lily, would you like to wait with me?"

Lilyana's face paled. "No, I should go." She turned on her heel and hurried into the forest toward her cottage.

Her reaction struck him as odd, but August didn't have time to stand here and question the witch's actions. He needed to get back to the castle and brief his father so he could return to Emery. He'd been away from her too long, and his body thrummed with the need to be near her.

As if on cue, his dick throbbed, and August imagined how he'd find her in his room, waiting on his bed for him to make good on his promises. He turned without another word and raced toward the castle.

Music and laughter echoed through the halls as the ball

raged on. It almost comforted him to know his people were enjoying themselves, unaware of the dangers that lurked outside their walls. Almost. He couldn't ignore the nagging feeling they were on the verge of something that would change everything.

Upon entering the war room, five pairs of eyes narrowed on him, the most prominent being his father's. The rest belonged to King's closest advisors. Stuffy old vampires who'd followed his father for centuries like hounds looking for scraps. August wasn't sure he'd even call them advisors considering they rarely advised his father on anything. Their only purpose was to agree with everything the king said.

They stood around a map of the greater Chicago area with markers for the locations of every similar death. Twenty-one in total, focused mostly in the district his club was in.

"Thank you for joining us, son. What did you learn from the body outside the castle?"

"The body was moved there, no blood on the forest floor beneath it means the murder occurred somewhere else." What that meant, he still wasn't sure and couldn't begin to venture a guess. "As for the magic, Lilyana confirmed it was witch magic surrounding the wounds."

"That's not exactly what she said," Callum interjected. "She said it was witch magic unlike anything she'd ever seen before. Someone other than the coven could be responsible."

The room erupted in a chorus of disagreements. No one, including August, believed the coven wasn't involved. They'd love nothing more than to get rid of vampires in their territory.

The king held up his hands, and the room grew quiet. "There is no doubt the witches are somehow involved. There have been too many coincidences as of late, and I'm inclined to believe they're planning something. The lives of twenty-one vampires have been cut short. I don't care who's responsible, that's twenty-one too many. The most likely perpetrator is the witches, therefore, I'd like for you all to start making plans to launch an offensive attack against the coven."

"But—" Callum stepped forward but halted when the king cut him off.

"I've made my decision, Callum." His father slammed his fists down on the table sending the markers flying from the map. "This is a matter of my kingdom. If I'd like your input, I'll ask for it."

Callum shook his head before storming from the room, mumbling profanities under his breath.

"Son, would you like to help with our preparations?"

Without hesitation August stepped up to the table and began assessing the options in front of him. It was the first time his father included him in any major plans for the kingdom, and August would not let him down. Not only that, but keeping the witches at bay would keep Emery safe. And that was his number one priority. He couldn't lose her. Not after she'd claimed him.

Not ever.

Chapter Thirty One

EMERY

Emery startled awake, sitting up and clutching the soft blanket with one hand while the other reached up and felt her neck. Her eyes darted around the room, trying to determine if she was truly awake or still in her nightmare.

She relaxed on finding her throat intact, but the phantom pains of a hundred fangs piercing her still lingered on her flesh. Her punishment for what she was.

Her fingers wrapped around the necklace August delivered with her dress, and she released the death grip on the blanket. Her panted breaths slowed as memories from the night before pushed out the horrid visions from her nightmares.

A hint of a smile tugged at her lips. Sometimes fangs were pleasurable. Especially when they were attached to the real version of the blonde haired, ocean eyed vampire from her dreams.

There was no telling how August would react to her

heritage, but he loved her. He hadn't outright said it, and neither had she, but there was no mistaking the feeling that flooded the bond they shared. She had no doubt they were meant to be together.

It didn't mean they would be, but she had hope. Everything depended on how August handled her confession.

"Emery, are you okay?"

She hadn't noticed August emerge from the bathroom, and she took a moment to appreciate the view. He was clad in only a towel, which hung dangerously low on his hips. Emery licked her lips, momentarily forgetting he'd asked her a question.

"Em?"

"Yeah, I'm fine. Just had a bad dream." She raked her eyes over him, drinking in every ounce of his body. Beads of water pearled and fell between the ripples of his abdomen, begging her to lick every one off until she'd quenched the insatiable thirst plaguing her

When her eyes reached his again, his piercing gaze was paired with a seductive smirk.

"Well, I've been living through a nightmare as well. I've yet to see you naked since last night, and that, Princess, is a fate worse than death. Although I must say, I do like the lust I'm feeling from you paired with the sight of you in my shirt."

Emery looked down at the shirt, the one she'd forgotten she put on. She liked the way it smelled of him. Like sandalwood and pine.

The weight of his heated stare mixed with the waves of desire rolling off him sent a jolt of electricity through her, landing in her lower belly. She should be focused on having the long overdue conversation with him of her heritage, but all she could think of was ripping the towel from him and reacquainting herself with his dick.

At the same time, he took a step toward her, she threw the blanket away and jumped from the bed to meet August halfway, crashing her mouth against his. The conversation could wait, and he'd be in a better mood after sex, anyway.

There was nothing soft about their kiss. It was filled with passion and need. Raw. Carnal. It tasted of the desperation filling the air around them.

August tangled one hand in her hair, pulling it and sending pain shooting from her scalp to her core. The other wrapped around her, grabbing her ass and lifting her, giving her room to wrap her legs around his waist and grind herself against his erection. The rough towel provided an amazing friction right where she needed it, and a low moan escaped as she pressed her breasts into his chest.

August smiled against her lips as he rocked her up and down, teasing her exposed flesh with his growing length. He sent vibrations through her body as a growl rolled through him, and he deepened the kiss.

Emery was lost in him.

And she didn't know if she wanted to be found.

She ground her hips against his shaft, stoking the fire burning low in her belly and sent the towel to the floor. The tip of his cock teased her entrance, and his hands tightened on her ass as he rocked her back and forth, slipping himself through her slick folds. Emery throbbed with need, wanting nothing more than to sink down until he was fully seated inside her.

August released her lips and pressed his forehead to hers. "As much as I'd love to push you up against that wall and take you hard and fast," he reached up and traced his thumb over her bottom lip, "I promised to take my time with you. And I'm a man of my word."

She swallowed hard when he unwrapped her legs from his waist and slid her down his body, his erection hard between them. His hands gripped her shirt and pulled it up over her head, tossing it on the nearby chaise.

"You're not too sore, are you?" Rather than throw her onto the bed, like she wanted, he cupped her cheeks gently and concern creased his brow.

"I'm fine." In truth she was a bit sore, but not enough to stop her from taking him till morning.

Her body hummed in agreement.

He leaned down until his lips brushed her cheek, until his mouth was dangerously close to her throat. "Liar."

"Doesn't mean I don't want you." Her answer was a whisper as she dropped to her knees before him. She'd show him just how much she wanted him. She reached up, wrapped her hand around August's cock and traced the tip with her tongue.

August sucked in a hiss, as Emery took him in her mouth and exhaled a groan. The sweet and salty taste of him rolled over her tongue as she worked in unison with her hand. A tender touch ran down the side of her face and snaked into hair, fisting in it. He didn't push initially, but as she ran her tongue along the velvet underside of his dick, his grip tightened, holding her steady as he thrust his hips forward.

Emery hummed around his cock as he continued to roll his hips, pushing himself farther and farther into her mouth each time.

He tipped his head back and growled. "Bloody hell, Emery. You're incredible. I've dreamed of this since I laid eyes on your pretty pink lips."

She peered up at him, savoring the lust and desire that permeated the air around them. She loved having him in her mouth. Could live on the soft groans escaping his lips as she pleasured him.

Gripping the back of his thighs, Emery continued sucking and licking as August pushed himself in and out of her mouth. The air around them grew thick, and the energy coming from August changed, charging like a tsunami approaching the shore.

"Emery, I'm going to—"

She didn't let him finish his statement. Her nails dug into his flesh as she inhaled and pulled his hips forward taking as much of him as she could. August growled, and with one final thrust, his seed warmed the back of her throat at the same moment the waves crashed down around her.

He slipped from her mouth, and Emery sat back on her heels, a satisfied smile etched on her face as she caught her breath.

August scooped her up and pressed a kiss on her forehead as she placed a hand against his chest. The rapid beat of his heart in his chest mirrored hers, as did his labored breaths. "I don't know where you learned to do that, but I'm pretty sure I've forgotten my name."

"Mine." She gave him a lazy smile. "Your name is mine."

"Funny, I thought that was your name." August chuckled as he tossed her onto the downy comforter and shoved her thighs apart. "As much as I loved watching your mouth around my cock, now I want to feel your heat clenched around me. The taste of your blood as I come in your drenched pussy."

"Yes," Emery mewled as her pulse skyrocketed.

He trailed soft kisses up her thighs, his breath hot on her skin. It fanned her mound, teasing, but never granted the attention she yearned for.

Her hips lifted, gaining a mind of their own in their bid to push her clit toward August's mouth. He growled and sucked on the swollen bud, until Emery cried out, a mix of pain and pleasure coursing through her as he raked his teeth over the tiny bundle of nerves. "This is mine." August released her and pushed up over her to caress her neck with the tips of his fangs. "This is mine." He trailed lower, skimming the tops of her breasts with his lips. "These are mine." He sucked her nipple between his teeth and pulled away gently, stretching the sensitive peak. Emery moaned as the pathway between her nipples and clit sizzled with need. She barely managed to catch her breath before August repeated the process on her other breast.

"Please, August."

"What do you want me to do, Emery?" His uncharacteristic playful tone undid her, more than the emptiness she felt when he pulled his body away from hers, waiting for her reply.

She swallowed hard, needing more than just his touch. "I want you to ruin me. I want you to remind me why no other man could ever take your place."

"It would be my pleasure."

In a single thrust, August seated himself within her, and she clenched around him, adjusting to his girth. "Fuck you're so tight."

Emery gasped. She needed him to move. Needed the

friction only he could provide. She reached up and dug her nails into his shoulders, using the little leverage she gained to rock her hips against him.

August pressed her down into the mattress, halting her movements. "Oh no, Princess, you are mine this time. I make the rules."

August pulled her hands from his shoulders and gathered them in one of his, pushing them above her head. He pressed a kiss to her lips, sucking her bottom lip between his elongated fang. Applying a small amount of pressure, he nicked the sensitive flesh and sucked. "Gods, you taste as incredible as you feel."

She moaned, the coppery taste of her blood dancing on her tongue mixed with a trace amount of August's caramel sweet venom. It tingled as it seeped within her, fueling her need.

Slowly, August pulled himself from her, and when she thought he might pull out completely, he thrust back in. He shifted, angling his hips as he pistoned in and out of her, hitting the deepest part of her while grinding against her clit.

Her cries grew with his quickening pace, each stroke of his cock stoking the fire within her. She lifted her hips from the bed, and her body jerked on the edge of release.

August released her hands and bit his wrist, pressing it against her mouth. The moment his blood hit her lips a wave of pleasure crashed over her, vibrating through her. She dug her nails into his arm, taking long pulls of his life force as her orgasm destroyed her, drowning her in bliss.

Seconds passed and August growled, slamming his cock deep within her. He buried his face in her neck, piercing her with his fangs, as his own release took him and pushed her over the edge once more.

Together they rode the waves of their union, until they both collapsed, a tangled mess of limbs.

Emery shivered when August licked the wounds on her neck, sealing them. He rolled over and pulled her to rest on his chest. "Mine," he whispered.

"Yours."

"I'm never letting you leave."

"You claimed me, not only here," she moved her hand to her heart, "but in front of your court."

"I did. And I'll do it again. Every day for the rest of our lives."

Emery stilled against him, and her heart raced. The need to be honest with August pierced through the post sex bliss she yearned to hold on to.

"I can feel your anxiety, Emery. I'm not going to ask you to marry me tomorrow. I know we have things to discuss, but make no mistake. You're mine, and I'll do whatever it takes to keep you and to prove to you that I am the man you deserve."

He pulled her on top of him, so she stared into his eyes. Eyes that held so much love and confidence. "What's worrying you, Em?"

"There are things about me that once you know them, I'm afraid you won't be able to see me the way you do right now."

"I want to know everything about you. Every memory you hold dear. Every dream you have for the future."

His declaration mixed with the devotion he sent through their bond warred with the fear she'd worn as armor her entire life. "My life before the castle was nothing special. It was just me and Ada, but like I told you before, she held no love for me. I did what I had to in order to get by. Sure, I had a best friend, and an uncle who tried to help where he could, but mostly I was alone."

August wiped a stray tear from the side of her face. "I'm so sorry, Emery. What happened to your parents?"

"My father was never a part of our lives, and my mother died not long after Sloane and I were born. She was run off the road by a drunk driver. Sloane was all I had left of my real family. Until she was taken."

"Taken by me." He tried to pull away from her, but Emery held on tight to him. She needed him close, needed to feel him in order to work up the courage to continue toward her inevitable confession.

"It's not your fault, August. The requirements for the Culling go beyond your family. I assume it's how it's always been for the Montgomerys. Actually, I don't even know if it's my mother or father's line that has the bloodline for the Culling, Ada never told me."

"We can find out if you'd like."

"It doesn't matter." She craned her head up and attempted to smiled. The last thing she wanted was him delving into her family tree. "All that matters is I ended up exactly where I was meant to be. I was only beginning to figure out who I was and what I wanted for the future when the mark appeared. I was thrust into a world I never expected to be a part of, one I thought I knew about, but I'm learning I didn't know at all. You were never part of my plans, but now I can't imagine a world without you in it."

August reached up and cupped her face. "I'll always be here, Emery. By your side."

This should have been when she told him her darkest

secret. But she couldn't bring herself to ruin this perfect moment. At least not yet. She needed him to look at her like he was her world for just a little bit longer before she shattered it. "What about you? I know your family history, but I know next to nothing about you."

August chuckled. "Well, I was born in the Scottish Highlands."

"Wow," She whispered, picturing him in the hills of Scotland. Tall. Strong. Dressed in his tartan. "They're beautiful."

"You've been?"

"It was one of the first places Wren and I went on our tour of Europe. I fell in love the moment we arrived."

August trailed his fingers down her spine as he spoke. "It's an incredible place. Rich in history and beauty. But history doesn't tell of the vampires of Scotland. The British Monarchy may have become the rulers in the human world, but as you know, the ruling vampire family of the isle resides in Edinburgh."

"King Lachlan."

"Growing up, my father was the spare. We lived just outside Inverness until my uncle asked my father to join the English in their quest to claim the Americas."

"So, your family is the Columbus of vampires?"

"Columbus didn't discover the Americas, Emery."

"I know that." She shrugged against him. "I was just testing you."

August's chest shook with laughter, and Emery drank in the image of the carefree man before her. Desire built within her once more, and she pushed herself up, straddling him.

His eyes smoldered, as she ran her hand over his chest, "I

knew you were a Scotsman, but I'd be lying if I didn't say I wish you kept more of your brogue. I might find it sexy."

"Two hundred years may have weakened my accent a bit, but never doubt I'm a Scot at heart."

In one swift motion, he flipped them, so his body was hovering over hers. Trapped between his hands, he leaned down and placed a soft kiss to her lips. When he pulled away, his nearly invisible accent gave way to the thick brogue she'd asked for.

"You're right to love the Highlands, lass. Fields of purple heather as far as the eye can see. Breathtaking mountain peaks that seem to bring the heavens to earth. Lochs with glittering surfaces holding ancient mythical secrets within their depths. Aye, I dream of showing you my homeland. But first, I intend to make you mi'own. Doona think a bonnie lass such as yerself can escape me. A woman has never belonged to a man more than you do me. Not because I aim tae own you. Oh, no, lass, you're wild as the golden eagle that soars through mi heart's home. I never want tae harness ya. You are mine because of the man I want tae be when I am with ya. I never want to cease being that man.

"Let me show you the Highlands. Let me love you. I am yours forever, lass."

Emery's lips trembled and her heart constricted in her chest. She'd love to make a joke about how she'd let him if he promised to wear a kilt with nothing underneath. Anything witty or funny to subdue the panic running through her.

August loved her.

He'd claimed her.

He'd all but put a ring on her finger.

And she was about to destroy the picture perfect image he had of her.

She placed a hand on his shoulder and gently pushed him off her. Once they were both sitting up, she took his hands in hers and inhaled deeply, trying to muster up every bit of confidence within her. "August, I'm—"

Before Emery could push the confession past her lips, a loud bang exploded through the castle, shaking the walls around them.

Her eyes widened, and faster than she could blink, August pressed her into the mattress and curled his body around hers.

"What was that?"

August twisted his torso to survey the room. "I don't know, but I need to go investigate. Stay here."

The phone across the room rang, and he sped to answer it. "What happened?" he roared.

His jaw tightened as he listened to the caller, and anger flooded the bond between them. "The Culling wing? Is anyone hurt?"

Panic flooded Emery's system. She slid off the bed and into one of August's shirts and a pair of sweats that were far too large for her.

By the time she'd dressed, August was off the phone and dressing himself.

"Is everyone okay?"

August continued dressing, ignoring her question.

"August. Is. Everyone. Okay."

"You need to stay here." The panic rolling off him scared her nearly as much as his avoidance.

"Who's hurt?"

His voice lowered, and he pleaded for her compliance. "Please, Emery. I'll be back soon, and I'll fill you in."

Emery dug her heels in. There was no way he was going to cut her out. Not this time. Not after what they just shared. "August, I swear if you walk out that door without telling me who's hurt, I won't be here when you return. What happened to being in this together, sharing the burden?"

"You're right." He raked a hand through his hair and sighed. "It's Chelsea. She's dead."

Chapter Thirty Two

EMERY

No.

Emery clutched her chest, swallowing the bile rising in her throat.

Chelsea couldn't be dead. Not the sweet lively woman who spoke a million miles a minute. The one Emery watched flourish into a woman with dreams beyond the Culling. Who'd become a sister to her. Chelsea promised they'd navigate the world of vampires together.

She couldn't be gone.

She met August's eyes, a sea of calm. If it weren't for the slight tightening of his jaw, she'd never know they'd just received the awful news.

His calm was unnerving.

Chelsea was dead.

She was in his Culling. He was supposed to take care of

her. Keep her safe. Keep all of them safe. But two of them were dead. Both of whom she considered sisters.

August took a step toward her, but she retreated a few steps back.

Emery turned to pace, needing to do something to quiet her racing mind. It didn't settle her, though. It only made her more anxious. She fisted and relaxed her hands repeatedly as images of Chelsea dying in a fiery explosion flooded her thoughts. Were any of the other Culling women hurt as well?

All air left her lungs as panic gripped her. Emery, Flora, and Chelsea had a tradition of staying the night together after eliminations. Was Flora dead too?

Without another word, she tore from the room, running as fast as her legs would carry her. Her bare feet slammed against the stone floor in unison with the mantra in her head.

Chelsea's dead.

Gone.

Never coming back.

Flora might be too.

It didn't matter how many times she repeated it, she wouldn't fully believe it until she saw the body with her own eyes.

Maybe the person on the phone was wrong.

Maybe she survived.

It was a near impossible thought. The explosion shook the entire castle. Still, Emery held on to the hope she'd find her best friends alive.

Both of them.

She'd made it to the entrance of the royal residence when two strong arms lifted her up.

Sandalwood and pine enveloped her. The scent usually

calmed her, but this time it did the opposite. August would likely lock her away in an attempt to keep her safe, and that wasn't what she needed right now.

Emery balled her hands and repeatedly hit his chest. "Put me down, August. If you think you're stopping me from going to find Chelsea, you've got another thing coming."

He pulled her tighter against his chest, and she wanted to melt into him, yet push him away in the same breath. She knew she should let him in, but there was no way she was going to wait alone and helpless for his return. He wouldn't sway her with his embrace or the concern that rolled off him in waves, she needed to see the truth with her own eyes.

"I'm taking you to her, Em," he whispered against her temple. "But I have no idea what we're walking into. Please stay close. I need to know you're safe."

She nodded against him and reached up, wrapping her arms around his neck, soaking in the comfort he offered.

The stone walls blurred, as August expertly navigated them through the halls of the castle. Servants huddled together in alcoves, the normal hustle and bustle of the morning hours nonexistent.

August slowed when he reached the Culling floor. A crowd of delegates, castle staff and the remaining Culling women were gathering behind the King on the opposite end of the hall. All Emery could focus on was the open door.

A shimmering purple residue around the doorway held her gaze. August set her down, but she couldn't tear eyes from it. The way it danced along the oak edges beckoned her. Called her. Willed her to take notice. Like the bond between her and August.

"Sloane?"

Her sister's name pulled her from the trance she'd been

in, and she turned to look into Malcolm's face. His brows were drawn together, and his jaw was tight.

"Come with me, so August can speak with our father."

Emery craned her neck to look up at August, sorrow evident in his furrowed brow. He leaned in and placed a kiss on her forehead. "I won't be long. Stay close to Malcolm."

The moment he stepped away from her, she shivered, missing the comfort of his embrace. But she understood he had a duty to both his family and everyone in his care.

Malcolm placed a hand on her back and led her toward where the other women stood.

Emery stood on the edge of the group, which provided her a glimpse into Chelsea's room. Her heart sank into her stomach, and all rational thought ceased when she saw the destruction.

Everything within the room was charred, leaving a fine black layer on every surface. From within the soot, the same purple haze that lined the door shimmered, giving the look of an amethyst trapped in charcoal. She followed the soot to where it stopped at the door frame. It didn't add up. Explosions didn't work that way. At least, none that she'd ever seen. She'd frequently watched the news and seen the carnage of an explosion several times before. They radiated from a singular point and not even the stone wall of the castle should have been able to stop its expansion. It almost seemed contained.

But that shouldn't have been possible.

The longer she studied the scene, the more she felt the urge to run into the room. To place herself within the carnage. Maybe then she could figure out why nothing seemed right.

Unable to tear her eyes away, she spoke softly, knowing

Malcolm would hear her. "Why is it contained to her room? It should have destroyed the whole floor."

"Magic."

She lifted her head to look up at Malcolm, his solemn gaze speaking volumes.

Fuck.

It explained why nothing made sense. Because this wasn't an ordinary explosion. Magic didn't have to make sense. It didn't have to act like anything else.

This was not good.

Not good at all.

If this was another attack by the witches, war was inevitable.

And she was smack dab in the middle of a witch hunt that had the potential to outshine centuries old Salem. She knew the outcome would be the same. Ask no questions, just destroy anyone that resembled a witch.

Her people did this. Not that she considered herself one of them, but the royal family wouldn't see the difference. Wouldn't care she was an outcast with no magic of her own.

Would August?

Emery returned to surveying the room, watching the purple magic that clung to every surface. When her gaze reached the bed, she noticed red ringlets peeking out from beneath the heap of charred blankets.

She brought her hand to her trembling lip as tears blurred her vision. "No."

Emery dashed from Malcolm's side and crossed the threshold, focusing only on reaching Chelsea. Her blood rushed to her head, and every cell on the surface of her skin began to vibrate. Stars erupted in her vision, obscuring her view, but she ignored them, stumbling her way over charred debris to the bed. She fell to her knees and carefully lifted the blackened blanket.

Chelsea, or what was left of her, lay beneath a pile of soot, her skin was badly burned and, in some places, nonexistent. What was left of her favorite pink dress was seared into her body, her face barely recognizable and patches of her hair were missing. Her beautiful red hair.

Emery's lips trembled, and she choked on a sob as she reached up and closed Chelsea's eyelids, covering the look of pure terror frozen in her eyes. She took Chelsea's charred hand in hers, feeling every blister and exposed muscle, and bowed her head. She was really dead. Gone forever. Her shining light would never grace the world again. She'd gone to be with Sloane.

She hated her sister, but at least Chelsea wouldn't be alone. She was in for a hell of a surprise, though.

A wave of relief washed over Emery as she realized Flora was not also under the blanket. Losing Chelsea was already hard enough, she couldn't imagine losing Flora too. She hoped Flora was already on her way to her new kingdom, far away from the heartache of the castle.

Emery leaned forward and whispered a soft goodbye to her friend, and as she pulled her hand away, a gold and blue amulet fell to the floor. Emery instantly recognized it as Sloane's. Chelsea had asked if she could keep it, and since Emery had no attachment to it, she didn't see any issue.

The amulet had the same purple glow as the rest of the room, but it pulsed around the object instead of remaining stagnant. Emery reached out and fingered the gold chain. It was hot, but not scalding and vibrated in unison with her body.

"Emery!" August shouted from the door. "Don't touch anything!"

She pivoted her head to see his eyes wide in terror. The purple shimmer previously dusting the room had thickened into a dense fog and was creeping toward her.

"What's happening?" she whispered, as much for her benefit as well as August's.

The purple fog surrounded her. Tendrils snaked out, licking her skin. The moment it touched her, Emery froze, unable to move or protest against the magic's assault. It was soft at first, almost pleasurable. The licks turned to caresses, and Emery couldn't stop a soft moan from escaping her parted lips. The magic hummed around her excitedly, and she watched in awe.

Then, the first drops of dew formed on her arm and seeped into her.

A blood curdling scream tore from Emery. The pain was unbearable. Like needles piercing her skin where every drop penetrated her skin. If it weren't for the magic's hold on her limbs, she'd be curled in a ball on the ground.

She shifted her eyes to the door where August now stood watching with wide eyes. He looked as terrified as she felt, and beneath the pain erupting all over her body, she felt his worry through their bond. He took a step toward her when a hand gripped his shoulder and stopped him.

A sardonic smile tugged at the king's lips. "You can't save her."

August shrugged his father off and tried to navigate through the magical fog, careful not to touch it. "I'm not giving her up, so I'll either save her or die with her."

He dodged the wayward magic until he stood a few feet from her. Emery knew the moment he registered what was happening. His eyes grew even wider than before, and his face contorted as if he were the one struggling against the magic. "It can't be. You can't be." His declaration came out a pain filled whisper.

"August, please, let me explain." This wasn't how he was supposed to find out. She was supposed to tell him. They were supposed to talk about it and work toward understanding together. Callum warned her it would be bad if she wasn't the one to tell him, but nothing could have prepared her for the hatred she felt rolling off him.

He took a step back, and she could have sworn she saw tears welling in his eyes. "What's there to explain?" he spat. "You're a witch."

She prayed for him to listen, to hear the words as she pleaded her case. "I can't access my magic. I'm not really a witch. I swear to you, I'm not what you're thinking. I was born with witch blood, but I am not a witch."

Rage flooded the bond, and August lost his stoic composure. He turned and flipped the charred desk behind him, sending soot everywhere. "For fuck's sake, Emery, the magic is seeping into you. It only does that to return to a source of magic. Which would mean you're a bloody fucking witch." His eyes narrowed, darkening until she could no longer make out the oceanic blue she loved. "I claimed you. Was this all just a game?"

"No. It wasn't. You know it wasn't because you can feel me just as I can feel you." She wished she could move. Could run to him and fall at his feet. Beg him to understand. "August, I tried to tell you."

"When? Before or after you made me love you?" He spat the words as if they were poison.

His words were another knife through her heart. He

loved her. Words she'd heard only once before, and now they were laced with disgust and hatred.

"I'm still yours. I still love you. I'm not any different than I was an hour ago."

"You're not?" He tipped his head back and laughed. "The woman I loved was honest with me, and I believed her when she claimed we'd tackle everything, together. She didn't absorb magic and conceal her identity. Most importantly, the woman I loved was not a *witch*."

"Please. August." She didn't know what to ask of him, he was right. She'd done all those things. It wouldn't matter why or that she had every intention of telling him.

Movement by the door caught her eye, and Jessi stepped into the doorway. "I'll bet she's the one who killed Chelsea. I saw her eyes glow last night, and now the magic is seeping into her."

August spun toward the door. "Get the fuck out of here. No one asked for your commentary." When he returned his gaze to Emery, he raised a brow. "Did you kill her?"

"I would never," Emery cried between shortened breaths. The pain of the magic grew to an unbearable level, but not nearly as unbearable as his rejection. It was so much worse than she'd imagined. "August, please. You know I would never. She was my best friend."

"That's the thing, Emery. I don't know you." He gave her his back and stepped toward the door. "Guards, when the magic is gone, apprehend her and take her to the dungeon."

"No!" she exclaimed, trying to find a way to make him understand she wasn't what he thought. Three guards surrounded her, and she struggled to see August through them. "Please, August. Search your feelings, my feelings.

Our fucking feelings, August. None of what you're saying is true."

August huffed a laugh. "Everything between us has been a lie, and I'd be foolish to trust it now. Likely more of your witch magic meant to weaken me, my kingdom. You are nothing but a witch whore to be disposed of."

Emery hiccupped a sob, her heart shattering into a million pieces. She lowered her eyes, unwilling to watch August walk away. She had nothing left to give and nothing left to lose. August owned every part of her. Her mind. Her body. Even her soul.

She focused on the last bit of magic surrounding her. It would be easy to blame it for the situation she was in, when in reality she'd done it to herself. She should have told August sooner. Forced him to sit down and listen instead of allowing him to brush her off each time she insisted they needed to talk. Instead of giving in to her lust every time she had the opportunity to have the discussion.

The pain increased, and room spun around her as the final drops of magic entered her body. It was too much. She couldn't house it all and felt as though she was ready to erupt.

When the last bit absorbed into her, she was released from its hold. Emery dropped to her knees, unable to hold herself up. Her skin continued to vibrate, pulsing as if it was ready to rip at the seams. The magic bubbled within her, looking for an escape. She had no idea how to control it, or if it would hurt someone if it escaped, but she willed it to comply with her wishes. August may not believe her, but she still would do what she could to protect those in the castle.

Using every last bit of strength she had, she warned the guards. "Get away from me. I can't hold it."

One of the three pulled her to stand and shoved her toward the other two. "We don't take orders from you, prisoner."

"Please, stop," she pleaded with them, worried what would happen if she let go. She was so close to letting go. She wasn't strong enough. Didn't have enough knowledge of magic to even fathom what to do with it.

They continued, pulling her toward the door where she came face to face with August. She tried to hold it in but the pressure of being forced to move was too much. She looked him in the eye and whispered, "I love you."

And then she let go.

The last thing she saw was August's eyes widening in fear as gold rays burst from her body.

Then, everything went black.

Chapter Thirty Three

AUGUST

How the hell had he fucked up so bad? Even looking back, he struggled to see the signs. Emery never gave any indication she was anything but human. Never gave him any inkling she was working for the witches. She never used her magic. In fact, she seemed scared by it. Terrified even. None of it added up, but he couldn't dispute what he'd seen. Emery absorbed magic, just as Lilyana had.

I tried to tell you.

Like hell she had.

She hadn't tried hard enough.

August finished the last of the blood in his glass and chucked it against the wall. It shattered, sending shards of glittering glass in every direction but did nothing to dull the anger and confusion churning within him.

"I don't see why you're so worked up, son." His father fingered the rim of his glass before taking a long sip. "You dodged a bullet when Emery got herself caught. I will say

I'm ashamed you didn't figure it out sooner, but now we know we have cause to retaliate against the witches."

August could practically hear the glee in his father's voice. It was what he'd always wanted, an excuse to go to war with the witches. To take out every last one of them.

Including Emery.

He scrubbed a hand over his stubbled face. Why hadn't Emery told him sooner? Not that it mattered. He was the fucking crown prince of vampires, he couldn't love a witch, let alone marry one. It didn't matter if she was unable to wield magic.

At least if she'd told him he could have avoided the current ache in his chest. The emptiness and longing. The way his traitorous body demanded he go to her. Claim her.

Forgive her.

What did his body know, anyway? She was a fucking witch. His enemy. Something he'd been taught to hate his whole life. Even if when he searched their bond, as she'd demanded, he found nothing but evidence she told the truth. None of it mattered. He couldn't afford to let it.

The bloodlust had returned with a vengeance as soon as her blood worked its way through his system. He was torn between his need to tear into any vein that approached him and his desire to tear into the one that would give him a temporary reprieve from the pain.

That would require going to her, and he was afraid if he took even the smallest pull of her blood, he might accidentally trip into her witchy vagina. No. He was sure of it. Which was the last thing he needed.

The door cracked open, and Callum peeked his head in. "You wanted me to report back any changes."

"And?"

Callum shook his head. "There haven't been any."

"How could she be asleep for two days?" August didn't miss the concern in his tone, but old habits die hard. As much as he tried to deny it, he still cared for her and didn't understand what was wrong with her. After radiating gold magic like a damn solar flare, she'd fallen unconscious and remained that way ever since.

Callum stepped into the room and walked to the bar, pouring himself a drink. "Lily seems to believe she took in too much magic and her body was overloaded. She also pointed out how incredible it was that Emery contained the flare as much as she did. She could have hurt a lot of people if she hadn't fought so valiantly against something she didn't even understand, let alone know how to control. Lily said Emery will wake once her body has recovered from the strain."

"Don't fall for their games and lies. Believe nothing she tells you," the King interjected from across the room. "I know you believe her to be a friend, Callum, but Lilyana is one of them. She brought the witches to our doorstep during Kipton's Culling. For all we know she brought Emery and Sloane here as well."

"I don't think—"

Rage bubbled within August. "I swear to the gods, Callum, if you or Malcolm tell me one more time Emery isn't like the rest of the witches, I will run a stake through your heart myself."

"But—"

August crossed the room and picked up one of the wooden chairs and broke it across his knee. He picked up one of the shards and pointed it at Callum. "You'd test me right now?"

"No." Callum swirled his whiskey nonchalantly, and August wanted to wipe the smug smile off his face. "It's just, we both know there is more to her than just her heritage. I tasted her blood. She tasted foul to me. It's how I knew."

"You knew? Knew what, cousin?"

He stopped swirling his glass and looked August square in the eye. "That she was your mate."

"We don't have mates," August scoffed. "We have Cullings and brides. Women we fuck until they give us what we want and then we are forced to be shackled to them for all of eternity."

"You're upset she didn't confide in you. I get that, truly I do. But you would throw away your chance at love? To be with the one person who could complement you in every way?" Callum looked pointedly at the wood in August's hand. "Did it ever occur to you your actions now are exactly why she was fearful to tell you? It seems her fears were well founded."

"Hold your tongue, cousin, my patience is wearing thin." August lowered the wood, hating the truth in his words. But his reaction was warranted, and she'd been right to fear it, his feelings were irrelevant.

He wasn't even sure that's what he felt for Emery. Not anymore. He'd loved who he thought she was, but he didn't know the woman who dwelled in the dungeon. She was an enigma. A mystery. As was her sister. It was clear they were playing the long game. Snag one of the vampire princes and report back to the witches.

Part of him wanted to believe that wasn't the case, maybe a tiny part of him in the dark recesses of his heart even did. Believed Emery was exactly who she'd said she was. But he couldn't live his life on wishful thinking. The facts were there staring him in the face. She'd lied, no matter her intentions, and couldn't be trusted. The bond they shared didn't matter.

Not if she'd use it against him. Which, in a way, she had.

His father chuckled, and August was surprised it took him so long to join the conversation. "Love is overrated. It's not necessary."

August nodded, his father confirming his inner thoughts. "What my father said rings true. She is our enemy now."

Callum sighed. "Malcolm and Sloane made it work."

"Don't you dare bring my brother into this." The asshole had yet to face him since accidentally admitting he'd known all along about Emery and Sloane's heritage. The prick had been working with her all along, concealing information from him about Sloane's death. "He chose her pretty face over his own brother. He knew what they were all along. From the moment she arrived, he chose her over us."

"He's right, though." Callum downed the remainder of his whiskey. "She isn't what you think, August."

He was done listening to people tell him what to think. If they knew Emery so much better than he did, they could have her. He opened his mouth to say as much, but his chest constricted, and the words wouldn't come out.

Bloody hell. Fucking traitorous body. The thought of sending her away nearly tore him in two, and he couldn't force the words past his lips. He didn't want to keep her. She would only serve as a reminder of what he lost. What he wanted so wholeheartedly until she fucked it all to hell. The memory of what they were was now tainted with the reality of what she was.

He couldn't send her away, but he couldn't keep her either.

He didn't want to.

Even he knew that was a lie.

The only way he'd ever be free of her would be to kill her, but he couldn't follow through with that either. No matter what she'd done, he couldn't harm a hair on her head. She'd embedded herself in his soul, and no matter what he did, she'd be there for eternity.

Unless he had no soul for her to reside in.

August closed his eyes and relaxed his mind. This was the only way he could ever hope to escape her. To do what he had to do to keep his family and his kingdom safe. He allowed his instincts to take over, pushing his humanity to the furthest edges of his mind. Far enough, he wouldn't let pesky things like emotions get in the way of what needed to be done.

When he opened his eyes, a weight lifted from his chest, and he knew what he was going to do about the witch problem in the dungeon.

He may not be able to kill her, but he'd keep her. Feed from her to curb the bloodlust. Use her to make himself better. He'd have a chamber made up for her next to his where he could fuck her and her magic pussy each night as he tortured her for information. She'd make the perfect mistress.

And it didn't matter what she thought about it.

Augustine brought his attention back to Callum with a malevolent smile. "So, you've chosen to side with my prisoner. That's disappointing, cousin, but I'm not surprised. You've always wanted her pussy. I'll admit it's a very pretty one, which is why I've decided to keep her for myself. She'll remain in my service until I have no use of her, then I'll send her back to the witches in pieces as a reminder not to fuck with our family."

The sweet prince within him warred against his words, but August wasn't in charge anymore. Augustine was.

Callum set his glass down and squared up with Augustine. "I knew you were stubborn, but until this moment, I hadn't thought you a fool."

"At least I'm standing with my kingdom. You can see your way out, cousin. In fact, it would be best if you take your leave back to Scotland. You're unwelcome here."

"As you wish, cousin." Callum gave an exaggerated bow and turned for the door.

Augustine stormed toward the fridge in the corner. He tore into a blood bag, not bothering to pour it into a glass. He'd need to summon a feeder soon, or maybe he'd pay the dungeons a visit.

His father appeared behind him and placed a hand on his shoulder. "You're doing the right thing, son. Your cousin is weak. He is swayed by a prophecy with zero founding."

That piqued Augustine's interest, he'd never heard of a prophecy. "You know what he's talking about?"

The King's mouth formed a grim line, and he nodded. "It doesn't matter, though, as I said, there is nothing to support it. You need to focus on the task at hand. Gaining information from our prisoner when she wakes and striking the witches while the iron is hot."

"Do you believe Emery killed Chelsea?"

"The facts are there. The women reported Emery gave Chelsea the amulet when she arrived, and it glowed brightest with magic in Miss Montgomery's hands. It's possible she'd been planning this from the moment she arrived. I'd hate to think it, but she could have been responsible for her sister's death.

"The witches understand the Culling magic as well as we do, it wouldn't be the first time they attempted to infiltrate a Culling. Not to mention the killings in the city began when she arrived. It's no coincidence the bodies also emit the same magic the explosion did."

His father was right. He couldn't trust anything about Emery.

It didn't matter August yearned to believe what they shared was real.

Every laugh. Every kiss. It had all been a lie. She'd played hard to get to trap him and get him to let his guard down. She'd gone so far as to woo him with her virgin pussy, and he'd willingly let her.

All Augustine knew was the witch would have to pay for her crimes, and he had no problem proceeding to take it out on the rest of her kind as well.

"You'll need to address the kingdom. It's time you take some of the reins. This is your fight, son. They attacked your Culling. Show them your strength."

Augustine picked up the phone and dialed his father's lead advisor. "Let the court know I'll be speaking tonight about the attack and the future of our kingdom."

"Yes, Your Highness. I'll make sure all are in attendance."

"Thank you." He hung up the phone, gleeful with morbid anticipation.

"We can't let this go unpunished."

The nagging emotions of August rippled through him. He was going to need to address his involvement and shove those emotions down further. They brought heartache.

Which was something Augustine didn't have time for. August let him out to play and play he would. It was time for a new approach.

Augustine nodded at his father. "Tonight, is the beginning of the end for the witches, and Emery will be made the example."

"So, it's true. You're no different than him."

Augustine looked up to see Malcolm standing in the doorway.

"Ah, my traitor brother has decided to show his face."

"It's not like that, and you know it."

The king rose and walked toward the door. "I'll let you two work out your differences. I expect a united front this evening in front of the kingdom."

After the king left, Augustine closed the distance, and before Malcolm could get a word in, his fist connected with his brother's face. It had been some time since he'd sparred with his older brother, and Augustine had a few grudges of his own to settle with Malcolm.

Chapter Thirty Four

EMERY

EMERY STRUGGLED TO SUCK IN A BREATH. REALLY, SHE struggled to do anything. She'd been in and out of consciousness for hours, but no matter how hard she tried to open her eyes she couldn't. She tried to scream, but her body refused to comply with even the smallest command. Trapped within her mind, she exhausted herself trying to wake the hell up and would inevitably drift back into the recurring nightmare that always ended with August sentencing her to death. A never-ending loop of torture followed by heartbreak.

Hers.

His.

"Is she awake yet?" A vaguely familiar brogue pulled her into consciousness.

How long had it been since she'd been overwhelmed by the magic?

Her head throbbed as she failed to put a name to the voice. She could scarcely remember her own name, let alone figure out anyone else's. That should have been much more worrisome than it was, but she didn't have the energy to dwell on it.

"Almost. One more pull of the excess magic, and she should come to. She's exhausted. I shouldn't even be trying to pull her out before her body is ready." A female voice answered, her brogue just as thick, but sounded closer. Or maybe she was just louder.

While she appreciated their accents, it would be nice if they'd call each other by a name so she'd know who the hell was waking her. She didn't know if the Scottish Delegation was still in the castle. She didn't even know if she was still in the castle.

"Good, I don't know how long Malcolm will be able to keep August distracted."

August? Panic rose within her. Was he okay? Why did he need to be distracted? What the fuck was happening?

The last thing she remembered was—

Emery pried open her eyes, and stars blurred her vision. Everything seemed hazy, but when her vision cleared, a pair of concerned amber eyes stared back. They belonged to a woman who looked to be not much older than her. She darted her gaze around the room. It was cold and unfriendly. The stone ceiling and walls, covered in cobwebs and dust, did not register as familiar at all.

"Where am I?" She tightened her core and attempted to sit up, but after rising only a few inches, her head fell back into the woman's lap.

"Shhhh…" The woman gripped Emery's arms and

pushed her up, helping her sit with a hand resting on her back to steady her. "You need to take it easy."

She didn't need to be told twice. She couldn't do much if she tried. Every muscle throbbed. Even breathing hurt.

Across from her, the glint of iron bars caught her eye.

Take her to the dungeon.

Emery's eyes widened. August followed through on his word. She was a prisoner. His prisoner. Locked in the dungeon where witches belonged. Witches like her.

She choked on a sob, almost wishing she could return to the catatonic state where August's hatred was only a nightmare. The reality hurt too much. His anger. His disappointment. It was all real.

Emery closed her eyes and searched for the bond they shared. She reached with heart where her love for August remained strong and sighed with relief, finding comfort in the fact it still connected them. A tiny bit of hope flared within her, even though the bond was stagnant, it was still there. Maybe she could fix things. Show him through the bond she wasn't what he thought. She'd deceived him, but it was never with the intention to hurt or use him. The goal was to keep breathing, there was no way she could've known she'd bond with him. She didn't understand how it worked, but she would fight for what they had.

She inhaled deeply and focused on how she felt for him before Chelsea's death, sending thoughts of love and unity through the bond.

The instant August received her message, anger flooded the bond. It assaulted her senses and filled her with a pain so intense she doubled over in agony. She never experienced such hatred. It took on a life of its own. A tangible, living entity that snaked all the way through her and left a bitter taste on her tongue. The exact opposite of the sweet caramel she'd come to expect from him.

Unable to bear it a moment longer, Emery cut the link between them. She didn't know how she did it, but she could no longer feel August through their bond. An empty void filled the spot where he should be.

"Are you okay?" The woman's eyes were wide with worry, and she was rubbing small circles in the middle of her back. "I'm Lily, dear. I'm here to help."

No, she was not okay, and the thought of help was laughable. There was nothing anyone could do to help. She'd just shut the door on the man she loved.

Emery's eyes flashed to Callum, as he cleared his throat and took a step toward her. Her jaw clenched and she narrowed her eyes on him. She was going to leave the night of the ball. He was the reason she stayed. He was the reason she let her guard down. He sparked a hope within her, making her believe August would accept her. "You were wrong. He hates me for what I am."

Callum cocked a brow, his signature smirk firmly in place. "I wasn't, he just needs time. Unfortunately, as long as daddy dearest is in his ear, we don't stand a chance at changing his views. Which is why we need to get you out of here."

"No." Her throat constricted, and her heart raced. She couldn't leave. Even if she wasn't safe in the castle, she had to stay. To convince him she wasn't a traitor. That she hadn't been working some grand plan to deceive him. "I need to see him. To explain."

Lily shook her head. "Callum's right, Emery. We need to get you out of here, preferably before August realizes you're awake. Who knows what he's capable of now."

Emery winced. Well, the proverbial cat was already out of the bag on that one. They weren't going to be happy about her little bond experience. "He already knows."

"How?" They asked in unison.

"Through the bond you didn't bother telling me about. Thanks for that, asshole." Emery turned to the woman who'd helped her. "Did Callum coerce you?"

"If you weren't part of a bigger plan, I'd leave your bonnie arse here to rot in the dungeon." Callum muttered. "No, I didn't force her to be here. She's important to the plan, and we can discuss that later. We need to move. Now."

Emery crossed her arms over her chest. "I might take my chances with August before I blindly trust you. August may be pissed and want me dead right now, but you've already betrayed me once, and I'm not foolish enough to trust you again."

"Enough bickering." The woman's eyes softened as they searched Emery's face. "We have time, Callum. Malcolm will keep him occupied long enough for me to explain."

Lily took Emery's hand in hers. "As I said, I'm Lilyana, but you can call me Lily. Technically, I'm your great great great great great great grandmother, but saying that makes me feel old."

"Wait, what?" Emery and Callum simultaneously echoed together.

"What the hell, Lily? You didn't think that was important information to share with me?" If her entire world wasn't being turned on its head, Emery may have enjoyed the shocked betrayal in Callum's voice.

At least she wasn't the only one taken completely by surprise. Did it mean Lily was a vampire? She must have been another Montgomery forced to participate in a previous

Culling. She could have made the choice to be turned. But she said she pulled the magic from her which would have been impossible as a vampire.

Emery pulled her hands from Lily's and crossed them in her lap. "As much as I'd love to believe you, how is this possible? You'd have to be hundreds of years old."

"I am, though a lady never reveals her age." A smile formed on Lily's lips, and she gave Emery a wink. "My grandmother was the original witch, marking our bloodline as royalty. Royal witches are immortal."

"I have royal blood? So, I'll live forever?" Emery looked to Callum, who only shrugged as if to say it was news to him as well. Living forever didn't appeal to her anymore, in fact it felt like the cherry on her fuck-me-sideways cake. Immortality might have been appealing if August was by her side, but he wasn't, he wouldn't be, and she'd rather not spend a literal eternity facing that. "I think you have the wrong woman. My magic was bound, a curse on my entire family, which would include you if this were all true. There is no possible way I'm who you think I am."

"Settle, lass, I'm going to try to explain as much as I can. It will be the short version, since we really must be going, but I promise to answer any questions you have once we're safe."

Emery nodded hesitantly.

"First, I'm going to show you what I really look like. I think it might help you to see I am who I say."

Lily closed her eyes and waved her hand down the front of her face. Her skin shimmered and a faint emerald glow appeared, similar to the purple magic in Chelsea's room.

Emery leaned away, hesitant to trust magic after everything she'd seen it do, but when Lily's features began to change, her eyes widened and her mouth fell open. She watched in wonder as the magic molded and contorted Lily's face, her nose narrowed, and her cheek bones sharpened slightly. Her pointed chin softened to a rounded square and her hair lightened to the slightly darker hue than Emery's.

Mesmerized by the transformation, Emery gasped when it was complete, and the magic faded away. She couldn't believe what she was seeing. It shouldn't be possible. Lily opened her eyes revealing whiskey-colored eyes, the same as Emery's, only they had the tiniest flecks of green around the centers. The resemblance was uncanny. Lily could be Emery's sister. Not her twin, but it was clear they were of the same blood.

Family.

Something she hadn't truly had since Sloane was taken.

Lily tilted her head, and Emery didn't need a bond to feel the love radiating from her. She reached out and pulled Emery into a hug and whispered softly, "I know you just met me, but I've prayed lifetimes for this moment."

Tears fell freely down Emery's cheeks. "Me too." She'd lived under the impression she was alone. Sloane was stolen from her at such a young age, leaving her alone in the world with no one to turn to. Chelsea, Flora, and most of all, August had broken down her walls and made her feel almost whole again. She should be skeptical, but Emery couldn't deny the missing piece Lily filled the moment she'd revealed herself.

"Holy shite," Callum whispered, ruining the moment as only he could.

Emery and Lily both turned to find him staring with his

mouth hanging open. "You look just like her. Does Malcolm know this?"

"He doesn't need to."

"Bloody hell, Lily." Callum cursed and ran a hand through his tousled hair. "He's your fucking mate. You have to show him who you are."

Lily bowed her head, shaking it. "He doesn't know what we are, and until he does, it doesn't matter."

"Doesn't matter? You're related to them. You look as though you could be their long lost sister."

Eyes narrowed, and Lily snapped. "How was I to know he'd be my mate? We've never seen a true mating. Not to mention, I've been secluded at the cottage for nearly a century. Up until last week, I believed mates to be a fairy tale."

"So, this is somehow his fault? Typical woman. Maybe we would all have mates if *your* grandmother hadn't kept it a secret," Callum lashed out and gave them his back.

"So, you could cull witches instead of humans?" Lily raised her voice, refusing to back down. She had a good point, though culling anyone seemed wrong to Emery. "My grandmother did what she thought was right."

Emery stood and threw up her hands. "Can you two stop for a hot second and explain to me what the hell is going on?" Callum and Lily both stopped and looked at her in time to see her start to sway on her feet.

Lily reached out and helped her back to the makeshift cot they'd been sitting on. "I'm sorry."

Emery wasn't sure if she was speaking to her or Callum, but she pressed on hoping for answers. "What does he mean Malcolm's your mate?"

"He was made for me. As August was for you."

Even if it were true, free will trumped fate, and August had used his to hate her. They were born on opposite sides of a history neither of them had a say in. Sure, they shared a bond, but it couldn't withstand the truth of her birth.

Emery's stomach rolled, and she grimaced. "It's a nice thought, but it's not possible. I've seen firsthand the hatred vampires have for witches. I've felt the hatred August holds for me, and it won't be changing any time soon."

"But the reason why is wrong. What I'm about to tell you is a closely guarded secret very few are privy to. As it affects you directly, I think it's time you know." She paused and took a deep breath. "My grandmother, the original witch, created vampires. They were intended for her daughters, and their future daughters, to ensure they would never be alone. The spell she cast ensured that every witch would have a vampire mate. It was said they'd be a perfect match, so in tune with one another they'd be able to feel each other at a distance and burn for one another with an intensity that rivaled the sun."

Lily's last statement wrapped around Emery's heart like a vise and squeezed, leaving her struggling to breathe. "I feel all that with August." She clamped her eyes shut and focused on forcing air into her lungs. As impossible as it seemed, it made sense. Coincided with everything she'd experienced with August.

That didn't mean fate didn't have a fucked up sense of humor.

"You knew, didn't you?" She opened her eyes and looked up at Callum.

"I suspected, but I didn't know about Lily and Malcolm." He shifted his gaze to Lily, and his brows furrowed. "You can't avoid him forever, Lily."

"I know." Her voice was barely above a whisper. "The way my body reacts to him, it's only a matter of time before I won't be able to fight the bond any longer. I'm just not ready."

Emery knew the feeling. She'd been fighting it for nearly a month. When she'd finally given in, took what she needed and gave August all of herself to complete the bond, she hadn't known that's what they were doing. Only that it felt right. Uniting them in a way that seemed unreal, magical even.

Because it was.

She wished there was a handbook on vampire-witch matings. Something to explain exactly what happened between them. And what to do when one mate hated the other. "Are there any other vampires and witches who have completed the bond?"

Callum shook his head and looked at Lily. "None that I've come across. Have you heard of any?"

"I've only heard of a completed bond once, my grandfather and grandmother, and he didn't give me much information. He started to go a little crazy after she died. Although, he did say something in one of his more lucid ramblings about needing her blood, I'm not sure if he meant when she was alive or after her death."

It made perfect sense, especially if the bond worked both ways

She craved August's blood as if it were a lifeline, and once she consumed it, all logic went out the window. What her heart knew to be true was all that mattered. August was hers, and she'd do anything to keep that bond alive. But what would happen if they stayed apart? Would they go crazy like Lily's grandfather?

Just the thought of leaving sent anxiety through her, but it was hard to say if that was the bond talking or her heart. Perhaps they were now one and the same.

Emery released a deep sigh and brought her leg beneath her. "What happens next? August hates me for what I am, I doubt he'll be welcoming me back into his life. Even if I am his mate."

"He'll come around, lass. For now, we're going to get you out of the castle to somewhere safe. The King is hellbent on blaming you for Chelsea's death, and right or wrong, August has decided to fall in line with his father."

"How could he believe I'd kill my best friend?" If he believed her capable of that, he'd believe her capable of anything. If he truly thought she killed her best friend, he didn't know her at all, and there was no way he would overlook the blood of a stranger.

"The amulet. It housed magic that killed Chelsea, and the king believes you gave it to her for that purpose. Even without Chelsea's death, you're a witch. That in and of itself is enough for them to kill you."

Emery dropped her head into her hands, testing their bond and finding the same hatred and rage there as before, and so she slammed it shut once more. Bond or not, he was lost to her. "I don't understand how he could think any of this."

Callum scoffed and crossed his arms over his chest. "You lied to him. We all did. And, right now, that's all he sees. He's likely fallen in line with King Lewyn because he's the only one who hasn't deceived him. And my uncle has only one agenda...end the witches."

Callum was right. August asked for her honesty, and she'd continued to lie to save herself. By the time she'd worked up the courage to give herself to him completely, it was too late.

Even if it hadn't been, there was no guarantee he'd ever see past his prejudice.

She couldn't compete with his father. Not when she'd hurt him so deeply, betrayed his trust so thoroughly. "How did I end up the pawn in a game I didn't know existed?"

"I hate to be the one to tell you," Callum walked over and tipped her chin up. "We're all pawns in this game, lass. It's high time we started making moves to ensure the endgame we want."

Emery looked him square in the eye, hoping he'd have the answer to her question. "And what would that be?"

Callum stared off into the upper corner of the dungeon. She followed his gaze, but nothing was there. "Freedom from the lies and prejudices put forward for us by our ancestors."

Emery hadn't a clue what that meant, and she was borderline too overwhelmed to care. There would be time later to work through the nuances of vampires and witches. At least, if she was going to be a player in the game, might as well fight for freedom.

She nodded in agreement, and Lily helped her stand before handing her off to Callum.

"Emery." Callum stopped moving and stared at her like she'd grown a second head as he inhaled deeply just above her hair. "Fuck, this changes things. We need to go to the wolves. She'll be safe with them."

"Wait, the wolves? As in werewolves? What changed?" Emery stepped away from him on shaky feet. "And why do you always have to sniff me? I'm sure I don't smell like roses, but I've been locked in a dungeon, asshole."

Callum chuckled. "You smell fine. And yes, werewolves. We have to take you there because it's the last place anyone will look for you. I've got a guy who owes me a favor. He'll watch over you until we can figure out what comes next."

"Why do I have to go there? I want to stay with Lily." She'd only just found out she wasn't alone, and Callum was asking her to walk away from the only family she had left.

"You're pregnant, Emery. If August catches one good whiff of you, he'll know, and with how angry he is right now, I don't want to chance he'd kill you on the spot."

Pregnant.

Her hands flitted to her midsection, and she looked down at her flat stomach. There was no way she was carrying August's baby. She knew how sex worked. She wasn't stupid. They hadn't used protection, but the odds of her being pregnant less than twenty-four hours after sex weren't likely.

"There's no way you can smell that."

"We can, lass." Callum's somber tone held her attention, an indicator he wasn't fooling around. "Your smell is sweet, while August's is pine. You have his blood within you, but you also have the faint smell of the ocean mixed with fresh blood. I've never been wrong about this sort of thing."

Emery's mouth fell open. Her baby smelled of the ocean.

Her heart raced and she struggled to breathe, as the idea took root. She wasn't ready to be a mother. As if the mess with August wasn't fucked up enough, now she had more than one life to worry about. Even if she couldn't leave for herself, she had to leave for her baby. Their baby. A baby whose father would likely hate it because of what Emery was.

"Calm your brain, lass, we'll figure this out." Lily

rubbed small circles on her back. "I'll go with you to the wolves, and we'll plan our next steps." She turned to Callum, who resorted to pacing the short width of the dungeon. "Let's go to my cottage. I'll portal us to Washington."

"Portal?" Emery didn't know why she was surprised by the notion Lily could create portals. After learning amulets can cause explosions, nothing should surprise her anymore.

Lily nodded and beamed a proud smile. "I can't wait to show you all the good things magic can do, lass."

Emery followed the pair down a darkened hallway lit only by the flashlight Callum carried. Her hands never left her stomach. She tapped a steady rhythm to her unborn child, willing it to feel the love and protection she'd provide, but also distracting herself from the anxiety coursing through her.

After winding through the underbelly of the castle, Callum pulled open a hidden door to reveal a gate. Light poured in through the vines that tangled themselves within the wrought iron, and she recognized the huge pink flowers that bloomed behind the stables. She'd admired them many times when visiting Shadowfell with Flora.

Things had changed so much since then.

Callum pushed open the gate and led them into the sunlight. He stopped behind the hedge lining the castle wall. "Wait here. I'll saddle up some horses."

Lily and Emery watched as he crossed the manicured grass and entered the barn. The moment he did, Emery's skin began to tingle, and there was a flash of light halfway between them and the stable. It was small, but started to grow in diameter, forming a sparkling teal circle, both beautiful and terrifying.

"It's a portal. Get behind me, Emery." Lily's voice was strong and firm.

Emery did as she was told, but it did nothing to ease her fear. Lily wasn't much bigger than her, and she could only hope Lily's magic could save them from whatever was headed their direction.

The glowing circle continued to grow, it's center rippling like lake water on a windy day.

Emery's jaw dropped as a woman, the spitting image of Lily, walked through the portal, followed by Dahlia.

Dahlia raced toward Emery, but before she could reach her, Lily threw her arms up and erected a green dome around them.

Dahlia halted inches before she crashed into the sizzling dome, and Emery didn't miss the pain in her eyes.

Emery tried to move around Lily, but Lily pushed her back. "Dahlia won't hurt me, Lily."

"It's not her I'm worried about."

The woman who looked like Lily stepped forward and laughed menacingly. "Hello, sister."

"Vishna." Lily nodded. "To what do I owe the displeasure?"

"I'm here for my niece. She's been victimized long enough."

"There was a misunderstanding, yes, but she belongs here. With me."

Vishna scrunched her face and scoffed. "You couldn't protect her, or her sister, from these blood suckers. What makes you think you can now?"

"I didn't know about Sloane, but if you'd enlightened me, I would have protected her. It's you who failed them, sister."

Emery stepped forward, almost touching the dome that protected her from Vishna. "How could you say you protected Sloane? It's your fault she's dead. You had her killed for falling in love with Malcolm."

"Oh, you naive girl. I did no such thing. It was my idea to have her go for the older prince. Your sister got herself killed by deviating from the plan." Vishna stepped forward, meeting her at the barrier. "You don't know what vampires are capable of. The lengths the king will go to further his agenda. The safest place for you is within the walls of New Orleans. Where no vampire can reach you."

She turned to Lily, hoping she'd contradict her sister and give her a reason to continue hating the coven. That hope was lost when Lily's hardened stare fell, and she shook her head.

"She's right. Although our plan is good, the safest place for you now would be behind the wards of New Orleans."

"But I don't want to leave you." She'd only just found Lily, and although Vishna was also her family, she didn't look at Emery the way Lily did. Like she'd move hell or highwater to keep her safe. Keep her baby safe.

Lily stepped forward and pulled Emery into a one armed hug, still keeping the dome around them. She leaned in and whispered in her ear. "Your life is about more than you now, lass, and your safety is paramount. Tell no one of the bairn. We'll send someone to protect you, and I'll be along as soon as I can."

Emery nodded against her cheek, hating the truth in Lily's words. Her life was no longer just her own. She needed to protect the child that grew in her belly, even if that meant forsaking August for the coven that never wanted her.

When Lily pulled away, she dropped the magic dome and led her toward Vishna. "I'm entrusting her to your care, don't make me regret it. I know I'm no longer welcome within the coven, but you will not keep my kin from me. Not this time."

Emery wanted to ask what she meant, but it wasn't the time, she only hoped there would be another chance.

Vishna gave a single nod and waved Dahlia forward to retrieve Emery. "You may not enter New Orleans, but I'll arrange for lodging on the city limits as long as Emery is in our care. She'll be able to visit you, but make no mistake, sister, we have not forgotten where your loyalties lie. I can taste the winds of war upon us. I suggest you think long and hard whose side you will be on."

Lily remained silent and handed Emery off to Dahlia who pulled her into a hug.

"I thought I'd lost you," her former handmaid whispered through a sob. "I didn't know what else to do."

"It's okay." Emery tightened her grip on Dahlia, savoring the love and devotion she had for her. "Thank you."

Leaving the warmth of Lily's unconditional love and being thrust into Dahlia's, Emery was forced to reconcile if war was coming, she too would have to pick a side. The problem was… both would include people she'd come to love. That she considered family.

The tingle she'd come to associate with magic crawled across her arms, and she pulled away from Dahlia to see Vishna creating a portal.

Emery glanced behind her at the castle. It loomed over her as it had the day she arrived, the same daunting figure, only it no longer represented her future. Rather, a past far more painful than the future had ever been. August's study had a perfect view of the gardens, and she looked up, immediately regretting the foolish action.

His blue eyes pierced hers, and for a moment, she considered reopening the door she'd shut on him, allowing her emotions to reach him through the bond. One last ditch effort to apologize and show him how much he meant to her. How much she needed him in her life. Not only because he was her mate, but because they were stronger together. His eyes narrowed on her, and his face twisted into an expression so full of pure hate it stole her breath.

Emery swallowed the sob that threatened to break her, he didn't deserve to see her cry.

She entered the castle as a replacement, but upon her dismissal, she was being reborn. It was time to embrace who and what she was. To rise into the witch she was meant to be.

Emery gave August her back and walked toward the portal with Dahlia.

She was no longer his Princess.

She was his enemy.

THANK YOU FOR READING

Thank you for Reading The Replacement!!
I really hope you have enjoyed August and Emery's journey so far. I have so much more in store for these characters and this world. In so many ways, this is just the beginning and I am so excited for more!
If you enjoyed The Replacement, or even if you hated it, I would so appreciate you hopping over to leave a review on Amazon and/or Goodreads. Reviews help tiny self published authors like me to gain new readers and get my books on fancy lists some day.
Thank you to everyone who reviews, recommends and posts about this series. I couldn't do this without you!

WHAT'S NEXT

Find out what happens next in Emery and August's story.

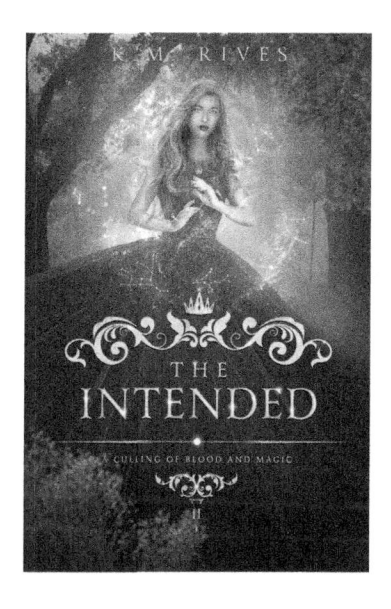

Pre-Order The Intended Today!

HYBRID MOON RISING

Want to find out what happened to Flora after Emery left the castle? Join her on her adventures with the Moon Ridge Pack in Hybrid Moon Rising.

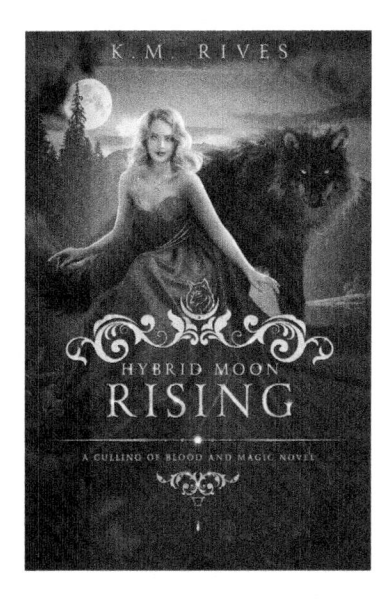

Hybrid Moon Rising

THE CULLING OF BLOOD AND MAGIC SERIES

The Replacement

The Intended

The United - Coming Fall 2022

Hybrid Moon Rising - Companion Novel

ACKNOWLEDGMENTS

They say raising kids takes a village. Writing a book is no different. It's this tiny book child that an author raises from just a tiny snippet of an idea into a full fledge story, with fantastical worlds and characters we love. I'd be nowhere without my village behind me.

None of this would have been possible without my amazing husband. From encouraging me to follow my dream of becoming an author, to allowing me to bounce hair-brained ideas off him, to hugging me when I was overwhelmed and keeping the kiddos out of my hair so I could edit for hours on end. He was an intrinsic part of getting this book done. Thank you so much for all you do, darlin.

I wouldn't be where I am today if it weren't for Veronica and Nana Logan. One phone call and a local author meeting changed my life for the better. I cherish all your advice, but most importantly your friendship. I could not ask for better mentors to help guide me on this journey.

Somewhere along the way I found my critique kitties. I can't thank these women enough for shredding my story apart until it was the best it could possibly be, as well as putting up with my drama llama tendencies. Victoria, Beth, Melissa, Siby and Mary, you are seriously the most incredible women and both myself and The Replacement are so much better because of you. Meowrl for fucking ever.

Most of all, I want to thank you, my readers. You are an essential part of my village and I wouldn't be here without you. I love creating worlds for you to immerse yourself in and can't wait for you to continue on this journey with me.

Krista is a California girl living in a North Carolina world… for now. After all, home is where the Army tells her husband they're moving next. She's a lover of dungeons and dragons, singing at the top of her lungs, ice cold beer and all things dessert. Most days you can find her wrangling her two young daughters and finding any moment she can to sneak away into the worlds she writes.

Check out kmrives.com for more information.

Printed in Great Britain
by Amazon